PARIS IMMORTAL

Atonement

S. ROIT

snowbooks

Proudly Published by Snowbooks in 2010

Copyright © 2010 S. Roit

Snowbooks Ltd
Kirtlington Business Centre
Oxfordshire
OX5 3JA
Tel: 0207 837 6482
email: info@snowbooks.com
www.snowbooks.com

British Library Cataloguing in Publication Data
A catalogue record for this book is available from the British Library.

Paperback Edition 9781906727567
Library Hardback 9781906727550

Printed and bound in the UK by J F Print Ltd., Sparkford

For the fans

There is a reason that all things are as they are, and did you see with my eyes and know with my knowledge, you would perhaps better understand.

Dracula, Bram Stoker, 1897

A smile dark enough to match his eyes formed, showing me two more fangs than I'd known he possessed, making it six. "You desire vengeance. Step aside, and you shall have it; it is a specialty of mine."

Fixed on those two very long, sharp teeth to the inside of his lengthened canines, it took me a second to register his movement. I pressed my hands to his chest again, for all the good it would do.

"Wait, wait. We have to finish the business, first."

"Step aside," he growled, the sound metallic, giving me a hot spinal monkey. "It is past time for him to atone for his sins."

Yes, yes it is.

But no!

"Aeshma, please, please, wait."

His eyes bore into mine.

"Listen. Just listen to me, please." My thoughts ran to a place I didn't want to drag him. But I had to. It might be my only shot at stopping him. "If you do this now, we fail. I don't want that. I don't want to fail Michel." My back contacted metal again. "Do you want to fail?"

I knew what saying this might do to him, God help me, but I had to appeal to him, and it was true. It was the only reason I could imagine looking at my attacker again—when I was able to look at him—the idea of letting Michel down otherwise.

Travis' reply sounded like boiling mercury.

"He does not deserve to breathe the same air as you any longer, Death Dancer."

Pressed, pressed harder into the metal. If the door opened, I'd fall inside, giving me somewhere to go.

But I didn't want it to open.

"You're right, Aeshma, he doesn't." His fangs, so close to my face that his other features were out of focus. "But we will fail if you do this now. Do you hear me, Travis? Fail."

The black of his eyes thinned, amber pushing its way through. A minute later metal wasn't chilling me through my suit any longer.

"*Fail...*" he said, but there was no rejoicing on my part as I witnessed the softening of his expression.

I still had to be certain the point drove home completely, damn it. There were still black slivers trying to swallow the amber in his eyes.

"Right, an absolute fuck up, Travis. We can't have that, now can we?"

"No, we can't have that. I made an oath."

"Exactly. We're both loyal to the end. So just a while longer, okay? After we've wrapped this up, I can't stop you, I know that. Just—wait."

All the blackness in his irises disappeared, and there was the laid back Travis I'd grown accustomed to.

"Will you want to stop me later?" Even his voice had shifted, I realized.

I also realized my inability to say yes to his question.

Hey there. Yup, it's me again.
You know the drill.

Chapter 1

SEPTEMBER 1

Michel

"You are quite close to boring me beyond death," said Gabriel, his voice dropping another degree, along with the temperature of his gaze.

A wisp of auburn drifted across her cheek with the defiant lift of her chin. "If you want entertainment, you can buy it on the street."

My dark angel's smile, frostbitten on its edges, grew a degree as he took a gliding step closer to the barstool on which she sat. I leaned back against the countertop, draping my arms to each side, admiring my lethal, longhaired beauty.

"I prefer a far higher class of entertainment, *merci*. More erudite pursuits, one might say," he replied.

She smiled up at him, the smile as flippant as her tone. "Guess that counts me out."

For this, at first, his smile merely chilled a wider path across his face.

We had arrived in *Phantasm*, a sanguinary club deep in the heart of Prague, through a chain of events both lucky and crafted.

Vita, the spy Elise had offered up, had been the first link in our chain. Vita had proven rather ballsy for a human, not to mention hardier than I imagined. It had taken more than I thought most humans capable of enduring, before a single tidbit of useful information spilled forth. Yet unfortunately— for I was enjoying myself at the time—she didn't prove as hardy as I would have liked.

She expired before I'd captured all the details I was having so much fun chasing.

No matter, this was no matter at all, as upon occasion I can be quite unselfish, and so I did not begrudge Trey his chance at satisfaction, and satisfaction we both did have, for much information did she give Trey.

From the Other Side, that is.

She'd certainly never expected the interrogation would continue beyond death, and she certainly had not imagined what manner of punishment a Death Dancer could deal, particularly when he felt righteously moved.

Of course, she hadn't known there were such things as Death Dancers either, which, since Travis had first uttered the words, had become our new term for Trey's *persona*. In the time since his possession, Trey was beginning to grow into this new skin in the most interesting fashion. I found the title fitting and elegant in its way.

But I digress. I often do so when I am being entertained.

My beloved hunter Travis Starke provided link two. I have often mused that there isn't a hole in the world in which one could hide that he would not pull one out of, and our next link was pulled out of a hole in Italy, after crossing the border from Nice. Quite literally pulled out of a hole, in fact, as this traitor had need of digging said hole before the sun reduced him to a bubbling slick of entrails, then ashes.

Link three was, admittedly, a stroke of luck, thanks to the faithlessness of link two's lover. The lover was having an affair with the third link, and so they were kind enough to be in the same location—namely her bed. I wouldn't have missed his expressions, nor the sounds he made when I crushed him beneath my boot heels, for anything.

I'm more than happy to provide other details later, perhaps, but we should expedite our return to the enthralling sight of Gabriel post haste.

As of now, here I stand, content to watch my Angel of Death conduct his interrogation; one that would, beyond doubt, end quite badly for the third-rate street walker named Phaedra, sitting on a stool in this bar she'd sleazed her way into owning.

"Truly now, your head is not fully vacant. Certainly you have an answer to the question that I have posed, one that might even suit me," he said.

"What would I know about the blood bags roaming your city, and why should I care about any of them?" she replied, her spine clinging to a straight line. She then laughed. "And why should *you* care?"

Gabriel's smile to her was pleasant— dangerously so. The more polite he became, in certain instances, the more life-threatening he was.

A slight flaring of his nostrils accompanied his next words, his calmly spoken words. "They have their uses, as I believe you know – indeed, know very well, and quite recently." As she offered only a shrug, Gabriel continued. "I have certainly found a use for one such creature even now."

On cue, her eyes flitted to the door, as also on cue, a mortal stumbled through it, aided greatly by Kar. Swiftly, she looked back to Gabriel, attempting to disguise her reaction.

"Some sport?" Her tongue slid across her front teeth, tasting each one. "If I'd known you were coming and that you were into this kind of thing, I would have made arrangements."

His bow shaped mouth, which I so coveted, curved ever so slightly. "A *faux pas* on our part, certainly, but not to worry. I have brought my own rabbit, as you can plainly see."

Said rabbit could not contain himself and made a desperate move in her direction, for which he found himself in my grip. I smiled sweetly, catching Phaedra's eyes.

"I might be of a mood to share," I said, "depending entirely on your next few words, of course." Her pet's fear wafted out through his pores and caressed my taste buds, delighting the devil within me.

"Save me a thigh, will you?" she said. "I love tender thigh meat."

I found the mortal's cry quite heady, quite pleasing, when fabric and flesh gave way to nails. So pungent the sudden release of blood was, I could trace its descent, taste every particle that paused to cling on the hairs of his leg.

"I don't know, Phaedra. I grow hungrier by the second, and the only thing better than a perfectly curved breast is a juicy thigh."

Trey
Germany

"Shit," I whispered. "This isn't working."

"That disc was supposed crack everything."

"Yeah, I know that; we all know that. Doesn't change the fact it isn't working."

"You need to figure something out; we've not much time."

"Know that, too, thanks." I waved my hands. "I'll take a shot at the password myself."

"Or we do it another night."

"Fuck that. Tonight's the night, man." In my head, I started going over everything I knew about the company and the dude whose computer I was hacking.

Trying to hack.

"By the way, I think you need to fire her software geek," I said. "Bill Gates he ain't."

"I was just thinking that myself, mate. Now get that brain working."

"I'm on it, I'm on it."

Fourth attempt, and I was so not on it.

"Of course. There's nothing remotely predictable about this dude. I can't figure it out, and I'm gonna trip something here; I just know it. It's gonna lock me out, and then we're well and truly fucked."

Travis was at the door one second, then standing behind me the next. "Let me see."

I leaned back to give him room. "Computer savvy, are you?"

"I might know a trick or five." The glow from the computer screen illuminated his grin.

"Yeah? So why don't you handle software next time?"

"I will."

And just as easily as he said those words, he had bypassed the security on the computer.

"You cheated. How did you do that?"

All I got for that was another grin. He started heading back to his post. "Copy that shit and let's get out of here."

Slipping the USB flash drive in, I set about finding the right files. "On it, on it."

"Shhh." He paused. "Our company's on the second floor."

"We're on the seventh, right? Still time, and I can't make this go any faster, you know."

He waved a hand at me.

"Maybe if you'd used that trick earlier, we'd be out of here already, Travis."

"Last resort."

"Why's that?"

"Shhh."

Sure. Fine.

Shhh.

Files. There. Copy.

"Almost there," I said under my breath, slipping the useless disc into my pocket. "Where are they?"

No response.

"Dude, where are they?" Copy next files.

Silence.

I looked up. Travis wasn't there.

"Shit. Travis?"

Click, open, copy. Hurry up, damn it.

"Travis...where'd you go?"

How would you say it? Stop tripping, man.

Scowl. (Definitely not a pout.) "I am not tripping."

Then be quiet.

Well where are you?

Focus on your task.

Grunt.

I grabbed the flash drive, slipped it into my pocket next to the disc, and proceeded to close up everything on the comp, cover my trail.

That done, I got up and headed for the door. I grabbed the doorknob and eased the door open, peeking out into the hall, and as soon as I saw that it was clear, cautiously, quietly, made my way out and started heading for the stairwell down at the end, to the right. Safely there, my feet started carrying me down the first flight.

Second.

Where the fuck is Travis?

Rounding the third, I heard a noise and just stopped myself from saying his name. Might not be him, after all. No, I was sure he wouldn't be making that much noise while he walked; this operation was all about stealth, for God's sake.

. The door below. Someone was opening the door below.

I turned and flew back up the steps toward the fifth floor exit, thinking *Travis,* hard. Hearing footfalls on the steps didn't give me much time to check out the hall before I bounded out and started down it, looking for a place to hide.

Office door, locked.

A few steps more, another door, locked.

"Shit." So where are you now, bodyguard and accomplice? Making a bloody trail? Is the gig up?

While reaching for the handle of a third door, something reached for me at the same time.

A hand clamped over my mouth, an arm gripped me around the waist, and whoever it was yanked me inside a pitch-black room and shut the door.

Fucked. That could be my name right now.

Gabriel
Phantasm

"I don't know, Phaedra. I grow hungrier by the second, and the only thing better than a perfectly curved breast is a juicy thigh."

My eyes traversed his person; it was Michel who I saw more keenly than the mortal he had caged, this mortal who was in the envious position of having his back to *mon lion's* chest—a powerful arm pinning him there, bruising the mortal's collarbones, most assuredly.

My gaze, it absorbed the vision of *mon amour's* fingers and the riveting way human blood lent a deep blush to the first knuckle of each one, his fingertips drilling more deeply into one of the mortal's quadriceps.

15

I found that I was quite envious of this human just then indeed, but soon, soon enough I would feel those nails splice me thusly. Foreplay, this, merely foreplay.

"He has two," said the whore in her grating way.

My Michel's lips, insidiously they pulled back; his upper lip, it made a slow ascent, revealing his gleaming, exquisitely sharp fangs, and I knew that I smiled, both for the thought of those teeth penetrating me, and their ripping into the mortal's flesh.

"Mistress," the human choked as Michel jerked his head back, set to strike. I freed myself from this too-tempting vision and found Phaedra's doe-eyed gaze, which wavered, and her pupils, they fluxed, and much to my satisfaction, she called out, "Wait!"

Yet I was disappointed as well when Michel stayed his bite.

"Wait for what?" asked he. "I'm thirsty."

With her eyes fixated on her human pincushion, who was, as we had surmised, a well-loved pincushion, she replied, much of her bravado fleeing. "I know something about your pets."

"This word, it offends me. Do not utter it again in reference to them," I said.

"Let him go. Then I'll tell you what you want to know about your…friends," she said to Michel.

He replied, "I'll let him go *after* you tell Gabriel what he wants to know."

Her gaze fluttered between us; it then settled once more upon Michel. "Do you swear?"

"Swear? *Mais oui*."

After gazing at him yet a moment longer, she returned to me. "Yes, I know something about your attorney."

"Something that you must assume I no doubt long ago surmised; otherwise, I would not have wasted my time in coming here," I countered.

"I heard he was special." She paused, and I reached a bit further for my patience during this pause.

"Might you speed this along? I find that I grow weary yet again, and your lover finds his tender flesh bruised by the second," said I.

"There was talk of him having talent."

I feigned a yawn. In the interim, a most pitiful groan reached my ears, which came from her lover. I had no need of feigning my smile, then.

She spared the pale-haired human a glance, a glance that shimmered. "Vita said it would not only upset Michel if something happened to his attorney, but—"

I adorned the back of her neck with my fingers, a light touch, even gentle, it was. "But?"

"But also that Vicont was interested in him."

Ice water coursed through my veins. "This I know," I spoke quietly. "The why – this I would have you tell me."

She made with a light shake of her head. Ice particles formed in the water.

"*Chérie*, I am not here by chance. Would you rather converse freely, or have me peel it from you, layer by layer?"

In that moment, there was an audible series of snapping, cracking sounds, and they did not issue from the bones in her neck. I followed her wild gaze to those standing behind me, one of which was now quite bereft of blood and vacant of life.

"You swore, you bastard!"

Michel gave off a light shrug, the gesture reflected by his golden brows. "Terribly sorry, Phaedra. I thought you were speaking of foul language. I've been known to use it."

Through grinding teeth, she hissed, "Bastard."

With another light shrug, Michel quite impishly stated, "He twitched. I couldn't resist."

The human melted, boneless as a feline, to the floor. I spared a moment to admire the flush of Michel's cheeks, to taste the heat further kindled within him, to listen to the fresh blood snake through his veins, before I fixed her with my gaze once again.

"Allow me to rephrase the questions in a way you might better understand, Phaedra. Or shall I find another whom you love? For my thirst, it now grows as well."

Trey
Germany

I immediately started to struggle, not that it did any good. I realized the immovable object that had me trapped must be a vampire.

Or a super strong human.

My struggling was soon cut short with the breath of words in my ear. "Be still, mate."

My entire body unclenched. I grabbed the hand he had over my mouth and yanked it away. "That is really *not* funny, man."

His hand immediately covered my mouth again.

Who said I was being funny? Be quiet; someone's close.

We were definitely having a talk about this later. You know, about his leaving and then nearly giving me a heart attack and almost having his balls smashed.

Well, in theory, anyway.

You know what else? Being tight up against Travis in a— closet, this is a closet— isn't a bad way to spend some time.

Typical. We're hiding, possibly soon to be caught—which is definitely not good—and I'm thinking things like that. Like about his fangs in my neck.

I. Have. Issues.

Hey, but there're much worse issues than this.

Travis started making a sound. Just a breath, really. A panting I could hear because his mouth was still close to my ear.

This did nothing for my issues.

Well, better than worrying if whoever might be in the hall was a vampire and whether or not we were – I mean Travis was gonna have to leave a trail. Right?

Ooo. Scenting. That's what he's doing. Uh, scenting me or someone else?

Sounds in the hall, and they don't seem too far away. Guess that answers that.

I felt Travis stiffen.

Great, just great. Don't breathe loudly, Trey.

Muffled footsteps, the flat carpet dulls the sound. The voice telling someone in German that he thought he heard someone on the stairwell, but so far hasn't seen anything on floor five, isn't as dulled, though.

The door. My door. Our door. He's right outside our door. Speaking on a walkie-talkie, no doubt. I wanted to ask Travis if they employed vampires as security guards, and cursed myself for not asking this long before we got here, and thought about cursing him for not telling me one way or the other to begin with. Then I remembered that as open as Travis was with me, he didn't offer certain information freely.

Too late anyway, I decided. If it was a vamp, and Travis had to off him, maybe he'd be tidier about it this time, and we could dispose of the body.

Doubtful, but I could always hope.

Listen to me: I'm talking about disposing bodies, and the possibilities in my head aren't even grossing me out. Gee, I'm a long way from where I started back in June, aren't I? And I have stolen information in my pocket. Got that promotion, all right. Promoted to corporate spy, dealing in corporate espionage. Mmm hmm. I certainly am getting more out of life and for damn sure have avoided anything mind-numbingly normal. Ah, well. If you want something done right, do it yourself.

More talking outside the door. The door whose handle just moved.

Shit. Sure, Travis was as still and quiet as, well, to be cliché, death, but I needed to breathe, and soon, and as far as I knew, Travis' talents didn't include invisibility. *I* sure as hell couldn't pull that off. Far as I knew. Be a damned handy talent, wouldn't it?

The handle moves again. Good, locked.

But naturally enough, a security guard would have the key.

I hear it slipping into its slot. *Shit*, I think and, *Travis, can't you do something?*

Turning, I think the guard's turning the key.

Turning.

Oh Traviiisss…

Static. A voice over the walkie-talkie. Come back to the lobby, it says.

Muffled footsteps heading away until I can't hear them anymore, and Travis keeps his hand over my mouth a couple minutes after that, even.

"He's going down the stairs," he finally said, dropping his hand, and I finally have to breathe—right after the sliver of air I could still spare for a sigh of relief.

"Lucky someone called him back," I said.

"Nothing lucky about it."

I turned and found the light of his eyes in the dark closet. "Oh, I think I get it. So something else you might have done sooner, unless you get off on what the suspense does to my—I don't know—scent or something."

He tapped his forehead. "I've been a bit busy here, mate. I'm *still* a bit busy here, *man*."

He opened the door before I could say anything else and led us out, down the hall, to the stairwell. Once in, he started up the stairs.

"Wait," I whispered. "Up?"

"Up."

"Okay, fine. Up."

Yeah, all the way up and out to the roof. Travis' eyes moved across the area. Then he gestured for me to follow, which I did, to the edge of the building and a view of an eight-story drop. He gestured across to a building of approximately the same height.

"We're heading that way."

"Eh…excuse me?"

He grabbed me, and I felt my stomach dip, that feeling when an airplane hits an air pocket and seems to drop, and suddenly I was standing—er, being held up on the opposite rooftop.

I took a breath. "Ya know, I'm not afraid of heights, and okay, that's totally cool, but a little warning next time might be nice, dude."

He didn't say anything, staring across to where we'd just been.

Another beat and he turned to me. "Right then, that's done."

"No one's following?"

"Nah."

Nod. "Good. Now you can tell me why you fricking disappeared, what you meant by *busy*, and why the hell your nifty trick in that office was a last resort."

His eyes moved over my face, he suddenly grinned, and he grabbed me around the waist. "I'll answer those in order in a quick. But first," and he jumped.

Down.

Straight down off the edge of the building, and there I was again, not standing fully under my own power, this time in an alley or some shit.

I took two deep, gut-soothing breaths and said, "Didn't I just say something about giving me a little warning?"

He chuckled.

I flipped him off.

"Now then," he said. "I left because someone was getting a few floors too close and they needed distracting; I've been multitasking during this entire operation; and that trick is a last resort because sometimes I fry the entire computer." He shrugged. "I haven't honed that one into an exact science, yet."

I assessed his words. "Multitasking?"

"Someone had to focus on the security cameras, the guards, the perimeter, and keep an eye on you, for starters. Especially when you struck out on your own and went down the stairs."

"You didn't exactly tell me to stay put."

"I repeat, I was multitasking, and I reckoned you might figure that out on your own."

I wanted to retort, but—"Yeah, okay. I got nothin'." Pause. "So your brain was still a bit divided when that guard just about caught us."

"Yes." Beat. "But I did like the scent of your adrenaline." He kept a straight face, but I could see it in his eyes, the humor.

"Asshole," I said, not quite stopping the involuntary grin.

He slipped an arm across my shoulder. "Come on, let's go home."

"I'm all for that. I've had enough fun for one night, thank you."

Sideways look from him as we started walking. "Oh let's cut the bullshit, mate. We both know you're rather keen on being a super-spy."

Couldn't help the smile. "Well, James Bond I ain't." I glanced at him. "You, on the other hand…"

"I was thinking more Steve McQueen."

I shook my head. "Not a bad choice, I'll give you that."

Michel
Phantasm

I observed the closeness of Gabriel's face to hers. The breath of space between, where the sepulchral chill of his words hung. When she made no reply, I looked to Kar. "You remember the address of the other, *oui*?"

"Yes, my Prince."

"Wait," Phaedra begged, and her eyes darted to Gabriel's,

his return look causing her to recoil. "I wanted to get back into Vicont's good graces."

My blood began to simmer in my veins.

"By attempting to murder one under our protection?" Gabriel asked in a way that raised my skin.

"He didn't want them dead," she offered, her shiver running deeper than mine, no doubt.

"And so you are informing me that you did nothing but spy, just as Vita did?" he pressed, whilst I turned the tidbit about Vicont over in my mind, wearied by the endless circular paths we had already traveled during this hunt for the one who had ordered the hit on Geoff.

"Answer me," I heard Gabriel demand in a low tone.

"You killed my brother," she shouted, and in the same moment, I felt the energy of the room shift.

I looked to her, finding her accusatory gaze not on Gabriel, but me, and arched a brow. I dropped my eyes to the body at my feet and then lifted them to her once more.

"Not him, you oaf."

I stepped over the body, heading in their direction, for Gabriel's fingers still rested upon her person. "Do tell," I said.

"Brute. Bastard. Monster!"

I folded my arms across my chest. "Flattery won't help you just now."

Her gaze moved to Gabriel. "You knew my brother."

Wafer thin interest gave way to a curiosity more insistent as I evaluated each of them. For Gabriel's part, he merely stared at her, his chill frosting the air.

"What are you on about?" I inquired, as he seemed intent on silence.

"Gabriel knew my brother."

"You already said this. Quit stalling before I snap your neck myself," I said, decidedly weary, yes.

"He knew him well."

I made another step in their direction, my patience near gone, but halted when Gabriel chose to break his silence. "Whatever it is you speak of bears little resemblance to anything relevant."

"Oh, but it does," she said, her mouth settling into a scowl. My curiosity swelled once more, as it seemed whatever she had to say had given her a last gasp of bravado.

Gabriel's smile to her was oozing honey, and my senses pricked sharply. "I shall humor you, if briefly," he said, his tone as sweet as said smile.

"My brother was one of your *erudite* pursuits."

My brows felt to knit, my hands to relax, and my arms to fall to my sides. Gabriel straightened, creating more distance between himself and her words.

"He must not have liked your idea of sharing," she continued in a snarl, thrusting her finger in my direction, "because he killed him in a jealous fit."

Gabriel did not so much as flinch, meanwhile my mind raced through years of memories and found one that detailed a rampage I'd gone on not long after Gabriel had departed.

There—there was one I had been led to believe was trysting, plotting, with *my* angel. So many faces I did not recall in my rage, but one, this one, yes, I could picture him now, clearly. I had torn him flesh from bone, limb from limb, tendon to sinew.

I had lost all knowledge of him having a sister until she reminded me, and even then, I only knew it must be her for the uniqueness of her name, which now echoed in the memory.

I felt my husband's eyes on me and met them with my own. Unreadable, his were—a generally rare thing. They were not vacant, nor inward, nor were they full of emotion.

Glacial green, this is what I was met with, though no sooner did I see this, than his fingers had broken through her flesh and splintered bone where they gripped along her jaw line; rivulets of garnet chased themselves over his fingers to splash upon the cheap white lace over her bosom, leaving tiny, poppy-like blooms.

24

Clawing at his wrist, she spat, "You betrayed him, and my brother died for it! And what did you lose? You're back in his arms – what did you lose!"

White-hot energy pulsed in the air; it filled my mouth and sat heavily upon my tongue, as the fingers of his other hand found purchase in the back of her skull and he lifted her, quite slowly, quite powerfully, from the bar stool. The flailing of her legs and arms, I knew he felt nothing of this as his eyes burned into hers like laser beams.

The flood of energy folded in on itself, still pulsing; liquid stretching a balloon. Yet his words, they were a blizzard. "*You* sent the assassin."

Lifted higher by him, gurgling laced her words, liquid rising in her throat. "I had a hand in it, *yesss*. I passed on all the information needed and agreed to the deal, and so?"

His tone now summoned a deep freeze with no hope of thaw. "If you wished revenge, you should have taken a more direct route."

The balloon of energy burst, sharply cutting through my thoughts of her words about a deal, causing my skin to crawl.

The dark blood in her throat bubbled up and through her mouth, soon spilling forth not only from there, but also her eyes. It oozed from the corners of those eyes, and her ears, soon they leaked dark matter also, and I knew that it bled from other orifices as well.

I knew, because the energy came from Gabriel. It was the darkest of his gifts, a gift even some of our kind thought evil.

Blood filled every cavity within her and overflowed, for the anger behind his thought was unleashed. It twisted, how it twisted, her organs, compressing and rearranging them. It knotted her dead intestines, it collapsed her lungs, and it wrung her heart. Quite literally, it wrung her heart like someone wringing water from a wet towel.

Before her body left off twitching, before her sounds of suffering ceased choking, gurgling and wailing through the cavernous room, he swung around, swung his arms with such force, that her body flew through the air and thumped against the far wall with a loud, wet smack, before shuddering to the floor.

Her head, still in his grip, he then launched in the opposite direction with a sinister growl. Bottles on shelves exploded in miniscule shards with the impact, as well as from the sound waves. Liquid of various tastes rained in all directions, dancing in the air with multicolored glass particles.

"You should have taken a more direct route, and left the gentle Sparrow alone. You've gained nothing from it, you see," he finished his previous line of thought, in the direction of her head.

Evil? Perhaps. This rests on one's point of view.

My point of view left me to smile the smile of the immensely pleasured, for my angel—he was quite simply the most beautifully lethal thing I had ever seen. It was rare, him losing his temper in quite *this* fashion, but when he did, it was fiercely magnificent.

Yet one thing lingered in my mind that ever so slightly dulled my lust.

His look to me before. A look that was not a look. Soon enough I had not even this to ponder, however, when he turned and strode to me. His eyes were an emerald fire, though deep within the fire, compassion sparked.

"How you suffered in my absence," he lamented through his lingering anger, his bloodied hands finding my face, cradling it. "How much more did you suffer?"

What lingered now in my mind was the thought that my suffering could be nothing compared to his.

In lieu of other words, I kissed him.

"You're freezing," I said, lips still to his.

"You're on fire," he breathed out.

"For you."

"I want you."

"I need you."

"Have me," he urged.

I inhaled deeply and spared Kar a glance.

"I shall handle it, my Prince." He moved toward the deceased human, to whom I also spared a glance.

"I truly am sorry, young man. But that's what you get, sometimes, when you play with monsters," I said.

I took Gabriel's hand and led him away, so that I might have him.

Chapter 2

SEPTEMBER 2

Trey
14ème

"Yet you made it away safely, and with all of the information you needed."

"Yeah, but it still isn't funny."

Michel looked across his shoulder at me, stopping in mid-stride by the giant desk, and that full mouth of his curved.

"It's not," I repeated.

That full damned mouth curved more, turning him into that green Maurin imp from the posters.

I looked away, looked back—and laughed. "Okay, it is."

He lightly winked and resumed heading for his chair. "And you had no objections to going, either. In fact, you were rather eager." He sat down, opened a drawer, pulled out a file, and tossed it on the desk.

"I had to meet with that one guy during the day. And...my going in with Travis gave him one less thing on his task list." Yeah.

"The way he tells it, you insisted on going in with him before you knew he'd be multitasking, and you don't lack confidence in his skills, do you?"

"No, but—yeah, I got nothin'." I returned his grin. "When you're right, you're right. Anyway, what's that? More intel?" I asked, striding to one of the chairs on the other side of the desk, where I sat.

"*Oui.* She just received these reports from her mole."

"This'd better be good." Grabbing the files."Her supposed software wizard was shit."

"She doesn't know the first thing about software, therefore whatever he said went over her head, I'm certain."

I arched a brow at him. "It might've been nice to know that *before* we went to Germany."

Damned.

Impish.

Grin.

"You're incorrigible." I opened the files and started skimming the papers.

"Yes, yes. I'm a lot of things."

Couldn't stop my own grin. "Shouldn't you be taking this a little more seriously?"

"Ah, but I am, Trey, I am. Yet there is no harm finding amusement in life's little bumps, is there?"

"Ohhh, I suppose not." Skimming another couple of paragraphs. "But I hope this spy of Elise's knows what he's doing." I slid forward in my chair. "This is some heavy shit." My eyes lifted. "If he gets caught, we're screwed."

"He won't be a problem."

"I'm glad *you* have faith in him."

He spread his hands. "He wouldn't be a problem even if he *were* caught."

"...right."

"He'd kill himself, first." He beamed me a smile.

"Oh. I guess that's what you call true loyalty." Don't think I could go *that* far, Michel.

"I would not wish for you to," he offered in response to my unspoken thought.

Which seems normal to me, now.

I studied his face, then moved on. "There's still the matter of electronic trails."

"Indeed. We shall see what we shall see. Certainly we can avoid being detected just long enough, don't you think?"

"Depends how good *their* software geeks are." He just gazed at me. "Oh well. More fun if you risk getting caught, I suppose." I set the files on the desk.

Head tilt from him. "They won't immediately know who hacked them in any event, correct? Not until it's clear who's taken over the companies, if we do this well."

"That's the idea."

His head righted itself and he nodded. "We've already got four in the pocket." A grin moved across his lips. "I knew you were talented, but you've exceeded even my expectations."

That made me puff up with pride, having exceeded a vampire's expectations—especially this vampire's expectations.

His grin grew.

"So," I said, unable to talk more business until I asked, proud or not. "How did it go in Prague?"

His next smile made him look like the King of Hell."That particular matter is resolved."

Heard that statement before. "Did *she* send the guy?"

"There may yet be one more involved, but reaching her was most satisfying, for she had a hand in the assassination attempt, yes."

"Why'd she do it?"

Strangely, he looked away. "Revenge."

Ruined that good vibe, now didn't I? Told myself it might be prudent to drop it. But per usual, I couldn't, and besides—it had involved Geoff and me.

"For what?"

He met my gaze. "I killed her brother a few years ago. She was still holding a grudge."

"I'd say so," I stated quietly.

"An eye for an eye," he continued. "However, she knew she didn't stand a chance against me, or Gabriel, for that matter." He rose and moved around the desk. "She settled for hurting the both of you as a substitute."

I turned in my chair, watching as he started pacing. Should definitely drop it, I told myself.

To no avail. "Why did you kill her brother?"

He froze in place. He hugged himself. I thought his fingers would drill through the suit-weight royal blue wool covering his sides and my eyes dropped.

"Jealous rage," I heard him say. I looked up when his presence felt closer. Looked up into his darkened eyes.

"He was named as someone who was trysting with Gabriel," he said. "Plotting with Gabriel. He played his part well. Shortly after Gabriel disappeared, I..." he sighed. "I lost my humanity." His gazed wandered. "It shouldn't have happened. Her brother had done nothing wrong."

"You were..." I whispered, then paused, "you were bereft."

"I should never have doubted." He drifted away, aimlessly walking across the room again.

I couldn't stand it.

I got up and went to him, cut him off and grabbed his shoulders. "Nobody's perfect, not even you," I said. "You were in pain, and pain blinds us." My hand went to his face. "But Gabriel *forgave* you, obviously. That means something. A very large something."

He tipped his head, touching his forehead to mine, and the colors of his eyes flooded my view.

"Yes, he did," he whispered. "And it does."

"Then you and I still have a common goal. We need to forgive ourselves."

His arms slipped loosely around my waist. "Yes; it saddens him that I haven't." Another sigh. "I'd known him so long, so long already. I knew *better*."

"Well. Emotions are good like that, Michel. Good at making us bat-shit crazy. Happens to the best of us, even ridiculously hot old guys like you." Especially *vamps* like you, I thought.

His shoulders lightly shook with a soundless laugh. "Thank you for that, my darling."

I smiled a little. "You've made me feel better more than once. It was time I returned the favor."

He took a step back and my eyes were able to focus on his face. "Emotions make us crazy, mmm. This could be why I'm allied with that woman," he said.

He'd told me the reasons Elise had given for what she'd done. I was convinced them hearing the reasons had made things worse. Hating her was easier. *I* still wasn't sure what I thought of Elise, so I imagined Gabriel and Michel must be uncertain times twenty, at least.

But so far, she'd kept her word and given them access to all kinds of things. So.

Here we were.

"I have to admit," I finally said, "she's provided some good information."

"Indeed," he said, moving toward the desk again. "She's not crossed us thus far."

"Well. Maybe she really is sorry," I surprised myself by saying.

He slid back into his chair, contemplating me. "I believe this is possible," he admitted, having not said this to me before.

Returning to my seat, my fingers walked the edges of the files on the desk after I sat. "Travis doesn't like her."

His following laugh stunned me a little. "This is an understatement. But he is tolerating her for me."

Forward lean. "It doesn't seem so much like he doesn't trust her when it comes to this operation as..." pause, "it seems personal."

He offered a slow nod. "Travis saw what it did to me." His face smoothed. "What it was like for me being separated from Gabriel."

I was sure I didn't want to know. But then again, I did want to know. "I saw a sample of how he is with you gone a short time. What happens to you?"

At first, he only gazed at me, his eyes moving over me, and I started to feel like he *did* see through clothing.

"I harmed myself far worse than you ever have," he said at last.

My eyes squeezed shut; it was almost a convulsion.

"Rages, I had a few more of those, as well."

Whisper. "I'm sorry."

"Don't be. What is it you would say? You didn't do it."

I managed to open my eyes. "For asking, then."

Slight shake of his head. "Don't be." He placed his hands on the desktop. "But please, don't bring this up around Gabriel. I never told him about mutilating myself. I'd already caused enough pain."

Head shake. As in no, I won't. "You were aware of it, though? That you were doing it. Gabriel wasn't aware of himself."

"I was. But sometimes I got carried away, even still."

Like I had once. But much worse, no doubt. My insides twisted a little.

"Let's move onto a brighter subject, shall we?" he suggested with a smile.

"Yeah. Yeah, that would be good. But just—just one last thing."

"Yes?"

"Did you sense from the beginning that I was a cutter?" Like calls to like...

33

A gentle look from him. "Yes, and I'm sorry that you know even half of this feeling, the need to release, the need to cut out the pain. And yet, it is another thing that drew me to you. Something that we share on a level, something that we both understand. For this I'm not sorry – does this make sense to you?"

Searching his eyes. "Yes."

His smile returned. "I knew that it would. You see?"

I had to smile back.

"Now, onto that brighter subject, beloved."

Hmm. I still hadn't asked about Stefan and landing my job so fast. But the subject of Stefan didn't qualify as brighter—well to Michel it might, parts of it anyway. No. Think of something else for now, Trey.

I studied him and smiled a bit more. "I got one for you, before we return to mission details."

He touched his chest. "I'm all a-twitter."

Laugh. Very close inspection. "How do you make fire?"

His brow arched.

Gabriel
Château Lecureaux

I turned from the French doors, my eyes alighting on Kar. "Elise. Where is she now?"

"Recent intelligence places her in Prague."

Certainly my brows must have risen. "Prague?"

"Surely we leapt to the same suspicion given your recent visit, my Lord, yes. Anticipating your next query, if I may, so far we have no indication she's met with anyone who knew Phaedra."

34

"You anticipated well, as always," I offered. "Tell me, how cold is the trail since Phaedra's unfortunate accident?"

"I'm sorry to say quite chill, sir."

A dull sound escaped me. "I killed her too quickly, I suppose." Though I felt no remorse over it. My mind flitted to her brother, whom I could not remember, and as Kar remained silent, I continued. "So then, does it appear Elise is there for pleasure, or on business concerning our joint venture?"

"Indications are that her visit encompasses both. She met with an ally in the employ of a mutual interest of yours. She's also been seen at parties, having quite a time of it."

I contemplated his reply a moment before speaking. "I wish to know *who* she is socializing with, and I do not merely mean names."

He inclined his head. "Of course. We're investigating this now."

"Very good."

I may not have sensed a lie within Elise when we spoke in Belgium, but this was an entirely different matter. Yet I had also realized, now that I had distance from those moments in her home, that I was not certain how clear my senses had been during pieces of our discussion. My detachment had wavered at the time.

Senses correct or no, I had not forgiven her, nor was trust inspired. Regardless of her reasoning, I had learned that she had lied even more in years past than I had surmised. How much she had lied to *everyone*.

"Did you require anything else this evening, my Lord?" Kar inquired for the second time. A second time, I realized, for I had begun to drift quite far in my thoughts.

"I think not, thank you, Kar."

"I shall take my leave, then. I have news to impart to your husband."

With a lift of a brow, I prompted him.

"We've nearly closed a deal on another company."

I felt a smile grow to match the one in the depths of his jet eyes. "By all means, you should speak to Michel at once, for he shall return to me in high spirits with such news."

He offered a bow, one which I was about to return, until my thoughts shifted yet again. "Just one thing before you depart, if it pleases you, Kar."

"Yes, my Lord?"

A smile rediscovered me. "I respect your heritage as always, and I appreciate the honor which you bestow upon me, but Gabriel is my name, and you have long known it. It is as Gabriel I should like to speak with you now."

For this, his own smile grew. "Very well, Gabriel."

"Please," I gestured to the seating area, "be at ease."

"Thank you." He moved to the settee and perched upon its edge. His hands, he placed in his lap.

I settled into a chair opposite him. "There is something on my mind, and I wish to ask you a question, perhaps two."

He inclined his head towards me.

"You were here during my absence," I began, and he could not contain the surprise that displayed itself with the sudden lift of his eyebrows. "I am in hopes that you may provide me with a detail or two."

Surprised or no, he inclined his head once again and I found myself hesitating. It was rather unfair to ask him what I was about to ask. It was even more unfair that I was not asking Michel himself. After the initial shock and pain of hearing Elise's words in Belgium, I now had some distance, true, and it caused me to ponder many things. But I could not yet bring myself to ask Michel directly and possibly cause him distress.

"I know that Michel suffered in my absence, Kar. I find myself seeking details of this."

He did not ask me why it was that I had need of knowing. His reply was merely, "If I am able to give you the answers, I shall."

36

I should have felt guilt over what I was about to ask, for it was not my way, being less than direct, not going to the source. I should have been ashamed over the hypocrisy of my action, but I could not feel such, just then.

"Do you know if he harmed himself?" I began carefully, to judge his reaction.

His gaze not once wavered with his soft-spoken reply. "I was not in his presence as often as Travis, to rightly know all of the details of his actions during that time."

"Michel asked you not to tell me, am I correct?" I should have felt remorse over placing Kar in the delicate position I felt certain that I was placing him in.

Still, his gaze was direct. "He asked that we not discuss those years."

"And so I have my answer."

I observed the lowering of his lashes.

"Forgive me, Kar. I shall take the blame, should Michel be displeased. After all, you did not outright say it. You have not broken an oath."

He met my gaze once more. "He didn't wish to trouble you with it. You'd borne enough pain."

"I'd borne enough pain?" A shadow of myself wandered down darkened hallways in my mind, hallways that led to walls of stone and steel, which encased memories. "In the finish, my pain must pale in comparison, for I have little memory of time passing. Michel, however, he remembers every moment, no?" I felt myself nod, for I knew that this must be so, and even as I was vaguely aware of Kar's gaze upon me, my shadow-self walked along a brighter corridor, colored in shades of pain, remorse and sadness. This other self touched reverently a conversation, its fingertips tracing the spoken words.

I realized that in my reconciling with Michel, I had not said these exact words to him. That though I could feel the ache in my heart and soul of his absence, I was in a way the fortunate one, for I could not literally recall how many days passed. My mind did not live through those days in full, as his must have.

Travis and Kar. Between the two of them, they must have witnessed much.

Kar. His name reverberated in my mind and reminded me of his presence. As I focused upon him once more, his lingering sympathy and worry over my mental retreat still registered in his expression.

"Tell me," I gently prodded, "how terrible was it?"

He searched my eyes, and seeing that I held a genuine desire to know, replied, "He used knife-blades most often, I believe. I don't know the worst of it, I feel." Sadness moved through his eyes as he confirmed what Elise had said to me.

"But Travis, he does," I said.

"He would not speak of it to me or anyone else, as it pains him to do so. I do know that the Prince often left Paris after he'd returned from Belgium, and Travis could not stand it for long, so often sought him out."

This brought another question to my mind. "Did Travis ever seek me?"

"Yes."

"At Michel's behest?"

He did not reply straight away.

"No, then." My gaze drifted. "Michel found me himself, the times we met. I knew this." I returned to gazing at his face. "Why did Travis seek me?"

"Because, Gabriel. He couldn't stand Michel's pain, and he couldn't stand the pain you must have been feeling yourself. He could not stand your separation – and he missed you. But he knew that he couldn't force the two of you to work through whatever it was, and so he sought you mostly for his own peace of mind."

I gazed at him a moment longer before rising. "Thank you, Kar." I had at last come to my senses, uncomfortable with questioning him.

He rose from his seat as well and bowed. "If it has helped you, then you are welcome."

I shortened the distance between us. "Forgive me for these questions. It appears that I lost control of my wits, certainly."

One of his hands bridged the remaining distance between us, finding my shoulder. "It appears nothing of the kind, to me."

"I should not be asking *you*," I replied. "Forgive me."

"If you require it, then you're forgiven." He lowered his hand. "But might I ask a question in return?"

"You might."

"Why are you asking these things *now*?"

"I do not mean to be evasive, but I think perhaps you know."

Lightly he replaced his hand on my shoulder, offering me a nod as he did so.

"Please, enjoy the remainder of your evening, Kar. I find that I require solace, now."

"As you wish. Good evening, sir." He wasted no time in turning to depart.

Soon I was alone, and I took a seat in my chair, pondering when I might speak to Travis, if I should speak to Travis on the matter at all. It was Michel to whom I should speak, but he had obviously buried certain events somewhere deep inside his mind, in a place that I had not found, and so could not open, though I had felt before there was something he was keeping for himself in the depths of his memories.

I asked myself another question, then. What was it I truly needed to know, I asked. All too soon, I heard my reply.

I damned myself for needing too much, and for even thinking to ask.

I returned my thoughts to Elise, why she was in Prague, and whether or not she yet retained enough moxie to cross us—and hoped Kar's news kept Michel in high spirits.

Chapter 3

Michel
14ème

I arched a brow at him.

"Kar sort of explained what the mechanics might be, but now I'm asking you. Unless it's a secret. Then never mind, I guess."

A chuckle left me, and I graced Trey with a smile. "Did he explain about consciousness?"

He made to nod. "I follow the logic. What I don't get is, even being super-conscious, how the hell do you make fire out of nothing?"

"You only *think* it's nothing," I corrected. "For which I can't fault you, as it appears from nowhere, to your eyes. No struck match, no flicked lighter."

"Didn't see any blowtorches, either," he quipped.

"A bit cumbersome, carrying one about." I winked at him and rose. I moved around the desk and leaned back on it, not far from the chair in which he sat. "Air is a gas. It contains,

40

amongst other things, oxygen, nitrogen, and carbon dioxide molecules."

"Yeah."

"I can manipulate these molecules. Their speed – "

"The warmer the air, the faster the molecules move."

"Yes, and so perhaps the faster I move them, the warmer the air, mm? Molecules generally spread out farther, the warmer the air. However, I bring them together, as well. I create friction."

He merely stared at me a moment and then said, "How do you know that?"

"These molecules. They are as tangible to me as they are intangible to you. I can feel them and taste them, though I could not explain precisely what they taste of."

He continued to stare at me.

"Of course, there is always existent heat to manipulate, to direct," I continued. "For example, we could be in the middle of the arctic, but your body will still contain heat, unless you've already frozen to death."

On he stared, speechless, the wheels in his head, turning, spinning.

"And I always have my body with me," I said.

A word left him at last. "Wow."

My reply was to offer him a wide smile.

"It must be practically automatic, this—mind trick. I mean, it seemed like it happened so fast, as if you weren't even concentrating. 'Course, I was a little messed up both times."

"I'm well practiced, Trey."

"But it's rare. Is that because it's such a fine-tuned manipulation?"

I contemplated a few things. "Perhaps. There is yet something that comes from within me, however."

His eyes made a sweep of my face and I could sense that his brain was working, working that logic even more. "You're warm. I said this to you before, that you always feel warm, and Gabriel's cool. Do you somehow project your warmth?"

"Yes, beloved, one might say that I do." I contemplated another thing or two, as he had such an insatiable desire for knowledge. "Have you not noticed that Travis is warm?" Perhaps I would offer him the undiluted truth.

Yes, I would.

His first response was to blink at me. His second was to say, "Actually, yes. Even warmer than you, really."

I graced him with another wide smile.

"Can he create fire?"

I made to shake my head, though Travis could warm a glass of liquid or a bag of blood, if not unleash fire.

"So why are you pointing out his warmth to me?"

I made a study of the reflecting light that made up the colors of his irises.

"Are you trying to tell me something? You are, aren't you?"

I could not contain my urge to play with him just a bit more. "Am I?"

He moved to the edge of his seat. "Are you and Travis *really* that different?"

I began to make for the chocolate-hued suede couch in the room.

"It's a different kind of warmth. Sort of," I heard him continue. I turned and sat, and as I did, witnessed his approach. He stopped approximately one meter from the couch.

"I once said to you that maybe you had special genes to begin with." His brows made a slow ascent. "Do you?"

I smiled up at him.

He just smiled up at me – more a shit-eating grin, really.

"What are you?" I persisted, moving closer.

"A ridiculously hot old guy, wasn't it?"

"Hah." I sat down beside him. "Yeah, but c'mon. You're not

42

usually this cryptic with me. Well, not anymore. Are you just gonna keep teasing me and leave me hanging, now?"

His nail moved across my cheek, giving me a shiver. "Would you like me to?"

"That's beside the point."

His lips curved. "Is it?"

Head shake and chuckle. "C'mon. Are you like Travis?"

"Yes, but then again, no," he relented. "It is in the same ball park, as you might say."

Travis had practically insisted they were different.

"It wasn't his secret to tell," Michel said.

"I was about to get to that thought," I replied. "I understand. He doesn't spill other people's information when he's not supposed to, and it's his job to protect you." I turned a bit to face him better. "So you're *special*, too. Is this why you knew what he was?"

He gave me a nod. "In part, but also because I had learned a few things from Vicont and others about such creatures."

I decided anything about Vicont could wait a while longer. First, "Are you some other kind of demon?"

"Mmm, many creatures have been lumped together under this label."

My next thought seemed far too radical. But then again, was it really? "Angel in golds. Are you…" Head shake. No. Well… "Are you an angel?"

He laughed lightly. "Angels have been called demons, but don't take this too literally. I am not in fact, Michael." He paused. "As far as I know."

Stare.

He winked.

Another headshake, laughing a little. "Uh, okay. Phew. So, it's in the same vein as Travis, you said. Basically." Er, pardon the pun.

"Yes."

"Just a—a different type of demon gene?"

43

"This would be the basic idea, yes."

"Wow." Head scratch. What to ask next. "How do you—or Vicont— know it's a demon thing? I meant to ask Travis, but then I didn't want it to come across as an insult."

"Insulting in what way?"

"As if I were suggesting he was lying, or I don't know, making a guess. I don't think he was lying, just—well, maybe explaining the best he could." Though he did mention testing, too. Still. How do you know you've found a demon's gene in someone's DNA?

"Ah, I see." A shadow moved through his eyes. "I assure you it's quite literal. Vicont was once acquainted with a woman who had herself been acquainted with an authentic 'demon'."

Blink.

"You don't mean the real thing...?"

"Indeed I *do* mean precisely that. One hundred percent so-called demon."

Whoa. Travis had said *ancient* race in a way that made me think B.C. at least.

"He also, supposedly, learned something of our kind from the Anima Mundi."

"Who are they?"

"Ancient vampires who were once said to rule all of us and are keepers of records. Many of the customs we yet observe— at least most of us do— are attributed to them."

"Wow. Nobody mentioned this before."

"You didn't ask." Before I could retort, he added, "We don't usually talk about them."

"Oh." I'd ask him why in a minute. "I'd actually wondered if there was a council or something. You know, like some group who oversees all you Princes, Kings and Queens, whatever."

Nod from him. "This all began with them, it is said."

B.C. was sounding more plausible in my head.

"So you answer to them," I said.

"Not directly. They keep to the shadows. They allow us to handle our own disputes, most of the time."

"They're mostly figureheads, then?"

"The very *idea* of the Anima is enough to keep many vampires in line, as these Ancients are quite respected and feared. They are liken to some of the old Gods; keep them appeased, but never, ever seek their attention, people say. Hope to be ignored, this is best."

"But Vicont wasn't or isn't afraid of them?"

"Oh," he laughed, "I don't know about that. They are certainly Gods in *his* eyes."

"Did you ever ask them for help with him? Couldn't they mediate or something?"

"*He* won't seek them concerning our affairs, because his hands are dirty. The same holds true for me. I'm not exactly a helpless, wholly innocent victim when it comes to dealing with him. So in short—no, I haven't and won't."

"Oh. No risking their wrath. I don't suppose they'd approve of what we're doing now—would they?"

"Likely not—if they're even around. But let's move on, lest we summon them by speaking too much of them."

He wasn't joking, so that must be why they didn't talk about them, and even Michel was afraid of this group, I realized. Could hear the fear in his tone. So I moved on, rather than asking him to clarify what he meant about them being around.

"All right, back to your special gene. Did it cause extra problems when you were turned?"

A dark smile then shadowed his features. "Somewhat, but as I am not *exactly* as Travis, the issues were more easily controlled."

"What kinds of issues?"

He super-beamed a smile at me. "So utterly fascinated, you."

I smiled back, not bothering to mention that he was stating the obvious.

He carried on. "My issues were more to do with learning what my powers were, learning to control them, and, oh," he

45

tapped his lips, his eyes sparking, "and getting carried away."
Beneath his fingers, his lips mischievously curved.

"Doesn't sound so different from Travis."

The mischief factor turned up several notches in his expression. "I *knew* what I was doing, and I was *reveling* in it. It doesn't cause the same conflict in myself that it does for Travis."

"Ah. So you were never feral."

"No." He gave off an elegant shrug. "But, give a boy some power, and he simply must test it, after all."

I chuckled, even though I imagined he might have been a very destructive adolescent.

"Mmm, yes. Petrov's patience grew as thin as tissue paper the fourth time I destroyed one of his mansions," he said.

Stare.

Then a shrug. "I'm sure he deserved it and could afford more mansions." I studied his dancing eyes. "How did you destroy them?"

He ticked them off on his fingers as he spoke. "Bonfire, mentally throwing objects around and bringing down walls, a combination of the two, and what appeared to him an act of Zeus, or some such."

Hand up. "Excuse me? An act of Zeus?"

That impish grin formed on his face again. I jumped when the hairs on my body felt like they lifted, as if I was suddenly sitting in a field of static electricity. Looking into his eyes, positive the gold in them was growing, I watched them flick up and followed his gaze just in time to see one, then two, three, of the light bulbs in the chandelier flicker, flicker, flicker, brighter and brighter, and then—

They all burst.

Blink.

My eyes shot back to him.

"Electricity," he said. "Which can also tie into fire, hmm?"

46

Slightly stunned, some words popped out of my mouth. "But there was no electricity back then."

He leaned close and the feeling of static increased. So did the gold in his eyes. "Not harnessed in that form, no," he said, gesturing to the chandelier. "Certainly Zeus could do more than explode light bulbs, in any case, hmm?"

Right, exactly, but—huh? Wait. "Nooo." My brain must have gone numb with surprise.

He leaned even closer. "What is Zeus most famous for, Trey?"

"Infidelity."

Laughing bells followed my blurted comment, then he said, "True enough, but really now, you know this is not what I speak of. Is it too much for your mortal mind to accept?"

Crackling. The air around him crackled.

Jaw, gonna drop.

"No way."

He gave me a mega-watt grin.

"Holy shit."

He kept on grinning.

There was nothing else to say but, "*Groovy*."

"Mmm, yes. It rather is. Such displays on my part can be a bit draining at times, however."

"I would guess it takes a lot of energy to, uh," wow, "toss lightning bolts." Jesus, can he *really* do that?

Airy hand wave from him and the static, the crackle, subsided. "It's full lightning storms that are exhausting. Mentally, more than anything else, particularly depending on what it was that set me off. I gather energy from such things, from electricity, which in turn helps me to unleash it. And of course one's body contains electricity. It's *expending* it that takes it out of a person."

Back to gaping.

More grinning from him.

"Dude. Would you show me sometime? Uh, not that I want you to hurt yourself."

"Ah, best not. Fully cutting loose, to use your modern lingo, is often a result of me being *mightily* peeved, shall we say? Hmm, yes, we shall."

"Oh. Uh, no, I'm not up for fried Trey. I'm sure you wouldn't like the smell, either."

Breezy chuckle from him.

"Jesus. Can Travis do something like that?"

Saucy reply from him. "Mmm, he can do a lot of things. Ask him."

"Fair enough." I thought of the conversation with Travis while fighting the urge to smooth my hair, suddenly thinking it must have stood up in places. "So I'll ask this. Do you feed off different things than Aeshma, besides electricity?"

"Yes, we have some different tastes. One that we share is a raging lust."

"Yeah, well. That one's not so bad, I think. As long as you can get partners, I mean."

His laughter tinkled around me. "No, not so bad. Gabriel is more than enough for me, though as you well know, I do *so* love to flirt. Sexual energy is so delightful to my senses, wonderful to feed on."

I'd call it more than flirting, but whatever. "Feed on? You need it?"

His laughter became bells again. "Define need." His hand went to his cheek as he calmed himself. "It *is* energizing, I must say, but rather than die from a lack of it, I believe I'd merely be decidedly insufferable."

"A grumpy bastard, eh?" He nodded and I laughed. "What's different about the two of you?"

"Travis carries a darker demon gene, one could say. An underworld demon, we might even say, to put it in your human terms. You may compare me to demons of light and fire. The lines may blur as we are both vampires, but generally I am drawn to the more pleasant aspects of the world, where Travis' demon aspect finds much pleasure in its underbelly."

"So we're back to fire." My eyes moved over his face. Then I couldn't help touching his cheek. "Radiance. That inner radiance of yours that—whoa. That's why your skin nearly glows the way it does."

And the electricity of his presence *was* literal, not just a human metaphor I'd come up with before. At last the full click and bam, right between my eyes. I practically *was* in the presence of gods. The thought hit *me* like a bolt of lightning. It was going to take me a little longer to wrap my brain around this, I ventured.

Vampires, Voodoo Marks, Ghosts and *Real Demons*.

Oh. My.

After the lightning strike, questions about Vicont returned while Michel continued to gaze at me, patiently waiting with a ghost of a smile that suggested he knew where my thoughts had gone, yet again.

"Sooo…Vicont figured out what you were after he turned you?"

Michel frowned and I figured *bad move*, Trey, subject dropped. But then he said, "He knew before. It is a reason he wanted me."

"How did he know? Travis said his Maker couldn't have known." But maybe that was his way of dealing with the abandonment. Or maybe Vicont was just older and more educated about it, where Clarice wasn't.

"I sincerely doubt Clarice could have known. Vicont himself didn't know about me straight away. He spent some time seducing me with his way of life, all the while cataloguing details about me. Comparing, contrasting. He tasted me a few times and I believe this sealed it in his mind."

Brows, knitting. "You tasted different?"

"Even as a human, apparently. More so now."

Travis had said his blood was very sweet to others. But he'd been talking about after his change—well, or so I thought. Interesting.

"So Vicont must have tasted it in someone else before then, right?" I asked.

"Yes."

"Damn. Did he want you for the power you'd have?"

"Powers he hoped I'd have, yes. I came to understand this after a time." His eyes narrowed. "He didn't tell me exactly what I was in the beginning. Special, this he would say, but he did not explain in what regard, precisely. Instead it was in the way one courts with the idea of bedding the other."

Sleazy.

Wait.

"You—you and him?"

"Yes of course," he said, as though it was ridiculous to think otherwise. "However, he would not consummate our relations until I was turned, much as it tortured me to wait." He actually smiled. "I was a randy mortal, which should not prove surprising. I had varied tastes even then."

Um. Well, yeah, okay. I should've already guessed it, since Vicont wanted them to be 'family' again, and human Michel probably thought Vicont was a wonderful guy. It was just hard to imagine Vicont as sexy enough to sleep with when all I'd seen was what a raging dick head he could be.

A darker part of me had also briefly thought Vicont might have forced Michel, used vampire magic. I shoved that away. Willing was certainly better.

If he caught that sick thought, he let it slide, because his laughter caressed me. "Don't worry; I understand completely that you find him repulsive."

Since he was laughing, which was a new thing when it came to Vicont, I said, "I can admit he's decent looking. Too bad his personality gets in the way."

Michel nodded. "I believe, as you might say, that you have said a mouthful. But I thought I loved him, Trey, and I thought that he loved me."

I cleared my throat, thinking of Travis, again. "Did he make you wait because he thought he'd hurt you?"

The grin fled his face. "So he said, but it was yet another seduction into becoming his Demon of the Night. I could have him *after* the change."

"Straight back to raging dick head."

"Mmm."

Mental head shake. Michel wasn't grinning anymore, but he wasn't upset. "But you chose to be a vampire, right? He seduced you well."

"Yes and no. I hadn't given him my answer when he took me."

Took him. Didn't like the sound of that. "Tell me you don't mean that he forced you."

"I'm afraid I must disappoint you." He leaned back into the couch. "He visited me much more often in the final months before my making. I believe now it's because he was finally convinced I was what he thought I was. I was truly considering being brought over, but then…"

But then…

"But then," he continued, "I witnessed his rather gruesome killing of a mortal, and it frightened me at the time. I'd seen people die, mind you. What truly frightened me was how literally monstrous Vicont became in his rage. I wasn't certain I wished for his gift when I saw this side of him. He knew it and took me immediately afterwards. It wasn't the lovely turning I gave to Gabriel."

My jaw set. It had been another form of rape, if you ask me.

"He spirited me away, and his apology was quite convincing," Michel continued. "Also, our bond was in place. I needed him after that. I could not go back to my mother or anyone else I knew. I may not have been feral like Travis, but a newborn vampire's thirst is very strong. Not to mention that my being a vampire would have given them heart attacks. No doubt I'd eventually have been hunted if I revealed myself, as well."

I searched his eyes. He'd lost everyone he knew before. Damn. All he had left was that bastard Vicont. "Your bond. You mean the one between Sire and offspring; you mentioned that once."

He nodded. "It's much stronger in the beginning. Over the next several decades, I became quite conflicted because of it."

I wasn't sure what to say.

"But I did come to enjoy my powers very quickly," he added. "Vicont's biggest mistake was reintroducing me to Gabriel."

Wait. What? "He knew Gabriel?"

"No, not precisely. He'd seen him in Paris. He knew that I'd fancy him. He brought him to my attention to assuage my restlessness, ten months after my turning. A pretty diversion to make me happy. He didn't know I'd met him as a young boy."

Ten months. And he was nearly a year older in vampire years than Gabriel, he'd told me. Short courtship, but that didn't surprise me.

I refocused. "How exactly was it his mistake?" I might have guesses.

His smile unfurled. "The loyalty Vicont so wanted from me, I gave to my Gabriel. Vicont's been attempting to retrieve it ever since."

That was swimming around in my guesses, yup. "You and Travis. You share that loyalty trait too, then."

"Yes."

Scowl. "How in hell does Vicont figure kidnapping me, or killing Clarice, or any of the other things he's done, will gain your loyalty?"

He waved his hand. "He became angry after a time of attempting nicer ways. He's tried threats, sugar and spice; all of it fails, eventually. Aside from this, he's, to borrow a word from you, twisted."

"I'd say so. How'd he get that way? Or was he always that way?"

"I don't rightly know if he was always this self-serving as a mortal. I tend to think it's highly possible. I also feel it's that the older he became, the more he detached from humanity, whereas I didn't. Something he didn't consider is that my demon aspect, if you will, is fascinated with the world, which amplified my *human* love affair with the world. I can be monstrous, but I haven't lost my socially acceptable emotions."

"This is where I say I'm really glad you didn't."

He patted my cheek. "I like you, too."

And that got me to grin. But I still had more questions. "Is Vicont *special?*"

"No. He is a rather ordinary, if very old, vampire. Powerful in his own right, but ordinary."

"Just how old is he?"

"He would never tell me. At least nine centuries. More, I'm quite certain."

Nine? I'd just (sort of) wrapped my head around eight. *Dayum.*

My mind, breezing through ideas, deciding we'd had enough of Vicont for now, because I needed time get over the fact he could be even older than *nine centuries.* Not to mention his raping Michel of mortality was still bugging the hell out of me, whether Michel embraced what he was now or not.

Let's go for different-yet-related questions, Trey. "So, this special gene. Is this why you can stand the sun? Did he know that, too? Because I could understand a vampire coveting that."

"I'm sure it's a reason I can, but he didn't have knowledge of it. As far as I know, he still doesn't. He would easily assume I fled his mansion just before he woke for the night when I visited before; I always woke sooner than he." A sly smile formed. "My ability evolved over time, perhaps first dampened under the gift of immortality and then equalizing. Longer and longer exposures were possible, but I did my best to keep some secrets. I learned the value of this from him."

I may have mirrored that smile. "Then he wasn't a complete waste of your time."

His smile took a dark edge. "Not at all, darling."

"Well. Since we're on the subject, is Gabriel *special*?"

He offered me a heated gaze along with a laugh that literally warmed my insides.

"That's not what I meant, and you know it," I said through my own sudden laughter.

He grew more serious. "So I *believe*."

Gazing at him, waiting.

"It really doesn't amount to more than my own musings, perhaps, Trey," he spread his hands, "but you'd no doubt find it interesting, as you are his descendent. Truth be told, I've wondered myself if there is a connection."

Exactly where my thoughts had blown. Did I have some special gene? Did it have anything at all to do with my gifts?

"I'm listening," I said.

"Very well. I've long felt he wasn't of this world. I felt this before his change. Though I don't have all of the pieces of the puzzle, I think—"

A knock. A knock on the big double doors. Michel's head tilted and I think he was feeling out who might be on the other side.

He stood up. "It's Kar." He strode to the doors and opened them while I just sat there pondering what might be *special* about Gabriel, thinking this was the worst time for Kar to interrupt.

"Pardon, my Prince, but I must speak with you." Kar's eyes found me. "Forgive me, Master Trey. I must speak with him privately."

Of course. He wouldn't have interrupted if it weren't important.

I got up and headed to the desk. "No problem. I'm sure you have business, and I should look over these files some more." I grabbed those files and headed toward the doorway, because Kar's expression left me incapable of protest.

"Thank you, beloved. We'll get back to our conversation soon," Michel said as I reached him. "Also, I shall, of course, keep you informed on those mission details."

"Sounds good." Yes, we're definitely resuming this conversation soon, man. I gave them each a smile. "Well. See you."

"Good evening, Master Trey."

"Just Trey, remember?"

Kar smiled at me. "Ah, yes. Good evening, Trey."

I nodded. Received a kiss to my cheek from Michel and headed out. As I headed down the spiraling stairs, I started listing what I knew about Gabriel in my head and comparing it to whatever legends popped up in the meantime.

And thought about acts of gods. And living for more than nine centuries. And ancient vampire councils. And, and—

Thought overload, brain smoking now.

Chapter 4

SEPTEMBER 3

Trey

I hastily strode toward the building, intent on a hit and run affair. I needed to pick up some papers from my office. Corporate espionage didn't halt my client's other business, and there were a few issues I needed to check up on.

I breezed through the front doors, quickly closing the distance to the reception desk, where, as it would happen, Odette was at her post. She looked up from her work, gave me a large smile, and I decided I could spare a few to talk to her; I mean after all, I liked her, and it probably wouldn't do to look anymore suspicious than gossip in the office already suggested I was.

"*Salut!*" she greeted me. "It's good to see you; you haven't been in the office for a long while. I began to worry you weren't returning."

I mirrored her smile even though her last comment struck me as odd, for reasons obvious in my head. "Hey doll, good to see you too." I glanced around as I came to a halt. "Robert in?"

"No, he took a personal day. Do you have a message for him?" She reached for a pen.

"Nah. Actually, I'm glad he's not here."

She chuckled and set her pen down. "So am I."

A grin formed on my face for that. "Well, anyway, I've been very busy. I've done a lot of work from home."

She eyed me up and down. "*Oui*, your clients have many accounts, and you also have a life to live, *n'est ce pas*?" She broke into another smile. "But still, even though you don't need to come into the office for all of your work, I missed your face." A coquettish bat of her lashes followed those words, and following that, a husky giggle.

"Ahh, well, I missed your pretty face too, doll." I tossed her wink.

"Will you be less busy soon, so that I can see more of you?"

"Eh, not for a while. I'm doing a little side work for my clients."

One of her brows lifted. "Oh? Seems you have so much work to do already, what now?"

"Sorry, I can't say." Apologetic smile. "Confidential."

She waved her hands. "Okay-doke." She glanced at my briefcase as I set it on the counter before looking me in the eye again, and her expression grew somber. "They ask a lot of their attorneys." She hesitated. "They treat you well, no?"

"*Si*." I studied her expression closely.

"*Monsieur* Lecureaux—Michel, he treats you well?"

Faint knitting of my brows. "Yes."

She discovered a small smile. "*Bien*." She nodded. "*Bien*."

I studied her a second longer, thinking about her comment on my not returning. "Odette?"

"*Oui*?" She perched on her chair.

"When I started here, you sounded as if you really liked Michel."

She nodded much too much. "He's nice to me always, very charming, *c'est vrai*."

57

"Then tell me," I leaned over the reception counter best I could, "why are you so concerned about how they treat me?"

She nervously straightened some papers. "I like you. I want to know that they treat you well, that's all."

I shook my head, lowered my voice. "No, it's more than that; I can tell. You seem genuinely worried. Why?"

She straightened the same papers again. "I hope that you stay. If they treat you well, then you'll stay."

I cocked a brow.

She looked at me a few seconds, then whispered, "They've lost a few attorneys since I have been here."

"Yes, I'm aware."

"Some of them, they disappeared."

"Like Stefan."

Solemn nod from her followed by a conspiratorial whisper. "He was bonkers, last I hear."

Heard that, too. "Is he still in Paris?"

She shrugged.

"Do you think *les Messieurs* had something to do with it?"

She turned to her computer, quickly saying, "I don't think anything."

I walked around the reception counter, touched her arm. "Odette, you can talk to me." I gave her what I hoped was an encouraging look. "I know how to keep secrets."

Her head turned; her questioning eyes lifted to meet mine.

"I've been getting to know them pretty well, so if there's something you're worried about…" I left it hanging there. I wasn't sure just what she knew or didn't, but I was certain they wouldn't hurt her. I was certain she might need someone to talk to who wouldn't say she was crazy—well, not completely certain. But maybe.

In her eyes, I could see the reaching of a decision.

She touched my hand. "Normal, I don't think that they are normal."

Voice, low. "In what way?"

"It's crazy." Her hands fanned air. "Forget that I say anything, ever."

Voice, lower. "They're not like other people." Her eyes jerked back to me. "I know that, Odette."

"No, they are not," she whispered.

"Not like any other people in the world you've ever seen or met."

Her whisper became a shadow of itself. "No. They are... unearthly."

Perfect word, that. "Do they frighten you?"

Her eyes bounced between mine. "Truly? Only when they are upset."

"They haven't been upset with you though, have they?"

Small shake of her head. "*Non, non.* It's true that Michel is always pleasant to me, but I have seen him angry." She fidgeted a little.

"Hey, remember, I can keep secrets. I won't tell them what you said, this is *entre nous.*"

"*Entre nous.*" Her head bobbed slightly. "Okay, between us, it's the other who is, is—spooky. That one, he's a beautiful ghost, to be certain, but spooky."

I could understand that statement easily. Gabriel was an enigma to everyone here, and he'd had a major confrontation with Robert in the offices.

She grabbed my arm as she exited her chair and once standing leaned in close, face tilted up toward mine. "I was here when he argued with Stefan and then met with *Monsieur* Bouchet."

Wait. Argued with Stefan? This was a previously unoffered piece of gossip. I decided to go past that for now, because my ultimate goal didn't involve freaking her out more.

"Yes, Gabriel can be rather direct and uncompromising," I said.

"Stefan was very frightened."

I went with, "I imagine Gabriel's temper isn't pretty, no."

"Stefan never came back to the office after that," she whispered.

Uh huh. Dead? No worries, Trey. They like *you* and you're *not* going to steal from them.

No. Way.

"Maybe he's in a mental institution somewhere," I offered.

Sure. Sure he is.

Thoughtful tapping of her chin with her index finger. "I don't know. Stefan, he did do bad things." Her face relaxed. "But you know, I must admit that Gabriel spoke to me another time that he was here, and he was quite polite, a gentleman, truly he was." Her lashes fluttered and closed. "*Dieu*, so strangely beautiful, that one." She shook herself and grabbed my shoulders, stretching to bring her mouth close to my ear. "Just, he felt *very* dangerous that night."

Dangerous, why yes. Yes he could be, no debating that.

She settled back on her heels and I studied her eyes. "I don't think you ever need to worry about them, Odette."

She studied my eyes in return.

"You've worked here a few years," I said. "Michel *likes* you, and I don't believe Gabriel *dislikes* you." I laid my hand on her shoulder. "I happen to know he doesn't speak to just anyone, so you see, it's good that he talked politely with you."

Her lips parted, sealed, and parted again. "I never gossip about certain things. I don't. I won't. Only to you."

They knew that, my employers—my family. They knew about the gossip that *did* go around the office.

"They trust you." I gave her shoulder a squeeze. "Don't *worry*."

"You," her eyes moved over my face, "you know them *very* well, now?"

Just a nod, that's all I gave her, keeping my gaze level. I knew them a lot better than she did, anyway.

She studied me some more, then found a small smile after she took a breath. "Then as you say. It's better since you arrived in Paris, I know this."

"Of course it is." I winked and grinned. She laughed a bit, which is what I was after. I glanced around the room, and back to her, about to fish for some kind of confirmation. "Does Robert think they're normal?"

She shook her head. "But maybe not the same as me." She gestured between us. "As we."

"But he's afraid too, I think."

"To say *anything*." Suddenly she let go with a bark of a laugh, covered her mouth trying to stop it, and then dropped her hand. "It's not nice, not nice at all, but sometimes I find it funny."

Which certainly had to be something Michel liked about her.

I offered a smile. "I'll tell you a not-so-secret secret. I think it's funny as hell."

Whisky giggles from her. Then a frown. "But still, if – no, he would have disappeared a long time ago."

I couldn't say for sure how Robert would – retire. For now it seemed like Michel still had too much fun playing with him, so.

"Probably," I said.

We both heard footsteps, then.

"Anything else to file, sweets?" she asked me for the passing attorney's benefit as she backed away and turned toward her chair.

"Nope, that covers it." I nodded to Guy as he walked through, went back around the desk, and grabbed my briefcase. "I'm gonna grab some stuff from my office, and then I've gotta split, so. See you."

Soft smile from her. "See you. Also, *merci*."

"*De rien* toots." Return smile. "*De rien*."

Michel

His voice slid like mink over my exposed flesh. "What takes you from our bed, my love?"

Turning my head from the window to look across my shoulder, the vision of him captured me before I could reply.

He now lay on his stomach, his head toward the foot of the four-poster bed, which brought him a closer view of me. Chin resting on the backs of his hands, bewitching eyes peeked at me from his perfect face, exquisitely surrounded by a cascade of black silk.

My eyes wandered the length of his body, over the lunar flesh and down his spine toward the gentle, rising curves of his buttocks, and traced every muscle, vein and sinew of his legs before stopping at his feet, which kicked up in the air. My gaze then shifted to where the now healed wound hid beneath the black silk, there on his neck. Only moments ago I'd been attached to him and he to me, swimming in the circling current of our blood, a perfect circle flowing out of one into the other and back, carried on musical, whispering sighs, our hearts providing the beat, and his soul opulent through my consciousness.

"*Mon amour?*"

"My thoughts," I replied at last, meeting his scrutiny.

"They must be something indeed, to take you from my arms."

"Indeed," I whispered, eyes drifting once more toward the darkened, shuttered window.

"*Dites-moi.*"

Tell him. My arms found my waist as I went over my last discussion with Kar. "You have something to ask me?" Kar had mentioned Elise during our discussion, but this was not foremost in my mind, and, certainly, Gabriel knew it.

I received several ticks of silence in response, which eventually pulled my gaze once more to him. It settled on his lowered lashes.

"Kar did not speak overmuch. He had no need of it, as I have sensed something in you," I said. "He was merely worried."

"I have no wish of upsetting you," were his words through scarcely moved lips.

"Yet it upsets me if you're troubled," I gently reminded him.

Slowly, he lifted his eyes. "Of course, yes of course."

I turned more fully, leaning back against the window's frame. "It isn't like you to be evasive in this manner."

I watched as he fluidly shifted to kneeling there upon the end of the mattress and attempted to tuck the heavy strands of his hair behind his ears, of which about half obeyed. He then looked at me with the eyes of a much younger man, nearly a child, accompanied by a childlike reticence, which admittedly was quite endearing, particularly as it had become an increasingly rare thing during our centuries together.

"It concerns our separation," he offered at last, his delicate hands finding a place to rest upon his thighs.

So that I would not look away completely, I focused on those hands, those thighs. I focused on the way his long nails flirted with polished flesh.

"What do you wish to say of it?" I asked.

I watched those nails flirt with denting the flesh just beneath their tips. "Ever since Elise made mention of certain things, I have not been able to push it from my mind."

These words ripped my gaze away from his hands, demanding it find his face. "What did Elise say?"

"I stayed a time after you left, before I found you by the river."

This I knew, yet it was now obvious I did not know the fullness of their conversation.

"She made mention of how terrible it was for you, my absence," he said.

My eyes took to studying the tapestry to the left of our bed. "No more terrible than it was for you."

"I don't feel this to be true, *mon amour*."

I rediscovered his eyes, but could say nothing. She had told him, she must have told him what I never would, and he must have felt there was truth to her words. I now felt more certain that I understood precisely what he had spoken to Kar about. My ever-faithful Kar had not wished to break anyone's confidence; he was not a teller of tales, and thus he'd not spoken in more than riddles.

"You and *mon* Trey, not so terribly different," said my dark angel.

"There's no point in denying it," I replied as my lids dropped. "How it's worse, however, I don't know."

"Other than the fact I greatly dislike your being harmed, you mean." Before his words ceased softly vibrating through the air, I felt his smooth palms gliding over my shoulders. "It seems that you harmed yourself terribly."

The weight of his gaze forced me to open my eyes, though the opposite felt more true, that it was an impossible thing to do. I looked into those now-shadowed green depths. "I healed."

"But have you? Have you truly?"

He and I both knew the answer to that.

"Tell me, *mon lion*. What did you do?"

I shrank inside. Shrank away from the question, this earnest question, and chanced one of my own, as he was in a soft mood. "Why must you know?"

"Forgive me, but I simply must. I must know more about these missing years. I must know what you haven't told me."

So apparent was this need in his eyes, in the tone of his voice, a swift pang of guilt struck me for what I was about to say—though the guilt would not stop me from saying it; the need, the reflex in myself, was too strong.

"I wasn't truly aware of it. There's nothing much to tell."

His eyes penetrated me fully, and I asked myself why I should believe that lying to him, even with the best of intentions, was ever an option. He could always feel it, and this time he wasn't allowing it to go by unaddressed.

"Nothing much to tell, you say." A cool hand came to my cheek. "Nothing you wish to tell."

I grabbed his hand and squeezed, desperate to divert the subject. "Why must we do this now? It's over, past, settled, yes?"

"But it is not." His look was gentle. "It is not a closed subject."

No, clearly it was not, and wasn't this my doing as well?

"I'm sorry, Gabriel." My vision blurred. "I'm sorry, but—"

"I'm sorry as well." He touched his brow to mine. "So terribly sorry, but please, *mon ange d'ors*, what exactly did you do? Why did you do it?"

Chapter 5

Trey

Having left the office with everything I needed, I made my way home, figuring I'd do some work from there, including some super-spy business. When I opened my door, the scent of baking bread greeted me. God, what a wonderful smell, and I knew it meant another wonderful thing was about to greet me.

"*Hola*, angel," I heard as I dumped my briefcase on the first sofa and headed toward the kitchen. He met me halfway with a bear hug that I returned.

"Hey, baby, fancy seeing you here." I pecked his cheek.

"You no mind? I felt like being here."

"Of course I don't mind. I gave you the key for a reason." I grinned down at his upturned face.

A smile brightened his features. "First time I use it."

"Yeah, I know. Took you long enough."

He chuckled. "Not so long; you are impatient, is all."

"True enough," I agreed, pecking his nose. "It's pretty cool, coming home to you, know that?"

"I do now." He smiled wider. "Is nice."

"Well then, we're in perfect agreement. You waited too long."

"Hee. Okay, if you say."

"I did."

He playfully swatted my butt and turned to head back to the kitchen. "I must check the bread."

"Hang on." I grabbed his arm and yanked him back, then pinned him around the waist. "First..." I planted a firm, wet kiss on his lips. "Okay, now you can check the bread."

He grinned sweetly at me before resuming his original path, and I headed for my bedroom to retrieve my laptop, then made my way out to the second sofa and plopped down, settling the computer on my lap.

Then remembered to get my feet off the coffee table before Geoff had a chance to see them there. I chuckled at myself and fired up the laptop.

Ah, domestic bliss, eh?

"What you doing?"

I glanced behind me to see him returning to the living room. "I'm about to do something I shouldn't."

"So why you do it?"

"Because in this instance, I really should."

He made himself comfortable beside me, peering at the screen. "You make no sense."

I grinned as I inserted the flash drive. "I'm doing something illegal, but it's for Michel and Gabriel."

"Oh, that thing."

"Yeah, that thing." I started typing.

"So what you doing?" He peered closer.

"Sending someone a backdoor Trojan." I looked over in time to see the confused look on his face.

"Trojan? I thought this a condom."

I laughed so hard I snorted like Scott when he laughed. When my laughter was close to stopping, I could finally see the confused look still on his face.

"What? You said that the kind," he said.

"Yes, I did, but this isn't the same thing. I can't send one of those through a computer."

He pushed at my shoulder. "I know this."

"Sorry, couldn't help myself."

"Oh…okay, I forgive you, if you tell me what Trojan this is." He batted his lashes.

"Keep that up, and I'll show you again."

He went for a *come on, Trey* look and failed when he giggled. "I like it better without."

"That's my boy."

He grinned. "So…"

"Okay, so." I started typing again. "A backdoor Trojan is a computer virus."

"What it do?"

"This one is going to collect information."

"How you send it?"

"Like this." A click, and off it went.

"Email?"

"Yup." I removed the flash drive.

"They only have to read the mail?"

"A little more than that. We know one of their computer programmers." Grin. "The back door's already there. A simple click on the harmless looking attachment I included with the email, and we're good."

His brows creased in concentration. "The back door is there? Is what?"

"The hidden path for the virus to worm its way through, which the programmer left for us in their computers."

"What if they know what it is?"

Head shake. "I'm able to make this look like official corporate business mail from someone else, thanks to some intel from a mole and my trip to Germany. Also, this virus hides itself damned well, and it constantly morphs. It'll take 'em a while to find it."

"Um. Intel from a mole? This is an animal."

I couldn't stop another laugh, though it wasn't a complete fit this time. I reached across and touched his face. "You're disgustingly cute, do you know that?"

"This is a good thing?"

Another laugh. "Yes, baby."

"Okay." He beamed me a smile.

"Anyway, in this case a mole is a spy; he's on the inside. Works for this company."

"Why to call a mole?"

"Moles dig around where lots of people think they shouldn't. Get it?"

"Ohh." He nodded at me. "Intel is…" he held up a finger. "Intelligence?"

"Very good, yes." I smiled at him.

His smile reversed itself. "Won't they know where it come from? They can trace, what is called…"

"IPs? Yes, they can, but thanks to Travis, I have software that hides my IP. With it I can change it, too."

"Um. Different IP every time you want?"

"Yes."

He looked very proud. "I learn much from you."

"Yeah, not all of it good." I chuckled, and he shrugged.

"I not going to do this, not to worry."

"Of course you're not; you're a nice young man, unlike me."

"I think you nice." His lips downturned. "Just I don't want you in trouble."

"Me either. Don't worry; we're all going to great lengths not to get caught."

"But in the finish, they'll know." Full-blown frown from him.

"It'll be too late, sweetie."

"But if they want revenge."

I set the laptop on the coffee table and put an arm around his shoulders. He pressed himself into my side. "Maybe, but I'm all the way in now, baby, and our little family isn't going to let anything happen to me. To us."

"I know they try hard to keep us safe."

I tightened my hold on him. "I'm sorry to worry you."

"No, it okay. I understand."

I couldn't stop the smile. "Of course you do."

"It all works out in the finish."

My smile grew as he tilted his face toward mine. "Well, see, there you have it, *bonito*."

He found his smile again.

"So, what else did you do today besides come here to bake bread?"

"Not so much. I clean my apartment."

"That couldn't have taken long," I teased. "It's always clean."

"Because I always clean."

Exactly. "Is that all?"

His fingers tapped at my knee. "I walk a little." He scooted away from me.

I cupped his chin in my free hand and lifted it. "I'm starting to have the feeling something's bothering you, and it wasn't my spy business at all."

"They call me today." His brows creased.

"Who?"

"My parents."

I searched his eyes. "Did you have an argument or something?"

His fingers fiddled with my lapel as he shook his head. "Mama asks if I meet anyone. I want to say, but I didn't say."

I let go of his chin and covered his twitchy hand with mine. "I haven't wanted to make you feel uncomfortable by asking, but—why haven't you told them you're gay?"

His teeth worried his lip a bit before he replied. "Papi might not like it, and Mama be afraid for my soul."

"So she's very religious."

"She wasn't before so much like this, but a new priest came." He scowled. "So strict. Mama changed. The old priest was much better."

"Fire and brimstone," I muttered.

"Huh?"

"He talks about the devil a lot and going to hell, right?"

"Oh." Another scowl with his nod. "I was younger when he first come. He sometimes scares me, too. Mama is a beautiful person. She is," he quickly added. "He's so *scary*. He think people are, what he say…going soft, sinning more than ever."

I shushed him with a finger. "Of course she's beautiful. She raised you, after all. Some people are just very convincing, like that priest. Maybe she lost her way, and he's taking advantage."

He grabbed my finger. "That it. *Abuelo* say that once." He grabbed my other hand. "I know he would like you."

I remembered what Geoff had said before. Hell, I'd never forget. "I'm the other soul."

A smile finally broke on his face.

"Maybe he could help your mother understand, Geoff." I touched his cheek. "Find her way back." I gazed into his eyes. "And you, what you are. Surely you can look into her and know that she loves you, will always love you, no matter what."

"I know she love me, but I don't want to say on the phone, about you. I should tell her when I'm there. Just hard to think what might be in her eyes when I say, and I don't know…I don't know what the priest will do." Then he nodded. "But you are right. It is okay in the finish."

I gave him a smile—my always optimistic boy.

"Angel?"

"Hmm?"

"Why you never tell your parents?"

I stopped to think about it. Why hadn't I? Why hadn't I *really*? All the scenarios in my head, what was it that frightened me most?

71

My eyes dropped. "I might have underestimated my mother, actually. I didn't want to disappoint her in any way. Maybe have them fight over me, because I felt Dad wouldn't care so much about my sexual preferences."

His arms found their way around my neck.

"I could give other reasons, things I thought, but it comes down to that, really. It was mostly me. I realize that, now. It was mine, something only for me, not something for her to approve of or not, or to be looked at with pride or shame. All mine." I paused. "She was good to me, really. Somehow it was easier to talk to Dad, though."

He pressed his cheek to mine.

I wrapped my arms around him and hugged him as tightly as I could with the way we were sitting. "Don't do what I did. Don't wait too long, if you can help it. You never know when it might be too late."

He moved his head back, brought his hands to my face, and kissed me softly. "Maybe not too late."

My eyes closed. I'd certainly thought of that, but I wasn't quite ready to truly think about that. Geoff didn't say anything else about it, just gently worked his fingers through my hair.

"I came here today because I know I feel better when you come home," he said.

I opened my eyes to see the tender look in his. "Do you?" I went happily along with his rearranging of the subject.

"Very much."

"Good." I kissed him. "You make me feel better, too."

"*Te amo*," he said, softly, and kissed me just as softly.

"*Te amo, bonito. Te amo.*" I went for a deeper kiss just as my cell rang. "Shit, I'm sorry; it might be business. I have—"

"Answer." He swiftly kissed my cheek. "I go to get the bread out." He got up as he said it and headed that way, while I pulled my phone out and brought it to my ear.

"This is Trey."

"Trey du Bois?" a voice I didn't know replied.

Pause.

"My name is Phillip. I have your number courtesy of Travis Starke."

"Phillip. As in?"

"Mistress Elise's emissary."

"All right, then. What do you need?"

"I have urgent information to impart. I am not privy to your Prince's private line and could not reach him currently in any case, so if you would please pass a message as soon as it is feasible, I'd be grateful."

"Go ahead. Make it quick; my cell's about to die."

Never knew when someone else might be listening.

"Understood. Please tell the Prince that area five has an employee who needs dealing with before he ruins our *department*. We need to speak to him as soon as possible."

I get it. Our department—one of our *moles*. Shit.

"Got it."

"Thank you, *Monsieur* du Bois."

The line went dead. Smart boy.

I hit speed dial for Michel, deciding I'd give it a shot.

Unsurprised by his not answering, I stowed my phone in my pocket and stood up, just as Geoff was coming back from the kitchen.

"I've got to go by Michel's and give him a message."

He looked a bit crestfallen, but just as quickly smiled. "Okay."

I strode to him and finished the kiss I'd started before the crap call. "You're the best, know that?"

He gave me a firm nod. "Uh huh."

My hand had to run over his hair. "Love you. I'll try to be back soon."

"Love you, too, but I guess I eat bread alone." He mock pouted.

"Save some of everything for me." After giving him a wink I headed for the door, nearly running into P.K. after opening it.

"Hmm, maybe you *are* psychic," she said, her lips tilting upwards.

I kissed each of her cheeks. "I was leaving, actually. So hi and bye."

She sighed. "Just when I'd arrived to hang out with you."

"*Your* sensors must be off," I teased.

"Apparently so. I feel like I've hardly seen you, lately. More business?"

Business? Yes. I hadn't exactly told her what kind of business, um…yet.

"Yeah, business. We'll get together soon as I can, promise. Right now I gotta split." And before she could get a word in, I added, "Geoff's inside. Go eat some of the bread he just made."

"Mmm, I smelled it before you opened the door." She smiled. "I can live with Geoff and bread for now."

"Come in, come in," we heard Geoff say.

"You heard him," I said, then as we passed each other, "Save some for me."

"Some of Geoff, the bread, or both?"

As I walked down the hall. "Bread. Geoff's not on your menu, and you're definitely not on his."

To the sound of her laughter, I headed down the stairs.

Michel

"*Ange*?" he prodded. "Please?"

I ran my fingers over my eyes, then gazed and gazed at him. I took a breath, stalling.

Stalling still more, yet truly wishing to know, I asked another question rather than reply to his. "When I said it wasn't more terrible for me than it was for you, why did you say you don't feel this to be true?"

He made a thorough study of my eyes before his lashes fell to half-mast. "Because I do not remember as you do."

I could only take in his expression.

"I didn't live it as you did. Why I didn't express this to you before—why I didn't consider your pain fully before, I can't say."

The way his mind worked pained me greatly when it came to our separation, for I had caused him to lose so much time, so much time. And yet, I was somewhat grateful for it. To hear him say this to me now caused a wider rift within me.

"No." I slipped my fingers under his chin. "No, don't do that. You've no blame in this."

He remained silent.

"Gabriel..." I nearly sagged. "It's because you didn't know what I was doing during all of that time."

His lashes lifted. "You never told me how much you truly suffered. Yet another thing you will no doubt berate yourself for." He took up my hands, and kissed the knuckles on the backs of each one. "I'm sorry to bring this discussion to you now." He frowned, but not at me. At himself. "I keep telling myself to let it go."

"But you need to know," I whispered.

"I would know everything of you, my love."

This I understood, as I felt the same of him. It was never that I *didn't* understand this, and I knew that this day would come. I had merely been practicing the art of procrastination, of which I was an otherwise poor student.

"You haven't forgiven yourself in all these years," he added.

My conversation with Trey flashed through my mind. I wanted to do this for Gabriel, how I wished it. But even for him, I hadn't been able to.

"Gabriel," I began, "During that time..."

I paused, and then I heard a tapping. Realizing it came from our front door, I knew then how deeply I'd been sinking in the current subject, for I'd not sensed a thing before the sound. I focused outward.

"It's Trey. There's a feeling of urgency."

"Then you should allow him inside," he conceded.

"Please, Gabriel. Give me a little more time." It was much to ask, I knew, considering how long I'd already been keeping it close.

But my Gabriel, he did not begrudge me this, and how I loved him for that.

"I can wait." He placed a kiss to my cheek. "Go, lest he thinks we are not about answering the door."

I found a robe, slipping into it as I left our chamber, very much loving Trey for his fortuitous timing.

Chapter 6

Gabriel

"When did he call?"

"Less than half an hour ago. I came straight here."

Their words drifted up the stairs to reach my ears as I descended. I more firmly wrapped Michel's robe about myself against the chill. A chill that did not come from without.

"Yes, I do know of whom he spoke."

More of Michel's words reached me as I descended the second flight of stairs, and I found that I was not perturbed by Trey's interruption, but grateful. My questions could wait, should have waited. There were more, concerning Phaedra's brother, but these questions, too, could wait.

A pox on my tongue; I would silence them.

"Greetings, *petit-fils*," I said as I entered the front room, my eyes alighting on Trey.

He turned away from Michel in mid-sentence to greet me in return. "Hi, *grand-père*." His gaze made a sweep of me. "I'm sorry if I interrupted something."

I held out my hands as I reached him. "It would seem important; no need to apologize." I kissed each of his cheeks. "It is always lovely to see you, and our not being clothed is nothing unusual."

Trey's laughter warmed me. "True."

"Do not allow me now to interrupt your business." I moved to my chair and settled. As I did so, I did not miss the grateful look Michel handed to me, nor the affection in his eyes.

"One of our moles is having some issues," my love informed me.

"Which?"

He first took the chair next to mine, gesturing for Trey to make himself comfortable. "Spain."

Trey placed himself on the settee. "Does someone need to go there and take care of it?"

"I have contacts in place. I'll send word to them shortly," Michel replied.

"You have people everywhere, don't you?"

At this, Michel only smiled.

"Guess I'll visit Spain with Geoff another time," was Trey's lighthearted comment.

"You may yet be able to take him elsewhere," I stated, looking to Michel.

"Yes," he concurred. "We may have need of someone in New York City."

I observed the faint shadow that darted through Trey's eyes. "To do what?" he asked, whilst I wondered at what I had seen.

"There is currently a merger on the table between one of my enemy's companies and one that belongs to a neutral friend. This friend does not yet know he is dealing with my enemy," explained Michel.

"Do you want me to run interference?" Trey offered.

"A bit," said Michel, "but also this is a chance to gather firsthand information and possibly acquire another company while you're at it."

I continued to watch their back-and-forth in silence.

"What's the plan, Michel?"

"Simple. Go in as my attorney with another offer. I've already spoken to said friend and informed him of my interests."

Trey's head made to nod. "All right. It'd be cool to take Geoff with me, but I'm wondering if it's safe for him to go."

"Travis would accompany you, but of course it's your decision."

My grandson appeared to turn several things over in his mind. "You're still not sure that you've found everyone involved in his attack, right?"

Michel replied, "This is true, and I must confess the trail has gone a bit cold. You're right to consider this."

"Well. If anyone's still gunning, I don't suppose it'll matter where we go, now will it?"

For my part, I rather supposed that it would not.

"Not truly," Michel agreed. "Our search has not ended, I assure you. We will make certain one way or another that all are brought to justice."

Mon Trey's eyes moved between myself and Michel. "I know you will."

"Certainly news of our retributions has spread," I offered. "I feel you safer from this type of threat than before."

Trey's eyes shifted to me. "I trust your instincts."

"Still, if you have no wish of visiting New York, we shall find another way," I could not help but offer, believing I had a grasp of what the shadow before had been.

"I can go," he was quick to say. "No one else knows your accounts like I do, and after the software crap, I'd rather do it myself."

I felt a swell of pride and love, which I felt emanate also from Michel.

"How I love you," *mon lion* said. "You never do things halfway." His following smile was very wide. "I should think none will be the wiser of your ulterior motives. It's merely business, after all."

"No. Because I'm damned good," Trey was swift to add, at which I could not help but smile, myself.

Michel's laughter, most precious to me now particularly, as I had caused it to flee earlier, seduced my flesh with its warmth.

"Indeed you are," he agreed. "Indeed you are."

"When do you need me there?"

"I shall pass along the details when I'm certain. However, I have some files I'll have sent to you this afternoon."

"All right, then." One of Trey's most enticing smiles, so enticing in its earnest nature, formed. "Maybe I could see Scott. I'll just be there for business, like you said." Yet this smile, soon it reversed itself. "Though if any shit hits the fan around him…"

"I have human allies in the city," offered Michel. "Day and night, you shall be covered. I leave it to you, whether or not you feel it safe to be seen with him."

Trey considered yet again, then commenced with his circle of thoughts aloud. "He was seen with me in Paris." He took a moment's silence. "If I see him, I'll keep it low profile." His hands spread. "If he finds out I was there and didn't at least call, that'll hurt him. I can't have any more of that. If I call, he'll insist on seeing me, so."

"Inform me of your final decision when the time comes. I shall place extra eyes on Scott."

"Thanks, Michel. That means a lot to me."

"You're most welcome. It wouldn't do to have anything happen to the friend you only just rediscovered."

"I'm not involving him in it, so maybe it'll be okay. As long as I don't have to lie, that is." I was relieved to hear Trey's laughter chasing after this statement.

My Michel offered him a gentle smile. "I should hope there will be no reason for him to see Travis shift, or some such."

"No way, no more situations like that." Trey gave off a vigorous shake of his head. "And he still hasn't wrapped his head around all that, or the idea of vampires." Of a sudden, he laughed. "He definitely doesn't need to see Travis in Wolverine mode."

My Michel merely gazed at him. As for myself, I supposed the animal in question could be a fair comparison.

"Uh, X-Men." Trey made a motion with his hands. "The claws, you know?" He paused. "Or you don't know – never mind."

Michel's smile burst free just as I recalled a film he had insisted that we view. "I understand the reference," he said. "I was simply musing over my own thoughts. One or two people sometimes call Travis *Taz*."

"Tasmanian devil," Trey said, laughing once more. "I can see that."

"It is also a play on his initials. Travis Angelos Starke."

"Ah. Angelos, messenger. Cool name. What are yours, by the way? You must have middle names, but you've kept them off your paperwork."

Michel widely grinned. "Which middle names?"

After a laugh, Trey rejoined. "All of them."

"Michel Jean Noël Lecureaux, at your service."

Trey repeated the full name, and it flowed perfectly from his tongue. "Noël is fitting, you being born in December. Beautiful." My grandson's gaze moved to me. "Yours?"

My lover replied before I had the opportunity. "He also has a beautiful name. Gabriel Benoît Christophe."

Trey repeated this also, and offered me smile full of warmth. "I love it. Hmm, if I ever have a son, I could name him Christophe."

I felt my own smile grow for the warmth his words added to my heart. Of a certainty, I was most glad for his interruption.

Trey

Gabriel's smile caught me up for a minute, and that smile shoved away any lingering thoughts I had about Michel's

81

demeanor when he answered the door. Thoughts about asking if they were okay, that is. I didn't want to spoil the upswing in mood. I was betting it was personal anyway, and none of my business. If Michel needed to talk about anything, he would.

I just wanted him to know that he could. He probably did, I told myself. I wondered if he knew just how much he could say to me that I'd listen to, if he needed. He'd been more than willing to listen to me before, after all.

"So what'll happen in Spain?" I asked, shifting my eyes to Michel. He'd taken it lightly, my message, but that didn't mean it was all peaches and cream.

"Once I contact my allies there, they shall assess the situation, deliberate on what should be done, then contact me for my decision. It likely isn't so dire; otherwise the message from Phillip would have been different."

Nod. "Wouldn't want to jump the gun and do something major when it's not necessary."

"Precisely. We should avoid grand gestures just now, if possible, lest we out ourselves. I have other spies in Spain to collect intelligence."

Couldn't stop the grin. "Of course you do." Another nod. "Inside?"

Mischief in his eyes. "But of course. One is never enough. What was it you once said? Always take back up."

Laugh. "P.K. said it first. I finally started taking her advice."

"Thankfully, yes." His eyes sparked with his half grin.

"But wait; are these Elise's spies, or yours?"

His fingertips fluttered to his chest. "I may have been frozen shy of nineteen, but I am not without sense. Nineteen was much older in my time, you realize."

I laughed again. He knew damned well I didn't think he was stupid. "Yes, not to mention you're closing in on four hundred, now."

"Indeed. Therefore, I have spies on her spies, darling," he said.

"Of course you do. I don't know why I asked."

He lowered his hand. "I do. It's because this is what you *do*." He didn't smile, but his eyes were dancing.

Grin. "Well, since you have that under control, I guess I'll head back home. Geoff's there."

Michel stood. "By all means, don't keep him waiting a moment longer."

I got up and strode to him, taking his outstretched hands and exchanging the customary kisses. Turned and did the same with Gabriel. Gazed into his eyes a moment, because I'd also felt earlier that something was bothering him.

But whatever was there before was gone now, so I widened my smile. "See you soon."

"Please, any time, my darling one," he said.

I'd gone from dreaming of words like that, to reality. Still couldn't get over the world I'd landed in. As long as my new family was in it, the rest didn't matter.

"Love you, *grand-père*."

"And I you." He stole my breath with another smile.

The unfinished conversation of mine and Michel's came to mind. Special. Something besides the obvious, that was special about Gabriel.

But now didn't seem like the time to bring it up.

My breath came back. "I'll see myself out. I know the way." I kissed his cheek again and headed for the door.

Michel

I made a thorough study of Gabriel whilst he was absorbed in Trey's departure. He had actively listened to my discussion with Trey; actively participated when moved to.

My darling Gabriel had given me a reprieve, assuredly, and I could only gaze at him with a heart so full it wished to burst.

His body turned in my direction, and his entrancing eyes found mine.

"You are here with me now, my love, and have no wish for your words to pain me," he began, his tone dulcet. "I understand this. Just as I would not bring you pain. And so, it seems a waste, futile, even, to dance this dance, for that itself causes pain. Do not dwell on the subject, nor shall I. I am sorry that I spoke of it to Kar, to anyone at all, just now."

I gathered him in my arms, pressing my cheek to his. "Thank you."

His return embrace lovingly caged me.

"This I will tell you now," I whispered. "Nights upon leaving her bed were the worst." I could tell him this. I needed him to know this more completely than he had before, and I realized that his relenting had removed the pressure of saying it. "The worst, because I always wished it were you. But it wasn't. No amount of mental retreat, conjuring your face, your touch, would assuage me."

His head drew back, and he studied my eyes. "She told me something of it."

Had she confessed even this? Had she confessed the truth of it to him? I wanted to be both grateful and yet worried, wondering what precisely she had said of it. Her words, had they made it seem worse?

He captured my face between his hands. "She said that you were never truly with her. She said much about your pain."

My gaze lowered. He knew, and the pressure lessened more. "Those were some of the worst scars I created, could you see them now," I confessed. At last, I confessed something of it. "I hated myself for giving in to some blind need for release with her."

"But as you just said, it was blind."

I looked deeply into his eyes. "Just when I thought it impossible to love you any more than I do, you give me even this."

"Because I understand, Michel."

Yes. He did. So had Trey.

"As you have offered these words to me," he quietly said, "you may pass on this question for now, but I do have just one, one in my mind this moment I wish to ask."

"Ask me, my love." You, who love me without condition, ask.

"I know that fear at first kept you from me. Yet I've never known how *long* this fear kept you from me. Will you tell me now?"

Too long, my mind said, yet I would tell him now. "Months, nearly a year, actually. I was petrified." How I detested fear in myself.

Fear caused me to do ridiculous things. Monstrous things. Detestable things.

"I am still not blaming you in this," he replied. "But you made yourself out to be a complete villain who was throwing himself at my mercy. It took you so long to speak of this fear, something you must have thought I'd understand."

"I *was* a villain. I didn't wish to make any more excuses. There were no excuses."

"Fear, it isn't an excuse." One of his fingertips traced my brow. "It was real, what you felt. So real even Elise told you to go."

I tipped my head, bringing my forehead to his. "That she did, to her credit. She gave me the final push. The fear of never seeing you again grew and grew, overpowering me. The way your mind works, I also feared you not knowing me one day, and I panicked. I set off to find you, before your mind obliterated me, hoping I wasn't too late."

He caressed my cheeks and let his hands slide to my neck. "I would not have forgotten you, no matter how long the passing of time, my love. Not you. I recognized you soon enough from when we were children, after all."

This brought a smile to me, though it wilted. "Yes, you did at that. But this time it was me who had hurt you, and you had gone, and –"

The dipping of his head cut my words short, and his fangs gently broke through the flesh around my left nipple.

I gasped, cradling his head in my hand, and felt the tears that escaped my eyes stroll down my cheeks.

He drank now from the exact spot his mortal lips had attached themselves when I created him anew so long ago. The place I had deeply pierced for him after draining him, our exchange dizzying in its intimacy.

I knew now without question that which I had always hoped during our separation.

He would not have forgotten me; he would never forget me.

Chapter 7

Trey

Out of habit I took a path that led me by Le Parvis on the way home from Michel and Gabriel's place. I gave a little wave to Remy, one of Geoff's coworkers, as I passed. I was only halfway by when I spotted P.K. heading toward me.

"Hey," I said as we caught up to each other. "I thought you were hanging out with Geoff. I wasn't gone that long, was I?"

"One of the other waiters called him, and the little darling agreed to cover the other man's shift, so our visit was cut short," she explained.

I looked back toward the café. "Oh. I didn't see him."

Her reply brought my gaze back to her face. "He just left for his place to get ready a few minutes ago."

"Well, damn. So much for coming home to him again today."

"Coming home?" She lifted a brow. "I've missed something, here. It sounds like things are getting serious."

Sheepish grin. "I gave him a key."

Her smile practically exploded on her face. "A key already. I'm really happy for you." She touched a finger to her lips. "But this illustrates just how *little* I've seen of you lately, that you didn't tell me sooner." Her brow arched. "Unless you gave it to him yesterday."

Chuckle. "No, it wasn't yesterday." I spread my hands. "Sorry? I've been busy."

Her smile grew again. "It's okay. Maybe your misfortune is my good fortune. Do you have time to catch up with me right now?"

I made a show of checking my nonexistent watch. "For you? I suppose I can spare a few ticks of the clock."

"Always so generous, handsome." There was laughter in her words.

"C'mon," I said, slipping my arm across her shoulders. "How about we just go back to my place?"

"Sounds good to me, especially since it still smelled like fresh bread when I left."

I gave her a smile, and we made the short walk to my apartment building.

"So what's been keeping you so busy lately, hmm?" she asked as she settled onto a sofa.

"Give me a sec. I haven't even sat down yet, or offered you a drink." Grin. "Or found out what you've been up to, not really." I was teasing. Sort of. During our short walk, I'd begun considering, once again, just how much anyone else should know about my covert operations.

Her chin lifted, and her eyes found mine. "You know what I've been up to and I don't need a drink right now, thanks. I'm sure whatever's keeping you busy is far more interesting, so you can stop stalling. Please." She gave a sweet little smile.

I shook my head at myself. Eyeballing her, I sat across from her on the other sofa. "I should just give it up, shouldn't I?"

"Um hmm. Fill me in on the secret."

I planted my elbows on my knees and prepared myself, still debating, but not wanting to say that aloud, because starting with *I'm not sure it's safe to tell you*, wouldn't inspire confidence. I was probably going to get a semi-lecture either way, too.

Well, maybe that's a strong description, semi-lecture. Slightly chastised little brother, that might be closer, when she reminded me about playing it safe and this and that. Though it wasn't a horrible feeling, having a big sister for the first time in my life.

"All right," I said. "I'm involved in some side business of Michel's that has nothing to do with regular business."

She arched a brow at me.

My reply to that was, "May as well call it what it is. Corporate espionage."

Faintly confused expression on her face. "How doesn't this relate to regular business?"

"Well." Pause. "Well, it involves revenge." Hand up. "Before you say anything, that's only a small part of it. It's also about asserting his position, knocking Vicont's allies out of the picture, and fully taking over France. You know. The usual Vampire Mafia sort of thing."

He arms crossed over her chest.

"Go ahead, lay it on me," I said.

She studied me a second. "Was your trip to Germany related to Vampire Mafia stuff?"

"Yup."

"Did it involve breaking and entering, computer hacking, file stealing? All of those interesting-but-illegal things associated with espionage?"

"So quick to assume nefarious deeds, my, my," I shot back.

"Espionage," she repeated.

"Yeah, I did say that. There was no breaking to the entering, though."

She stared at me.

"Travis went with me," I explained.

A quirk of her brows.

"I know, I know. Dangerous. These are big time players. Mm hmm, I know all this," I said. "Travis is still looking after me."

"But what happens if you get caught? He rescues you, kills them all? What about during the day? And will he silence anyone who starts asking questions?"

I lifted my hand again. "I'm not entering any more buildings without permission." That I know of. "And most of the stuff can't be traced to me." Although logically, someone might wonder about their attorney somewhere down the road.

"Most?"

"Um. Well." I pushed at my hair. "I'm probably going to New York soon." And I told her why, before she could ask.

And then I said, "I'd been thinking that the fewer people who knew about this, the better. I don't want to put you or anyone else in danger, if I can help it. But I can't keep much from Geoff, and it's nearly impossible to keep things from you for long." Head shake. "Can't hide shit from this new... family of mine." I smiled a bit. "Not that I'm really complaining."

She gave me gentle look. "I understand why you didn't mention it before. I'm just worried about you, but you know that. I even understand your wanting to help."

"But I'm getting in deeper than necessary, right?"

She placed her hands on her thighs. "I can't deny this crossed my mind."

"They didn't force me. I freely offered."

Neutral expression on her face. "I'm not surprised."

"These other vampires messed with me and Geoff. It could get worse before it gets better, I know, but in my way, I'm trying to help Michel keep things safer for us, too."

"With a little vengeance of your own, handsome?"

No point denying it. "Yes."

Her expression darkened. "What will all this spying do for you guys that you can't do legitimately?"

"It helps us find their weaknesses and exploit them. Find loopholes in clauses. Have advance knowledge of new deals we can jump on. Get to people on the inside who we can sway to our side. He wants to take over Vicont's companies, hit him the wallet. And I remind you, he doesn't want Vicont to know what he's doing."

She contemplated me. "What happens to anyone who considers ratting you out? Or taking advantage in some way? Offer to pay them off, and if that doesn't work…"

"Go ahead, say it. You already said it once."

"Kill them?"

"I'm not killing anyone, P.K."

"Your employers might."

My hand went through my hair. "Yes, and they've killed a lot of other people, long before I was ever born."

"You're privy to it, now."

Stare. "Am I supposed to reform them or something?"

She hesitated. "No."

"You think I could stop them, anyway?"

Her eyes remained level with mine. "No."

"Am I a bad guy, now? I know I'm doing illegal shit, but I'm not a murderer."

A long sigh from her. "No, you're not. Michel sucked you into all of this, pardon the pun. Can you stand by while they do what they do, though?"

I felt my eyebrows come together. "Hang on. First, it sounds like you changed your mind about them. Do you wish I'd stayed away, or that he'd pushed me away?"

Her hand drifted toward her face. "Well. Gabriel's your relation –"

"Yeah. How about all that fate-talk of yours?"

"Yes, I have spoken about Fate. I haven't changed my beliefs on that."

"What about me standing by, then? You think I'm an accomplice."

Vita's death hadn't exactly distressed me, but I wasn't the one who flayed her, and I couldn't have stopped them anyway.

"Well…" she smoothed her hair, appearing to think about it, and I bristled a little.

"Listen, they'll do what they do with or without me around. I've let some stuff slide, yeah. I know they're predators. I also know my morality isn't theirs, and that's just the way it is." My connection to the Dead was apparently expanding my horizons, all right, and I had been thinking that even with my gift lying dormant before, it had affected me in the past.

I was not without my own dark side, never had been. It just happened to be growing since I'd gone in with vampires and grew into my powers.

Apologetic look from her. "You're right, and I didn't really mean any of that the way it sounded."

"Then why are you saying it?" I persisted, still a bit surprised by the turn of conversation. "After I told you about the trial, you said that girl would've died anyway. You reminded me after the thing with Geoff that it was Adele's time, that I was never a murderer. So maybe whoever they kill, it's just their time." Pause. "Even Lucien's told me things happen as they happen, and that's that."

No reply from her.

"You said my gift will give me understanding, right? Well it has, and I refuse to take any blame for who they kill."

She met my gaze. "I did say those things. I'm glad you're not blaming yourself, I really am. You've blamed yourself for enough things in the past already."

"Yes, I have. I figured I'd stop adding to the list."

She almost smiled, but it faltered. "I've also said that everything has a purpose."

"If you don't want to be a hypocrite, then this includes vampires." My eyes dropped to my hands. I didn't want to debate this with her any more—if we were really debating. "They're my family, whatever they are. I don't want to lose my family again. Nothing's truly forever." I lifted my eyes. "I just found you all."

Whisper soft, she said, "I understand, and it's wonderful to hear you say family." More volume returned to her words. "It's just starting to feel scary; it's so broad in scope." Her eyes moved over my face. "Grandma's voice is going off in my head, and it's making me tense; that's why I lost my mind there for a minute. I'm sorry I spoke to you that way. Thanks for talking some sense into me."

My eyes moved over her face. "Wow. I actually got to return the favor."

Soft laugh from her. "Hey, it happens to the best of us."

"To your credit, you didn't try telling me I was rationalizing everything away."

"How could I? You rightly tossed my own words back in my face just when I considered doing that."

My eyes flicked over her face. "I wouldn't say tossed. Reminded. I reminded you."

Her eyes dropped and lifted. "Yes, you were being kind. You are what you are, too, and there it is. Honestly, I'm proud of you for taking charge of your life."

Smile. I scooted to the edge of my seat. "Thanks. But now tell me, do you think something'll go wrong in New York, or wherever? Because seriously, if you do, we'll find another way. I'm not so stubborn that I'd ignore a warning from you—or your grandmother. I listen to Lucien when he's actually being helpful." Well. I try.

"I'm not literally hearing her. It's mostly my upbringing kicking in—which makes me extra sorry for rolling up on you that way."

"It's cool. I forgive you. I know it's because you care."

"Thanks." She smiled fully.

"Still, tell me what you're feeling."

I gazed at her in silence while she seemed to be considering what that might be.

Finally, she said, "I don't know that I have any strong feelings of danger to you. But you know I'm not a master prognosticator."

"So what *do* you see?"

She shook her head slightly. "I should read the bones. I'm not able to really separate what's just a worry and what might be a genuine feeling, right now."

"I know that feeling from questioning myself. Still, kinda strange to hear you say it, even though I know you don't have some magic looking glass." I asked myself if I should be worrying more. Actually, I was already beginning to worry more, because I started thinking this vague feeling of hers could have something to do with Scott or Geoff. Maybe I needed to leave Geoff at home and risk offending Scott by not seeing him.

"I'll read the bones today. I'll have a better answer then, hopefully. You're not leaving immediately, are you?" she asked.

"Not today, as far as I know. Michel's having some files sent over that I need to look at first."

She tapped her teeth. "As far as you know. Then maybe I'll get to this right now. Just in case."

My brows lifted. "You're not even going to try to talk me into staying here until you read them? Just in case?"

Suddenly, she laughed. "What would be the point? You are you, after all."

"And there's nothing for it, right?"

"Not a damned thing." She offered a crooked smile. "You're not holding out on me this time, though. This is progress."

"I was *trying* to, useless as it is."

"You weren't trying that hard, face it."

My grin slowly formed.

"Just try not to run off before I get back to you about this feeling, sound fair?" she said as she stood up. "See? Not insisting, just asking."

"I think I can handle that small request." I got up from my seat, too. "Hey, I just realized. Aren't you usually open today?"

94

"One of my friends is looking after the shop."

Brow waggle. "Which one?"

Her laughter oozed through the room. "You always have your priorities in order, now don't you?"

"Well duh. Isn't this the first thing you learned about me?"

Her eyes swept over me. "The first? I don't know about that." She moved to me and kissed my cheek. "See you later."

"Okay, beautiful."

After she left, I sank back into the sofa and worried some more about what the bones would tell her.

Chapter 8

OCTOBER 13, 1989

Michel

Restless. I was growing ever more restless, pacing about the front room. I could nearly hear him, his mellifluous voice, lightly admonishing me. *You will carve a trench in the flooring, mon lion.*

Except he wasn't here and hadn't been for what seemed an eternity. I longed, how I longed to hear those words, spoken in this very room I had been close to destroying only moments ago, it seemed, in my sudden fit of despair. Fits that had grown, not subsided, over time.

He had not been to our home for years, now, and I myself had taken to avoiding it often enough, for it was far too empty, regardless of our belongings, our treasures. Only one thing had truly filled it. And so, I had nearly followed the urge to tear it down, bring down the very walls, hoping at the very least, this particular emptiness would flee.

It would not flee my heart.

The smallest sliver of hope had kept me from destroying it in times past, a hope that waxed and waned with each encounter he and I had, once I had finally scoured the earth for him. It waxed and waned, for there was tension between us each time. Certainly, I expected this, but just when it might lessen, the next meeting would kindle brighter these tensions.

How long since I had seen him last? Each meeting ended with his parting. Each parting shattered whatever piece was yet left of my heart.

Months. It had been months and agonizing months since our last meeting, and all too brief, it had been.

I was such a fool. Just when it seemed we'd make progress, invariably I said the wrong thing, and next I knew, we were arguing. Arguing over everything and nothing. As I stood, still at last, and stared at his favorite painting, I realized I couldn't even blame him for the times he may have started it. Did it matter who started it? I was the one who created this hell to begin with. Did he not deserve his barbs?

I didn't always understand where some of them came from, what moved him to moments of coldness just when it seemed he had defrosted, but what did it matter in the end? It was all of my doing, my making.

Perhaps it was because I had not yet truly *begged* him to return. I hadn't truly *asked*, for fear he'd say no.

I heard a laugh. It was mine; I was laughing humorlessly at myself. I had not sought him at first, for fear he'd turn me away. Then knowing well in my heart that the greater fear was never seeing him again, I'd found him.

I was now afraid to beg his forgiveness.

How rich and completely ridiculous. I was an utter fool, an emotionally tangled fool.

Yet still, were he to refuse me forever, I could not live with the pain, therefore was I truly such a fool? At least this way, there was always the hope of seeing him again. The hope that he would choose to stay if I did not push, did not beg. Better to fight, than nothing at all, if only to hear his voice, to look upon his face. Better to bear the slice of his words, than not. Did I deserve any less? Carrying on this way, it at least assured me that I would see him again, that I would bask in the flames of his ire. That he was yet *feeling* something.

I sank to my knees, burying my face in my hands. "He'll stop meeting with you if you fight, you idiot. Let him slice you without recrimination, you yet deserve it, yes." I lifted my face, wiping at the sticky tears. "Even if he doesn't like it when you surrender the conversation." New tears swiftly followed the old tears, and I nearly wished to curl up like a baby and weep, the fierce pain in my heart seeking to replace its emptiness.

"What have I done?" I wailed. "It doesn't matter what you thought. It doesn't matter how well they lied. Just beg and be done with it—oh God, why should he ever trust in me again, what have I done!" I longed for a release, a different pain, however temporarily, to supplant the one in my chest.

Nearly in that fetal position, I flashed on the ceremonial blades I owned. I flashed on the foils, the swords and the daggers, the lot of them.

Intent on grabbing the first one that came close to my hand, there was a prick to my senses as I rose—a small sound. I was certain I'd imagined it, until the sound came once more and seemed far closer than I'd realized, once I focused.

Yet once more, a rap on my front door. Perhaps I'd lost all control of the volume of my voice, I thought. Perhaps the entire city had heard me, and someone had sought out the source of the sound. To see if someone were literally dying, perhaps this.

Though I made swift work of cleaning my face on a nearby throw, I was, at first, intent on ignoring the door. Whoever it was could damned well go away and leave me in pieces.

I then regained some manner of my wits. None knocked at my door without invitation. None would make it beyond the fence, unless they shot Loki repeatedly first.

Heart wishing to thunder in my chest, I made my way out of the front room and down the hall towards the front door. Before ever reaching it, my senses spiked with something I would have recognized before; my core warmed with something I would have noted far sooner, had I not been about to lose my mind—and my heart received its wish.

When I opened the door, at once wanting to toss it aside, yet doing so slowly, there he was, revealed to my eyes, and after a heart stopping moment of being captive to his gaze, my own dropped to his form.

So much the same as when last I'd laid eyes on him. As every time I'd seen him. Blue jeans, tattered, aged. Boots, their heels worn down a few centimeters.

But it was the faded vermillion pullover he wore that fully captured my attention. This wasn't as all the other times. It was mine. I remembered it well, the first time he'd ever donned it. He had grabbed it from the armoire one night after making love, and when I remarked that it draped him wrongly, as most of my clothing did, he informed me that he didn't care. He wished complete saturation in my scent, as always. His usual reply to my usual, affectionate jest.

This particular event had occurred over fifty years ago.

My mind left off wondering when and where he'd retrieved this article of clothing when he spoke. The hope it sparked, his wearing my nearly threadbare cashmere, didn't subside in the slightest.

"Michel. I felt that you were here."

Years. It had been years since he'd set foot on this property. That he was here must be significant, my heart dared to say. I wanted to crush him to me. I wished to tell him how damned beautiful he was, standing there in those god forsaken clothes. But I was too overwhelmed and the words would not make it past my lips, my limbs would not obey.

He must have sensed this, yet he merely said, "Might I come in?"

"Yes of course," I was at last able to speak, even though I near swooned with his question. Why, I even managed to move aside so he could enter.

"Thank you," he said as he passed me.

An automatic reply left me. "Always so polite."

"Not always," he rejoined.

No, not always. But I did not say this. He was here, in our home; I would not say this. We were not to the point of jest, not yet. I resolved that it would be different this time. So very different.

I so desperately, desperately needed him to stay. I was a wealth of feeling, balanced on a pinhead. Something I had often said of Gabriel's heart in the past.

I followed as he drifted towards our front room – could it be ours again? – he the phantasm of a panther, and I stopped as he paused before the very painting I'd been gazing at not long before.

"It hangs here still," he said.

"But of course," I whispered, this being the only reply that came to me.

"How long since last I saw you?" He turned, and his bewitching eyes dazzled mine.

He'd asked me this before, and I didn't wish to answer anymore than I had the other times. It was better not to know, perhaps. Yet, his clouded memories slivered my soul.

"Months," I said at last.

His left hand lifted, drifting to his chest. "It feels longer."

I was both saddened and joyous over this statement. "You haven't been here since…" I stopped, the words sitting like low clouds in the air.

He lowered his hand. "I left you. *Je sais*. I would remember being here with your scent enveloping me."

It was an earnest question, the one that left me then, but once it did, I wished to recall it. Reword it or even erase it. "Why have you come now?"

"I missed you."

I certainly could not regret it after his reply. I wished to ask, *would you stay?* But it was too soon. I couldn't, and in lieu of this I said, "You're always welcome here."

In a blur, his hands were at my chest and his face, so close to mine. "Time is dark for me, only spotted with meetings, ours, yet it feels like forever since we parted. I feel you always, but all I feel is pain."

My eyes closed under the weight of his words. Certain that he spoke of his pain, the pain of what I'd done, I was otherwise paralyzed in fear of saying or doing too much—or too little. In fear of his having come to say goodbye for all time.

His sudden, short sniffs came to my ears. "I scent blood; it is fresh. Yours."

"I…" For the love of any god admit it, I told myself. "I was weeping."

"Why?" he asked so earnestly.

Still, I could not look upon him, though I ached to. "I was thinking of you. Of what I've done."

Silence greeted me for three beats of my slow heart.

"What you've done," he whispered.

"How wrong I was," I managed to say. "So terribly wrong. I was quite ready to pull the house down around me and be done with it." Quite ready to inflict more pain upon myself as well.

Yet another silence, which caused my heart to tremble.

"The hour is early," I both heard and felt him say then. "May I stay?"

The breath for my reply caught in my throat. I slid a hand over one of his.

"Mon lion?"

I squeezed his hand, swallowing thickly. How long since he had called me thusly? Far too long.

"Of course."

But no. No, I said to myself. This isn't enough.

"I *want* you to stay," I amended, lifting my lashes to look upon him, my heart, my soul. "I miss you *so*."

Whether he meant a day or a lifetime would matter to me again the next night. For the moment, I could only focus on the wisp of a smile that touched his lips, and that he'd asked me at all. And as I gazed into his bright eyes, I understood why I truly hadn't begged his forgiveness, or rather, knew what I hadn't fully admitted to myself.

This too, was part of my self-punishment. My penance was to long for him but not quite have him, for I'd soiled our union. But I could not stand it a moment longer, and it struck me how my need to punish myself also hurt him, though it was not my intention.

The situation was untenable. As we moved farther into the house, I resolved then to do everything in my power to convince him to stay longer than a day, which included placing myself at his mercy.

SEPTEMBER 4, PRESENT

"Once again I find you deep in thought."

I turned from the Botticelli toward the sound of his voice. "The night you returned," I said. "I was thinking on this."

"I remember it well," he replied, his feet consuming the distance between us.

"As do I." My arms snaked their way around his waist. "You didn't leave."

"*I'm incomplete without you, Gabriel; I'm dying a slow and agonizing death without you, my love*. This is what you said to me the next night." His lips brushed mine. "It is not a bad memory at all, but what other thoughts have I brought to you with my previous questions, *mon lion*?"

"Nothing terrible, my darling, not to worry. Just now, this painting's done it. It often reminds me of that night."

He graced me with a smile. "Of course. It has long been my favorite."

"I'd been gazing at it before you returned, that night. It was as if my doing so summoned you, I later thought. I don't know that I ever mentioned this."

His fingertips created a path along my shoulder that travelled to my neck. "Ah. No." He pressed a kiss to my cheek.

It was me who changed the subject, then, before it might possibly swerve in the wrong direction and rob me of his fondness for the memory. "I'm considering a visit to Spain."

His eyes made a search of mine. "Can they not contain things? Has it already progressed too far? Should New York be abandoned?"

I took a moment to collect my words, the moment needed, as Gabriel didn't often ask so many questions in one breath.

"Don't fret, my love." I traced the tip of his nose with a nail. "For the most part, I'm feeling rather like Trey. If you want something done right, do it yourself."

"But?" he prompted—because of course, there was a *but*.

"I'm not fully confident of Elise's man. I don't trust that his being discovered is truly the problem." As I knew where his mind might go, I added, "I've no sign of any double cross, but I would like to restore my confidence."

The green of his eyes darkened.

"I'm keeping my visit secret from her until I have more information," I said. "I told her there was nothing to worry about, just now."

He offered a slight nod. "I will accompany you."

"But of course," I agreed.

"What of New York?"

"I yet feel Trey to be safe in going. *Et toi?*"

"I do not have a feeling of death, at least."

My brows rose.

"My feeling now is merely that it will be quite uncomfortable for him," he clarified.

"I know his past, yes."

"I feel something awaits him, Michel."

A silent moment passed between us as we both pondered this.

He resumed a previous thread. "Though you lack proof, that Elise knows of New York—"

"She doesn't know of New York," I interrupted.

One of his finely made brows sharpened itself on an arch. "You have been suspicious for a time, then? Even before I told you that I wished to spy on her myself?"

"Merely taking your advice, my raven."

His lips pantomimed a smile.

"Of course, she still has her *own* spies as well," I continued. "Therefore mine have been doubled."

"When will you send Trey?"

"Soon, very soon, I think. Perhaps as early as tomorrow. I await the last bit of information I require concerning the company."

"We may be in Spain, then, whilst he is in the States."

"Travis will be with him."

"*Oui, oui.*" His brows made to knit.

"I'll have them set up in one of my havens."

His head made to nod. His focus then sharpened on a related detail. "In what capacity shall he say that Travis has accompanied him, should Scott inquire?"

"The same as Scott already knows," I answered. "To see about security in the business I am thinking of taking over."

He inclined his head, satisfied that I had followed logic.

"Gabriel," I made a study of his features, "do you honestly feel Elise knows more about the past business with Trey than she admits?"

"I cannot say it is an honest feeling, no. Merely that I am suspicious of her being in Prague so soon after our visit to Phaedra."

"For which I don't blame you," I said. The knowledge had caused me to lose my control for a moment in Kar's presence when he informed me.

I could not bear the thought of being a fool yet again where it concerned her.

"Should I find out otherwise," he said, "you may have need of racing me in order to murder her first."

Gazing into his eyes, the chill gleam that sparked in the green did not escape me. "I believe you'd best me on this particular score," I said.

His expression at the prospect was dark. Lethal.

The sound of Loki at the French doors brought to mind another detail, blessedly putting a halt to whatever else I might think, feel, if she betrayed us. After a kiss to my angel, I strode in that direction, and dropped to a knee beside my reliable companion after opening the doors and pausing to feel the sun on my face, as Gabriel was at a safe distance.

"You, my pet, must once again remain here," I said as I began finding all of the places that begged for scratching. "No *oncle* Travis to keep you company this time, but you always have fun with Shane and Dane, no?"

He agreed with a delightful little squeak of sound, and I rubbed my cheek along the slick surface of his head. "So like your mother, my good boy." I lifted my head. "Hungry?" I received a much more exuberant reply that came complete with a full body wiggle on his part. "Aha, yes, steak tartare for you, darling."

"I returned last night with a lovely and very fresh cut of meat," my Gabriel said. "I shall retrieve it from the *cuisine*."

I looked into the eyes of my guardian, the friend who kept this house from being utterly empty for me in Gabriel's absence. "He takes such good care of us, doesn't he? You were so happy to see him that night as well; I remember this." I knew that he also remembered.

For it meant that his master might at last be himself once more.

I sank all the way to the floor, Loki doing the same and rolling over onto his back beside me.

"You wish to play?" I tickled his broad stomach. "To wrestle, do you?" He barked and I grabbed at his paws, laughing. "You are by far the finest of your line that I've bred. But I've told you this countless times, now haven't I?" I made a bid for his muzzle and then rolled with him, his playful growl bringing one of my own, until I heard a very different sound.

"I really should answer that," I said to my furry companion, looking up at him. "Give me my hand back, will you?"

He released his bite and leapt off me.

"*Merci beaucoup.*" I rose and made a beeline for the offensive-sounding device. The device that I paid more attention to these days, as there were important matters afoot.

"*Oui?*"

The voice on the other end sounded entirely unnatural to my ears. Foreign in its way. I did not like the way phones changed the tones of people, nor the way I could detect every other sound in the background, or of the machine itself.

"*Señor* Lecureaux?"

"Who else would it be, my good man?"

"Excuse me, my friend. I'm unaccustomed to reaching you so easily."

"Of course. Forgiven." I snapped my fingers at Loki and pointed in the direction of the foyer. He sprinted in that direction. "How's the weather there, Emanuel?"

"The temperature in Spain is abnormally high, even for this time of year."

"I see..."

Trey

Poe

"So no, I didn't get a read on anything specific going wrong," P.K. said, coming out from behind the counter. "No impending doom of mass proportions."

"I'm gonna live, then. We're all gonna live, right?" I grinned, starting to feel better about the whole New York thing.

"Yes, yes, I think so." She smiled a bit. "I remind you, though; it isn't a specific science, reading bones. The future is always shifting, depending on what choices you and others make."

"Yeah, I know. So what's the *bad* news?"

She closed in on my personal space and looked up into my eyes. "It seems you may have to face something when you get there."

I studied the emotion in her eyes. "I know it's not exact, like you said, but even still, that's pretty damned cryptic. There're a lot of things I might have to face." Pause. "So I should let you finish what you were saying, huh."

She chuckled softly, the concern in her eyes lessening. "Yes. Now, let's see." She snatched up my hands, giving them a slight squeeze. "Your past. The reading went in that direction. And before you interrupt me again, yes, this sort of thing seems obvious. New York is where a lot of your past lies, right?"

I just nodded this time.

"Things you haven't come to terms with may be forced on you."

Butterflies. In my stomach. There were a few of those *things*.

"Now, we always have a choice, but I think you're going to be in a position that leaves little choice, if you don't want everything to crumble."

Swallow. Knowing is better than not knowing? Starting to doubt that. "Everything? Like everything what?"

"If you can't confront your past, your mission might crumble."

Sarcastically, "Exactly what I was hoping."

She touched my face. "I don't always like telling people possible future outcomes, Trey. I read the bones mostly for myself, when I'm worried, or just want a general idea of things around me."

Another nod. "You know how to interpret them for yourself best."

"It's that I understand how things shift. I don't always like to share what I see, because then it sticks in people's heads until it becomes a self-fulfilling prophecy. They worry. They think everything's set in stone, so even if it's something good, they're more upset if it doesn't happen. I knew you'd ask for the bad news, though."

Breath. "Yeah. I'm good like that."

She nodded. "And that's okay. But I can't necessarily tell you how to prepare for it, either. That frustrates people. They want all the answers. I can't give them."

"I know. It's up to me, anyway. It's not like you can wave any magic wands."

"Right. So, I'm just going to say again, there could be a very uncomfortable situation. And I believe you'll have to make a very tough choice. But I'm also going to say, I think you can handle it."

I squeezed the hand that still held one of mine. "That helps. Really. In a way."

"Good. But are you sorry you asked, now?"

"Well. Yes and no. Everything you said about sharing what you see, I understand. I know all that's true. I could have imagined a bunch of shit on my own anyway, though. I'm good like that, too."

"Has this made it worse, though?" She slid her hand away from my face to stroke my shoulder.

"I don't know yet. I'll get back to you."

"Honest enough answer. I can tell you one more thing." Her brows lifted with their own question.

"Tell me," I said.

"I have a feeling it's the last thing in the world you would expect to face. Want to face."

I felt my brows knit while I asked myself what I'd least expect. What would suck the most to face? Then my cell vibrated in my pocket.

"I should answer my phone. It's buzzing."

She stepped back. "Go ahead." She moved away, towards one of the far bookshelves, giving me some semblance of privacy.

Fishing my phone out, I saw who the caller was. Flipping it open, I brought the phone to my ear. "Hello 'Chel."

"Why hello, du Bois."

Chuckle. From both of us.

"What can I do for you, 'Chel?"

"Many things, I've no doubt."

Another chuckle, from me. Sure, I stepped into that one on purpose.

"So is this a business call, or something else?"

"Pity that it happens to be a business call."

"New York?"

"*Oui*. I need you there tomorrow."

"I'll be there."

"Can you leave tonight? I'd prefer Travis fly you."

Oh. Yeah. I'd about forgotten Travis was a pilot. "I can work it out, yes."

"It need not be too early. You have plenty of time to ready yourself."

Nod. Glance towards P.K., still busying herself with books. "I'm as ready as I'm gonna be, aside from packing."

A pause on his end.

"I know New York City is likely not your favorite place," he said. "Likely the state itself is not on your list of favorites."

"Oh, I love it. And hate it, yeah. But I'm still going."

"If it's truly too much, darling—"

"Michel. I know that you have an idea why I hate it." Pause. "More than an idea." Breath. "I can't run away from it. It doesn't work, anyway, and I can't waste any more time trying. I'll be okay."

I swore I saw P.K. smile in my peripheral.

"Very true. One can't run away from one's own past. We're both learning."

I puzzled over this, then realized I knew what he was talking about.

"Will you be calling Scott?" he asked.

"Yeah. And I'm taking Geoff."

"Very well. I've arranged a place for all of you to stay, in the event this was your decision. Travis has the pertinent details. Scott's apartment is too small for all of you. I shouldn't imagine it will be a problem."

I didn't bother asking how he knew that about Scott's place. "Okay. When do I have my first meeting?" Let me guess.

"Likely tomorrow night."

Thought so.

"Did the courier get the files to you yesterday?"

"Yeah."

"Very good. Travis has extra files he'll hand over when he retrieves you later."

"All right. Well, guess I'll see you when I get back, then."

"We may yet be in Spain. We are also leaving tonight."

Back up.

"Spain?" I lowered my voice. "Is it a problem, after all?"

"There is a problem, yes."

I turned and strode away from P.K.'s location, stopping closer to the door of her shop.

"I'd like to know more about it, since I'm going to New York for you." Soon as I asked, I wondered about discussing this on the phone, but he answered me cleverly.

"One of *her* employees. I'm not confident he hasn't already attempted to share investor information that is not his to share."

Bristling. "How does she feel about this?"

"Not well, I'd hope. I've recently learned he may be considering handing in his resignation, and she can't afford that. If we lose this one, we may lose more, and there goes the deal. Things tend to go more smoothly when I see to it myself. *She* doesn't have a head for business."

110

The mole might be a turncoat. Might stir up others. Got it. And he doesn't sound confident of Elise, nope. *Merde*.

"You focus on New York. That's my deal, nothing to do with our joint venture," he said.

Nothing to do with—

Elise doesn't know about it.

Well.

I trusted him. He wouldn't send me if I were in danger. Doubtless, my activities wouldn't be secret very long if she had half the spies Michel did. But he thought of these things, too.

Besides. If the mole in Spain had succeeded in screwing us, we were, or some of us were, already in someone's sights.

"I'm sure I'll be fine. P.K. says there're no expiration dates on this one. None we need to worry about, anyway." Please catch my reference.

His laugh lilted through the connection. "Splendid."

But then he let some of the code-speak drop and got right to it.

"Trey, right now I don't believe the information possibly shared was with our enemies. Just now, it appears more a question of blackmail; he's reaching for his own piece of the pie. I am capable of paying him off; however, I won't on general principal."

"And that would send the wrong signal." Heck, even in regular, human business dealings, there was a lot of posturing. I totally understood this. "You'll appear weak. Easily ruffled."

"Indeed. An open target for the next one daring to consider such a ridiculous thing as blackmailing me. If this is truly the case, I shall enjoy him in courses."

Ehem. Right.

"If you're wrong? Scratch that. If you find out it's more?"

"I shall enjoy him in *courses*."

Right.

"But then?"

"We'll reassess the situation. I have, as you say, a backup plan, if necessary."

"Right. Okay." I'd ask about back up plans later. It could be anything, with him. "You'll be okay down there, yeah?"

I could imagine his expression after that comment.

"Kar will accompany us, as well as daytime allies."

"You've got everything covered, as usual. Sure you do."

"You're sweet. Don't fret."

Ah-ha. There's what I was waiting for him to say.

"By the by, you may be interested in knowing that *Monsieur* Chomette will be in New York City at the same time as you."

"Oh? Are you saying I'm going to see him?"

"It's a possibility. Can you handle some side business along with everything else?"

"Can I handle it? What do *you* think?"

"That's my boy. You may summon Travis when you're ready to leave."

Summon Travis. That gave me a way wrong mental picture. "Uh. I'll do that."

"Have a safe trip, darling. We'll keep in touch. Ciao for now."

"Ciao."

I closed the phone and stowed it in my pocket. "I'm leaving tonight, P.K."

She approached me, not bothering to pretend she hadn't heard some of the conversation, which is something I liked about her—no fricking pretense.

"You sounded very confident," she said, reaching me. "That's good. Will you humor me on one little thing, though?"

"Tell me, I might."

"I have this charm I'd like to give you for the trip…" her brows lifted.

An insincere rolling of my eyes. "Ohhh, all right. If you insist."

Chapter 9

Michel
Madrid

Kar escorted us through the lobby to the private elevator, which would lead us to a floor with a private office, where one Emanuel Varela, my most trusted ally in Spain, waited patiently.

Once the doors slid firmly shut, I turned to Kar. "Where was she when last you checked in?"

"She had returned to Belgium, my Prince. This very evening, in fact."

"Mmm. It might have been better had she yet been occupied in Prague." I dismissed it with a wave of my hand. "No matter. We'll see to this and return to Paris before she notes our absence, hopefully." Thoughtfully, I tapped my lip. "Keep her informed with other details; we'll simply pretend we're in Paris."

"Yes, my Prince."

"Is there word from Travis?" my husband asked of Kar.

"Yes. They were to depart shortly after we did."

"Very good."

"And Shane and Dane are seeing to Polly," I confirmed aloud. "Our latest arrivals are seeing to the Fall Out."

"Drake seems a fit acquisition," Kar commented.

"I knew him in Lyon. He's always been a good friend, even from a distance."

"I can't think how I missed this information, sir."

"He changed his name, and I didn't tell you, Kar. Not to worry, your reputation is safe."

He graced me with a smile. "May I ask how he was formerly known?"

"You remember my speaking of a certain musketeer by the name of Charles, don't you?"

"Oh *yes*." He graced me with a much larger smile. "I must have a proper conversation with him once we return."

"Once you get him started, the stories never end." I simply had to wink. "Do remember that he is prone to exaggeration when it comes to me. He was by far the more promiscuous one."

My Gabriel's low laugh softly vibrated the metal doors. "So you say."

I feigned offense by his words and his laughter. "I certainly never bedded an entire regiment, my dear. Nor an entire court of ladies."

"I am stunned," Gabriel said. "You are saying that he bested you? Are you quite well, my love?"

This brought the sound of Kar's laughter, merging with Gabriel's own. A most pleasant sound indeed.

"Bested me?" I countered, as if this were the most ridiculous thing I'd ever heard. "I simply have a more discerning taste. Can he claim royal bed partners—which include a king and queen, in the same bed, on the same night at the *same time*, no less?" I let go with a snort. "The answer to this question would be no."

The green of Gabriel's eyes sparked. "So you say."

"Tut." I folded my arms over my chest. "It seems I shall have to show you those personal artifacts of mine once again."

"You may have stolen those. I did not know you then, after all," he dryly quipped.

"How does one steal hair, my love?"

"From brushes or clippings, for example. You were already Vampire, if I am to believe you. Stealth came easily to you. I imagine that you pilfered many things – whatever took your fancy."

"This is not the hair we're speaking of, and you know it." Reflexively I traced the locket that was beneath the fabric of my shirt, which contained a small curl of human hair belonging to Gabriel.

"It could belong to anyone," he rejoined, lifting his gaze from the movement of my fingers.

"This is not all that I have."

"All of it could belong to anyone."

"Fair enough. But you must admit the jewel is impressive."

"Oh yes, utterly authentic, I grant you this." His expression at last gave way to his amusement and then to affection. "Alas, perhaps I must concede, for I know that you are not truly a thief." He reached, tapping my locket through the silk with his index nail.

"I *do* steal hearts."

"That you do."

"I was not always above other forms of larceny, either."

All of us were yet laughing as we reached our floor. Once the doors opened, we resumed the appropriate mind frame, that of business, and stepped out, making for the office.

"*Señor* Lecureaux, very good to have you here."

I strode to him, my hand out, and received a firm shake. "How goes it, Emanuel?"

"It goes, it goes." A smile lit his face, softening his look. He had a proud, square jaw and heavy brows, Emanuel.

After making his greetings to Kar and Gabriel, little time was wasted. He came directly to the point of my visit, just as he knew I'd prefer. There would be time for niceties later.

Emanuel gestured for me to sit. "I have more information than I did when I called you before."

I settled into a high-backed chair, Emanuel kitty-corner to me. Kar remained by the door, whilst Gabriel settled himself at a polite, yet close, distance.

"I am, as is said, all ears," I replied.

"Our suspect met with Lucas Demetrius last night. My men say his flight originated in Belgium. I mention this, because as far as I've heard, he usually stays in Greece, letting others do his business outside of the country."

Without doubt, my eyes must have narrowed as I felt a tremor of tension along mine and Gabriel's bond. "Do you have information on who he may have visited in Belgium, or what he was doing there?"

"No, my friend. We were only able to trace his flight. It's possible it was a mere vacation." His hands spread as his shoulders scrunched up. "But it's always good to turn every stone, no?"

"Indeed." I shifted in my chair, eyes moving to Kar. "This name seems vaguely familiar in some way. Do we have information on this Lucas?"

Kar's hesitation was subtle, yet not subtle enough to escape me. Nor was the subtle sense of Emanuel's confusion.

"Not currently, my Prince. But soon we shall." He produced his iPhone, his fingers moving over the touch screen.

I had little time to ponder Kar or Emanuel's emotion before my human ally commanded my attention as he spoke again. "I can tell you, my friend, that I've heard this name Lucas Demetrius here in Madrid. He does long-distance business with some of the resorts."

"In what capacity?"

"Kitchen supplies, this kind of thing." His elbows went to his knees as he leaned forward. "He's not a day person."

The tension within Gabriel increased.

"I'd already had the suspicion, but thank you for confirming it, Emanuel," I replied. "Now tell me, what do we know of Lucas and Diego's meeting?"

"Oh," a laugh animated his features, as it was often wont to do, "all very secretive. They went to great lengths, changing cars three times along the way to their destination, and then stopped far away from Madrid in the middle of nothing. After fifteen minutes, another car came, and they each went their own way."

The rapping of my nails on the chair's arm reached my ears. "He certainly isn't doing anything for my confidence, now is he? Where is Diego now?"

"Drinking himself to a promising hangover, I hear. Maybe he heard you were coming, aha."

"We shall see," I responded, "we shall see."

"There is one other detail, my friend."

"Do tell."

"I'm almost certain one of those cars belonged to Ricco."

My brow arched, and quite sharply. "Oh. Really."

Emanuel nodded. "But I'm also certain he doesn't know you're here, not yet."

My smile unfurled. "Splendid."

"What else can I do for you, Michel, tell me." Emanuel leaned forward yet again. "Your accommodations have been seen to and the right people know already of your arrival."

"Just be certain Diego doesn't leave Madrid in a drunken stupor. I've just decided to pay someone else a visit, first. Diego can wait a while longer, particularly as my first visit may help to decide his fate."

"Hoh! Pity I won't see the look on his face." Emanuel offered me a winning smile.

"Kar can take pictures on that contraption of his. I'll have him send you one."

Yet another laugh from Emanuel, and he rose, looking between myself and Gabriel. "There is nothing else, then?"

I considered this a moment before replying. "Actually, there is one more thing. Call Jonathan and inform him that I'll be visiting the vault shortly."

"I shall do so. Anything else, you know who to call, night or day, Michel."

Gabriel rose as well. "You sleep little, yes," he said to my Spanish friend.

"But I do sleep, sir, I do. Many siestas during the day. Maybe one day I should come all the way over to your side. Already I keep your hours." Emanuel offered my husband a smile.

Gabriel returned this smile with an intensity that negated its sincerity. "Perhaps someone will provide you with what you need, one day."

With that, he turned and made for the door, which Kar opened to allow his passing.

Emanuel turned rounded eyes in my direction. "No disrespect my friend, but your man still makes me nervous. Always so quiet, until he says something like that, and then he walks away."

My grin was hastily conjured. "He's not always so quiet—but you're not the first to say this."

My comment hastened the return of his rotund laughter.

"But if you'll excuse me now, I must see about my other business, Emanuel."

"Of course. We'll keep in touch, Michel."

I nodded and made for the door, exiting with Kar. Gabriel yet stood in the hallway, still agitated, though not because of Emanuel. Certainly mention of Belgium had done it; I'd felt it in him the moment Emanuel spoke of it, and though I was once again wondering at Kar's hesitation before, Gabriel's tension was more pressing.

"Lucas in Belgium, Elise in Belgium," Gabriel said under his breath as he glided away, heading for the elevator.

Kar and I shared a look, following a few paces behind. Once at the doors, Gabriel turned, his gaze stabbing me.

"I know this name," he flatly stated.

My brows lifted. This I had not expected.

"I remember this name, and I am certain that Elise knows him," he continued, and Kar's surprise at Gabriel's words, not quite hidden, mingled with my own.

"How do you know of him, my love?" I asked as the distance between us lessened.

A shadow darkened Gabriel's eyes, his face. "I remembered. When he said the name, I remembered."

Feeling the tightness in his posture, I merely stared at him, for once capable of waiting for his next words.

"I remember her speaking of Lucas Demetrius. She sounded quite upset. She spoke of him just before our separation." His gaze drifted. "I overheard it...She was speaking to Vicont on the telephone."

My vision narrowed. I did not press for further details just then, sensing it was yet foggy in his mind and not wishing to distress him. Instead, I rifled the files in my brain, as the name had been familiar to me as well. At last a picture formed. My gaze shot to Kar.

"Make Lucas a top priority. I remember, now, seeing him once before. I believe he's old and possibly powerful."

"Yes, my Prince." His fingers were already flying over the touch screen.

My eyes returned to Gabriel as his focus sharpened on me. "I once saw him leaving one of Vicont's mansions," I said. "Vicont refused to utter much more than his name when I inquired, but I very much had the sense that Lucas had just been tossed aside in some manner. Associate, lover, I'm not certain, but it doesn't matter. To Vicont they're interchangeable."

But how was it, I silently wondered, that I didn't remember more?

Gabriel's gaze hardened. "Then perhaps he yet carries a grudge."

"The remaining questions are," I said, giving our shared thoughts voice, "did he meet with Elise in Belgium, and which grudge is *she* yet carrying? I will not have this operation failing over a personal matter."

"We should, perhaps, think on speaking to Elise about Lucas. Carefully, of course."

"Yes, perhaps we ought, my love."

Gabriel's thoughts then shifted to a previous subject. "By the by, I am curious as to why we are visiting the bank this evening."

I gazed deeply into his eyes. "I'm feeling less and less confident by the moment. I may wish to tie a loose end, and I thought it best to be prepared if so."

Trey

I was in the jet and ready to take off at 10:27 p.m., with Geoff tucked in beside me. By the time we landed in NYC, it'd be about midnight, and I was deciding whether to call Scott during the flight or wait until morning, since no meetings were happening during the day anyway, due to Travis' situation. He refused my having mere humans as escorts during my covert operations, unless it was an absolute necessity. I knew it was because he still thought he'd failed Geoff and me when we went underground.

Travis wasn't personally acquainted with all of the human allies Michel had in the city, either, and even though he trusted Michel, it was like he said—one never knows when one of them will lose their bleeding minds and fuck off.

120

Like David.

Travis didn't suggest that Geoff and I should stay locked up inside during the day, though. He still wasn't about us feeling like prisoners; he thought sightseeing wouldn't be dangerous. I figured if we caught any heat during our meetings, that could change, but this was okay with me. I'd probably want to lock myself up with Geoff if that happened, anyway. And Scott. Just in case.

Geoff, previously a chatterbox of excitement at the prospect of seeing my New York, as he put it, started drifting off not long after the jet leveled into its flight pattern. He'd finished his shift, packed fast, and bam, we were off to the airport. My brain was overloaded with different thoughts that made me restless, but not wanting to disturb Geoff, I waited a few more minutes, until he was completely under. Then I carefully slipped away from him and headed for the cockpit.

Knock. "Okay if I come in there, Travis?"

Sure thing.

I let myself in and sat down in the copilot's chair, eyes bouncing over the lighted panels and crazy instruments that didn't make much sense to me. If I studied them long enough, they might, but that's not where my brain was.

"Geoff's asleep," I said.

"Why aren't'cha cuddled up to him?"

"I don't generally sleep on flights and I didn't want to disturb him."

"What's on your mind, then?"

"Well, there *is* something I've been wondering, yeah." I glanced at him. "Why didn't Michel have you guard me until *after* I went New Orleans and all that?"

"That was about trust."

"But he trusts you."

"Yes, but *you'd* just accepted a world with vampires. How many could you honestly trust all at once? You'd just begun to trust him."

"Oh. Well, yeah."

"He wanted to look after you himself, anyway."

I smiled a bit.

"I don't think that's what was on your mind though, Trey. You're smarter than the question you asked me. You already knew the answer."

Yeah, I did, and naturally he noticed my stalling. I did it again anyway. "Michel said you had some files for me."

"I don't think files are on your mind either, mate." The edges of his mouth upturned. "You can look over the rest tomorrow, during the day."

I settled back, gazing into the darkness and letting out a breath. "Yeah. Okay, so I have other things on my mind."

"Such as?"

My fingers started tapping a tattoo on the chair arm.

"Go on, fire away, Trey." Soft chuckle from him.

"I'm deciding where to start."

"Well don't dent the leather there."

I flattened my hand. "Sorry. Bad habit, I know. Probably irritates vamps more than humans."

He chuckled again. "It's not so bad. I'm somewhat used to it. Michel taps his nails all the time during meetings. Usually when he's impatient or irritated. Damned loud on that desktop, those nails."

Laugh.

"Now tell me why you're dancing around the subject." He glanced back at me when I glanced at him.

"'Cause I was about to ask you something I should ask someone else."

"Maybe. May as well take a shot, just to be certain." He turned his head and winked at me. "Or are you testing a new form of self-control?"

"Hah hah, yeah, I know, it's so unlike me." Slight shrug. "Oh well, I tried. It's about Gabriel."

"Okay. What about him?"

"First, I know about Michel. He told me."

Travis shot me another glance.

"About his own special gene."

His brows lifted. "Ah, that. I had to go on as if I were the only one, before. I hope you understand."

"Oh, totally, no worries."

"Carry on, then."

"He thinks Gabriel is special."

He looked at me, arching a brow. "This could cover a lot of things."

"Kar interrupted before Michel could tell me how Gabriel was *different*."

"So you're asking me what's *special* about Gabriel."

"Yeah."

"I don't know exactly what Michel was going to tell you."

"Well, I haven't really told you what he started to say; that might help."

He shook his head. "It's not just that. I honestly don't know his precise *differences*. Or the source of them, I should say."

My brows shot up. "So, as far as you know he's—well. Regular?"

He contemplated me from the corner of his eye. "I didn't say *that*."

"Well, no, not exactly," I interrupted.

"And if it was a matter of loyalty, at this point I'd just say that I can't tell you."

"Yeah, I know. Maybe it's Michel's own secret, then." Pause. "He did say it was just a theory, basically." But he was going to tell me, even though he hadn't told Travis? Had he told anyone, ever?

"I know Michel has some kind of theory. I've never pressed the issue. I reckoned if he ever wanted to discuss it with anyone, he'd get round to it."

"You're pretty good about not prying." I offered a smile.

He returned the smile. "I do my best. Gabriel's never said

anything about his precise nature, either, which is another reason I never asked."

Totally understood that. Then pondered just how special it apparently was that Michel had been about to share his theory with me. Now I was more curious than ever. *Was* there something more passed along the family line to me?

Travis broke my internal reverie when he cleared his throat.

"There *is* gossip about Gabriel, sometimes," he said. "For whatever it's worth."

Perked me right up into a sideways lean. "What's the gossip? Kar's not here," I joked.

"Some of the shit that goes around is kinda silly." Beat. "Then again, anything's possible, I reckon. I'm here, and Michel is what he is, after all." He took his eyes off the instruments and gave me a level look. "And there you are, Death Dancer. You and your realm."

All ears, that's me.

His gaze shifted forward. "It ranges anywhere from him never being human, which we know is false, to him being a reincarnation of a true wizard, alchemist, some such, to being the embodiment of—what was the last one." Beat. "Petro... something. I don't always pay close attention to unimportant, random gossip. I reckon I've some idea where they get the wizard thing, though. Still—"

"Wait. Did you say Petro?" Bigger sideways lean.

"Yeah, I did."

"You said Petro *something*. What's the rest– can you think of the rest?"

His brows creased. "I'll try. Does it mean something to you? Seems like it does."

Oh yes, it could definitely mean something. "I know what Petro is, well, depending what else you remember."

His brow line stayed creased. Meanwhile, I about held my breath waiting for him to reply.

His brows finally shot up. "Jean. That was it."

My brain raced through pages of P.K.'s book, the one she'd given me about Vodou. "Ti-Jean-Petro?"

"Yeah, that was it," he said. "Is that a title, a name, or what?"

I fell back into the seat. "You could say both. Holy shit, now wouldn't that be interesting." Maybe there *was* a connection to my Mark—or Gabriel knew a lot about Vodou, maybe.

"Care to let me know what's so interesting about it? You scent of nervous excitement and such."

"Ti-Jean-Petro is a *lwa*."

"'Ang on. You mean like that Legba guy?"

"Uh huh." I recited some of the words I'd read. "Jean's a so called snake-*lwa*, loves fire, is very passionate, and is apparently friend to sorcerers and black mages, to put it in general terms. Not strictly good or bad, he just is. Like the rest of them."

"Well. How about that." He chuckled. "Maybe that's why they think he's a sorcerer, and such."

"Maybe that's why he's colder than Michel," I muttered.

"Eh?"

Hand wave. "Snakes. Just being silly out loud. Michel's abnormally warm like you." I didn't know if Vicont was cold. He hadn't touched me. The twins didn't give off the same warmth as Travis and Michel, but I'd not really touched them either—not skin on skin, anyway.

He gave me a one-shoulder shrug. "Maybe you're not."

"How many people know his exact ancestry? Because I do, and—definitely interesting, this gossip, considering his mother."

"Me, Kar, Michel, and the twins know about it. They don't tell most people. But like you said once, we've got that immortal grapevine thing going, so who knows where the gossip started, who else might know who's still alive, or who just passed it along before they died."

"I have got to ask them when we get back."

"Let me know if the snake thing's true," I caught his wink. "Because even though he's cat-like, I can see a snake thing going on, too."

"Man, and like you said. Here I am, with this crazy gift, whatever, and—I wonder how much he could tell me about Vodou. I wonder if his father…"

Oh. No, no. His memories around that might be crap. Not just painful, but gone, blocked out, even.

"Wouldn't hurt to ask," Travis said.

"It might."

"I know what you mean by that, but listen. Even though he doesn't talk about it much, I do know that Gabriel has a few memories of these Vodou ways. Some things he learned from his dad and studies and other people he met."

My eyes rolled up toward the ceiling. "He was in Louisiana, too. I wonder if there was more between him and Lucien. If it was more than a family tree that made him go there."

"I wouldn't count on his time there being clear."

My eyes shifted towards him after his soft words.

"I wouldn't ask about *that* particular time," he said. "If he offers, okay, if not—don't."

My eyes dropped. "I know. I know why." I lifted my eyes, and he was staring at me, seeming to consider. What, I didn't know, until he decided to speak again.

"I saw him there a few times."

"You went after Gabriel?" I asked.

He nodded. "I just wanted to see if he was okay, you know? So I tracked him down a few times."

Nod from me.

"I've realized I saw your grandfather there. I didn't know who he was until you and Gabriel put it together. Never seemed a good time to bring it up before. Not till now."

Blink. "Did you talk to him?"

He shook his head. "But I know that Gabriel spoke to him a few times. Gabriel just doesn't remember how many times, or what about. Only the diary now, same as he told you."

My mind dove into a far less exciting side subject. "He may never remember the rest. You saw how bad off he was."

"Yes I did," he whispered. "He was completely—he wasn't himself at all. He was lost."

Return whisper. "Lost. You saw how bad off Michel was, too."

"I did."

"I won't press, because I have a feeling you don't want to talk about it."

"Thanks. Because you're right. I don't, not just now, anyway."

With that, his eyes glued themselves to the instruments for a few minutes, then straight ahead through the glass to the starlit sky.

I'd started fiddling with the charm in the meantime and pulled it out of my pocket, studying the 'double machete' done in iron. One hilt green, the other red.

This attracted Travis' attention. "What's that?"

"Something P.K. gave to me." I held it up for him to get a clearer view. "Protection charm. Supposed to help give me strength, too."

"It's an interesting looking charm. What's with the machetes?"

"For Ogoun, another *lwa*. My grandfather, Lucien? He was dedicated to him."

"Let me see, I think Michel said something about that. He's a *lwa* of power, great power."

"Yeah. Strong Father. Warrior. Protective of his 'children.' And other nifty things."

"Cool of her to look out for you, and with something so appropriate."

A smile to myself. "Yeah." The charm actually felt good in my hand the moment she had given it to me. I couldn't deny that it seemed infused with her intention. Certainly couldn't write such things off as only psychological, not these days. But any psychological effects were just as beneficial.

Placing it back in my pocket, I said, "Lucien approved."

"Even better, mate. Does he still treat your mind like a swinging door, by the way?"

Laugh. "Not so much, now."

"Progress, then."

"Yup. I started showing him a little more respect. I'm sure that helped."

He laughed. "Hey. You could ask him about Gabriel."

I supposed I could, at that.

"Yeah, you're right. But for now I think I'll head on back to Geoff. He's gonna wake up any minute."

"Yes, he is. Were you guessing, or did you literally sense it in your own way, too?"

Pausing mid-rise, I looked into his eyes. "Now that you mention it—yes, I sensed it. I can't find the words to explain, but I just—yeah."

He smiled up at me. "Something beautiful emerging from the tragedy." Beat. "Goes for Michel and Gabriel, too. One day I'll talk about it."

After giving his shoulder a squeeze, I left the cockpit to check on Geoff.

Chapter 10

Michel
Madrid

Kar approached the conspicuously armed man by the gate, who asked him in Spanish who he thought he was and what he thought he was doing here—though he did not ask so politely. Kar then stopped less than a meter from the guard and trained an even gaze on him, for which the guard drew his darkly gleaming weapon, once again asking his question whilst aiming the gun at my escort.

"I suggest you put that away before someone gets hurt," I said as I moved forward, Kar stepping to the side to allow me a face-to-face view of the gun-wielding man.

My words had flowed in perfect Spanish, but he opted to reply in English. "Who the fuck are you?"

"What will you give me if I tell you?" I became aware of the arching of my lips.

"Maybe some of this." He shoved his weapon in my direction.

"Tsk. I'm disappointed. This isn't what I had in mind at all, darling."

"What do you think you're playing at, mister? Do you know where you are? Whose place this is?"

"I'm quite aware, but thank you for reminding me. Do you have any other redundant questions for me, sweetheart?" I offered a coquettish bat of my lashes.

"I should shoot you right now," he directed his aim closer to my chest, "*cabrón*."

With a lift of brow I said, "Shoot me or kiss me, the result will be the same, I assure you." I graced him with a very wide smile.

"You're *loco*, mister." He laughed, though not with humor, as his eyes flitted over my companions, no doubt wondering if we were armed and considering his options.

He did not pull the trigger, but with his other hand he reached for one of those wireless devices Trey called walkie-talkies.

"Don't do that," I said. "I've not finished with you yet, and it would be a shame to bother the others just now."

He leveled the gun's barrel in the direction of my heart, slowly lifting the walkie-talkie towards his face, his eyes once again moving betwixt the three of us.

"You don't wish to do that," I said, exuding a bit of *'charm'*.

His hand paused in its movement, the fine muscles quivering, begging to deny my suggestion.

"Now, be a good boy and put it away."

His hand obeyed, clipping the walkie-talkie back onto his belt.

"Thank you ever so much." My eyes assessed his form. "Pity, however, that you don't have manners on your own."

He could only gaze at me stupidly.

"Mm. You've already bored me," I said, releasing him. "We're going inside, but not to worry, I'll announce myself soon enough."

I stepped around him, reaching for the gate. I began to open the latch, and in what was a blink to him, slow motion to me, he squeezed the trigger—and found that I'd placed my palm against the barrel just as he fired.

"How rude," I commented with a lift of my hand, and then smiled—impishly no doubt—for the bafflement in his eyes as he watched the wound knit itself. "Hmm, such things do still sting, you realize, though certainly I am capable of finding pleasure in pain." After a pursing of my lips, I added, "Are you?"

He was about to make a stunned second attempt when I captured his gaze and looked deeply into his eyes, mesmerizing him more strongly than before.

"Stop. You've moved past boring to *irritating*, young man. This is not wise."

His hand froze and his eyes glazed.

"You are most assuredly threatening the *wrong* person."

My puppet echoed me. "I'm threatening the wrong person."

"Do you know who this," I tapped a nail against the blue steel, "should be pointing at?"

"Who?"

"You. You should be aiming this gun at *yourself*."

"At myself..." His elbow bent and his hand turned.

"Simon says a bit higher, darling."

"Higher..."

My tongue darted out to wet my lips. "Mmm, and in the interest of getting it right the first time, place the barrel to your temple, *s'il vous plaît*."

He placed it to his temple.

A smile discovered me. "Very good, poppet, very, *very* good. Living is hard, don't you think? Dying," my index nail learned the line of his jaw just below his ear, "is so much *easier*."

In his glassy eyes, there was yet a deeper understanding. Devil that I am, I'd left him just enough wits that he knew what was happening—and that he could do nothing to stop it.

"Now..." I moved back a step.

My puppet's next breath was a shuddering one.

"*Bang.*"

His brains painted the white stucco surrounding the dark door various shades of red, pink, grey, and others not defined, his body jerking sideways and dropping to the ground whilst I admired the artistry of his skull matter.

"*Gracias.* I have now been *properly* announced." I spared Kar a glance. "I didn't like this one's tone."

"He was rather crass."

"Terribly uncultured. Common thugs bore me, you?"

"Yes, my Prince, they do."

"I don't believe we need to ask Gabriel his opinion." I looked to him, and he merely smiled at me.

"Ah, here they come," I said, turning toward the tall door that split the stucco, which was now opening. The first of them already had his weapon drawn, which I grabbed, pinning his fingers to it beneath mine in a bruising embrace. "Do it and I shall consume your intestines from your warm body as I would a large bowl of spaghetti, all whilst you watch."

As his eyes widened and his pulse quickened when more of my façade evaporated, my senses counted three more, one of whom was the man I'd come to see.

My left arm shot out, my hand finding purchase on the second thug's neck, my grip *just* shy of crushing his windpipe. This was to be only a warning, after all.

"Stop," said Ricco from behind them.

"Surely you're not speaking to me," I commented with a lift of one brow.

"No, no. Boys, back off." Ricco pressed his hand to the chest of the man beside him.

"He shot Bobby!" the one whose hand I was near to crushing said.

"Correction: he shot himself." I offered him a sweet smile, or as sweet as it could be when I was of a predatory mood. "You won't find a single fingerprint of mine on that weapon, should you like to investigate it." Not that they would even *had* I handled it.

Ricco spoke once more, spoke very wisely. "He'll kill every one of us before you fire a shot, if you could fire a shot right now. Let it go."

The one who was having trouble breathing continued to struggle and claw at my hand. The one whose fingers were throbbing under my grip scented of just enough fear that he might fire mindlessly. This was more than fine with me, for I always enjoyed a bit of sport, and my hackles were raised.

"It might help if I let go, yes?" I released both men. One gasped for air and choked on it; the other immediately gripped his badly stinging fingers, his gun clattering to the ground, which briefly disappointed me. I leaned, retrieving the weapon, and then straightened, holding it out to him.

"Tut. You could've shot someone's foot off. Now move, if you please." As he couldn't seem to let go of his wounded hand, I slipped the pistol into his pocket for him as I passed, striding directly for the wiry human with thick wavy brown hair named Ricco, who was quite clearly startled and more than a bit worried, judging from the damp shine of his flesh.

As he well ought to be, I thought, as I spared the third of his goons a glance.

"I wasn't expecting you *señor*—"

"Of course not. Why should you?" I interrupted Ricco. "I deal with common drug lords as little as possible, and since when do I inform you of my visits to Spain?"

"Since never, sir."

I gestured to his injured men who even now scampered to his side, glaring at me, one coughing violently and even more wary than the others. "Why do you insist on employing such pathetic little men? I mean really, Ricco. You ought to teach them some manners along with a little finesse. Bobby, was it? He was a particular brand of Neanderthal." My lips arched, for I knew the other three men desperately wished to retort.

133

Self-preservation, however, would not allow it. Either myself and the two with me would kill them, they surmised, or Ricco might later.

I continued. "Apparently *these* three have learnt to hold their tongues lest they be ripped out of their heads."

Ricco's Adam's apple did a jig for my eyes with the nervous clearing of his throat. "They are my brothers, and this one is a cousin." He gestured to the short, dark haired man I hadn't injured. "Fine men, truly."

A rich laugh left me. "Ah, yes. I see it, now."

The confusion over Ricco's submissive display registered in the fluctuation of his brothers' pupils and the twitching of their pulses.

"What may I...do for you, Mister Lecureaux?"

"Aren't you going to invite me inside and offer me a drink?"

Ricco nearly choked on his own saliva, and for this, I laughed.

"Ehh, this way, sir."

Ricco grabbed the arms of two of the men, his cousin following on his own and casting wary glances at myself and my companions as he walked.

"I do hope you're well stocked for company," I said, and once again laughed for Ricco's reaction.

My laughter quickly died once reaching the house and entering the front room, however.

"Sit," I commanded. "All of you."

Ricco's brothers and cousin looked to him. Ricco sat, and his prompt compliance brought to them a clearer understanding. His obedience would have been sufficient cause to show me respect and fear. My earlier display of power merely drove home the fact I was definitely not one to fuck with, as obviously, I was a hot-blooded killer. Perhaps even a psychopath. Assuredly, they had been previously acquainted with those they deemed such—but this was before they had met *me*.

Two sat on Ricco's left on the large, rose-colored sectional couch, and one to his right. All of their eyes trained themselves on me.

"Such obedient dogs," I said. "You're more intelligent than you appear, which is not saying much."

The one to Ricco's immediate left tensed, and his hand twitched. Ricco grabbed his arm. "Be still, Mauro," he said.

"I would do as he says were I you, Mauro." Mauro shrank back into the cushions in an attempt to escape my glare.

"Now then," I addressed Ricco, "I'm here for some information. Depending on said information, this visit may end on a much brighter note for you."

He managed a slight nod.

"What has Diego been up to lately?" I inquired.

"Diego? I haven't seen him since the last mess," Ricco had the nerve to lie. His cousin, Mauro, had the gall to back him up.

"We fixed him good after his last fuck up. He knows if he comes back, he's dead," he said.

His lying I could understand. Ricco, however, had met me on other occasions, and should have known better.

"Are you certain this is the story?" I stared each of them down. Neither responded. "Lies don't escape me, you realize." I took a step closer, the force of my gaze pressing Ricco farther back into the cushions.

"I don't know what he's doing these days," Ricco persisted. I rather supposed that if I were feeling generous, I might have given him credit for bravery. As generosity was not within me, however, I deemed it suicidal.

My feet consumed more of the distance. "You know I can scent the change in your body chemistry, Ricco, and you positively reek."

Words appeared to fail him, then.

"I can see the fluctuation of your pupils," I continued, "the miniscule shift in the blood vessels." Yet another step I took. "I can hear it your voice, and I can nearly taste the beads of perspiration forming at your hairline; not to mention, your heart has added a beat."

135

He lifted trembling hands as if to protect himself. "Forgive me, forgive. My entire family…" he glanced at his brothers, his cousin.

"Whomever threatened you is not standing where *I* am right now, Ricco," I said. "Tell me what I wish to know, and perhaps I'll feel charitable and offer some protection."

It did not take him long to weigh his options. "Okay. Okay," he said, and even his family seemed to understand the gravity of my earlier statement, none of them protesting. Ricco then said, "Diego came to see me yesterday. He wanted to borrow a car."

"And?" Impatiently I prompted.

"He wanted some back up," he nearly stuttered. "Truly I don't know exactly what he's into, sir. We don't keep in touch much since I disowned him."

Gabriel came to life, his voice slicing through the tension in the room. "He must have informed you somewhat as to why he needed back up. After all, if you are no longer close, why should you do him any favors?"

"Unless he paid you well," I finished for Gabriel. "Which I'm fairly certain he's not in a position to do." I folded my arms. "Though someone may have fronted him a bit of cash, hmm?"

Ricco's eyes darted nervously betwixt Gabriel and myself, whilst his cousin's dazed stare remained on Gabriel. Meanwhile, his brothers were keeping their eyes on Kar.

"He said he was in on some big deal," Ricco offered. "That he would pay me everything he owed with interest, once it was done."

"You believed him why?" I pressed.

"Because," he swallowed hard, "because the man he was dealing with is rich and powerful. And anyway, if Diego didn't pay up, I told him I'd kill him myself, this time."

I had no trouble believing this. "Who is he dealing with?"

A nervous twitching of his fingers followed.

"Ah, I see," I said. "The one who threatened you, correct?"

"His name is Lucas."

Gabriel stiffened whilst I pressed on. "You know what he is, don't you."

"He's like you," Ricco said. His family members, however, had no idea what they were dealing with.

My eyes narrowed. "What else do you know, Ricco?" If he were helping Diego and Lucas in their attempt to undermine me, and whatever else was afoot, Lucas wouldn't have need of slaughtering this family; I'd do it for him.

Ricco said, "They're smuggling weapons."

Certainly, my brows rose on my forehead, and I paused as I judged the truth of his words. As Trey might have said were he present, this was out of left field.

"To do what with?" I inquired.

Ricco replied, "To sell."

"What manner of weapons?"

"Mostly guns," he said. "Maybe more. He's not selling them all. He said something about a big job. That he might need explosives."

"Did he now?" I gazed at him a moment. "What, do you suppose, needs exploding?"

"I don't know; he said he's not supposed to say."

Contemplating, I said, "Seems to me he already told you more than he ought, which is all the better for me." Yet it was still so little.

Ricco's Adam's apple danced another jig.

"Listen to me carefully," I said. "As you can easily surmise, I'm not here on holiday. As I believe you can also easily surmise, weapon trafficking is not the only thing Diego is into these days. In fact," I gave him a hard look, "I'm thinking this is merely a convenient side project. You know him well." My arms re-crossed themselves. "What is he really doing, hmm, Ricco?"

"I—I think he gave Lucas information about you."

"What manner of information?"

"Sir, I don't know exactly what. But you're right not to

trust Diego. He didn't tell me what he was doing for you, but intimated he was doing something. Now it seems he sold you out. "

I judged his words as truth. This did nothing for my mood, which darkened. Diego collecting weaponry yet niggled at me as well, regardless of my previous words, which certainly didn't help matters. So much for blackmail. Ricco had the right of it. Diego had already sold me out. But why and where did Lucas figure in?

"Have you met Lucas?" I asked him then, as it was becoming increasingly apparent I ought to know more of this vampire, and had wonder as to why I didn't.

"Once, sir. It was enough."

I looked to the others. They shook their heads. My gaze returned to Ricco. "When did you meet him?"

"Maybe..." His brows tightly furrowed. "It was..." His entire face twisted in concentration.

"Never mind," I said, realizing Lucas likely fogged his mind, which instantly frustrated me.

Ricco's face relaxed as much as it could, given my ever-descending aspect.

I came to a quick decision. "I have a job for you," I said as I gestured to Kar, who placed the case he'd been holding on a table close to Ricco, opened it, and then resumed his position several steps back. A growl of a laugh managed to find me as Kar's movement had caused every human in the room to flinch.

"This is a down payment," I said. "There will be twice this when the job is complete and you comply in a manner I find satisfactory."

The humans then boggled at the amount of crisp bills they spied stacked in the case. As they were dumbfounded, I carried on. "What you will do for me is this: You will exterminate Diego and make it appear that his cause of death was a drug deal gone horribly wrong. If there is collateral damage, I don't care; I'm not paying you extra for it. I only care that no one ever traces this to me, that you never speak of my visit, and that you make damned certain no one else knows what you've done."

All eyes had moved to me.

"You will not do this *yet*, but I want you to be prepared, so that when I call in this favor, you may take care of it post haste." I gestured to the case. "In the event I change my mind and do *not* call in this favor, this is yours to keep." My feet brought me closer to the sectional couch, and I placed my hands on Ricco's shoulders, bringing my face within an inch of his. "And if this doesn't ensure your forgetting that I was ever here, perhaps a promise that I shall return and take it out of your hide if you don't – *will*."

Though I could also merely fog all of their minds later, however, if they crossed me, I doubted I'd be in such a generous mood.

Ricco made with a shaky nod.

"I knew you'd see it my way, Rrrricco." I straightened and backed away. "As a courtesy, do keep a hidden eye on Diego for me in the meantime, will you? And for you and your family's sake, do not inform him of my presence ahead of me. You will speak of me to no one."

He offered another nod. "Sir…if Lucas contacts me and—"

"I'd be more concerned about *me*, if I were *you*. You had best shoot yourself before he gets you to tell him anything, because you see, you're nothing to me but an annoying flea I can split with a fingernail." My tone descended along with my mood. "That you still draw breath all these years is only because you were beneath my notice, generally. Cross me, and I'll split you so *very* slowly that you'll be begging for a gun. Do we have an understanding?"

"*Sì.*"

"*Très bien.*" I glanced at the others. "Gentlemen, enjoy your night. Ah, and you may wish to clean up that mess outside before someone notices."

"Who *are* you?" the one named Mauro suddenly asked.

"*El Diablo*," I stated as I took Gabriel's hand and we made to leave.

Apparently, Mauro believed me, as I noticed him crossing himself as we went through the door.

"Did you take a picture, Kar?" I asked after exiting.

"Yes, my Prince."

"Emanuel will be so pleased." The three of us continued on our way, laughing rather darkly as we walked—though I was more than simmering on the inside and my teeth were on edge.

Trey

I looked over the new files a bit, noting Michel's changes to his proposed deal as well as inside info on the company, and then Geoff and I talked about this and that for the rest of the flight, putting aside thoughts of business for a while. After landing at JFK and grabbing our luggage, a sedan with a driver Michel had hired whisked us off to Manhattan. Since we were heading for E. 63rd, we didn't have to get near the Brooklyn Bridge. No way was I going over that bridge, so thank God or whoever for that.

Michel's 'haven' turned out to be the penthouse suite in one of the most discreet hotels in NYC. The Lowell. It's a bit more like a residence than a hotel. Honestly, I admit surprise over him not setting us up at the Pierre hotel, or the Waldorf Astoria, or heck, even a private residence, but I'm not complaining. Discreet is good. It's just the Pierre—well it's very French, really. Totally his style, and the Waldorf— it's the freaking Waldorf.

But the Lowell is *very* nice. Our suite is cool, and certainly pricey, of that I have no doubt.

The living room has cream sofas and chairs, love that, and for a touch of that French style, a white Louis XV *fauteuil* with olive green velvet upholstery. We have slates, blues and browns provided by pillows and other accents, and alabaster lamps.

A very cool thing is the dining conservatory, with a ceiling partially enclosed by glass. Potted palms frame the doors that lead to a terrace and several flowering plants. Don't suppose Travis'll spend much time in there.

The kitchen's probably too bright for a vampire, too, with its wall of windows. Gotta love a built in espresso machine, though. Well, maybe Travis doesn't drink espresso.

Unless it has blood in it. I think I'll stick with wine and blood, myself. That is, if I ever get another swig of zippy-juice. Not that I'm going to injure myself or anything in hopes of it, I swear.

Anyway. There're three bedrooms. Each one's got a flat screen TV, not that I think we'll be watching much of it. Geoff and I got the master room with orchids and bamboo hand painted on the walls, a metal four-poster bed with raw silk headboard cushioned by a sea of pillows, and dude, there are even cashmere blankets.

Niiiice.

Speaking of nice, I've encountered marble yet again. The master bathroom. Green, blue-green and yellow runs through its milky background—every single wall.

I'll stop right there. It's swanky as hell.

Travis opted for the bedroom that's more masculine. Not surprising. Darker colors almost make the walls look like natural stone. There are black and white sketches and photos hanging in there, too, and a black metal framed mirror. Suits him, I think. Of course, the most pressing reason he chose it is that it's 'vampire safe.'

There are some other cool details, but enough about that. It's damned nice. The end.

Once we'd settled in, there was plenty of night still left. 12:57 a.m. Geoff had already slept on the plane, I was still wide-awake, and Travis is—duh. But instead of TV (or hey, sex, even), I got a mini-debriefing and a third degree on my daytime plans.

"Before I retire for the day, I'll give them a call and set up the meeting for tonight, hopefully," Travis said from his place in the chair across from me and Geoff, as we cuddled on the sofa, quietly listening.

"I'll finish looking over the files in the morning," I said.

"I believe we'll just be meeting Mr. Blake and his attorney."

"I know Blake's got controlling interest by a long shot, but still; he's kept the board out of the loop so far." Hand up. "Last minute affair, I know. Just a comment, nothing to worry about."

"No worries here. Michel told me that Blake wants to hear about the offer first, before going to the board."

"Who's his attorney?"

"I don't know which is coming with him, yet."

"Oh. Right. Other people need more than one to do the job."

He grinned back at me. "Apparently so. I think you already know this deal was hush-hush from the beginning, so I expect they'll be somewhat cautious with us."

Nod. "Likely. Don't worry; I can be charming, really." Wide grin. "If that doesn't work, I just do it the old fashioned way."

"Which is?"

"Stupefy them with my mad skills. They'll surrender before they know what hit them."

He chuckled, Geoff giggled. "I'd like to see about getting close to one of their computers," Travis said then. "We'll probably be meeting with them more than once, so I'll feel out the best opportunity."

"Hey. I can help with that, you know."

"Yeah, I do know. After Germany, I think we both know who's the better man for that job." He tossed me a wink.

I pointed a finger at him. "I don't fry computers."

"Not so far, anyway," he retorted.

Hand waving. "You're faster anyway."

"If nothing else, I might want to install a key logger."

"Ahhh, nice. Hey. I can definitely do that."

"I reckon you'll be too busy, since you're the attorney, not *me*. You get to distract them and stupefy them, remember?"

"I think he like this too much," Geoff said, nudging me.

"I'm inclined to agree, precious," Travis said.

Let's try for innocent. It'll probably fail. "No, I just want to be especially useful." I glanced between them. Failed. "And in on it." Grin.

"You're knee deep already, mate." Travis started laughing. "But it's good you're not afraid, not wound up over it."

"Who said I wasn't wound up? I'm all wound up and ready to go."

"He is," Geoff said and his face suddenly turned pink. "All the time."

Travis just waggled his brows while I hugged my boy to me.

"Um. What is a key logger?" Geoff asked.

"Here I go, teaching you bad things again," I said with a grin. "Basically it'll let us track whatever they type on their computer keyboards."

His brows shot up. "Ohhh." They furrowed. "Ew. I hope no one ever do that to me."

"No worries," Travis said. "I know all the different types, so I could remove them. I doubt anyone will get close enough to your computer to spy on you that way, anyway."

"Don't even tell him about wireless and software types," I said, and before Geoff could ask, I redirected. "You know something? I've never seen you use a computer, *bonito*."

"That no mean I don't." Geoff's deadpan reply.

"Heh. *Touché*."

He smiled. "I don't use it much."

"Somehow I didn't think so."

Travis said, "Now we have that sorted. What are your plans for tomorrow?"

Geoff and I both looked at him. "After I finish with the files in the morning, I figured I'd call Scott. If he's free, probably go see him," I said.

"If he's not?"

"Take Geoff sightseeing."

"Where?"

Oh yeah. Travis was all business now.

"Well, since it's close, Central Park, for a start."

"And then?"

Glance to Geoff. "We could be in there a while, actually. He wants to see the zoo."

Geoff nodded at Travis.

"And if you do see Scott, are you staying in his apartment?"

"We'd hang out there a while, probably, but I'm sure he'd be up for going to the park."

Travis studied me a moment, then said, "I'm going to give you a number for a bloke named Richard. Check in with him every time you change locations, or if anything goes wrong." Beat. "Just in case. Please."

"Hey, no problem, Travis. I figured we'd be followed, too."

"Abso-bloody-lutely. But they'll try to stay out of your way."

Geoff leaned a little closer. My one arm hugged him a little harder.

"I don't sleep late. I'll be up and about an hour before sunset, at least," Travis said. "Sunset is at 7:23. I'd love it if you were back here around seven, or thereabouts."

Of course. He knew the exact times. "Sure." My eyes moved to Geoff. "Are you afraid, baby?" Maybe I should have left him at home, but that might have driven me crazy, wondering how he was. He'd already told me he would've gone crazy wondering about me.

"No. I just not used to this." He looked to Travis. "But you take care of us."

When I turned back to Travis, the blip of regret that registered in his eyes didn't go by me.

"I'm doing my damndest," he said.

"You do good," Geoff assured him, and wonderfully, Travis almost smiled.

So I decided to go fishing for my own details, see if that smile would grow.

"You know, if you're hungry, Geoff and I can look the other way while you duck into an alley, or something," I said.

Score. His smile grew. "That's mighty decent of you, but no worries. The fridge is stocked, same as any safe haven."

"What, you've got bags of blood in there?"

"You've the right of it."

Geoff piped up. "Where you get them?"

"Donations." Travis' eyes moved to Geoff. "I own a blood bank."

Laughter struck me hard. Geoff was still staring at Travis when it let go of me.

"Good one, Travis," I said.

Stone cold, straight faced serious, his reply. "I'm not having you on."

More laughter. "Oh God, that's rich. A vampire who owns a blood bank."

"Um, wow," from Geoff.

"Michel's got his resources," Travis said, "but this time I decided to bring my own along." He looked at Geoff. "We pay better than other blood banks. Some of it still goes to humans in need. I'm not entirely selfish." He winked at Geoff, who beamed him a smile.

"So that's what was in the black case!" Knee slap. "But wait. Don't you—do you feed off live prey?" I asked.

"Yes. But one never knows when an emergency will arise. Not to mention, some of my lovers need blood transfusions when I'm finished. Depending, I might be low myself."

My eyes narrowed.

He still wasn't joking.

"Dude." I paused. "Nope, I still got nothing." A glance to Geoff showed me his wide-eyed look. "Vampires heal, remember? Don't worry, *bonito*."

He just nodded.

"Any road, sometimes we just like a quiet drink at home, same as you." Travis smiled at me. "Warm it up a bit, it's not so bad."

Shrug. "Sure. Why not? Is it same as, uh, live?"

"No. It's a softer buzz. There's no pumping heart, there's not as much life left in it, it isn't the *complete* essence of the person. Nothing's better than live." He grinned wide.

While I swallowed thickly. More to do with my fetish than anything else.

"Do you…" pause. "Michel's sampled me." Yeah. That's a way to put it. "Do you do that?"

"I do." His gaze heated. "Are you making me an offer?"

Mouth—full of spit. "I probably wouldn't mind."

Chuckle from him. Then I noticed Geoff was picking at the fabric over my thigh.

"Trey says it…it very nice."

Mine weren't the only eyes that moved to Geoff's face after that.

"Maybe sometime…you…"

Geoff never finished the sentence, instead planting his face in my shoulder, hiding. Travis and I shared mutual look of understanding and amusement.

Though Travis also looked touched right after that.

"You honor me," he said to Geoff, then. "When you decide, I'll be even more honored."

Geoff peeked at him.

"Meanwhile," Travis said, redirecting, "I'll be awake till after sunrise, which comes around 6:26 a.m. If you guys want to do something…"

No mistaking what Geoff was thinking, I replied, "Uh, yes. I think we do want to do something."

Geoff giggled in my shirt.

"I'll *try* not to listen, but it's not easy, you know," Travis said with grin and a sparkle in his eye.

"I'm not shy and Geoff forgets to be shy when I'm driving him crazy."

The heat coming off Geoff then could've singed me.

"But maybe I shouldn't have said that." Chuckle from me.

"Maybe not." Travis' soft chuckle joined mine. "Though this one's on me. I started it."

"If you'll excuse us, I think I'll finish it, now."

"Oh, do carry on, carry on. I'll be fine. They have porn channels, here."

I lifted Geoff's chin. "Hear that? And we've got our own TV in there."

He took a deep breath and blurted, "We make own porn." Then got up and headed off. "Don't make me wait. Maybe I watch porn without you." He couldn't contain the giggle, but he kept walking.

"Oo, you heard the man," Travis said. "Go get him, tiger."

As I stood up. "I'm on it. I am so on it."

Chapter 11

SEPTEMBER 5

Trey
Brooklyn Heights

"So this is your new place," I said, looking about the living room. "How'd you score a deal in the Heights that didn't break you? I heard prices were getting even higher here."

"It's pretty small, man." Scott said.

"It's still in the Heights."

Scott laughed. "I saved up, but I've still got debt, trust me. For the neighborhood, though, this actually wasn't bad. They hadn't renovated yet. I did some of this myself over the last couple years."

My eyes moved over the dark blue sofa and chairs, the cherry wood tables and bookcase, and the soft beige carpeting that cut away in a graceful arc, giving way to hardwood flooring, which then met a red brick wall on the other end of the room.

"You're doing a good job of it so far," I said.

"Thanks."

Geoff's comment beat mine when his eyes moved to that brick wall. "Wow, so many pictures of angel. They really nice!"

I gazed at the black and whites of all different sizes and different periods. Different facets of my personality captured, frozen. Expressions, clothing, every part that made me, me. There were a few other subjects framed and hanging there, but mostly he'd done a display of Trey.

His best friend.

Too touched to say anything, Geoff's speaking up first was a good thing.

"Thanks, Geoff. I'd love to take some of both of you, sometime," said Scott.

"Okay!" Geoff turned to me. "Okay?"

Swallow. Smile. "Absolutely."

Geoff turned back toward the wall, the photos. "You could be a model."

Scott's laugh easily flowed out. "I told him that all the time."

"I always said no. C'mon, lawyer and model? Nuh uh."

"Why not?" Geoff asked.

Shrug. "It's just not my thing, and I was already too busy."

"You liked posing well enough," Scott teased. Then to Geoff. "He's just cheap. Works for free, the hussy."

Geoff laughed; I rolled my eyes, then gave up my own laugh.

"Oh hey, you guys want a drink?" Scott asked.

"I've still got coffee running through me; don't know about Geoff."

"I'm okay right now, *gracias*."

"Well I'm thirsty. Make yourselves at home, I'm just gonna run into the kitchen. You'll still be able to see me, don't worry." He chuckled and headed that way.

Geoff lingered over the photographs a little longer, while I sat on the sofa, looking through the cut out in the wall, or butler, as people called it, into the kitchen. Three very nice bar stools sat on the living room side of it, the countertop between being big enough for cozy dining.

"So how's Polly?" Scott called through the opening.

"What," I said, "you haven't called her?"

"Well, yeah. But that was about four days ago."

Chuckle. "She's doing great. She said to tell you hi and give you a kiss, but I told her you wouldn't allow the second part."

His laughter wafted through the opening in the wall. "But she had to try, right?"

"Yup. She also said she wanted pictures and detailed notes if I managed to convince you."

Another laugh from him complete with snort. "She's something else. Anyway, didn't expect to see you again so soon, but this is really cool," he said, striding back in and settling in a chair on the other side of the coffee table, a glass of OJ in his hand. "Perfect timing, too, since I have some free days while you're here. You didn't say how long you were staying, though."

"I'm not sure. Couple days, anyway." Geoff finally wandered over and sat down beside me.

"Why didn't you call from Paris, dude? I only have one bedroom, but I would've handed it over. That sofa's pretty nice," said Scott.

"Yeah, it is. But Travis came with us, too, so that's why we got the hotel. Company paid. Couldn't pass that up."

"Company paid. *Michel* paid, you mean. He spoils you."

Spoil is a word.

"Lowell's a nice place," Scott continued. "Don't blame you. Besides, someone would end up on the floor here, and I only got one bathroom. You're in a much better situation all around." A hopeful smile hit his lips. "But maybe next time you can stay with me, even if I can't spoil you the same way."

"Sometime, sure."

"So why'd Travis come along this time? I thought he was the security man."

"He is. He wants to check out that department, assess the company and figure out what he'd have to do, if Michel takes it over. He also keeps an eye on me."

Holy crap, truth! Though I wondered why I'd added the last part. Suppose it was forward planning in the event Scott had reason to notice Travis shadowing me everywhere—not to mention it *was* exciting, telling the truth.

"Why, don't they trust you?" Scott asked, his lips quirking.

"I mean like an escort. He makes sure I get what I need, and gets me where I need to go. He flew us here."

"La-ti-da. You have an escort."

"Spoiled, that's me," I said. "Even still, with accounts like these, I wouldn't take it personally if they kept an eye on me, y'know?"

"True. But you told me they were like family, too. So escort sounds better. And he flies? That's cool."

"Yeah, totally cool." And Michel can fly without a plane – how cool is that, Scott? At least I could tell the *whole* truth in my head.

"Sounds like Travis doesn't mess around," Scott said. "I mean, he doesn't even *know* if it'll be Michel's company yet, but he's already checking departments?"

"That's why he's Michel's number one."

Truth, glorious truth, how I love thee.

"Will you be tied up with your business the whole time you're here?" Scott asked.

"I don't know. I'm free *today* till about 6:30."

"Gotta late meeting or something? Is that why you're dressed up?"

"Yeah, I planned ahead."

"Where's Travis?"

151

"He's stuck inside doing other business most of the day."
Hey, even more truth. (Sleeping counts as business, I say.) Let's
see how long we can hang out today, truth.

"All day?" He sipped his juice. "I remember he said he likes
to work hard, though."

Nod.

"Well, since you're free today, did you want to do something?"
Scott looked between me and my boyfriend.

Geoff answered. "Can we go to Central Park?"

Scott's smile lit up his eyes. "Sure. I love Central Park."

"And the zoo!" Geoff added.

Scott's smile widened. "You got it. I can think of a couple
good restaurants close by, too." He nodded to himself. "We can
grab the subway, no sweat."

Subway, how I love you. No bridges. Scott was much too
close to bridges—to *the* bridge.

"We rode subway here," Geoff said. "I don't know. I think
metro nicer."

Scott and I both laughed and Scott said, "It's cleaner, I'll
say that."

"Not so scary, too," Geoff said. "Maybe at night, but
daytime is okay."

Scott laughed again. "Well here it depends on which lines
and what time of day, too. It's still better than some cab rides.
Cheaper, too."

Emphatic shake of Geoff's head. "Taxi driver in Paris, some
are loco."

I suddenly thought of our lie about the taxi, our accident.
Looked to me like Scott did, too. But neither of us commented.
I sure as hell wasn't gonna push that subject right now. He was
still digesting it, far as I knew. Neither of us mentioned anything
about vamps or other related strangeness on the phone, either.
'Course, we didn't talk long.

He could bring it up; I'd let it lie until then.

Scott said, "Since you guys already had breakfast and everything, guess I'll get off my ass and finish dressing, 'cause I'm sure you're ready to go." Pointed look at me. "Damn, you called early. At least for me, nine-forty-five is early, since I was up way late."

"Heh. Sorry, dude." Travis was—whatever, and I was fighting looking into his room, for one thing, and I'd finished the files and paperwork quickly, not having slept all that much.

"Nah, it's cool. I'm glad you called me first thing." Scott stood. "Just chill a minute and I'll be right back."

After Scott was well on his way to his bedroom, Geoff leaned and whispered, "Travis okay, you think?"

"Of course he is. Michel said it was a haven."

"No maids?"

"Why, did you want to stay there, like you did in Baton Rouge?" Wink.

He smacked my arm, but not hard.

"I don't think he's up for watching porn anyway." Another wink.

"Too bad." His hand covered his bubbling laugh.

At the Zoo

"Man, it feels like forever since I was here."

Tearing my eyes away from Geoff, where fruit bats had him completely enthralled, I looked at Scott. "You *live* in NYC, dude, and not *that* far from here."

"Yeah, yeah. I get busy, y'know. And there's a lot to do and see."

"I'm just giving you shit."

"I always did like this part. I see Geoff does, too."

"Yeah, we might be in here a while. He totally digs the bats."

"They need some vampire bats." Scott nodded.

I stopped myself from gawking at him. "I think Staten Island has some." Didn't mean a thing, Trey. We're in a zoo, talking about bats.

"They don't live on fruit like these flying foxes," he said and pointedly gazed at me.

"Nope."

"They drink blood."

Holding his gaze. "Yup."

"Ever been bitten by one, Trey?"

Uh, hmm. He *has* been thinking about it, now hasn't he? "No." Nope, never bitten by a *bat*, Scott.

He started laughing. "Just giving you shit."

No laugh from me. "I kinda think you're not."

His eyes darted around, then back to me. "Do you really believe they are?"

"Yes." No need to ask who he meant.

"Ohhhkay." He pushed his hair behind his ears. "Right, whatever."

Now I laughed. "Don't sweat it. You can keep thinking I'm nuts." Shrug.

"No, no." He lowered his voice as some people walked by. "You're not. Well maybe you are. Hell I don't know. Maybe I am, too." He paused then spoke even lower. "Is Travis...um."

Leaning in. "Is he what?"

"Okay. His eyes flipped me out. And dude, okay, I saw teeth," he whispered.

Couldn't resist. "He's got a mouthful, like the rest of us."

He blinked. "Oh, fuck you."

"Hey, hey." I patted his shoulder. "I'm just teasing." Pause. "Guess maybe I shouldn't. It just seemed like you were gonna wind yourself up."

One of his hands fanned the air. "No, sorry. It's okay." He looked deeply into my eyes. "But tell me. Is he really here for business?"

Didn't have to lie. "Yes, really. We both are. Why do you ask that?"

"Something about him *watching* you didn't – what I saw in Paris, you know – I don't know, it didn't sit right. Not that I think you lied, earlier. Just – you're still okay, right?"

"Dude really, it's okay, chill." I gave him a smile. "I'm absolutely fine. He's not here to see if I wig out, I swear. I said that wasn't happening again, and it's not like he's a doctor or something, man."

"Okay." He nodded. "Okay, cool. I don't know what I was thinking, really, anyway." He moved closer, more people passing around. "I still don't know what to think of that, I mean, the way he looked in your apartment. But I'm curious. Do you think, uh – do you think I could talk to Travis while you're here?"

I contemplated. "I'll see what the schedule allows. He said he wouldn't mind seeing you again."

"So, say, if I asked some really weird questions – "

So could not stop my laugh. "He won't think you're being weird."

"You sure?"

"Pretty sure, yeah."

"Okay, now stop laughing at me."

My hands went up in surrender. "Sorry, sorry." But I was still laughing.

"Pff. Screw you."

"Offering?"

"Nope."

"Didn't think so. But you know me."

"You had to ask."

"Uh huh."

"I'm gonna tell Geoff."

"Go 'head, chile."

"*Chile?*" Now he nearly man-giggled. "What was that about?"

Oops. Seem to be slipping – even I heard that. "That's probably about Lucien. Or something." Maybe it was just my

155

Mark. I remembered how when meeting Gabriel the first time, he'd made that strange comment about detecting something other than just 'New York' in my accent. Had it started even then? Just enough for vampires or maybe super attentive humans to notice?

Scott craned his head around to spot Geoff – who the bats still had caught up. Looked back at me. "I did say you didn't sound New York last time I saw you."

"Nasal ass Upstate New York is what I think you said, yeah."

"You really don't sound New York now, and I don't just mean the chile thing. Your entire accent's different, every time you talk. I'm thinking even more than the last time I saw you, in fact."

Brow lift. "Really?"

"Totally."

"No one else has mentioned it. Well, P.K.'s commented on it before, but more like how it slips."

"Ask all those people you know now. I can't be the only one who noticed. Though, okay, they haven't known you that long, but still."

I supposed if I had asked P.K. before I left, she'd have said the same. She would know. But it wasn't a pressing issue. We had things more important on our minds.

"I will," I said. "Gonna start calling me a hick, now?"

"Maybe. But it's kinda cool. Weird, but cool."

A bit weird, yes. Seemed this Mark of mine had done all kinds of things to me, I thought as I smiled at him.

"So anyway…"

Whatever he said next escaped me when I heard a multi-layered whispering. Just resisting the reflexive urge to look around, I focused inward, trying to parse the words.

"…maybe if there's time…"

Female, the whispering sounded feminine as it condensed somewhat, but I was having trouble understanding it, which puzzled me. I'd gotten good at turning the Dead into background noise, as Michel once suggested, and better at focusing on singular sounds, but I couldn't separate this one whisper from the others enough to make out all of the words.

"Yo, Trey. Something wrong?"

Focus, snapped back to Scott. "Nothing's wrong, no."

"Where'd you go?"

No omissions. To gain his complete acceptance of what I was, best to keep *confirming* what I was. Treat it as normal. It could only help.

"I was listening to someone on the Other Side."

His response at first was to gape at me. Then, "What did they say?"

"Couldn't quite make it out. I'm not sure why."

"What do they want?"

Nearly a repeat of his earlier question, not that I blamed him. What else could he ask while wondering if he and his friend were sane?

"I don't know, yet," I said. "And relax. No one's taking me over."

"'Course not."

"So stop looking worried, pal." Nudge.

Nudge back. "I can't help it, pal."

"S'okay. You're just too sweet."

"You can shut up, now." He shook his head. "But no, really. You honestly hear…them. You really do, don't you?"

"Yes, Scott, I do."

"Dude, no offense, but I kept telling myself I'd had a fucked up nightmare after I left Paris. One big, long, vivid nightmare with an all-star cast."

Shrug and chuckle. "I don't blame you. It was fucked up, all right."

"But it really happened." He studied my eyes.

"It really did."

"And Geoff is really here."

"He really is, thank Papa."

"Because of you."

My eyes dropped. "Yes and no. There were other paths. His time didn't have to end."

"But if you hadn't been there..."

"Don't say it."

His hand came to my shoulder. "Sorry, I'm sorry."

"I'm mostly holding on to the beauty of the after effects, but sometimes I can't get the scene in the catacombs out of my head."

"I wouldn't think so. I know it would mess me up, for sure."

Eyes, lifting. "But let's not be morbid, yeah? He's here, I'm here, you're here – it's all good."

A full smile found him. "Yeah, it's all good. I'll untangle my brain later. This means you should be prepared for questions in the near future."

"Heh. Thanks for the warning."

"I'd like to hear more about these after effects, too, if you're up to it."

Warning. There. Whispering, again. Was it a warning?

"Yeah, I'd be up to it, Scott. What I've noticed so far is pretty cool, actually."

"Speaking of your boyfriend, we'd better grab him now and talk about that later. He'll never see the rest of the zoo at this rate," he said.

"Yeah."

"Though there is one quick question I'd like to ask you right now."

"Shoot."

He studied my face. "Did you ever notice weird stuff before you moved to Paris? Voices, whatever?"

"P.K. asked me a similar question not long ago, and I've been thinking about it in the few free moments I've had."

His look was expectant.

"There might have been some stuff when I was in rehab," I continued. "But I was a mess, and I might've been imagining things. I figured it was from the detoxification, y'know?"

"Well...What do you *think* happened?"

One of my hands just had to push at my hair. "When I stopped trying to block all that out and really thought about it, I realized there might have been a ghost around me back then. It was more a feeling of being watched, really." Humorless laughter left me. "Then again, I was being watched by real people all the time anyway."

"Yeah, but were they watching *every* second? Did they watch you on video, even?"

Headshake. "No. But I was in a druggie hospital, eh? You tend to get paranoid about a few things."

"Sure, but was there anything else, besides feeling watched, that made you think ghosts?"

"I don't know, Scott." Pause. "I think I might have heard some voices." Another headshake. "Still, that and everything else can be explained as the DTs."

"True...But ya know, you did die and come back. There're lots of stories about that altering a person, changing their reality. Most of the world doesn't believe it, but look at you."

"Yeah. I dunno. It's so hazy," I said. "But it *has* occurred to me that Lucien sounded familiar." Big wave of my hand. "Eh, but Dad used to imitate him. I got nothin' solid, see?"

"Okay, so how about before – and of course, I mean before all the drugs."

Shoulder shrug.

"Nothing at all, really?" he said.

"I've been spooked out in a place or two before, but who hasn't?"

"True, but we're not all like you." He touched my shoulder. "I just figure there must've been something before, something hinting at this power – or gift, thing, whatever."

"Nothing that really stands out indisputably, Scott. It was kinda like *bam*. Woke up."

"How about weird dreams? Weirder than weird, y'know?"

"Well…"

Soon…

…me.

Hurt…

…can help.

"Trey," a very different whisper.

Blink. "Yeah, Scott."

"Gonna answer me?"

"Uh…what did you ask me?"

His eyes searched mine. "Never mind, I'll ask again later. Were you listening to someone else just now?"

My turn to study him. "Yes."

"Anything understandable this time?"

His eyes held honest curiosity. "Nothing that makes much sense. But I'm sure I'll find out eventually." Shrug. "If someone needed me that bad, surely I could reach them and they me. Let's go get Geoff now and figure it out later, when I can focus better."

"Sure, but just *one* more thing. Will you keep me updated on this, this voice?"

A smile slowly formed on my face. "You're getting really fascinated with this."

"Well. It wouldn't be the first time, now would it?"

"Oh, so I'm on the list of oddities now, I get it."

He lightly slapped my back. "Yup. So will you?"

"Sure, why not." I gave him a push. "Now, onto dragging Geoff away from those bats."

You…

…happened…

Queens…

That was the last of the woman's whispering I heard the rest of the day.

Numbness slowly ebbed whilst the miniscule pulsing of sensation flowed, spreading from my center along my torso, then through my limbs. Words previously drifting through a haze of purple-black hues along unseen channels began to find purchase in my consciousness.

I took breath and my eyes opened. Distant murmurings merged with clear, crisp words now spoken as I awoke, and as in my dreams, they belonged to Michel.

"I don't care how. I need this information sooner than yesterday."

My gaze wandered languorously about the room until it found his form. Clad in a vermillion robe not secured by its ties, he had his portable phone pressed to his ear. Impatience not only writ itself upon his face, but through the tension of his muscles. Pacing soon followed, and I sat up in the bed, pulling my knees to my chest, watching and listening keenly. I could hear the voice that issued from the mobile, though I did not recognize it.

"Where did he go after this?"

Sections of the conversation that had found their way into my subconscious whilst I slept surfaced completely. Michel had been speaking to this someone for several minutes, and this person – this human, was calling from Belgium.

"What business would he have with *Miles*?"

This piqued my interest sharply. Miles was one of Michel's men.

"You're absolutely certain?" He paused whilst listening. "Exact? Were these the exact words? Think carefully; it's of great importance."

After the next brief pause, his sharply spoken words gave

me a start, which I attributed to my yet being groggy; though still, his ire was rather great.

"Have him detained *immediately*. I swear I'll skin him slowly, by gods."

His following low growl caused the fine hairs at the nape of my neck to crawl. No doubt, the mortal hearing this growl may have soiled himself. The thought amused me, if briefly.

"Yes, I mean Miles, you imbecile! You've no need of knowing why, just have it done!"

Michel snapped shut his portable phone; it cracked. This apparently did not provide adequate satisfaction, as he flung the device down, where it shattered on the flooring. I moved from the bed and went to him, my hands finding his shoulders in their attempt to still his movements, to soothe him.

"Something is amiss," I commented. A simple and obvious statement, but such was often better when he was in this particular mood.

"Hah! Amiss?" He moved away, the energy within him not allowing stillness, not yet. "Oh yes, something is *amiss*."

I remained silent, allowing him to go on as he would, judging it best not to interfere whilst he expended this energy, his need to do so, rather great.

"Ohh, Miles, Miles, Miles." He made another turn, feet retracing the circle he had commenced marking upon the floor whilst yet speaking on the phone. A circle that wove around me, as I now stood in the center of it. "Guess what I've found out, my love, can you guess?" His steps did not pause as he inquired, nor did he spare me so much as a glance, but he was waiting for a response, any response, this I knew.

"Betrayed you in some way, I would venture."

His gaze flickered to me, his eyes intensely gold. "I do believe we have a winner, why yes, I do believe he's about betrayal, yes indeed." Yet another turn did he make, the wall of electricity about us growing, his aura extending – golden, but dotted with blue, liken to that of a gas flame. "Were he here just now, I would begin with his eyelids, peeling them free of his face. Mmm, yes, this would be a *fine* start," he snarled.

My eyes, my senses, they tracked his movements. "What has he done, my love?" I had yet to string the bits of conversation into something completely coherent, his demeanor now claiming all of my attention. He was doing nothing to tame his energy; we were alone, there were no immediate witnesses to consider, but I began to worry that his energy was becoming volatile.

He came to an abrupt halt and I could feel my hair lifting farther away from my scalp.

"He met with Lucas Demetrius." He moved closer, and his aura bathed my skin, which prickled, tingled, felt to crackle. "Lucas Demetrius, who was there asking after Elise." His own hair shifted, lifting as if in a breeze. "It would seem Miles offered him some information."

This most certainly did not sit well with me, not in the slightest. Yet, rather than indulge in questions or my own ire, I opted for a shift in subject, knowing well what may manifest should Michel's anger continue to grow. I cared not what happened to Miles, held no emotional tie in my coming defense of him – it was merely a bid for preemptive damage control. Though presently there were no witnesses, should he unleash what truly was two days worth of irritation, the wreckage would draw much attention.

"Perhaps Miles was threatened, coerced, forced into such," I carefully offered. "Perhaps he had no choice."

There was a popping sound, followed by three more, extremely close to my ears. It was the very air, the currents which flowed through and from him, nothing yet broken in the room – though the lights were dimming as the source of their power was drawn to him, collecting and merging with his own.

"He was under no duress when they were spied," he said. He then appeared to consider. "They may have found means to coerce him in some way, at some other time." This did little to assuage him, however. "It doesn't change the fact that he opened his mouth, and words fell out." His eyes flashed brighter still. "Everything I've done for him, yet he talked." He flung his arms away from his body. "Apparently he also stirred up my men in Liège. Finn was caught attempting to defect. By the gods, I cannot trust anyone these days!"

My tactic having failed, I commenced with my previous questions. "What information did Miles share?"

"That we're in Spain, that we're considering a power play of some sort, and we're utilizing our spy network extensively. Even more distressing is Elise. What the hell does she have to do with this? That's something I'd dearly love to know!"

A lamp on a bedside table burst.

"Michel…" I moved to him, even as I wished to inquire how it was that Miles knew we were in Spain, the question dying on my lips, as well as my statement of the obvious – that Lucas had wasted little time in leaving Spain to return to Belgium.

"Michel," I purred, caging him from behind, and my hands found his thighs, the touch giving me a jolt that felt as if it lighted my spine. "Let us take a moment to think upon this rationally."

He did not recommence pacing. However, yet another lamp burst.

I moved a hand to his groin and gripped him whilst bringing my lips to his ear, my tongue slithering out to taste it. "*Mon amour*," I purred as my hand moved upon him. "*Mon amour*, there is a better way to expend this energy." My very veins felt like electrical wires, and I knew that I must calm him before he drew attention to our hiding place. Before he *destroyed* our hiding place.

I gripped him harder, moved my hand faster. "Better ways," I whispered, though quite truly excited. Were it not for practicalities, I would allow his energy to grow, yet I was assuredly excited with the prospect of his turning it on me.

Of a sudden, he groaned and his hips shifted, finding the rhythm. "Better ways," he near growled.

"Several and several ways," I replied, tracing one of his dusky nipples with the nails of my other hand.

He then spun and laid into my throat, drawing a cry from me, and before I could move past the sudden pain into a place of pleasure, he shoved me back with enough force that I found myself prone on bed.

There was no time to blink as he was then upon me, pinning me, claiming me mercilessly.

I had a moment to understand that his aura had condensed. A moment to comprehend that we had evaded disaster, before his energy flooded my being.

Disaster evaded, which was for the best, to be certain, though I could not deny it had been too long since I had received his daemon energy in such a way. Since I had drawn it in such a way.

It was gloriously dangerous.

Chapter 12

Trey

Geoff and I didn't end up going back to the hotel. Travis called while we were finishing dinner after finally having seen the rest of the zoo, and he said he decided he'd come get me, take me straight to the meeting. He also decided it'd be good if Geoff hung out with Scott while we took care of business. I'd already considered that, since there wouldn't be anything for Geoff to do while I was at the meeting, and I didn't like the idea of him sitting alone in the penthouse – secure or not. I had thought to suggest it to Travis, but naturally, he was already on top of things, and he said Scott and Geoff in one place worked better for keeping an eye on each of them.

Scott didn't get a chance to talk to Travis, though. Travis phoned me again when he'd reached the apartment building, saying we had little time to waste and that he thought it'd be more rude to do a 'hi and bye' with Scott. So, making my apologies and my goodbyes, I took the elevator down and hit the street.

"A cab?" I said when I saw Travis standing next to a familiar, piss-yellow car with my briefcase in one hand and a tie in the other. Good thing I'd worn most of a suit in the event I wouldn't have time to change at the hotel.

"Our previous driver is otherwise occupied and I don't know the area. I took the subway here; it was quick." He grinned. "Then I called a cab. I reckoned it might be a spot of fun, anyway."

Eye roll. "Fun?" Laugh. "I thought we were in a hurry."

"The place isn't that far." He shrugged. "I take this business seriously. I have it all worked out."

"Fair enough. I won't begrudge you your moment of sightseeing."

Laughing, he opened the door after handing me the tie. "Get in."

"Get in. Not *please get in*. I see how it is."

"Yeah, I'm pretty commanding." A wink from him and a gesture to get the hell in, already. The cabbie took off shortly after Travis slid in beside me and gave him the address.

"It's good these guys weren't weird about meeting late," I said as I worked on the tie. "Though there's still the possibility of a day meeting, you know."

"Yes, I know. Any road, it wasn't a problem at all. Business types are used to working all hours, right? We'll see about the rest after this first meeting."

I nodded and then really looked which way we were heading. "Wait." The address finally clicked. "We're going back to Manhattan?"

"That's where they wanted to meet. Some private office there," Travis replied.

Glance to the cabbie, tie forgotten. "Don't take Brooklyn Bridge. Take the Manhattan."

"Don't take it? S'right there, dead ahead," Joe Patrioni barked back. Typical cabbie, at least, typical American NYC cabbie. "You see how bad traffic is the other way? Prolly a wreck or somethin'."

167

"It's a little late for that," Travis said, giving me a curious look. "We've enough time for that bit of sightseeing, but just a bit. Reckoned I just wanted to go over this famous bridge of yours, ya know?"

"The Manhattan's right *there*," I said, pointing at the appropriate window.

Joe barked, "Did ya hear what I said, or you got wax in those ears?"

"It does look all backed up, Trey," Travis said.

Panic wanted to set up house already. "How about a ferry," I said. "That's a much cooler ride, plenty to see. Or a train."

"Trey, what's – "

"You want I should stop right now?" Joe chimed in, cutting off Travis. "I thought you was in a hurry, but whateva, we can stop now."

"Stop," I ordered.

Joe swerved, and amidst a chorus of horns and squealing brakes, the taxi bumped to a halt at the curb.

"It's definitely too late for ferries and the like, Trey," Travis said. "The building isn't far from the other end of the bridge, as I understand it." His eyes were asking me what was wrong.

"Yeah, yeah, s'close," Patrioni butted in. "But listen, I don't care which way you wanna go. You want I should find you another bridge, gonna cost you more, whateva. But if you're in a hurry, your funny talkin' friend's right. It's Brooklyn Bridge or nothin'. Make up your mind." Joe looked over his headrest at me. "In or out, this way or that. Stop yankin' my chain."

My back pressed to the seat, and my eyes closed. "Fine, take the fucking Brooklyn Bridge."

"Right, Einstein, we take the fuckin' bridge I was gonna take." Joe jerked the car away from the curb and cut through the traffic, horns once again issuing in stereo.

"What is it, Trey?" Travis asked in a low tone.

"Nothing. No big deal," I tightly replied.

Yes it was. Still, surely crossing a bridge wasn't going to kill me.

Travis' stared burned into me. "I'm not buying what you're selling, mate. Nervous?"

Not over what you think, Travis. "About the meeting? No."

"What is it about the bridge?" he asked. Then in my mind, *I can feel it, the dread rising in you.*

Or he does think.

Hitched breath and a whisper. "Accident was on the bridge. My parents died on *that* bridge." I hadn't even been able to *look* at the Brooklyn Bridge since my parent's accident.

"Damn," Travis whispered back. He started to say something to the cabbie, but I grabbed his arm before he could get all the words out.

"It's too late. It's fine," I said through gritting teeth.

"Lots a' people die on that bridge," Patrioni commented.

"Obviously it's not," Travis said to me.

"We'll be late," I said.

"We'll find an excuse. We'll take the ferry if you like." *I can get you there an unnatural way, if I have to. Shit, I'm sorry, Trey.*

"No." My teeth clamped and my eyes squeezed themselves shut again. "Gotta go over it someday, don't I?" Maybe not, but maybe it was time to face it and I didn't want to screw things up by being late.

Maybe this was the something P.K. had mentioned. She said I could do it. I can do this.

"Trey it'll be fine, really. We'll go another way," Travis said.

"I said no." I opened my eyes and looked straight ahead. "Keep going," I ordered Joe.

"I was plannin' on it, mister."

Travis sat back and said nothing for blocks. Neither did I. Then we were approaching the Bridge, that fucking monster of a suspension bridge whose main span was 1,595 feet, the total length of the bridge around 6,000 feet. Those feet seemed like miles to me before the car was even on it, making its approach. It felt like impending doom, and my chest tightened. I tried, how I tried, to look at the water as we progressed forward. Tried, how I tried, to admire the skyline, one of the best views in the city. Tried so hard to admire the construction of the old bridge just like so many other times crossing it before my world had caught on fire.

Instead, even before I closed them, my eyes filled with flames and wreckage. A newscast imbedded in my brain moved behind my dropped lids in slow motion. After this, all I could see were black and white photographs. Photos of the other victims who died when the tanker hit them, photos shown to me because their family members were suing over insurance settlements, and their lawyers had sought me out for any extra information I might have.

Had sought me out to convince me to go in on the lawsuit. Waved photos at me to punctuate the point, since they knew I was a lawyer. It reminded me at the time of how those girls' families must have felt in court when I defended a murdering rapist, them having to stomach repeated viewing of photographic evidence. Here came lawyers who said they wanted to help the victims, and in their eyes, I was a victim.

But no. They just wanted their cut.

No, I'd said. If I wanted that, I could represent myself, and I was too devastated to give a shit about money. Didn't give a shit about the money either way.

The visions and thoughts morphed soon enough. Images like full color portraits of my parents looking the same as when I'd identified them, blazed through my mind foot after foot (mile after mile) of the crossing. They merged with the damned black and white photos those lawyers had wielded.

Snapshot: My father's hands grafted to a melted steering wheel. The Tag Heuer watch I'd purchased for him with my first success as a lawyer, welded to his wrist. The watch gave him away immediately in the morgue; no pretending it was someone else after seeing it. His once beautiful profile, something from a horror film. Tiny sprouts of hair still coming out of his skull.

My mother. Snapshot: Her dress, nothing but scraps littering a form that was nearly skeletal in places, nearly indistinguishable from the seat it blended with – damned lawyers and our details. One dangling ruby earring taunted me from one nearly perfect ear in an otherwise torched visage. A set I'd given her for Christmas one year. A shock of hair, the blond she'd always colored it, twisting its way around that ear. One shock of hair left.

I could smell it. Roasted flesh. Gasoline. Could hear my mother scream and my father saying *I love you* one last time. My mind conjured these things over and again. I could even hear him say my name, but it wasn't his ghost.

Smelling it. Gasoline. Burnt hair. Roasted flesh. The seat dropped out from beneath me and my stomach lurched. Sweat broke out. I think Travis grabbed my hand and he probably said something, but my lips wouldn't move to speak in return, because it felt like I was on a runaway rollercoaster. The bile rose in my throat. I tried to take deeper breaths, but I was going to be sick. I willed myself not to be sick in the car, willed hard, but was certain I'd lose the battle.

So I held my breath forever.

Years later the car stopped. I stumbled out, wrapping my own arms around me. My feet tripped me into an alley, I think. Wasn't really seeing where they were taking me. My hand found what felt like brick. Travis must have run after me. I'm sure he said something, but my ears didn't parse the words, because my guts couldn't hold out any longer, and my body was doubling over, retching.

"Trey." I felt his light touch to my back as the last of the dry heaves finally loosened their spasmodic grip on my stomach. "I'm sorry, I'm so terribly sorry. Are you going to be all right?"

"It's," I spat against the wall. "S'okay." My body tried to straighten up. His arm went through the one I wasn't leaning on. "I'll get a grip, I will." My other hand moved off the brick to swipe at my mouth.

"I'm sorry it was so awful, Trey."

"Not your fault." I stood up fully. "You didn't know. But thanks."

"Maybe I should've insisted that he stop, regardless of what you said, though."

I looked at him, finding the tender expression that went with his words. "I can be a stubborn bastard. We're here now, and it's over. Let's go in there and do what we came here to do." I smoothed my hand over my hair.

"Do you need a few more minutes, first?"

I took a deep, deep breath and let it out. "I don't want any more minutes." I searched for words. "I'm just...I guess I'm just such a person of place, know what I mean?" I gazed into his eyes.

"Places trigger memories hardcore for you," he said and set about fixing up my tie.

"I build it up so much over time. Sights, smells," I said. "Some things don't take much. I think I'll be okay now that we're off the bridge. I just want to go inside, because, well. Because I don't really want to think about it anymore right now. I need the shit in my head to go away. I need to think about this meeting. I need a different surrounding."

He nodded. "I get you." He placed his hand on my shoulder. "The entrance is just around the corner."

Buck up, Trey. "Lead the way."

He nodded again and picked up my briefcase, handing it to me.

The charm. I'd forgotten. I stuck a hand in my pocket, touching it. Better late than never, maybe.

"Trey?"

Refocus. "Yeah. Let's go." I reached into a different pocket to find a breath mint.

Okay, something faced. Good. I handled it. Yup. *You're fine*, I told myself as we walked.

You did it, son. You're all right. There are finer memories of that bridge. Think on those.

172

Oh...Dad.

Briefly closing my eyes, I took a deep breath and his scent tickled my nostrils. When my eyes opened, I realized that rather than feeling grief, my stride was much smoother. Confident.

Thanks Dad. I love you.

But he was already gone.

"Trey, were you just communicating with dead people?"

I glanced at Travis, noting extra brightness to his eyes, guessing he'd sensed it in some way. A smile, a real one, found me. "Dad popped in and out," I said.

He returned my smile. "That's a beautiful thing." But his smile started to fade as a thought apparently struck him. "Do you think you could..." he abruptly looked ahead, his words dying off.

After studying his profile a minute, I decided not to say a word, let him pretend he'd never considered asking me a damned thing. I had an idea what the question might have been, and he obviously wasn't ready for me to answer it, yet.

****

Once inside, we strode across a small lobby that looked like something out of a mid-to-low-rate hotel. Dull, flat ochre carpet, rather sterile, cold walls with a few uninspiring paintings here and there, and one small, unmanned, reception/security counter.

As we hit the elevator, I tried not to make too many snap judgments about the meeting place. Maybe the offices were nicer. It was a small, unassuming building, for sure, but maybe this big-shot businessman had spent his money in other ways. In fact, as we were about to reach the third floor, I decided that maybe he wasn't flashy, didn't want to advertise his status. I could respect that. I just wasn't accustomed to it in previous dealings; people I'd met with in the past weren't terribly subdued about their money, though some were classier about it than others.

Michel also spoiled me something fierce. Flashy, yes. The only thing remotely subdued about him (compared to everything else), were his most casual jeans and shirts, but even they spoke money. At least he had good taste.

We stepped out onto an understated, but nicely polished off-white marble floor. As we walked down the hall, I noted that the paintings hanging at precisely measured intervals were a bit nicer than the lobby's, but too painfully organized for my taste.

"You don't seem too impressed," Travis said low, breaking the silence.

Shrug. "Mostly just curious why we're here. I'm starting to wonder if this is someone else's building, and they're just borrowing a room. So much for getting to their computers, maybe, huh."

He mirrored my shrug. "Maybe. Wouldn't be the first time. I've been to some meetings where the others insisted on such things out of paranoia. They had buckets of money, flashy homes and cars, but liked to meet in obscure places. Like warehouses, in fact."

"Makes sense for vampire shenanigans." Chuckle. "Warehouses. So stereotypically low-grade mafia. Ranks right below Italian restaurants." I looked at him as we approached a plain brown door at the end of the hall. "But it makes sense for humans too, if they're intent on keeping secrets."

"They're not on to us," he whispered.

"I mean from the press, too." Another shrug. "Competitors. Shit like that. There're ways to spy that won't get a person arrested. They all do it."

He grinned and rapped a knuckle against the door. "You mean like dating a secretary on a temporary basis?"

I grinned back, but the door opening cut off my reply. On the other side was a man all of 5'6" maybe, with closely cropped brown hair graying at the temples, and a pleasant enough face with rounded features that showed just enough wear and tear for me to decide he might be in his fifties.

"Mr. du Bois and Mr. Starke, I presume?"

My arm went out. "I'm du Bois."

He took my hand, giving it a firm shake. "Prompt, a very good way to begin a meeting. I'm Mr. Blake; good to meet you."

"Likewise," I said as I dropped my hand and watched him shake Travis' as they exchanged pleasantries. Blake then moved back and gestured for us to come inside.

It was your average meeting room, nothing too special. Small and sedate, though as I looked around, it was clear the highly polished dark brown table in the center of the room wasn't exactly cheap. Neither were the softly glowing wall sconces on the coffee-with-extra-cream walls, or the shiny, long table against the right wall. They must have brunch there, I thought. There was a coffee maker and a set of decanters and highball glasses sitting on that table. Water glasses and a pitcher full of water, too. I had time to glance at a couple of paintings in the room, judging them far better than any I'd seen yet, before Blake was gesturing yet again, this time toward another man at the far end of the room. The man's back was to me, but I could see he was engrossed with digging around in a briefcase he had set on low cabinet, so I assumed it was Blake's lawyer. I followed Blake in that direction after setting my briefcase on the floor by the center table, while Travis hung back in that area.

"Mr. du Bois, this is my attorney, Mr. Brantley," Blake said.

The other man turned just before his name registered. When he did, his light brown eyes punched the wind out of me, socked me right in the gut. The rest of his face appeared to me in soft focus and it felt like all of my blood dropped to my feet, icing my veins along the way. Had I not set my briefcase down already, I'd have dropped it.

"Good to meet you, Mr. du Bois."

I could only stare blindly at his face. The features several years still couldn't erase. The short, meticulously coifed, dark brown hair. Not terribly changed; he was just dressed better than the last time I saw him.

"Mr. du Bois?"

A sliver of logic that hadn't fled when the rest of it did told me he was waiting for me to shake his hand. Both of my hands said *no way, we're not touching him.* Even if I hadn't just become petrified wood, I wouldn't touch him, except maybe to punch him.

Someone cleared his throat. Wasn't sure who.

Time split; I was standing in two places.

"Mr. du Bois?"

Take your turn or take his place.

"Is something wrong?"

Take your turn or take his place.

"Trey?" Whisper in my ear. Or was it in my head?

"Young man, are you ill? Can we get something for you or do something for you? Some water, perhaps?"

Look at the older guy, the one I don't know intimately. Not so difficult after all, because staring at *William* was making me nauseous.

"Mr. du Bois, what is it?"

Can't form a sentence, Blake. Yes, you're Blake, right.

"Is there something wrong with him; does he have a medical condition?"

He must be asking Travis.

Attempt sentence, Trey. "I'm…" I have no idea. Sentence not forming. No, I do have an idea. I'm going under, that's the problem. Someone toss me a life preserver.

Trey, what is it?

Oh. Is that a life preserver? "Pardon me," step back. Step back again. Hold onto that preserver for dear life, Trey. Where is it again? "I feel ill."

A half laugh reaches my ears. It doesn't help. I've heard it before. "You look like you had some bad sushi. I can sympathize."

Funny. If it came from someone else, anyway. I'm drowning. Help. *Help me, someone help me.*

Trey, I'm losing you, I can feel it. Hold on, I'll get you out of here.

There. There it is.

Still half here, half there, I somehow manage to find the door, somehow manage to go down the hall, and somehow manage to keep going who knows where.

Fled. I fled. Like so many other times. I was a master by now.

My trembling hands reach for who knows what.

Take your turn or take his place.

Billy, no!

Go on, scream, queer-boy.

I can't breathe.

Can't breathe.

Stop, nghgh, please! STOP!

Mouthful of grass.

Why don't you fight harder, huh? C'mon, fight, you scrawny little shit.

Can't move. I can't breathe.

Raw throat.

I can't move.

"Hey…hey there, Trey."

Hands on me.

Can't struggle.

"Trey, can you hear me? Trey?"

"No," gasp, "Get away."

Hands.

On me.

"I'm not here to harm you. Do you know where you are, for God's sake?"

Gasp. "Get away!"

No more hands.

I get up.

Get up?

Yes, up. I get up and realize it's Travis' voice. Those were Travis' hands. Those are Travis' concerned eyes. The understanding I was on the floor moments ago hits.

"With me now, Trey?"

I can only stare at him while seeking air for my lungs.

"Take it slow," he says, meaning my breathing, no doubt.

Hands to my chest, I take it slow and feel him studying me while he waits.

"You blanched when you saw Brantley," he said after the eternity of me learning how to breathe again.

Someone let out a sick laugh. That someone was me.

"You're beginning to really worry me, mate. Say something, anything."

Anything? "Vegemite."

His brows furrow more tightly. I see the crease it makes between his eyes, just above his nose. "You know him, don't you," he says, and I surmise he damned well knows the answer to that.

So I nod.

"He scares you."

Different synapses fired in my brain. "*Scares* me?" My fingers clenched. "I hate the son of a bitch." I turned towards the – reception desk? Fucking hell, how did I end up here, wherever here is – and gripped the counter. "How could he stand there just looking at me, *looking* at me with that fucking polite smile on his smug fucking face? He has to remember, he must remember my name!" I whirled on Travis. "I haven't changed that much since I was sixteen!"

"Trey, I…" he took a step towards me, but it looked like he was afraid to.

Afraid to startle the babbling mad man.

I rubbed my face. Rubbed it again.

Jesus. Oh, *Jesus*, this was the *last* thing I'd expect to face, want to face, fuck, yeah it was. My hand found that charm of P.K.'s.

178

Hang onto it, man.

Travis spoke again, his tone dropping. "He harmed you in the past."

Slowly, my eyes turned toward him. It wasn't just the low pitch of the words, it was the underlying sense of threat that made me look at him, and when I did, I saw it reflected in his eyes.

Get a grip get a grip, Trey. Fingers, furiously stroking the metal in my pocket. I can do this. P.K. said so. Here's my life preserver – maybe.

Oh. God. Dad, please don't pop in. I'm sorry, please don't. I lied to you.

Jesus, get your brain together, Trey. One thing at a time.

"Doesn't matter right now. I need to get my shit together, go back in there, and salvage this meeting." Jesus, did I just say that?

No sooner had I said that, than Travis was so close there couldn't have been an inch left between us, and he was scenting me. He then moved his head back, his eyes nailing mine. Eyes swallowed in blackness, not a spark of moonlight there.

"He violated you."

Thick swallow. Had he seen it? The visions that rushed behind my eyes? Had he heard it? The words repeating in my head? How long had he been here before I knew he was here?

Did he smell the lingering affects just now?

All of the above?

Whatever the case, he knew. Anyone could see that he knew.

So I nodded.

His lips pulled back with a low snarl, revealing fangs, and he turned for the elevator.

In my brain, click click click.

"No!" Shit. "Wait, wait!"

He didn't stop, now striding towards the elevator, and all I could do was throw myself in that direction and toss myself in his path. "Wait!"

Suddenly I found myself sliding backwards across the floor, my hands still at his chest, because I was no more than a feather in his way. His eyes were impossible black holes, and I could feel the thick, dark tendrils of energy rising in him.

"*Stop*. Please. I know what you want to do, but you can't. You can't do this right now...*Aeshma*."

Saying Aeshma, this brought a little of his focus back to me, and somewhat to my surprise, I privately rejoiced.

"He has violated you and should be judged," he said. But even with those words, he moved back, just as my spine contacted metal.

While his sharp baritone seemed to echo in my ears, my brain scrambled for my own words. "Yes!" I moved forward. "Yes, he should, but not right now. We can't right now."

"How long has he enjoyed freedom already, Death Dancer?"

Too long.

No, can't say that. "A long time. A little while longer won't matter." Jesus, as much as a good chunk of me wanted to see Billy torn to shreds, this couldn't happen now. But still, standing here negotiating for Billy's life was making me *sick*. Hadn't I already had enough of that because of the damned bridge?

A smile dark enough to match his eyes formed, showing me two more fangs than I'd known he possessed, making it six. "You desire vengeance. Step aside, and you shall have it; it is a specialty of mine."

Fixed on those two very long, sharp teeth to the inside of his lengthened canines, it took me a second to register his movement. I pressed my hands to his chest again, for all the good it would do.

"Wait, wait. We have to finish the business, first."

"Step aside," he growled, the sound metallic, giving me a hot spinal monkey. "It is past time for him to atone for his sins."

Yes, yes it is.

But no!

"Aeshma, please, please, wait."

His eyes bore into mine.

"Listen. Just listen to me, please." My thoughts ran to a place I didn't want to drag him. But I had to. It might be my only shot at stopping him."If you do this now, we fail. I don't want that. I don't want to fail Michel." My back contacted metal again. "Do you want to fail?"

I knew what saying this might do to him, God help me, but I had to appeal to him, and it was true. It was the only reason I could imagine looking at my attacker again – when I was able to look at him – the idea of letting Michel down otherwise.

Travis' reply sounded like boiling mercury.

"He does not deserve to breathe the same air as you any longer, Death Dancer."

Pressed, pressed harder into the metal. If the door opened, I'd fall inside, giving me somewhere to go.

But I didn't want it to open.

"You're right, Aeshma, he doesn't." His fangs, so close to my face that his other features were out of focus. "But we will **fail** if you do this now. Do you hear me, Travis? Fail."

The black of his eyes thinned, amber pushing its way through. A minute later, metal wasn't chilling me through my suit any longer.

"Fail..." he said, but there was no rejoicing on my part as I witnessed the softening of his expression.

I still had to be certain the point drove home completely, damn it. There were still black slivers trying to swallow the amber in his eyes.

"Right, an absolute *fuck up*, Travis. We can't have that, now can we?"

"No, we can't have that. I made an oath."

"Exactly. We're both loyal to the end. So just a while longer, okay? After we've wrapped this up, I can't stop you, I know that. Just – wait."

All the blackness in his irises disappeared, and there he was, the laid-back Travis I'd grown accustomed to.

"Will you want to stop me later?" Even his voice had shifted, I realized.

I also realized my inability to say yes to his question.

He gave a short nod. "Later." Suddenly, he touched my face, tenderness setting up camp in his eyes. "He will suffer, if it will give you peace."

"I don't know if it'll give me peace. I don't know that I want to watch you do it, even if I think I do. I don't know if it's right or wrong. But I know I've wanted to do it myself more than once, so I couldn't stop you even if I *were* strong enough."

"It's selfish, but it'll give *me* peace. And I very much doubt Michel would mind."

My eyes dropped. "He knows what happened to me. I never told him, but he knows. I don't think Billy's death would choke him up, no. Also," I took a slow breath, "I can't say I wouldn't feel the same in your shoes." My eyes rose to meet his. "The truth is, thoughts like this are another reason I'm not a defense attorney anymore." Mental shake. This wasn't the subject at hand. "I need to go back into that meeting room."

He accepted my redirection. "I told them that you had a blood sugar problem."

"You knew that detail about me, good."

"I also know that you don't have the problem any longer."

No, I didn't. Not since having their blood a few times. Still worked a charm as an excuse, though.

Charm. The charm. My hand found the charm again.

"If you need more time, I'll go back and tell them that you had to find some food," he said.

I ran my hands through my hair. "I...yeah. This time I do. Just a little more time. But not too much, or I might lose my shit again."

"I'll go on ahead, then."

I moved away from the elevator and headed for the reception desk, wishing there were a sink behind it, aching for cold water.

"Trey."

A glance back in his direction. "Yeah?"

"You're very brave, you know."

My eyes shifted forward, seeing nothing. "We'll see about that in a few minutes," I whispered.

"I think you *will* see," he said. "Remember. Courage isn't the lack of fear. It's doing what needs to be done in the face of fear." The elevator dinged. Soon I heard the doors slide open, then close.

Doing what needs done. Right.

The elevator pulled me back in its direction. I stared into the metal, into the warped reflection of my eyes, still able to see the familiar haunting that greeted me after waking from a nightmare. Part of me *was* still a little scared of Billy. He'd pinned me, battered me, humiliated and violated me; he had so much power over the others, and I'd felt so weak. Weak to my soul.

Billy fucking Brantley.

Strangely, I suddenly couldn't decide if I was happy with this twist of fate, or ready to rail at the bitch and then throw up whatever my stomach still held. Because as twisted as it was, when I thought about it, it *was* –

Fate. It came to me that my entire life up until now had been stretching towards this point – everything of the last three months. All of it truly sank in as I stared at the fun-house version of myself. It sank in how large the sum of the parts really was.

As fucked up as some of my past had been, it also led me to a city I loved, with a job I loved, and a chance at a new life. I'd found out that what I'd seen in that cemetery was not only real, but discovered he was my ancestor. There was Geoff – a second chance with a sweet little angel. P.K., the sister I never had.

I'd set foot in my parent's house again, and fate had brought Scott back into my life. I'd been growing into powers that had lain dormant within me until I met them, Gabriel and Michel. Powers that might still lead me to answers I'd told myself I didn't want, but needed.

Powers connected to a world unseen by most, and which I was beginning to think had been affecting me in subtle ways my entire life.

And now Billy, here in New York City. A full circle. Had I not taken such a screwed up path through some of my life, would it have been completely different? Would I have run into Billy some other way?

Inexplicably, I think I would have, eventually. So maybe my previous thoughts about fate weren't terribly strange, after all. So far, I'd survived everything the bitch had chosen to throw at me, after surviving everything I'd done to myself.

Maybe that was the point.

If I could handle dealing with Billy for a little while, then just maybe I'd truly put the past behind me. All of it. Maybe that was the purpose of this, in the end. Forced to face it all, I'd stop pretending to run away.

My reflection gave me a warped version of a smile. As much as I hated forced situations, the fringe benefits of my new life were damned good, and I *was* stronger than I realized, now wasn't I? I was still here, after all.

Besides.

I'd chosen to come here. It just wasn't what I'd expected.

The last thing I expected.

After telling myself that by now I probably should have learned to expect anything and everything, I pushed the button calling the elevator, and when the doors slid open, stepped inside. Short moments later, the doors opened again, and I stepped out, intent on doing business and finding a way out of my past completely.

However painful it might be.

It wasn't until reaching the end of the hall that it struck me I'd exited on the wrong floor, hell, hadn't even chosen a floor, I realized. There were no brown doors.

Painful? Messed up, that's what it was. I headed toward the elevator once more, trying to retrieve the rest of my brain and my bearings.

Michel

Madrid

With his purr still roiling through me, my vision cleared at last, the colors of the room, the bed linens, and his porcelain skin appearing normal, as a false pinpoint of sunlight no longer cast them in sun spot negatives.

"My love?"

My eyes moved to his face at his still euphoria-tinged words, and he shifted slightly beneath me as I pushed a strand of hair away from his cheek.

"*Oui, mon ange foncé.*" I pressed a gentle kiss to his lips. "I seem to have regained myself. This is thanks to you, no doubt."

His lashes fluttered, flirting with his cheekbones, before he was at last able to focus on my face.

"I would do it again." His words were husky, seductive, and a smile discovered me. "Yet I imagine it would be best if you did not have the need again, just now," he said.

I made to shake my head.

"Your eyebrows." His fingertips came to said brows. "They are creasing."

I sighed and took his hand, pressing a kiss to his palm.

"Belgium," he said, his gaze cooling. "*Dites-moi.*"

"There's nothing much more to tell, my love. Not yet." I slipped from him, rolling onto my back. Soon enough he was astride my hips, peering down at my face.

"I have worry, *mon lion*."

"As do I," I whispered. "As do I."

"Perhaps we should call the whole thing off, as you might say."

Staring into those green eyes, I replied, "Let's not be hasty."

"You are being double-crossed. It is not safe."

My brows made a swift ascent. "Safe? Indeed it's not, for I'm going to perform a vivisection on every last traitor."

"What of Trey? Should Vicont find out, what of Trey?"

I made a study of his eyes. "It'll be me Vicont goes after this time, if he yet possesses the nerve. Or his minions will, I should better say." Gabriel merely gazed at me in silence; I slid my hands up his arms, and then lightly grasped his biceps. "Trust me in this, please. He won't go after Trey, I just know it."

He contemplated this for a moment. "Very well. I cannot say that I sense imminent danger to Trey. I do wonder of others, however. Are you so certain that Vicont will come for you?"

Opening my mouth to speak, I soon closed it, knowing suddenly that I couldn't truly answer this question. Yet I remained certain of Trey's safety. Why, I could not explain, but for once, I was certain of someone's safety, at least from Vicont.

When at last I found words, I chose a different route. "Thank you for not suggesting Vicont managed to manipulate my feelings in this arena once again when last we met."

He traced the corner of my mouth with a sharp nail. "I do not believe it is so, and so I did not voice the opinion." He then covered my lips with that finger before I could speak. "I know that you were emotionally confused last you saw him, but it had nothing to do with this, and furthermore, it did not stop you from setting your plans into motion."

I brought a hand to each side of his face and of a sudden, he presented me with a smile.

"Also, I noted the shift within you," he said.

My brows rose once again.

"Within you a chain broke free," he explained. "You would have killed him then, had I not intervened."

"How you long for that day," I replied. "Yet you stopped me, which as I said before, was right and proper."

"It is yet right and proper, Michel. One day…one day." He then, as he was often wont to do, switched subjects. "We should yet speak to Elise."

I forced my jaw to relax after I felt my teeth begin to grind. "I rather suppose we should. This Lucas, his name is popping up in far too many conversations as of late."

"Why is it we do not know more of him? The more I ponder it, the more it seems that we should."

"Precisely my thought, *mon amour*."

Yes, it was prickling at me, my ignorance concerning this vampire. It seemed to me he might have power other than physical, therefore I could not imagine why I'd not heard more of him over the years, regardless of having relinquished my position for a time.

Kar's demeanor in Emanuel's office came to mind, and I decided I should perhaps ask him about it. My thoughts then returned to Gabriel.

"You said before that you remembered a phone call, Elise speaking of this Lucas," I said. "I don't remember her speaking of him. Either she was keeping other secrets, for whatever reason, or he's used many an alias – or both. It makes little sense for him to use the name Lucas Demetrius now, if he were about remaining hidden." My head made to shake. "But then, *none* of this makes sense, as the name jogged a memory of my own, a very old memory."

Why did I know so *little* about this vampire?

"I wish that I could remember more," Gabriel said. "If there is more to remember, that is. I believe that we should ask her directly and be done with it, *mon lion*."

A sigh escaped me. "Yes, we will. I will. I shall contact her as soon as possible. It may drive me to insanity, otherwise." I gazed into his eyes. "We may as well inform her we're in Spain – that is, if she doesn't already know. Because I'm not yet ready to leave this place. Ends are still trailing loosely."

He offered his agreement by way of a nod.

Yet another weary sigh escaped me as I prompted him to move so that I might rise. "I may as well contact the human network and get the ball rolling, as is said."

Moving from the bed and across the room, I made note of the shattered cellular phone. Redirecting my steps, I came to a halt at the dresser and retrieved a shiny new phone from the drawer.

"Thank goodness Kar thinks of these things," I said, turning to face Gabriel as I dialed the number.

He graced me with a smile, though it belied what was in his eyes – the same as what was in my mind.

That this mission was quite possibly falling apart and much sooner than I wished. I had no true back-up plan, regardless of what I'd said to Trey.

Not one that involved companies, in any case.

Chapter 13

Trey

I made it through the door after pulling those miniature machetes out of my pocket and nearly praying to them. It actually seemed like it helped. I also paused to beg Fate for the absence of security cameras in the lobby while thanking her for keeping Blake and Brantley away while I was down there with Travis.

Once inside the meeting room, my focus stayed on the table and chairs so I wouldn't have to focus on Billy just yet. Thankfully, Blake spoke first.

"Your associate explained the situation, Mr. du Bois. If you're not well enough to continue, we can reschedule."

My focus shifted fully to Blake. "Thank you. However, I'm much better now." It helped that he'd sounded sincere. "My apologies for the delay. Shall we begin?" Kicking into business mode helped, too.

"By all means." Blake gestured between himself and the man I felt was looking at me, but whom my eyes still didn't want to view directly. "We're interested in the details of Mr. Lecureaux's proposal."

After a glance to Travis, who took a seat at the table and placed my briefcase on the floor next to his chair, I situated myself in the chair beside him, following his cue.

"Let's be comfortable, gentlemen," I said. "This isn't a high school English class."

Blake almost smiled. He took a seat, his cretin of an attorney choosing a chair next to him. The arrangement left them sitting across from Travis and me.

Billy directly across from *me*.

Still focused more on Blake, I opted to get to it. "I'll come straight to the point," I said. "You've already been romanced by those proposing a merger. *Monsieur* Lecureaux has decided he's not interested in a merger."

Blake's brows drew themselves together. "Then why am I here, young man?"

Letting the young man comment slide, I replied, "He's interested in buying you out."

The asshole across from me swiftly added his worthless pence. "My client isn't interested in selling. You're wasting our time."

I kept my eyes on Blake, knowing it wouldn't appear strange. After all, it was him I was romancing, not his bastard attorney.

What's that sound?

Focus, Trey.

"This isn't what your employer and I discussed. The board is expecting a possible merger with someone," said Blake.

"*Monsieur* Lecureaux is willing to offer terms many others won't," I said.

Blake said, "I don't care what kind of pension plan he thinks to offer. This business is a family legacy. I've no interest in losing it."

I noted his choice of word. Losing. Even if I didn't know what I already knew, this would've been a good first clue.

Business, blessed business. I can do this. Yes, I can. Stop fiddling in your pocket, Trey. You don't have to touch the charm for it to work.

Sound.

Wait. I know that sound.

Damn it, I have to focus on this room.

"You're already losing it, Mr. Blake," I said. "We're aware how dangerously close you are to welfare status, and the others courting you aren't as interested as you've been led to believe."

Blake gave me a hard look. My idea of romancing was often brutally direct and not to everyone's taste. But you always knew where you stood with me, something many appreciated later on, if not immediately. Not to mention after flipping out earlier and then having to be in the same room with the head rapist of my nightmares and reality, I couldn't help myself. The sooner this was over, the better.

So I went for the throat.

"You've been misinformed at the water cooler," Brantley said. "I suggest we resume negotiations with the other company, Mr. Blake."

Eyes trained on Blake, gauging his reactions, I ignored the obligatory remark from the attorney. A very weak lie, that remark.

"I respect you enough to dispense with the bullshit dance moves, Mr. Blake. Mergers aren't always what they first appear to be, as you well know." I chanced a glance at Billy to punctuate my statement. "As does your attorney." My eyes moved back to Blake while I briefly rejoiced over not flinching a second ago. "No doubt your business will end up resembling little of what it once was by the time someone backs you into a merger, only to enact a hostile takeover later."

Blake's eyes narrowed. "My business is stable, and I'll see that it remains as is. I have been doing this for some time, you realize. Now, if your client is no longer interested in a merger, I'll find someone who is."

"This is contingent on two things, Mr. Blake. One, if you could afford to wait. Two, if anyone thinks a merger with your company as-is will be profitable, which I'm sorry to say, is highly doubtful."

His expression soured, but I carried on, particularly when I felt Billy so ready to interrupt.

"You don't have the time or the leverage to hold out for the sweetest deal, the biggest player. There are already signs of a flight to cash," I said. "This certainly does nothing for your portfolio."

Billy interjected. "Again, you're horribly misinformed, not to mention ill-mannered. If what you said was true, why then would your client be so interested in this company?" He looked to Blake. "They obviously think they can bully you into a deal. Frighten you, rather than negotiate. It's past time to end this meeting."

"If I'm so horribly misinformed, how could I possibly *frighten* him into a deal?" I asked.

Asked Billy directly. Spoke to him directly for the first time since seeing him.

Without losing my shit.

Holy crap.

Billy's flat, brown eyes found mine. "Figure of speech. Clearly, you *think* you can ruffle him."

Figure of speech, my ass. But then, he never was that bright.

"I don't care for these tactics in any case," Blake said. "I'm inclined to agree with my attorney. You're far too sure of yourself. It would seem Lecureaux has hired himself an upstart."

My eyes snapped back to Blake. "Upstart, no. Cocky, yes, and as I told you, I'm sparing you the bullshit. With all due respect, I didn't fall off the turnip truck yesterday, either, Mr. Blake. I've done my research. I'm confident in my assessment and cocky because *Monsieur* Lecureaux is happy to make it a sale-manage-back with a tidy share of the profits. I'll wager my own money that no one else will offer the same."

Both sets of eyes – make that three as Travis was intently following the discussion – glued themselves to me.

"He's also quite willing to have your company retain its original purpose. He feels that given a little time, a little guidance, and with a safety net in funds, it will reclaim its former glory," I said. "Certainly the extra overseas business is in your best interests, as well."

"Back to figures of speech, though this certainly fits – too good to be true." Billy laughed. "If I see it in a contract, I might believe it."

I shot Billy a glance. "Oh, you'll have it on paper, and you in *particular* should know that no one else is going to offer such terms, if you've been doing your job."

Blake, recovering swiftly and cutting in before Billy could retort, asked, "Would I merely be a figurehead?"

Head shake, eyes shooting back to Blake. "You'd do the same as you do now, but with more money. *Monsieur Lecureaux's* money, not to mention his clout."

"But what does he gain from such a deal?" Blake asked. I'd hooked him just enough to keep him sitting in his chair. "Certainly there's a catch."

"He'll take it over completely in less than a year," Billy said. "There will be some special clause pertaining to performance, just grey enough that he can give nearly any reason and change your status, Mr. Blake." I felt Billy's hard look. "Just like du Bois suggested someone else would do."

I treated Billy to an icy look. "You've not seen a contract, yet. Getting ahead of yourself, there."

"Exactly. We've not seen a proposal, either. We only have your empty words."

Would so love to punch him. Even though any other lawyer would've been smart to question it – though any other lawyer would've done a better job of it.

Blake held up a hand, shushing the asshole rapist. "Mr. du Bois. What are your client's interests in this?"

My eyes shifted back to Blake. "Occasionally he bails out businesses he feels are worth saving." Shrug. "He likes your company and he can afford it. Naturally, he's also interested in profits. These profits will, of course, extend to you and the shareholders. I should also mention that there wouldn't be any mass house cleaning, either. Everyone can keep their jobs, as long as they're doing them well."

Billy's next words were dripping sarcasm. "If he's such a philanthropist, why not merely offer a loan?"

"He doesn't do *loans*," I snapped back, but quickly reigned myself in. "He prefers for reliable people like me to have access to the company files and funds, to help Mr. Blake restore it."

Mental smirk as Billy gave me a hot glare, catching every one of my between-the-lines accusations. Seems he could still surprise me occasionally by catching a clue.

Stupid should be painful, if you ask me.

That's it, Trey. He's just a fucking lawyer. You eat other lawyers for breakfast, lunch and dinner. You can do this. Are doing this.

Damn it, I can't listen to your message right now, whoever you are. Wait. Please.

Billy repeated himself, essentially. "I'd like to see this in writing. A detailed proposal. Then we'll see if you're worth negotiating with."

Blake only nodded, no doubt very used to lawyer posturing. "Yes, I wish to see a proposal. Get me one, and I may be happy to arrange another meeting. I admit you have me intrigued."

With Blake's words, Billy had started to rise. This was his attempt to dismiss me, signal the meeting was over. His way of saying there wasn't anything else for me to offer right now.

So in the meantime I lifted my briefcase, set it on the table, opened it, and pulled out a file, which I dealt across the table. It slid to a stop on the polished wood in front of Billy's chair.

"It's all right there," I said. "As well as a sample contract."

Blake's brows shot up.

Billy nearly smirked, which made my stomach turn. Mostly because I'd always hated that particular smirk. Even before he raped me, I hated it. Yet another reason to punch him, but of course I didn't.

The smirk said he didn't believe there was anything impressive on the papers in that folder. That there was some hidden, bullshit catch.

He lifted the file. "I'll be going over these very, very carefully, du Bois."

"Of course," I replied, keeping my irritation at bay. "I'd give it the acid test, if you were handing it to *me*." But not my inner smartass.

Though I meant it. It's exactly what I would do, and really, always did when other lawyers offered me files. But for Billy I'd do it twice.

"This is rather abrupt, and your method rather unorthodox," Blake commented. "Though I *did* say I wanted a proposal."

"I'm always ahead of the curve," I said. "Just in case. I also don't believe in wasting people's time. Do know that both my client and I hold you in high esteem. This is a reason he's offering you manage-back."

A bit of a smile discovered Blake's mouth. "I know enough of your employer to know he's not one to waste time, either. He's also been rather congenial the times we've spoken. I feel I must retract my earlier statement. It would seem he may have found himself a decent attorney at last, one that suits his style, in any case."

"You can fully decide that after you see the paper work," I said, offering a smile. "And yes. When he makes up his mind, he wants it done yesterday. Therefore, this is the part where I tell you it's an exploding offer."

Blake nodded as he rose. "I thought this may be the case," he said, while Billy stared at the files. If he had any other words for me, he was saving them for another time.

"We'll look over the papers," Blake then said, "and contact you either way."

I stood. "Very good."

"If you'll excuse us now…"

Travis stood. This was our cue to exit, leave them alone to talk.

"We know the way out," I said. "Good evening."

"Good evening, Mr. du Bois, Mr. Starke," Blake said, and Travis returned the sentiment.

"Mr. Starke," Billy gave a small nod. "du Bois."

"Mr. du Bois if you don't mind, Mr. Brantley. *Mr.* du Bois."

He just gazed evenly at me. I grabbed my briefcase, turned, and headed for the door.

* * * *

During the ride down in the elevator, Travis told me how impressed he was. That it was brilliant, the way I handled myself. Said that he sensed Blake actually appreciated my kind of directness. Mostly I just nodded where appropriate. He likely knew what was going to happen, but it wasn't until I, just short of sprinting, made it through the door and outside, that he said anything about it.

"All right then, it's okay, Trey. You've breathing room, now. Do what you need to do."

I had no idea what I needed to do. I was shivering violently from nonexistent cold. Gulping air. Gripping the charm in my pocket just short of breaking it.

"Can I do something for you, Trey?"

Breath. Breath. "Take this before I drop it."

He took the briefcase from me.

That now free hand flew to my face. "Jesus. Ugh! Fuck."

His hand moved over my back.

"No, don't touch me." Half second's pause. "Not right now."

196

His hand left me. Knuckles to my knees, charm still in one fist, I sucked in some more air. "Agh, I can't believe I just did that. I can't believe I just...urrghh."

"That's just it. You *did* it."

"It still sucks!"

"Abso-bloody-lutely. So let's walk a bit, ay? Walk a bit, and you let it out. Scream if you need to. Whatever you need. You can let it rip, now."

Violent head shake, clearing cobwebs. Memories. Another, trying to shake them loose. Sharp inhale through my nose. Exhale through my mouth.

Again.

"He has to know who I am. I hardly looked at him, but it doesn't seem like he knows who I am."

"Trey."

"I haven't changed my name. He has to remember my name."

"Trey..."

"I mean seriously, no way he doesn't remember me."

"*Trey.*"

I managed to glance at him.

"Do you want him to know you?"

Breath. "God damn it, he damn well should. Somehow, it's worse if he doesn't."

"Because it wouldn't be fair, him not recognizing you...?"

"So fucking convenient. So conveniently going on with life."

"Maybe not having one moment of remorse...?"

"Yes, damn it. There's a good reason. He should look me in the eye, knowing who I am, and realize what a bastard he is."

"What if he does recognize you but still doesn't regret it, Trey?"

Teeth. Gritting. Another glance. "Then it'll be even easier to deck him when this is over."

"Fair enough."

197

Another hard shake of my head. "Damn it," I said, straightening. "Maybe he's just better at this than me. Maybe he does know. Maybe he really doesn't give a shit. Damn it."

Travis' next questions were gentle. "Would it be better if he was sorry? Would it make a difference?"

"No. But yes. But not enough to redeem him. I just want to know if he's still human. Has feelings, I mean. Or something. But he'll still be an asshole either way."

"Believe it or not, that made sense to me."

"Good, now explain it to me."

He offered a sympathetic smile. I squeezed the charm some more.

"Hey," he said. "How about a drink, ay?"

"My stomach can't take a drink. Or food, before you suggest it."

"All right. Why don't we get you to Geoff?"

Geoff. Yes, he could make me feel better. Except he's with Scott. Do I wanna tell Scott about this just yet?

"I don't know if I can – Scott. I should calm down, first." Finally, I fully looked at him. "Walk. Let's walk for a while."

He nodded, and we started walking.

"Oh God. No, don't let me see the bridge again so soon."

He changed our direction, then suddenly stopped and faced me. His wrists came to rest on my shoulders as he looked down into my eyes.

"You know, I reckon there's a drink you can stomach."

"Huh?"

"Michel had me pack something special, said to give it to you if you needed it." Beat. "I reckon this is appropriate. It'll help calm you down, help you forget about Billy for a while."

Fucked up or not, my mouth started watering.

"So we'll stop by the hotel, first," he said.

Swallow. "We can't go directly to Scott's after that. It makes me high and he'll notice."

"We'll walk some of it off, no worries. Unless you want to save it for another time?"

"No," I answered too quickly. "I mean, yeah, I could use it."

Nodding, he started walking again and I fell into pace beside him.

I tried to focus on something besides Billy and zippy-juice. "I heard whispers while we were in there. At the meeting, I mean."

He looked at me, arching a brow.

"Dead. A dead woman."

"What did she say?"

"I think she wants me to...to find her."

His brows lifted. "Her remains?"

Nod.

"Do you know her name, anything?"

Head shake. "I had to focus on the meeting and staying calm." Then a nod. "Wait. Maybe I do know. Mmm...Myra."

"Myra. So her body's missing. How did she die?"

It was working. I was calming even more. Thank you, Travis, for engaging.

"Uhh. Murdered." Yes, I knew this. Even if I hadn't heard all the words, I knew it.

"Does she know who killed her?"

"I think she might."

"Is this the first you've heard from her?"

"Yes." Wait. "No. Actually, I don't think so." I stopped walking and faced him. "It may be the same voice I heard at the zoo."

His brows creased. "Today?"

"Yeah. While I was talking to Scott. I told him, by the way. He's still not sure about everything, but he's trying, and he's intrigued."

"Cool. So what did she say at the zoo?"

"Nothing that made sense. It was just random pieces. I couldn't figure out why I was having trouble reaching her. Or she was having trouble reaching me, whatever."

"But more came through during the meeting?"

"Not exactly. But I know what I said is true."

"I understand that. Sometimes we vampires, we just feel it, I reckon you'd say."

"Sounds good to me."

We started walking again.

Travis said, "Is her body in New York?"

"I'm not sure. But at the zoo she said something about Queens."

"Maybe it's there."

"Guess I'll find out more if I'm supposed to." A smile actually found me. Small, but a smile all the same. "Just another thing added to the task-list, I guess."

He smiled back, much wider, and slung an arm across my shoulder. "I reckon you can handle it."

Placing the charm back in my pocket, finally having loosened my death grip on it, I nodded. "Yeah. Maybe so." Sideways look in his direction. "I still might throw up again, though. Just sayin'."

He offered another smile, more a grin, really. "I'll hold your hair back for ya." He gestured with his free hand. "The fringe, anyway."

"Well, ain't you sweet."

"Every once in a while, mate. Every once in a while."

A bit of reasoning ability returned to me, then. "Oh, by the way. Do you think there were security cameras in the lobby?"

"Nah. I checked that first thing."

Thank you, Fate – for placing Travis at my side.

Chapter 14

"No way. No. *Way*."

Keeping my eyes on Scott while he absorbed everything I'd told him, I leaned back into Geoff's touch. He was moving his hand in circular motions over my back. Though the walk Travis and I took had brought me down a few notches, and the zippy-juice had made me giddy for a while, a mental state had crept back in, comparable to when you've had a dream too vivid not to be real, even though it couldn't be. Geoff was smoothing the rest of it away.

"Yes way," I replied, and Scott's previously widened eyes narrowed with his deep scowl.

It really wasn't just in my mind and never had been.

"Dude...I..." his jaw clenched as he struggled for more words, which didn't seem soon in coming.

"I shouldn't have to deal with him much longer," I said.

Hoped.

"Do you have to deal with him at all?" Scott angrily asked, his eyes speeding to Travis who was sitting in the only other chair. "Seriously, does he *have* to do this? I know it's business, but...damn it. Do you know what this fucker did to Trey? Do you?"

"Scott – "

"No," Travis said before I could spit out another word. "Actually, he doesn't have to do this. Michel would understand. And yes. I've *some* idea what Billy did."

Scott's eyes shot to me. "Just what I was thinking, or hoping, anyway. Family would understand."

Sigh. Knew all this, I did, but, "No, Scott. I *do* have to do this." My hand went up to halt Scott's coming interruption. "Travis is right, yeah, Michel would understand, but I'm going to do this because I said I would, and besides..." Breath. "I have to get over it eventually."

Scott studied me, then his head shook. "Maybe so, but it fucked you up. There's better ways to get over it, yeah?" His turn to hold his hand up. "It's cool you want to do your job – you're dependable, I get it, but if Michel would let you off the hook, why keep wriggling on it?"

"Scott." I leaned forward, elbows to my knees. "I deeply appreciate your concern, I really do, but besides wanting to finish this for Michel, ain't no way in hell I'm leaving here with *nothing* after what I had to do tonight."

"Well..."

"Seriously. No fucking way I'm letting this deal go after having to breathe the same air as Billy. I'm finishing this."

Holy crap, I am.

"I'd like to finish it," he muttered. "Open him up like a FedEx shipment."

Scott could and would never do such a thing, of course, but the vampire sitting not far from him would, and Scott's words must've sparked the dark energy in Travis – I could feel it. Started wondering if Scott could. Thought he might have, in a way, when he gave off the slightest shiver. The type of shiver people refer to as someone walking over their grave.

Travis didn't utter a word, and Scott didn't really seem conscious of the cause of his own shiver, turning his eyes to me and saying, "I don't know how you dealt with all that, dude, but wow. Really, wow. I don't think I could've kept my cool."

"Trey was quite impressive," Travis offered, his voice thankfully normal. "He's very resilient."

Scott's face brightened a little. "Yeah, I always thought so."

You have *no* idea, Scott.

"But can we possibly beat the shit out of Billy when you're done with the business, though?" Scott said then.

Uh.

Take a number, Scott. Get in line. Have a feeling that if Travis tells Michel about this, the line is gonna grow.

Again I felt the energy shift in Travis. "I'm certain something can be arranged," he said.

This time Scott turned to stare at him in such a way that it left me certain he'd noticed. Whether he could name what he noticed was another matter. Still, it's not like people don't sometimes give off vibes when they're angry, right?

Except Scott had seen strange things happen to Travis back in Paris, whether his brain had wrapped around it yet or not. Not to mention Scott's hand then went to the back of his neck, and since this wasn't a habit of his, his neck hairs must've been prickling.

Travis' eyes didn't leave Scott, but it felt as if he were seeing me plainly at the same time.

Sorry. I can't completely choke the energy so soon after the meeting. It's feeding off Scott's disgust and anger over Billy.

Surprisingly, or maybe not, my first thought was *don't sweat it*. Scott did say he wanted to talk to Travis about some things, after all – so maybe this was a strange blessing in disguise. Forget about Billy (which I wanted to do myself) and let's ponder the big Aussie in the room who is giving off strange vibes, yes.

Okay, so not just vibes. I then noticed Travis' eyes were just a bit different. Given Scott's direct view of those eyes, surely he noticed before me, so it wasn't like Travis was gonna hide anything now, anyway.

I sat back and waited for whatever was about to happen next, Geoff seemingly doing the same, also watching Scott and Travis closely. Personally, I was hoping Scott would start asking Travis questions, because the distraction might mean Scott would stop unintentionally feeding the Demon, which would be a good thing. I didn't think I had any strength left to stop Aeshma a second time. Was still amazed I'd managed it once as it was. On the walk back, one of the things my brain managed to ponder was the fact I'd placed myself in danger back in that lobby, getting in Aeshma's way. On my side or not, there had been a primal feeling to his energy – *primal*, the word that couldn't make its way into the rest of my screwed up thoughts when it was happening.

God, if Scott's emotions were feeding into the Demon right now, I could only imagine what would've happened if I hadn't managed to convince myself, as well as appeal to Travis, that business had to come first.

Scott interrupted my rambling thoughts when he blurted, "Did I see what I thought I saw that night at Trey's?"

"Depends," Travis replied. "You'd have to tell me what you think you saw."

Scott's hand lifted, gesturing around his mouth. "Uh... teeth."

The way he whispered it, well, I suddenly wanted to laugh. I just stifled it, while Geoff barely contained a giggle.

Travis, however, kept his gaze even – even as amused as I figured he was – and said, "Mine, you mean? I have a mouthful I'm rather proud of. Nice and straight. They're very white too, don't you think?"

Definitely amused, and there was no stopping my laugh, then. Scott nearly smacked his own forehead, which made Travis' chuckle break loose.

"Pff," Scott exhaled. "Fangs, okay? I swear you had *fangs*."

Travis gave him a serious look. "Oh *them*. Yes, I have some of those as well."

About two beats of my heart passed before Scott said, "*Dude*." He leaned forward a bit. "Real ones? Not those custom made caps?"

Travis so wanted to grin – and finally did. "I grow them myself, yeah."

Scott, "No way."

Travis, "Yes way."

Scott, "For real?"

Travis, "No bullshit, mate."

Scott, "...show me?"

Travis thought about it while Geoff and I kept sitting quietly. No way were we gonna interrupt whatever was about to happen now.

Scott broke the silence first. "Was that too personal?"

A smile itched at the corners of Travis' mouth. "No, it's not that."

"Then what?" Scott leaned a bit more.

"I could show you," Travis said. "I don't mind showing you. But I'm not responsible if you faint or run away screaming. After all, you're the one asking for it. Certain you want to see them?"

Scott's eyes dropped to Travis' mouth. "I don't faint." His eyes darted back to Travis' eyes. "Not gonna run away, either." Then his words dropped to a whisper. "But uh, you don't mean anything by 'asking for it', right? Like, if you show me, you'll have to kill me?"

A round, warm laugh escaped Travis. "I'm not threatening you, no. But some people find them quite frightening."

Couldn't help myself. "Believe me, you'd know it if he was threatening you."

Scott's eyes flicked to me.

"Ignore me. Carry on."

"Have you seen them?" he asked.

205

"Yes, Scott."

Scott's eyes flicked back to Travis. "I can take it, if he can."

Now I about held my breath along with Scott, wondering if Travis would show him two, four, or six fangs. The bottom ones were kinda scary. That is, until I saw the third set. Scary, but cool as hell at the same time.

Travis tilted his head. "Whaddya think, Trey?"

Blink. "About what?"

"How many?"

Scott glanced at me and gaped at Travis. "How many what?" he asked.

I looked between them, then focused on Travis. "You're asking me? I don't know if some of them are – I mean, *I* didn't even know you had – uh, your call."

"Your friend," Travis said. "I'll share as many as you say."

"What're you guys talking about?" Scott asked.

Two seconds contemplation from me. "Ah hell. May as well go for it then, Travis. There's scotch in the place. He wants to see, after all."

Scott couldn't be bothered to glance at me then, because Travis' lips had parted and he started, very slowly, to smile. His smile broadened until six, yes six, fangs showed, and that tooth-parted smile was more disconcerting than if he'd chosen to grimace or snarl, which seemed more appropriate with fangs.

Scott must've found it disconcerting too, and much more than me, because his body pressed itself hard into the back of his chair – and then there was Geoff, who gasped.

Guess I didn't stop to think that he hadn't seen them before, either. Still, he relaxed easily compared to Scott, who couldn't tear his eyes away even if his elbows were trying to escape through the back of the chair.

"Should I get the scotch?" I asked, my discomfort very short-lived because I'd seen the fangs up close before, and cool was winning over scary.

Travis relaxed his smile a bit, but you could still see the fang-tips. Then he spoke.

"You okay, mate?"

Scott kept gaping – and then in a delayed reaction jumped out of his chair, scrambled around to the back of it.

"Uh oh. I think I should get the scotch," I said.

"Maybe I should put these away," Travis said.

"Wait," Scott blurted while his hands gripped the back of the chair so hard I expected fabric to tear.

Travis waited. Heck, we all waited.

"Holy shit," Scott breathed out. "Holy shit!" His fingers stopped drilling the chair so hard. "Holy shit, no way. They just, they, those, wow."

Travis laughed along with me, there was just no help for it, and Geoff added his light tones to the musical.

"Why, thank you," Travis said. "I think." He gave a fangy grin to Scott.

"Do they, does that…" Scott paused and tried again. "Does it hurt when they, Jesus, they grew, they just – yeah."

"No, it doesn't hurt," Travis answered.

"They just…how…"

"Magic." Travis lightly winked.

Scott finally blinked. "Really?"

Travis laughed again, and by Scott's reaction, I wasn't the only one who could literally feel the warmth. "Well. They just slide down, basically, from my gums."

"That's uh, well that's kinda magical, if you ask me," Scott said.

"Reckon so."

"Do you need the whiskey, Scott?" I repeated.

He waved me off. "I'm cool. I think."

Geoff and I looked at each other. I was certain we were thinking the same thing.

Wonder if Scott will ask Travis what else he can do.

"Um," Scott started. Then restarted. "Um, okay, you can put them away for now. Please."

Travis' fangs receded – definitely fascinating – and now his smile was normal.

Scott slowly moved around his chair and (sort of) relaxed back in his seat, that is, after a small shudder. His eyes then sped to me. "So Michel and Gabriel have those too?"

"They have fangs, yes." Not like those, exactly, and I'm still not ready to talk about the bottom ones, fascinating or not. Those are some serious, *will-fuck-you-up-to-Mars-and-back*, teeth.

But the top ones are sexy as hell.

"Like that, really? I mean his?" Scott asked.

"Vampires aren't all the same," Travis answered for me, which was good, because I wasn't certain what I could share. "Their fangs are different than mine."

Scott's eyes sped back Travis. "Do I even want to know?"

"I don't know, do you?" Travis grinned anew.

"Maybe not just now. Besides, we're talking about you." Scott leaned forward. "I think I saw something else that night."

Travis' brow arched.

Scott continued. "Like…claws maybe."

Travis' other brow joined the first, and mentally I nodded. Confirmation Scott had seen his claws, too, in Paris. Travis lifted a hand and we all watched in fascination as the index nail of his right hand grew and shifted.

Except it wasn't black. It was the Beast claw. Natural colored, and with a curve the black claws didn't have – more cat-like. I'd seen the Beast claws at the Fall Out. I wasn't certain which ones Scott had seen, and got to thinking about whether or not Travis had to be in the right mode for different traits.

Maybe he had to be in Demon mode for the black claws and Beast mode for cat-claws. I figured his extra set of fangs were Aeshma inspired, so maybe –

Scott interrupted my ponderings.

"Whoa. But wait, I thought they were black," he said.

Hocus pocus, presto change-o and Travis' claw shifted to jet and straightened, so it looked even longer.

Well. That put a stop to my ponderings. Obviously, he could whip either of them out any time.

"Fuck. Me," said Scott.

"Sorry," Travis said. "You're not my type. You've too much between your legs and not enough up top."

That made me snicker, and it worked on Scott, too, who snorted. "That sounded way too much like Trey."

Travis shrugged. "Or he sounds like me." With that, the black claw shifted back to a normal fingernail.

"Dude," Scott said. "Just, dude. No way." He stared hard into Travis' eyes. "Is that why you were inside all day, then?"

Travis' lips quirked. "You've got the right of it. The sun and I don't get on so well these days."

"So that's true." Scott mulled this over.

"Don't even talk about garlic," I said. "Or crosses. That's movie shit."

"Actually," Travis said, "you can occasionally find a vampire who has a problem with crosses or other religious symbols."

My turn to stare. "But I thought that was all bullshit. Michel said it was."

Travis said, "He did? You certain about that?"

"Well, maybe he didn't precisely say that. He was talking about himself. Implied the rest, more like." Yeah, I was probably – okay definitely – having trouble concentrating during the Vampire 101 discussion. Michel clothed will do that to a person, let alone Michel naked.

"He doesn't imply anything, remember?" Travis said.

Smirk. "*Touché.*" Scott was watching our back and forth intently. "Okay, so will you explain that for the room, please?" I said.

Travis spread his hands. "It's psychological. Some carried their religious beliefs into their new life so deeply, that they are convinced holy symbols, churches and all that will have an effect. They actually believe they're damned – the devil's creatures."

"*Can* it hurt them?" Scott asked. "I mean, did they test it on themselves, or someone came at them with a cross and it was all AHH! It burns it burns, help, I'm melting!" Then to himself, "Did I just say that?"

Travis' eyes moved to Scott, and he ignored the last bit. "The mind is a very powerful thing. As a vampire, you have much more control over it. Believe something strongly enough, yes, it effects you even physically. You humans do it to yourselves all the time. Stuff like making yourselves sick because you're paranoid about your health. Stressing out, emotions all over the place. All sorts of ways to muck yourselves up."

"Good point," I said. "It also seems like some vampires don't move ahead with the times. Admittedly, I don't have much to compare, but I'm thinking of Gabriel. He's very old-fashioned in some ways, where Michel seems to keep up with the times a lot more. So I could see some old world vampire being trapped in his dogma."

"Sure," Travis said. "It sometimes depends how well prepared you were when turned, what your Maker teaches you, and really, how much of that you accept."

Scott's eyes bounced back and forth between us before settling on me. "Old world. Dude. How old are Gabriel and Michel?" He suddenly rubbed his face. "I can't believe we're having this conversation." He shook that off. "Okay, really. How old are they?"

"Is it okay to say?" I asked Travis.

He nodded.

My eyes returned to Scott. "Almost four centuries, or close enough, anyway."

Scott's faced nearly drained of blood.

Well then. We'd keep it secret for now that I'd met one way older. Easy enough, since he was a dickhead, and oh no, we weren't going over that fucked up mess yet if I could help it.

"How old are you?" Scott asked Travis, thank goodness.

"Not so old. Seventy-one, all totaled."

"Well. Shit, you look good for an old man."

"One of the perks."

Unfortunately, Scott would then ask me, "Are there older ones?"

I just nodded.

"You've met older ones?"

Opted for another nod.

"No one important," Geoff said, before Scott could ask me another question. "Not a friend, just a…a…"

"Acquaintance," Travis offered.

"Yes, that word."

"Vampires have been around a very, very long time," Travis said to Scott. I think he knew I wanted the conversation redirected, not to mention that he wasn't fond of Vicont at all. "And we're everywhere, mate."

I think Scott gulped. "I don't suppose they're all as nice as you."

Travis gave off a dry laugh. "No, they're not. I'm not always this nice, either."

Scott gulped again.

"Now don't panic," Travis said. "I've sworn to Trey I'd protect you whenever you're around, or I'm around you."

Um. Travis? What are you doing?

Geoff patted my hand.

"From…what?" Scott asked, his eyes bugging.

"Anything at all, because you're his best mate. Since I care about him, and he cares about you, I won't let anything happen to you in general, if I can help it. It's a big, bad world with speeding cars and muggings, shit like that, ay?"

Oh. Well. That's not so ominous. I should have known better; Travis knows what he's doing.

Scott scrutinized him a minute. "You protect them, too?"

"Yes." Travis shot me a look. "Unfortunately, I was a bit late last time." His eyes moved back to Scott. "But Trey's special in his own right, thank God."

"Oh my God," Scott's words nearly exploded from him. "That's why you were so concerned about Geoff and – I knew something wasn't right with that car wreck story, even before I was told the real deal." His hands smacked into his face. "Oh my God, it's all really, really, real, and Gabriel healed Trey, and oh shit. Shit, you're really vampires."

I cleared my throat. "Sounds like you've actually caught up this time, Scott."

"Oh my God." He dropped his hands and looked at Travis. "So can you fly, turn into a bat, or mist, or a wolf, or you know, shit like that?"

There was a round of laughter that I was grateful for before Travis could begin to field those questions.

Chapter 15

SEPTEMBER 6

Trey

"Dude, you can stop staring at my neck any time. Marks are not magically appearing no matter how hard you look."

"What? I wasn't..." Scott tore his eyes away from my jugular for the bazillionth time. "Uh, sorry."

Travis had answered all the questions Scott fired at him last night. The ones he could and would, anyway. Random remarks about Gabriel and Michel he mostly skipped, since Scott's queries had come in groupings littered with stuff about Travis himself – and apparently it was now left up to me to field questions about them. And them and me. And Travis and me. And all that jazz. Seemed Travis trusted my judgment in this.

"What did it feel like?"

Head shaking, I was unable to stop the chuckle. "I already explained, Scott. If you want better words, you'll have to find out for yourself and make up your own."

Not easy, describing what a vampire biting and drinking from you feels like, since it's less to do with fangs than you'd first expect – in my experience, at least.

"Uh, I think I'll just imagine it for now," Scott said.

"You do that, buddy." I grabbed Geoff's hand and laced my fingers through his as we strolled around Central Park. Yes, we were there again, but not at the zoo. It's a big park. We had some other plans, too, I swear. That is, if Scott ever downshifted, and we made it *out* of the park.

"You really weren't scared?" Scott asked for about the zillionth time.

"No." I didn't tell him about Gabriel's biting me in distress. Seemed prudent.

"You totally trust them?"

Geoff smiled at him, answering in my place for the thousandth time. "They love him."

"To death, maybe," Scott mumbled.

I stopped walking, which meant Geoff stopped, which then meant that Scott stopped, since he hardly took his eyes off me. I looked into those eyes of his and decided to offer a whopper of a detail.

"Yeah, they are what they are, but they'll never purposefully put me in danger, particularly since I'm literally family."

"Huh?" Wide-eyed look from Scott. "What do you mean literally?"

"I mean literally, you think?"

"That's impossible."

I took a step closer to my bud. "When your ancestor is *immortal*, it's not impossible."

He stared hard.

Finally had to blink.

"Dude...oh *wow*. Which one? Or both?"

"Gabriel."

He continued gawking. "You're actually related to him?"

"Yup."

"Fuck." A grin suddenly split his face. "Wow. Well that's cool, yeah? A walking, talking, living history of your family line."

Well. What Gabriel remembers, yes. Very cool.

Scott snatched my left wrist and before I could react, said, "This is blood, isn't it. Is it?" His eyes had glued themselves to my bracelet.

After giving a nod to a passerby with a quizzical expression on his face, I returned to Scott. "Yes," I whispered. "It's theirs."

"What's it for? Like, what does it mean, or does it do something?"

Geoff shared a look with me.

"It's a sign of affection," I said, leaving out the rest for now. Scott's brain, like it had been last night and all morning into lunch, was racing through details and questions. I could nearly see the smoke coming out his ears, and sure enough, he bounced subjects yet again.

"You're really here for business? Vampires do that?"

"Yes," I assured him for the hundredth time. "I really am. They like money too, and besides, it's sort of a hobby for Michel." I leaned in. "You gotta have something to do with eternity, right?"

"Well. Yeah."

"Right. So he does some business when he's not doing Gabriel."

Geoff laughed and Scott snort-laughed, then turned very serious and whispered, "Dude. Have they killed people?"

I answered with a dramatic eye roll and a "Duh," which he nearly missed, being in hyper-mode.

"What I *really* mean is," he said, "have you seen them do it?"

Geoff and I shared another look.

"Yes."

Scott's voice went all church quiet. "The whole bite, drain the blood, bam, they're dead thing?"

"Yes." We'd skip the Fall Out deaths for now. Seemed prudent.

"What were you doing when it happened?"

"Standing there like an idiot, wondering what had just happened."

Scott gazed evenly at me, waiting for more words.

"Gabriel just – well, he was a bit agitated at the time, and it was really swift and unexpected," I said.

Yeah. That would do for a summary.

"He killed someone, just like that," he said with a snap of his fingers.

"Pretty much." And right in the middle of Paris. But we'd skip that too, if possible.

"Did you follow him or something, or did he take you with him, or – hell I don't know. Why were you there? And where were you? And what do you mean agitated?"

Whoa, one at a time, Scott. Geez.

"Well…" How to explain this without getting into the entire psychology of Gabriel, of which I knew relatively little, comparatively speaking. But if I didn't explain, he'd sound like an outright monster.

Right?

Geoff squeezed my hand.

"We'd been walking along," and then my cell rang. It was Michel's ringtone, which startled me because I hadn't been expecting a call from him. Offering Scott an apologetic look, I reached into my pocket. "I gotta get this, it's business."

Taking a few steps away, I slapped the phone to my ear. "'Chel. What's up?" Behind me, I heard Geoff talking to Scott.

"Are you well, beloved?"

My brows were itching to knit. "Yeah." I took a few more steps. "Is something wrong?"

"I wished to check on you myself. To hear your voice."

Flattering and sweet as that was, something in his tone was off. "Michel, what's wrong?" I whispered. "Are *you* well?"

"Not to worry, darling, not to worry."

"Too late."

There was a long pause on his end.

"Michel?"

"How fares business in New York?"

His ignoring my question worried me more. But I said, "I'm inches from closing the deal, I'm certain. Just one more meeting, maybe. They're looking over the proposal and contracts." As far as I knew, Travis hadn't mentioned Billy to Michel.

So I didn't mention it.

"*Très bien.*"

Geoff still had Scott occupied, but I lowered my voice more anyway. "Michel, talk to me. Please. I know something's wrong." I could feel it, or it seemed like I could feel it. "Did things get hotter in Spain?"

His sigh slithered through the connection, making it seem he was standing right next to me, rather than a few thousand miles away.

"There is more than one traitor and a mysterious man, long of tooth, whose name keeps appearing in all the wrong conversations. I'm concerned as to what he's about."

Shit. More than one?

Long of tooth?

"A mosquito you don't know?" I asked.

"Gabriel remembers hearing the name a few years ago. I have some memory of the man, a trite memory from centuries ago, connected to Vicont. Strangely I know nothing of him in the time since."

"Michel..." I pondered for all of two seconds what I was about to say. "This really troubles me, that you don't know anything about this vampire. So maybe you don't literally know all of them in the world, but you mentioned him and that raging dickhead in the same sentence."

Another sigh from him that was far too tangible. "You're right." He sounded almost weary. "It's all a bit off."

"Then call it off, Michel. Let's just call it off. Traitors and a strange hemo-lover popping up from the past connected to Vicont? Not cool. I'll finish here; we'll call it good, and we'll all go home where you can tell me about plan B."

"I can't do that, Trey."

My fingers white knuckled the phone. "Yes you can." *You're making me anxious, Michel, though I'm uncertain precisely why.*

"There is no plan B."

Pause on my end. There were no words forming in my mouth.

"Not one you may participate in, in any event, and it's a last resort – also I cannot leave Spain yet."

Yet. He said yet. I clung to the yet, trying not to freak out over the plan B comment.

"Okay, not yet. You want to tie up loose ends, right?"

"For the most part. I must investigate this further, darling. I must know how far this betrayal goes and why they are crossing me. I can't leave things in this state. It leaves cracks for others to worm their way through. There is a bigger picture here that I can't presently see."

Really worried. Though everything he said made sense. Nothing there for me to debate, even if I could debate him.

Not dwelling on that certain comment didn't work. Now I had to know. "Michel. What do you mean about no plan B?"

"I must go now, beloved."

"No, wait!"

I glanced at my companions. Yup, they were looking at me, their conversation halting.

Resuming a calmer level of speech, I turned away from them. "Michel..." Michel what? He wasn't going to answer the question, which did nothing for my nerves – my nerves? It was like I could feel *him*. Okay, in person their emotions had always seemed tangible to me, but over the phone? Could they carry so well even over the phone?

Whether they could or not, it was different in some way. It was more *precise* in feeling.

"You had something yet to say, Trey?"

"Um. Just make sure you come back in one piece. I'll kick your ass if you don't."

"You'd not find me on the other side, Trey."

My blood chilled, because he'd taken my comment as meaning death, his death. But maybe he was reading something in *me*, since my brain had gone there already.

Find some levity, Trey. Even if you do mean what you're about to say.

"Of course I would. You have a soul, and I'll kick your incorporeal ass if I find it wandering there."

The lilt of his laughter soothed and warmed me. "I believe you. However, you shan't find me there, as I do not intend to lose my body or my soul. The situation is not so dire, darling." Pause. "And I love you as well, my dear, sweet boy."

My eyes closed. "You're the only family I have. You and Gabriel."

"And this is a gift without price, beloved. Do not fret. We'll return soon, but I can't tell you what may happen, not yet. I don't quite know myself." He drew a long breath. "I called to hear your voice, truly. You're one of a dwindling number, it seems, whom I can trust. I trust you with my life, Trey."

The words breathed out of me. "That still awes me."

"I must go now, Trey. Close the deal swiftly, if you can, and return to Paris. Forget about Chomette. I want you in Paris."

"Am I in danger?"

219

"No. But I want you in Paris, where you belong."

Where I belong. Yes. It was where I belonged.

"I've got it covered, 'Chel. And hey. Will you keep in touch? Don't leave me in the dark. I hate not knowing."

"I understand. I will keep you informed, or Travis will. Give him my love, will you?"

"Sure."

"Do take care."

Damn. It felt all wrong. "You too, Michel. You too."

"Ciao for now."

"Ciao."

The line went dead, and I slipped the phone back into my pocket. Turning to face Geoff and Scott, there was no missing the look on Scott's face. He'd heard just enough to puzzle and concern him.

"Trey," he said, taking steps toward me. "Is everything okay?

Madrid
Michel

I slipped the cellular into my pocket and wandered farther down the sidewalk, a heady mixture of human scents having flooded my nostrils in the small club, until I was ready to fang the first person who crossed my path. This as much as needing to hear Trey's voice had driven me from said club.

Yes, I was quite ready to sink my teeth viciously into the throat of the first person I came across, until that first person outside of the claustrophobic space scented as vampire. A vampire with coppery hair and golden-green eyes, wearing chic jeans and a smart little chemise in pale blue.

"Elise," I said as I strode toward her, stopping close enough to kiss her cheeks, which I did not actually do. "My, you certainly arrived quickly. Have you at last mastered flying without aid of metal and engines?"

Her reply followed a half tilt of her lips. "Michel. So good to see you as well."

My gaze swept her form once more, before settling upon her eyes. "Yes, yes. Sincerely, how on Earth do you come to be here in Madrid so quickly?"

"Well," her painted lips spread into a sly smile, "I was already here."

Before the intention registered in my brain, I had her slender bicep in my hand. "Already here, you say?"

"Ohhh, stop narrowing those pretty eyes and stop manhandling me, Michel." She easily pried her arm free of my grip, which was lax, as I was stunned, affronted and suspicious – and because there were witnesses all around, and I was in no mood to glamour the lot of them.

I lowered my voice accordingly. "Why were you already here, and why didn't you tell me when I called?"

Her chin made to lift. "Why didn't you inform me that *you* had come here? Or that the situation is worse than it first appeared?"

"Truthfully?" I brought my face closer to hers. "Because I don't trust you."

"Now, this I can I believe, *petit-père*."

"Do *not* call me that."

Her laughter trickled along my nerves, and I grabbed her arm once more, leading her farther away from the club.

"Why were you in Spain?" I asked again.

"Because you were in Spain."

"Fine. Your spies are nearly as good as my spies."

"As good."

"No." I stopped and forced her to face me. "Nearly, for I know you can't have been here long. You've been to Prague, back to Belgium, mmm, and while we're at it, how is Lucas?"

He expression froze, along with her entire body.

"Know him well, do you?" I pressed.

Her words became feather light. "This is not the place for such a discussion."

221

"Yet here is where you chose to come upon me – and with me being so *hungry*." Vampire was becoming a more tempting entrée by the second.

She attempted to ignore my comment, a slight shiver along her flesh giving her away. "Where is Gabriel?"

"Why? Don't tell me you'd rather face his interrogation."

She made with a thorough study of my face. "In this instance, perhaps."

I released her from my grip. "As you like. He's in the club just there," I made with a sweeping gesture. "Take your chances."

She let go with a sigh. "I'll explain, Michel, I will. To both of you. You both wanted to see me after all, and here I am."

"Yes, here you are, when you were supposed to be in Belgium."

"Don't be a hypocrite; it doesn't suit you, mister *supposed to be in Paris*. Let us go somewhere, and we'll talk privately."

"Oh, by all means, retrieve Gabriel yourself." I folded my arms across my chest. "It should prove amusing, if nothing else. I can't wait to see the look on his face."

A rather sour expression marred the usual loveliness of her mouth. "How can you possibly dance at a time like this, anyway?"

"You're asking me, you who could spend money on trivialities when bombs are dropping from the sky?" I waved a hand. "Believe me, dancing wasn't on my agenda."

"And you're going to explain this agenda, correct?"

"Doubtless I'll have little choice as the night wears on," I muttered, irritated that I hadn't fooled her into thinking we were in Paris at all. Though were I not suspicious, I might have felt more than a spark of pride for having taught her well.

"What was that, Michel? I don't believe I heard you."

I spared her a thin-lipped smirk.

"What rocket ship did you commandeer?"

We both turned toward the sound of Gabriel's voice.

"How long is it that you've already been in Spain," he further inquired as he glided in our direction, his expression smooth, his eyes chilled.

I captured the portrait of her in my peripheral. "Not quite as amusing as it could have been, Elise, but amusing enough," I said. "More so when you reply, perhaps."

Her spine became rigid. "Gabriel." Her eyes flitted between the two of us as he came to my side. "I'm prepared to explain everything, but this is not the place, as I was telling Michel. Where are you staying?"

"Where are *you* staying?" I inquired.

With a lift of brow she replied, "You don't already know?"

"Do not irritate me any more than I already am, Elise." I laced my arm through Gabriel's, more irritated nonetheless.

With a toss of her hair she replied, "Your haven or mine, I don't care. But we obviously need to get this over with."

"Indeed we do," I said and took steps in the direction of the corner. "Keep up if you can."

The clicking of her heels was far too evident as we strode across the street.

Chapter 16

We'd returned to Scott's apartment, where I decided to come clean. Nothing I said in the park was gonna convince him everything was okay, and frankly, I didn't want to dance around the truth one second longer. I'd promised I'd never lie to him again, and omitting so many details was starting to feel too much like lying. Felt too much like what I'd done in the past with him. I figured it would be safe to talk, since it was broad daylight, and Travis had already deemed Scott's place clean – no bugs.

No one was interested in us here, anyway, he also said. Not that he'd heard.

So. Scott accepted vampires were real now, and he'd accepted that everything he thought had happened in Paris, really had happened. With Geoff giving me moral support, I told him everything.

Okay, most of it – including my kidnapping and my other technically-illegal-business-dealings. I skipped stuff that might not be kosher for him to know, whether I liked it or not. Stuff pertaining to vampire secrets, that is. I made certain it was clear I'd volunteered for the mission Travis and I were currently on. Hell, said that I'd insisted on being part of it. Didn't want Scott blaming Michel.

He listened in stunned silence. It took him a few minutes to begin digesting everything. Took a little longer for it to sink in after he picked his jaw up off the floor.

And then he read me the riot act, after I assured him it wasn't all some fantastic leg pulling exercise.

Are you insane, Trey? You fucking nuts? Some vampire almost killed you once already. What happens if they catch you this time? What if there're more assassins? What if they shoot *you* next time, are you coming back from the dead? They gonna make you a vampire? Are you fucking kidding me with this? Fucking Vampire Mafia, all right; you got a death wish?

"Travis'll protect us," I said to that.

Scott pointed at Geoff. "Didn't manage to last time."

Wincing, I said, "Don't ever say that around Travis, please. He already feels bad enough."

Scott tossed his hands out. "Whatever. It was sunny. But that's a good point, isn't it. What happens in the daylight, huh?"

"Humans look after us."

Scott looked between Geoff and me. "I haven't seen anyone following us."

"That's the idea, but trust me, they are."

"Sounds like Michel has people all over the place, the more you talk, which tanks my confidence, actually. They have way too many connections." He pointed at me. "They really *are* mafia, aren't they?"

"Nooo. Well…"

"Dude." Scott sat back. "What's Michel, the Godmonster?" He made a derisive snort.

225

"He's a Prince to his people, and he's not a monster. Monsters don't have hearts, damn it." That he can behave monstrously is a different story.

Scott didn't reply to that, so I dug out my cell and held it up, reeling the conversation back in. "Those calls I make every time we go somewhere? I'm checking in with the lead day guy. We're covered, just in case."

Scott's face went into his hands. "Jesus, you're in some deep shit, Trey." He lifted his face and let out a humorless laugh. "Friggin' power plays between what, vampire *royalty*? Shit. I don't even know what to say. There's gotta be some way to talk you outta this."

"Nope."

"You always were stubborn."

"What do you want me to say? That I'll quit my job, quit Paris, and move back here?"

"That's a good start. You can bring Geoff with you." His eyes shot to my boyfriend. "I'm sure you'd like it here."

Geoff looked at him a second and said, "It okay, but – "

"I can't do that, Scott. I *won't* do it," I said.

His expression suddenly softened. "Yeah, I know. You went to Paris and found a new family." His eyes rested on Geoff a moment. "A new everything." His eyes shifted back to me. "I get it, I do, and that part's cool, especially after you lost so much before. But holy crap. They're *vampires*, Trey. And you're not immortal, man." He looked hard into my eyes. "I don't want you dying on me, damn it."

"I am not gonna die on you."

Geoff's arm went around me. "He not."

"You can't promise that," Scott said.

"We didn't," I said. "But I'm not dying on this trip. P.K. even said so." Unless that had changed. "And Geoff just said so. That's two people who are good about knowing certain things."

Scott's brows went up. "Polly knows about all this?"

"She's helped me with my Mark, my adjusting to all this. Yes, she knows."

"What about the shit you're into *here*?"

"She knows everything."

Scott stared at the two of us a moment.

"Dude, I – shit," he said. "And she's okay with it?"

"Not *perfectly*. She worries, of course."

His head shook. "This is some crazy, fucked up shit."

"It's a whopper of a tale, I know. But I'm tired of leaving you out of the loop, and you were gonna keep asking – so I told you. Was that wrong?" I asked.

"No," his head shook again, "no, I'm glad you, well – trust me with this. I'm glad you're not keeping secrets from me. But yeah, dude, one fucking whopper of a tale. How'd you expect me to feel about it, anyway? Don't tell me you're surprised."

"I'm not."

His fingers started picking at the denim over his knees.

"It'll be okay, Scott. One more meeting, and we'll call it good, all right?"

His mouth grew a scowl. "All this is why you have to deal with that fucker Billy, too."

"Which I chose to do."

"I know, I know. Like I said, stubborn bastard, that's you."

I could only shrug a little and offer a contrite face. We'd already gone over the Billy thing before.

"But then there'll be other meetings, right?" he asked. "You'll get in deeper."

"Maybe."

"Shit. I don't suppose there's much *I* can do," he said. "I can't even help. Everyone else is helping you, doing something, seems like."

A smile sprang to my lips. He scolds me, yet wants to help me. But that's what best friends are for, after all.

"Just keep being my friend," I said. "That's a big help."

"I'll always be your friend, Trey," he said. "So, you're just closing a deal here, nothing else? Honest?"

"Honest, nothing else. I'm not on anyone's radar." My hand dove into my pocket, producing the charm. "And look, P.K. even gave me a protection charm. Dude, I'm covered in every possible way, even mystical."

Scott scooted to the edge of his chair. "That's interesting." He held out his hand. "Can I see it?"

I reached and placed it in his palm. He turned it over a couple of times.

"I think I actually feel something," he said, lifting his eyes to mine. "Is there something I should know about her?"

"She's not a vampire," I said.

"No," Scott said. "But is she special in some other way? Y'know, does she have some sort of freaky power like you?"

Geoff said, "She much empathy."

"She's sensitive," I added. "Senses things, but not exactly psychic."

As he handed the charm back to me, Scott said, "I kinda got that from her, yeah. And she's said some things that remind me of Mom in a way. I'm not completely ignorant of superstitions."

"I know. But it's not all just superstition, as you're finding out," I said.

"In a big fucking way," Scott replied. "I feel stupid for not knowing already – but then, Polly always directed the subject back to me, now that I think about it. But anyway, what does she believe in? I mean, like that charm. What's the tradition?"

"Vodou. And don't feel bad; she did the same with me in the beginning."

"Crap, wait. You said something about her being sort of a Mambo, that's right."

"You were still messed up about things at the time. I'm not surprised you forgot."

"Yeah, that must be why. So what about vampires? What's she think of them?"

228

"She heard all about the old men growing up. That's what they call vampires. She knew about Michel and Gabriel before I did. I'm sure she'll tell you a lot more about herself once she knows I filled you in on everything. Just ask her."

"You better believe I'll ask." He pushed at his hair. "You don't suppose she worked some mojo on me, do you?"

"Why, you in lurv?" I said with a grin, wanting to lighten the subject. "Nah, that wouldn't be ethical; she wouldn't do that."

"Didn't say I was in love." He shrugged. "I don't know what I'm saying. Feels like in I'm in a movie."

"Welcome to the club, Scottie."

"Do I get a special card? What's my salary on this one? I think I want a back end deal, too." He smiled for the first time since hearing my story.

Geoff said, "I make you nice cake."

"It's a start," Scott said with a laugh. "With your cooking, a good start."

"I make it two," Geoff said.

Scott gave him a smile. But it faded. "You said some things are fucked up in Spain on Michel's end. You sure you're not gonna catch heat from that?"

"It's Michel I'm worried about," I said.

"You said he was super powerful."

"Yeah, but that doesn't negate me worrying, because I love him, and because…you just never know."

"So can Polly work some magic?"

"Scott, it's not like she can say abracadabra and poof, there it is."

"It's called a joke, Trey. Even if that would be cool. Anyway. This Vicont guy." Scott paused. "Dude, I cannot process how old he is. But anyway, does he have an army of people on his side, too?"

"Well. Yeah. I think so. He's a big shot, too." I glanced at Geoff and back to Scott. "But he hasn't made a move since he kidnapped me."

"No? Maybe he's just waiting for the perfect moment," he said. "You said they weren't sure they'd found everyone involved in the shooting. What if he's still after you?"

"No, they didn't, but they have something over Vicont," I said to that. "Besides, it wasn't him who ordered the hit." Okay, so I didn't tell Scott about Vicont's heart, partially for not grossing him out, possibly.

Queens...
...it's dark
Help me...
"What do they – "
Hand up. "Wait. You wanted me to keep you up to speed on that voice."
Scott said, "Yeah, but – "
"I'm hearing it again."
Geoff and Scott both stared at me.

Michel
Madrid

I settled in next to Gabriel on the divan, and leveled Elise with my stare. "Very well, we now have privacy. Start talking."

She pressed her hands to the tops of her thighs. "The hospitality of your home has certainly suffered in my absence."

"This isn't my home," I retorted.

"Why *aren't* you in one of your homes, by the way?"

"Because I wasn't about announcing my presence in such a fashion, and I wished to be in the city. Now stop being purposefully obtuse and get to it."

First, she made with a flip of her hair. She then gave me a sickeningly sweet smile. "I shall, but first let me remind you not to be a hypocrite."

I let go with a snort.

"I've been trying to *help*, Michel," she said. "I've only been here since last night." She met my gaze directly. "But your spies are still better, I admit it. I don't know how long *you've* been here. Happy?"

My lips began to curve.

"I thought that might please you."

Before I could make with a snappy remark, Gabriel broke into the conversation.

"Letting go for the moment this business in Spain, what I would most like to know is precisely why you were in Prague," he said, and I felt him stiffen beside me. "We shall proceed from there."

She managed to hold his gaze with her reply. "Doubtless you already know."

"If he already knew all he wished, do you think he'd be asking?" I inquired.

Her gaze wavered. "I suppose not."

My dark angel said, "I care little about your socializing. I wish to know why you were there so soon after we, and what your other business was."

"As I said," her gaze moved between us, "I'm trying to help."

Gabriel's simple query was, "With what?"

"I know you're trying to capture everyone involved in Geoff's unfortunate incident." She placed a palm to her bosom. "I wanted to help. Consider it another attempt at making up for the past."

"If this is the case," I leaned forward in my seat, "why not merely inform us of your intentions to begin with?"

"I was hoping to come to you with a warm body. Or cold, as the case may be." She offered me a contrite smile. "I wanted to surprise you."

"That's it?"

"Yes, Michel. That's it."

This actually sat me back, for I believed her.

"As you have not produced a body, did you gather any

information of use?" Gabriel asked, perhaps wishing to believe her, but not quite there as of yet.

She let go with a sigh. "No. I've nothing but dead ends; I'm sorry." She gestured to herself. "I wish I had something to offer." She directed a tentative smile in Gabriel's direction. "By the way, rumor has it you tore Phaedra up quite nicely. It's a shame I missed it."

Gabriel made no reply. I had wonder as to whether he was thinking of Phaedra's brother, the things said in Prague, but I quickly moved past that to more pressing matters.

"Why are you now in Spain?" I inquired yet again.

"I thought I had a lead in this direction." She let go with another sigh. "It was another dead end."

"And?"

"And because I heard that *you* were here. I decided to see what you were up to myself."

Again, I believed her, but said nothing in response, lest she gloat.

"You see, Michel?" She smoothed her hair as she spoke. "Nothing subversive, nor anything at all impressive, as I've failed completely in my search."

That she so far appeared to speak the truth didn't lessen all of my suspicions. There was yet another troublesome matter.

"Hmm. You may yet have something to offer, Elise," I said. "I wish to know what your relationship to Lucas Demetrius is."

"I haven't spoken to him for years," she replied, this time keeping a rather calm exterior at the mention of his name.

"No? He's been asking after you."

Her brows made a swift ascent. "To whom, and when?"

"You truly do not know?" Gabriel asked.

Her eyes moved to him. "I truly don't."

"Recently," I informed her. "He was in Belgium."

Her fingertips fluttered to her cheek. "I sincerely can't think why. I've been avoiding him for a few years, now."

"So you *do* know him," I said.

232

"Of course. Why would I deny it?"

She was giving me the strangest look, and her words, as well as their tone, baffled me. I carried on with my previous thought. "Gabriel remembers you speaking of him a few years ago. A phone call. Apparently you were rather put out."

She lowered her hand and laced her fingers together in her lap. "I see."

"You may, but I don't," I said. "Enlighten me."

"Then you still haven't remembered, have you?" Her stare was wide-eyed.

"Pardon?" I spread my hands. "What is it you think I should remember?"

"Gabriel must have overheard...yes." A fingertip came to her lower lip. "Shortly after I remembered."

"Would you do me the courtesy of dropping the riddles and make some sense, woman?" I was growing quite impatient. Meanwhile, Gabriel's eyes bored into her.

She placed her hands on her knees whilst sliding to the edge of her seat. "Lucas' brother is the one who brought me as a party favor to Vicont's mansion those long years ago."

My expression certainly must have reflected my disbelief.

"You fought Lucas as well as Declan," she went on to say.

Gabriel's gaze was now boring into me. For myself, I yet dangled in disbelief.

"I well remember Declan, your killer, but Lucas? There was no Lucas," I said.

"Yes, there was and is. Vicont stopped you from killing Lucas. As he still had his uses for Lucas, he also..." she paused.

"He what?"

"He knew you'd kill Lucas elsewhere eventually, and so he tampered with your mind, to protect him after the event."

My stomach knotted itself even as my mind wished to suggest she was feeding me a line of horse manure – yet her words slithered through my brain, brushing against things I could sense but not see, not parse.

My love said, "Vicont erased this memory?"

"Yes, and I believe changed parts of the memory," Elise confirmed. "He mentally raped me as well. It only came back to me those few years ago. I ran into Lucas unexpectedly, and certain conversations seem to have jogged most of my memories surrounding him. I say most, as I can't be certain of everything Vicont erased. You may have overheard one of the conversations I had with Vicont about Lucas, Gabriel."

"How would you know of his tampering with Michel's mind, then, if you can't be certain of your own?"

"Because he made me watch what he did to Michel, this I also remembered." Her hands went to her arms, as if she were catching a chill. "To give me few more moments of fear to finish off the evening."

"Preposterous," the word escaped me below a whisper. "Vicont can't get into my – "

"Blood link," Elise spoke my next thought aloud, and I felt my nails puncture my palm. "He reached into you through blood sharing. I didn't quite understand *then*; it was all so new. But I understand now."

Gabriel's hand came to my shoulder. "*Dieu*. She is telling the truth, isn't she? You feel it to be true."

My attention remained fixed on Elise. "But even then I knew how to shield during blood sharing. Even then," I nearly exclaimed.

"Michel...you'd run a gamut of emotions that night. Everything from anger to sorrow. He caught you up in the midst of it, I venture."

I rose and strode across the room. "I have only a vague memory of Lucas leaving one of Vicont's mansions, and it didn't come immediately." Halting in front of the mirror, my arms went about my own waist. "I know nothing of him in the time since." Pivoting, I looked to Elise. "Why do I yet know nothing else of him, as apparently he does much business?"

"Oh, Michel." Her expression spoke of sympathy mixed with horror. "Vicont must have left triggers in your mind as well."

"*Mon lion?*"

My gaze slid to Gabriel, my insides feeling strange, wobbly. Was this nausea, something I'd not felt since I was mortal?

"One of Vicont's best talents is mind meddling, fogging. He could make it so even Lucas' name was a trigger. That the moment I heard it, I'd forget it," I said. "You remember my speaking of his talent. I inherited it."

"Yes I know it well, but you remembered Lucas Demetrius this time," Gabriel said, horror creeping through his gaze as well. "However small the memory, you did recall his name and you don't seem to be forgetting now."

"It's been centuries," Elise commented. "My memory came back. Perhaps there was a trigger for me, so that I *would* remember eventually. Something in seeing Lucas, I don't know. Maybe there's yet another trigger for Michel, or perhaps it's because Vicont's hold is lessening, what with his current state?"

His whisper drifted to my ears. "Perhaps."

I held myself more firmly. What else had Vicont taken from me? I felt queasy, if I yet recalled such a feeling.

"*Mon lion,*" first his words, then his arms came to me from behind, and he held me tight.

"You didn't tell me of this before," I said to Elise.

"We weren't on speaking terms until recently, Michel. And until now, I wasn't certain it was something I should burden you with. I knew it might be painful for you. But as Lucas is making himself known, it seems, and spying on me..."

"He's involved with Diego's treachery."

"My God. I can't think why, I really can't. I have no intelligence suggesting Vicont is aware of what we're doing, and as far as I knew, he and Vicont were through, anyway."

"We have no clear indication Vicont is aware, either," my husband said. "But one can't be certain with him."

"Tell me what it is you've remembered," I said to Elise, a finger of coldness attempting to sketch a line along my spine. "You must tell me absolutely everything."

Chapter 17

Trey
New York

Strangled...
...dumped in the...
Told me he loved me.

"Myra, is that you?" I said. "You're not coming through very well."

Scott got up and squished into the couch on the other side of me.

Such a good liar.
...good liar.

I focused on the whispers, the snippets, and concentrated on her name – if it was in fact Myra.

...Queens, then...

"Queens," I whispered in return. "You said this before."

Through Queens and there was...

"There was what?"

Scott's hand started lightly gripping my arm, so I gave it a pat.

"Trey – "

"Shh."

Smells horrible just horrible...

"I hear you," I said to the voice. "But can you hear me? Can you tell me if this is Myra, the woman from before?"

Stench and...yes.

Yes!

Myra is my name.

I felt the need to move and got up. "Okay Myra, now we're getting somewhere." I paced a tight circle. It had to be, there wasn't a lot of room.

Help me!

"Whoa, now that was loud and clear." Glancing towards the couch, two sets of eyes met mine. "How do I help you? I need you to tell me, Myra."

Help...

Find me.

"But where?" A bit more pacing. "Can you tell me where and how? Are you in Queens somewhere, is that it?"

Compost...but no, water, water.

I could feel my brows knitting, and I could see Scott and Geoff's brows doing the same.

"Is your body covered with these things, Myra?"

Scott's eyes widened at my question.

...river...water...

"In a river, Myra? Which river?"

Scott suddenly chimed in. "Oh, dude. If ever there was a place to dump a body, East River would work. Well, or the Hudson. Matter of fact some girl was found there like, last year." He paused. "Not a Myra, though."

"I didn't figure it was, or she wouldn't be asking me for help," I said.

And I knew all about the Hudson, thank you very much.

"Maybe she knew her? Anyway," Scott said. "The girl was all...eaten up by fish and stuff." His head shook and his nose wrinkled. "Disgusting."

Yeah. Like that poor, sixteen-year-old girl.

Who are you?

Back to Myra. "My name's Trey."

You weren't here and then you were here...or I wasn't and then...I don't know. I feel drawn to you. Pulled to you. And...

...come...

To tell you...

"Myra? I think I'm losing you."

Come...

...make sense...

You...to...

...need to tell you...

I listened.

Listened some more.

"I lost her," I said to Scott and Geoff. "We gotta go to – to Queens. She keeps mentioning Queens."

Scott's hands flew up. "Dude, maybe we should wait for Travis."

"It's daylight, Scott."

"Duh, that's why I said we should wait. It's not that much longer until sunset, is it? Couple hours, three?"

"Why wait?"

"Could get dangerous."

"Dude, Queens isn't bad. Not along most of the water."

He just stared at me.

Resisting the urge to laugh I said, "I've got those people looking out for me, for us, remember? I'll give Richard a call."

Slowly Scott rose. "I think I'd rather have something more bad ass than humans along, man."

Geoff stared up at him, then looked at me. Moving my eyes to Scott I said, "You sure you wouldn't be more afraid of Travis?"

Scott shook his head. "No. I mean, yes, I'm sure. I think. He said he'd protect me too." He nodded. "Yeah. Why don't we wait for Travis?"

My eyes moved over Geoff again, then back to Scott. "I might have a meeting tonight, and Christ, we're not heading into a war zone." My brows lifted. "Unless it's really, *really* changed since I left. "

"No, it ain't a war zone," Scott said. "But..." he paused. "I guess this is just spooky."

"It's not like her ghost is gonna hurt us, bud. She's asking for help."

One of his hands lifted and tucked some hair back. "Yeah. I mean, no. But still, are you so sure? After that stuff in your apartment, man, the idea of going to meet some ghost kinda creeps me out."

Spreading my hands. "I'm positive. Unless I give up control, it's all good. Which means no ghost is gonna be jumping in your body either, okay?" I took a step toward him. "And another besides. What would a vampire do against a ghost, huh?"

"Hell if I know," Scott conceded. "But maybe they have special shit to deal with that, and you just don't know about it. Travis did *something* at your apartment. And he'd have our backs for living problems." He stopped just short of slapping his forehead. "Am I having this conversation?"

Travis didn't tackle *Adele* in Paris, though he'd done something, yeah. But I skipped Scott's comment on that, since whatever Travis did wasn't about ghost wrangling.

"Yes," I said. "You are having this conversation, but you're still overlooking one very important thing, dude."

"What?"

Couldn't stop my grin. "Don'cha think it'll be creepier and more dangerous at night?"

"Uh. Well. But see, that's what Travis is for. Yeah."

Geoff giggled. "Scary cat."

Scott shot him a look. "I'm not a scaredy cat." He moved his eyes to me. "But you never know about some places. I mean, we don't even know where in Queens. Or maybe she'll suddenly tell you to go to someplace fucked up like – like Spring Creek or some crap."

"Scott..."

"And you don't really know if anyone else is watching you; maybe today they are, huh? Travis is bigger and badder than anything out there – isn't he?"

"I'd have to say yes," excepting maybe some other vampires, "but c'mon. I need to get to the bottom of this. Maybe if I go there, she won't fade in and out and I can get this – whatever – settled. Then I can focus on wrapping up business."

"Dude." A frustrated sound escaped him. "Obviously I'm way more freaked about everything you told me than I pretended to be. Okay? There, I admit it."

Taking steps closer, I placed a hand on his shoulder. "I don't blame you. Listen, you don't even hafta go with us. No one said you did."

He eyeballed me.

"Really, Scott. I didn't even ask you, cause hey, I get it."

"But, well – you're my best bud." He straightened his shoulders and his chest puffed up. "You don't have to ask. Queens ain't scary, man."

My smile formed anew. "Actually, maybe you could just hang out with Geoff while I take care of this."

"No!" Geoff's exclamation startled both Scott and me. Neither of us had ever heard him yell like that.

Geoff calmed himself. "Um. I go with you. I must go."

"Okay, baby, don't panic. You can come with me."

"Good, okay."

Scott and I exchanged a glance.

"So..." he said. "You have to find her body so you can hear her, is that it?"

"I don't know for certain," I replied, refocusing on Scott instead of wondering about Geoff. "I tried asking Lucien why I was having trouble getting her messages – "

"What'd he say?"

"I was about to tell you. He said because maybe I don't want to hear what she has to say." Pause. "So then I was a smartass and said that if I don't even know what it is, how or why would I be blocking it?"

Scott's eyes moved over my face. "There's a small, valid point in there, though."

"I thought so. So Lucien said," doing my best to imitate him, "*it be dat sub-consurse ting, prolly.*"

Scott couldn't help laughing along with Geoff.

"He also said I'd know when I'm supposed to know, and that sometimes those who are dead and still lingering form their own traps," I said.

"Something's...something's holding her back, maybe," Scott said.

"Maybe." Shrug. "She might not really know how to reach out, or understand that she can. When I was talking to her she seemed surprised someone answered, that someone could actually hear her."

Scott's previous hesitation was turning to genuine interest. "Maybe she doesn't have the energy – she can't really project herself farther than New York. Or even Queens, hardly. I don't know if that makes sense, since you – you can go to this other side, or whatever, but maybe it's something like that."

Nod from me. "I do have a feeling that if get closer to her, it'll be easier. She *is* trying to lead me to her. And maybe it's also because that's the closure she needs."

"For someone to find her body," Geoff said.

"That does seem logical," Scott agreed.

"It okay to go," Geoff said. "Trey must to help her; it his purpose."

Scott's hands signaled his surrender. "Okay, okay. This could be really interesting, anyway, so yeah, let's all go." He pointed at me. "Just don't forget to call that guy."

"I'll do it right now."

"Does he have a car? 'Cause dude, that'd be much easier if we're gonna end up going in circles. Lots of places on the water to dump a body."

Michel

Madrid

With the tightening of my jaw, my words had need of forcing their way out. "Declan did. I attacked him for it; I remember this."

Her head made to shake. "No. It was Lucas."

"But..." My fingers flew to my temples, their fingertips pressing, attempting to dent the flesh. "But I can see it even now."

"Vicont must have changed their places in your memory," she said.

"Are you so certain you can trust *your* memory?"

Pain lashed her eyes, and her words were tight. "Unfortunately, I've recalled this event in great detail. I most certainly know who did what to me."

My eyes shut themselves tightly. "Forgive me. Yes, of course you do." Once again I left my seat, opting to pace. There was nothing for it. "*Merde.*"

"You attacked both of them, and Vicont stopped you, though not before Declan was dead by your hand."

"Ah! Yet another brother I have killed. Perhaps Lucas too wants revenge," I said, nausea or some approximation thereof still lingering within me.

Vicont had violated my *mind*.

"Pardon?"

I ceased pacing and looked to Elise. "It's not important just now. I'll explain later."

"Is none of this jarring your memory?" she asked then.

"No." I forced myself once again to sit. "Perhaps if you tell

243

me more about Lucas. Tell me...tell me of his business. Tell me where you saw him those years ago. Tell me anything."

One of her palms came to her stomach. "Oh, Michel, I'm so sorry. This has completely unnerved you."

"I can't imagine why," came my dry words.

Of all the things Vicont had ever done to me...

She continued to gaze at me with so much pity that I could no longer stand it, and so left my seat yet again, striding for the door.

"*Mon lion*," the currents of air shifted behind me. "*Où vas-tu?*"

"Out!"

I reached for the door handle, finding Gabriel's hand in its stead, as he had insinuated himself betwixt me and the door.

"*Mon lion*, stay, wait. We can work through this."

The irony slapped me hard across the face. Gabriel, whose mind erased memories for him, informing me that we could work through this.

"Now I know how it is for you," were my tense words in response to him. "Except, it doesn't disturb *you*. You don't *want* your memories." My fingers wished to clench, to curl. "They weren't stolen from you." I stumbled back a step. "I want them back!" My hands then flew to my face, obstructing my view of him.

My mind, Vicont had violated my *mind*, the one thing I thought he couldn't touch, that I had thought he *wouldn't* touch, yet he had, and the feeling of *knowing* he had left me on the verge of panic, now.

"What if..."

No other words would pass my lips.

Gabriel's touch to my hands was gentle, light. "What if he took more," he whispered. "This is what frightens you." Gently he moved my hands away from my eyes. "You are frightened, afraid that you have lost memories that you might cherish. And you are frightened of his acidic touch yet lingering in your mind. I understand, *mon amour*."

I gazed into his eyes.

"Oh...Gabriel."

His look, terribly gentle. "I have long known that the workings of my mind frightened you as well as fascinated. But we shall find *your* memories, Michel, as it is not a natural occurrence for you."

My emotions thickened, swirled, and came to their own sudden conclusion. "I must speak with him."

My Gabriel merely nodded.

"Yes, I must speak with Vicont."

"Michel." Elise's voice came from behind me. "If this is what you must do, then do it, for I also understand your need to know. But what of the situation here? And if you mention Lucas to him, who knows what will happen?"

Directing my gaze over my shoulder, I found her eyes, my thoughts yet bent upon one thing. "I don't know how you stood it. Realizing you had lost parts of your life."

"I didn't have long to fret over it." Her expression became apologetic "I remembered quite swiftly. That was the unnerving part, and besides – some memories I wouldn't have missed."

As her words lingered in the air, there was a knock upon the door. Kar's voice soon followed.

"My Prince, I have news."

I looked to Gabriel, who turned and opened the door, likely more for giving me a distraction than urgency on Kar's part.

"Pardon, my Lords. I have news I knew you'd wish to have immediately."

"Yes of course, Kar, do come in," I said, retreating a few steps with Gabriel to allow Kar's entrance, Elise's last words still in my mind."What news do you bring?" I inquired.

It was obvious that Kar sensed something was off, yet ever my calm lake, my stoic general when needed, carried on with his business.

"*Señor* Varela informs us that Diego has again been in contact with Lucas, who is yet in Belgium," said he.

My eyes narrowed themselves.

"He also informs us that Diego is planning to make a trip to Barcelona this evening," Kar continued. "We believe he may have caught wind of your presence."

"Barcelona." My mind interrogated itself, seeking enemies and allies in Barcelona, past and present. "Obviously the idea of blackmailing me left his thoughts, if it ever was in his thoughts. Anything else, Kar?"

"No other information, my Prince. Would you have me detain Diego in some way so you might interrogate him, sir?"

My gaze travelled from him to Gabriel, where it paused as we shared an unspoken thought, and then found a final destination in Elise. "Hand me that cellular, will you?"

She retrieved it from the side table and exited her chair, giving it over after reaching me. "What are you going to do?" she asked.

As I entered the numbers, I spared her a glance. "I'm making an executive decision." Admittedly, it was also a decision borne of agitation and impatience.

The one I was contacting answered on the second ring.

"*Buenas noches*, Ricco. Need I say why I'm calling?"

"N-no sir."

"I want it done yesterday, Ricco."

"Yes sir. Sir – "

I snapped the phone shut before suffering another word from him.

"It may or may not work, but all outcomes may be satisfying, *non*?" Gabriel said.

"What are you talking about?" Elise inquired.

"The possibility of drawing Lucas to us whilst ridding the world of someone I've come to despise," I answered. "I do so love killing two birds with one stone, as is said." My gaze shifted to Gabriel. "And yes, I believe I shall be satisfied with all the possible outcomes, though three birds would be delightful."

246

"Certainly I would not shed a tear for Ricco and family," he replied.

Elise's eyes bounced between we three males in the room. "Will someone explain to me what's going on, please?"

"Certainly, Elise. Just give me a moment." I turned toward my emissary. "Kar, I'd like you to send two messages for me." Contemplating an earlier question mark yet in my mind, I then added, "Also, I'd like to ask you something."

Chapter 18

Trey

Richard, the bodyguard, who didn't look like he could put the smack down on anyone (yeah I know, looks are deceiving), initially wasn't too keen on driving me around on some wild goose chase (his words), particularly without Travis knowing what was up. So, I reminded him that technically he was also working for me. But what really convinced him was my telling him that if he didn't drive me around, I'd find another way, so he may as well make it simpler by being my escort instead of following me around.

He did of course want to know exactly what it was I needed to do and why. I opted to tell him the truth. He worked for vampires after all, so I figured my being, uh, special, probably wouldn't sound too out there.

This also worked.

Glorious truth. So glad we're pals again. Not that any of it impressed Richard, because I – well, Myra – had him driving through the city like a drunk crow flies, and Richard didn't give a damn about my apologizing and telling him I was doing my best to zoom in on her while she did her best to lead me. At least I think she was doing her best – didn't think I was blocking her in some way 'sub-consursely' or not.

Richard's a bit of a bristly character, actually. Not that anyone could blame him in this instance, really. Even I was getting impatient with Myra.

Geoff had sat quietly through most of our tipsy turtle ride, letting me do my thing. Scott, on the other hand, was visibly doing his best not to ask me questions like *What's she saying now? What do you see?* every five minutes.

His record was eight minutes, I think. Thing was, there wasn't really that much to tell him every five minutes, as it felt like I was mostly following some hidden beacon more than anything coherent.

Eventually we made our way to Third Ave and ended up at Francis Lewis Park. Now, here we stood on a dingy strip of beach in the shadow of the Whitestone Bridge.

"This it? The trail just stops here?" Scott asked.

"No," I said, feeling incredibly drawn to the water – the East River. "Out there somewhere, I think."

"Uh huh, see, good place to dump a body, I told you," he replied.

Geoff then queried on the state of our crooked path to the river for the first time. "Why you think she bring you long way here?"

Turning to him I said, "Her memory was scattered maybe? Either that or," pausing as the epiphany struck. "No, no wait. I understand."

Everyone's eyes burned into me.

"Her killer," I explained, "took her through the boroughs that way. That's what she remembers, or can see of it, I mean. She was doing her best, showing me the fucked up path as she knew it."

"She was riding along with her killer as a ghost?" Scott asked.

Myra's voice suddenly struck my brain hard. "Whoa, okay I heard you," I said under my breath in response to that. Then to Scott, "Yes and no, she was alive for parts of it."

Richard chimed in before the conversation could possibly get morbid, asking, "So now what?"

My eyes shot to his. "I need to go out there."

"I'm supposed to play captain now?" His small hands gestured around us. "We don't even have a boat."

"Sun's going down soon," Scott added. "I don't know if I wanna be stuck out there in the dark."

"You don't hafta go," I said. "You can wait here."

"Hang on," Richard cut in. "Who says *anyone's* going? No boat, remember?"

Before a reply came to me, a vision struck me between the eyes.

Michel

Madrid

"Sir?"

Not accustomed to Kar lacking an immediate answer to a question, my rephrasing was a bit terse. "Lucas Demetrius. What do you know of him that I don't?"

"That you don't? I'm sorry, but…" Uncharacteristically at a loss for words, he appealed to Gabriel with a look. "I don't believe I understand."

"Bear with us Kar," Gabriel said, whilst I attempted to find a less caustic state of mind. "Michel met with other news before your arrival that did not please him. Tell me please, had you heard the name before?"

Kar's gaze shifted between us. "Yes, I had."

"This is why you hesitated in Emanuel's office, no?" I inquired. "You were surprised I hadn't at first, weren't you."

His chin dipped though his eyes remained on me. "Somewhat, my Prince."

"Explain." Tension resumed its winding way through me.

"His name has come up in years past," he said. "Sporadically, but it has. You," he spread his hands palm up, "well, sir, you yourself never brought up the name, never appeared interested in him, therefore I thought him unimportant."

Turning away, my gaze found Elise. In her eyes pity formed once more. "Who mentioned him, and in what capacity?" I asked Kar, eyes remaining on Elise, as I had no wish to see surprise on his face.

"It's been decades now, but I remember that generally it was some other who would mention him in passing, usually in a meeting. Nothing outstanding or suspicious seeming that I recall. Business matters, generally. Buy, sell, trade. You understand. Most of this business concerned resorts, kitchen supplies, just as Emanuel related."

"Have we purchased supplies from him for any of my hotels, or such?" Good gods, I knew nothing, even, of these things.

"No, sir. Demetrius made random overtures through his attorneys in times past, but you have always preferred doing business with Chomette and others, and..."

"And?" Elise's gaze was the only thing currently keeping me steady.

"As I said. You never appeared interested in the Demetrius branch, not in the slightest. It was as if it didn't exist for you."

"It must be as you guessed," I said to Elise, my eyelids dropping. "I remember nothing of it, nothing of what Kar speaks to."

"Sir?"

I turned at the sound of Kar's softly spoken word, a word holding a measure of concern.

"Should I have known more, paid more attention?" he said.

"You've missed nothing, Kar." Moving closer to him, I placed a hand on his shoulder. "You've missed nothing. Forgive my short temper, please."

"Of course, sir. Should I give you all of the minor details, sir?"

I waved this off. "It doesn't matter. If you felt it unimportant, it doesn't matter."

"Are you…" Words failed him once more, apparently, and he merely gazed into my eyes.

"I'm fine. You may leave us now."

With an inclination of his head, he said, "Yes my Prince," and made his exit.

"Michel – "

"*Pas maintenant*, Elise. *S'il te plaît*."

Gabriel's hand came to the small of my back.

"Very well. Then perhaps you'd rather explain the rest of the situation to me, now?" she said.

My eyes turned in her direction. "Now is as good as time as any, I suppose."

And so, once seated, I explained everything, including my plans for Diego. Elise, for her part, didn't initially take this well.

"Michel!" was her soft exclamation. "Even if Ricco pulls this off, what makes you think he won't tell Lucas all of it, threats or no? He'll bargain with whichever vampire has his fangs closest to his neck."

"I'm past caring if Ricco informs Lucas that I ordered the hit. My hope is that Lucas will come for us, then. If not, perhaps he'll at least out himself, make a misstep, or give up whatever his plan is, if he knows I've information on him."

"But you don't. You don't really have much information on him, Michel."

"Thank you ever so much for reminding me, Elise."

Her lashes made a partial drop.

"In any event, this matters not," I said. "*He* doesn't know this."

252

"Fair enough." Her eyes lifted. "But what if he's yet associated with Vicont?"

"I find myself caring less and less what Vicont thinks or knows."

She came out of her chair in a blur of motion. "We've barely begun! Are you intent on sabotaging the entire affair?"

Gabriel interjected. "Michel is being double crossed. This means you are as well."

"Well," she flung a hand to her hip, "do something about the traitors, fine, but surely you could come up with a better plan than this."

"It's too late," I said. "I've made the call, and Kar is sending word to have Miles silenced forever."

"You're so damned impulsive. This is reckless, don't you think?"

"Eh *bien*, at least I'm consistent," I replied.

A gliding step she took in my direction. "Seriously, Michel. Why such grand gestures now?"

"Because I am serious, Elise, and again, the point is moot."

Another step she took. "Why not inform Vicont of your plans, then, hmm? You may as well get it over with." After a short pause, she continued. "Did you even speak to Diego?"

"Ahh, my spies are better than your spies," I could not help but nearly singsong, offering up a half smile.

Her arms went across her bosom. "I see. No interrogation, nothing."

"Ricco told me enough."

Her expression turned petulant. "Too impulsive. I'm guessing he told you little."

"Come now." I rose, Gabriel's fingertips sliding across my arm as I did, and then closed the remaining distance betwixt Elise and myself. "Did you truly believe we could win? That we could gain everything of Vicont's before someone grew suspicious? Months upon months, with none the wiser?"

Her lips formed a *moue*. "Perhaps not. But it's been short weeks, Michel."

"Yes, and we've done rather well in this short time."

"Precisely, so why dance with danger now?"

"As if we haven't been from the start. You said Vita had already given you up to Vicont. He knew that you wanted to go after him."

"Yes," she replied. "Though no doubt he laughed and thought I was delusional. As I said before, and even you confirmed, there's no sign he's aware of our activities."

"This doesn't mean that he isn't."

Her hands flew away from her sides. "True, but – "

"And I might have added to his suspicions."

Her arms relaxed. "Might have? Meaning what?"

A bit of guilt crept through me. "Well. I may have informed him last we spoke, that you wished him dead."

"You told him about our private meeting?" Her eyes narrowed. "Did you?"

I managed to hold her gaze. "Yes. I was angry at the time. It was just before – "

"You showed up at my house and destroyed my living room with my body. Ohh," her foot stamped with her final expulsion of sound. One of her hands then fanned the air. "Well, fine, whatever. I'm sure he had another laugh over that."

"He did. But you and I did have some fun, didn't we?" I teased, her current demeanor amusing me, for which I was grateful. "I know I enjoyed it."

"Fun? For who, my decorators? No doubt they loved making the money."

"The room needed updating anyway. I did you a favor, demolishing it free of charge."

Her hands flew to her hips. "What exactly was wrong with the room?"

A tinge of impatience emanating from Gabriel caused me to drop our banter. "*Rien, rien.*"

Her gaze flitted to Gabriel, and then returned to me. "Fine, we'll finish that later. Now really, Michel…" Of a sudden, her hands came to my arms. A light touch it was, an affectionate touch. "If anyone could have accomplished this mission, it was you. I had faith in you."

"Save your flattery, please," I replied, though my words had softened.

"It's true. So why does it seem you're giving up?"

"Did I say that I was?"

"No, but it seems that you are." One of her hands drifted towards my face, stopping shy of actually touching it.

After searching her eyes, I moved back a step. "It's no longer safe."

"I have told him that it feels unsafe," Gabriel hastened to add.

"But I feel it as well, now," said I.

Deeply she looked into my eyes. "So you've been intimating. But is this the only reason?" she asked, closing the distance I had created. "I'm having trouble believing it is."

So many things moved in my mind, so many slithering shadows. Centuries of this dance, the repeated chess games of life and death; the lies, the angst. And now...now I knew that Vicont had bested himself when it came to *betrayal*.

"Gabriel, my love." I pivoted to face him.

"*Oui?*"

"You said to me once before that you'd tell me."

The green of his eyes darkened as he caught my meaning. "If you wish it, I shall show you."

I turned back to Elise. "We're returning to Paris tomorrow night. You should return to Belgium."

"But what are..." Her eyes widened. "Are you – "

"Yes."

"But you said – "

"I know what I said. I've had enough. Enough of it all." After a pause, I added, "This was always foremost about putting him in his place. I've decided to stop pussy footing around and get on with it."

The corners of her Cupid's bow mouth lifted. "Would you like some help? I'd be more than happy to provide it."

Trey
Francis Lewis Park

I realized that Scott and Geoff were holding me as if I were about to fall over – which maybe I had been. The vision and feeling, brief as they seemed to be, had been powerful.

"Whoa, Trey. You okay?" Scott asked.

"I," started (or kept) coughing and hacking.

"Maybe you should sit down," Scott said, sounding concerned. "Seriously, dude, you sound awful."

I waved him off, making a gesture to give me a minute.

"Angel, you need something?" Geoff asked, patting my back.

My hand went up again. "Hang on." My throat tried to clear itself. "Okay." My lungs pulled in a slow, deep breath. "I'm okay."

Scott's turn to question. "What the hell happened?"

"I just got slammed with a visual that came complete with a feeling." My eyes found him. "Like I was choking. No. Being strangled."

"You were choking all right. Fuck me," he said. "Was it Myra? What did you see?"

Head shaking. "It was like…" understanding hit, and I looked at Geoff. "I think it was the killer. But it was dark, and I couldn't make out the face."

"Wait a minute," from Scott. "The ghost of the killer?"

My attention returned to him. "I'm not sure. Don't think so, though."

"Dude. Maybe he's after you, doesn't want you to find out who he is."

"Don't panic, Scott. If he's a ghost, he can't hurt me."

"Oh yeah? You weren't doing so well a minute ago. I'd call that hurting you."

I contemplated. Tuned into my senses. "No really, it's okay, Scott. Myra's just coming through better, I think. I've let her in just enough to help her."

"So if it was her, why the choking?"

"I think she was showing me what happened to her."

"Whoa. That's one way to make a point, I guess."

"Hell of a way, yeah." I looked at Richard. "I have *got* to get out there, man."

He said, "I hope you're a good swimmer then."

"What time it is?" Geoff suddenly asked. "Travis maybe awake now."

"Oh, yeah, right." I dug out my cell.

"If he was awake, he'd have called one of us by now," Richard said.

Right after I said, "Well, it's six fifteen," Richards' cell went off. He pulled it out of his pocket, glanced at it, and held it up.

"He's up," he said, and put the phone to his ear. "Yo, boss." Beat. "Yeah, everything's fine." Beat. "Oh, we're all just hanging out on a crap beach, because your boy Trey – "

Travis must've interrupted him, because Richard cut himself off, squinted at me, then pushed the cell in my direction.

"He wants to talk to *you*."

I took the phone and slapped it my ear. "Hi Travis."

"Where are you and what are you doing?"

Brief seemed best because of his tone. "We're at Francis Lewis Park trying to figure out how to get on the river without a boat."

"Why?"

"Because I need to find Myra. She led me here."

Silence on the line for a minute, then, "Stay put. I'll be there soon as I can."

"Okay. Are you – " Click.

Er. Are you put out?

I handed the phone back to Richard. "We're supposed to wait here."

Michel
Madrid

I led Elise out through the door, having opted to escort her to her hotel; I was in need of fresh air. Gabriel did not begrudge me this, though he chose to remain in our lair.

We had gone precious few steps before Elise chose to speak. "We're no doubt asking for trouble. You are, really." She briefly paused. "Which I know I intimated already, yes. There could be a fight."

"*Une bagarre ne me fait pas peur.*"

Her eyes slid in my direction. "*Je sais.* I'm not afraid of a fight, either."

We took a few more steps in silence.

"Still, you may place yourself in great danger."

"Ah, so you *do* still care."

"You know that I do. That I always have." Her feet paused. "Don't you?"

My steps did not falter. "I'm not afraid."

Her response as she caught me up was, "So you already said. This isn't what I asked."

"I heard you, Elise. I heard you."

"You don't believe what I said in Belgium, do you. You still don't believe me."

This time I came to a halt and looked her in the eye. "Not much time has passed since this revelation of yours."

"No. But I can't help hoping, being impatient in my wishing." She reached to touch my arm. "I can't help hoping you'll remember how it was before all that."

258

"Pah." I resumed strolling. "You think I've forgotten? If I had forgotten, it wouldn't have seemed such a betrayal, what you did."

She moved alongside me, cloaked in another silence, and for my part, those times she eluded to began swimming through my thoughts. The years in which we were like siblings.

"I shouldn't press," she quietly said after we'd walked the equivalent of two city blocks. "On my end, so much time has passed with knowledge of the truth. But for you, it's so new, I know. I'm sorry."

A spot in my heart softened yet again. "Elise..." Once more, my feet paused. Once more, my eyes found her face.

"One day, you'll believe me. I can wait," she stated, as if to convince only herself it was a certainty. "After all, I have time."

A sigh escaped me. "I believe you now." Too many things unresolved, I thought. What would the harm be in admitting it to her in this moment? Too much unresolved, and my heart wearied of such things. What good had keeping things too close ever done? I had kept secrets from Gabriel for what I thought were good reasons, only for them to return and haunt me.

Her brows creased with an expression of uncertainty.

"I believed you when you said it that night." My hand drifted, finding one of hers and grasping it. "I believed you, and so – "

"You fled. It was too much to feel after everything else, and you fled, oh, Michel." Her free hand came to her lips. Red sprang to her eyes.

"Yes, I fled. It seems you do yet know me."

A smile was dying to appear on her lips, though it was yet hesitant to do more than hint at such, and as this moment itself became suddenly a bit too much for me, my eyes fled her face, moving in the direction my feet would now carry me – forward.

Apparently, she could yet manage to count her blessings and quit while she was ahead; perhaps too, she remembered how it was for me in such moments, allowing what passed between us to stand in silence when next she spoke.

"Michel, I know what you said in front of Gabriel, but there must be something I can do for you here, or in Paris. Belgium will keep; there's no need for me to leave Spain so soon."

"That wasn't for Gabriel's benefit. I want you on your jet tomorrow night, Elise."

"But why?"

"You're in my way. This is man's work."

"Still a misogynistic prick, I see."

A chuckle left me. She'd caught my jesting tone and thrown it back at me.

"And man's work, are you certain? You're quite the fop at times," she continued.

Full laughter accosted me. A very pleasant feeling indeed. "Do I not have taste?"

"Most of the time."

I offered her a smile.

"But seriously, Michel. I could speak to Lucas, perhaps. Since I remember him now, I might be able to find out exactly what he's up to."

"But you said you've not spoken to him for years."

"I haven't, but I can come up with a reason to now easily enough. I could tell him – "

"No."

"I won't mess things up, I swear. You already know how convincing I can be."

Our eyes met.

"Unfortunately," she added. "You know too well."

"No."

She flung out a hand. "I understand if you don't trust me, but – "

"It's not that."

Her hand drifted back to her side, her eyes widening. "It's not?"

I made to shake my head.

"Then what?"

"I..." pausing, I drew another breath. "You'd be in too much danger."

There was no need on my part to see her expression. I felt the tenderness of her emotion. "So you do still care."

My reply followed a light clearing of my throat. "Yes, damn me. You know that I do."

After a time, after she had regained herself, she changed the direction of our conversation somewhat.

"I'd still like you to take care of Belgium. No matter what transpired between us, I've always held to that."

My widened eyes moved to her. "Don't be ridiculous. You'll be its Mistress for many long years."

"Please, just tell me that you'll still honor my wishes. Please?"

I looked away. "Very well, though nothing is happening to you any time soon."

"Do you swear?"

With great reluctance, I met her gaze. "I swear."

"Thank you." She offered a small smile. "You yet posses the paperwork?"

"Yes," I whispered, thinking suddenly of her will, but just as swiftly, I steered my thoughts in a different direction, one less...depressing.

"Good." After a pause, she shifted the subject even more. "You're not going to see Vicont alone, are you?" she asked, her tone becoming quite serious. "Don't you dare go alone, if he accepts."

"Last we met, he wasn't surrounded by guards."

"He may not feel as secure this time."

"As far as he'll know, I only wish to speak to him."

"You know better. He can't be trusted; you don't know what manner of greeting you'll receive."

"It's between him and *me*. Always it's been between him and me. So much I could've prevented, if only I'd – "

"Michel, stop it."

Our eyes met once more.

"Please," she said.

Silently I held her gaze.

"Promise me you won't go alone. Take Gabriel, take Kar, and not because I think you weak. I know you're not."

"There's nothing to debate, in any case; don't worry. Gabriel wouldn't allow it," I conceded. "Not even were I to insist, I think. Not this time."

"Good." Her lips began to curve. "We both know he's more of a man than you, anyway." With those words, she winked at me.

A smile found me once more.

Chapter 19

Trey
Francis Lewis Park

After about an hour and a half of us trying to look like guys just enjoying a night on the beach, guys who weren't at all *dressed* for the beach, Travis showed up.

On the water, in a boat.

Make that a dinghy.

"There you are," he said as the boat drifted to a stop on the shore. "Now, where is it you need to go, Trey?"

Um. Okay. He didn't sound put out, but, "Hold on, hold on," I said. "Where'd you get the boat?"

He gestured. "Down that way. Someone had it tied up to a small pier."

"You stole it?"

"Borrowed, mate. I'll return it when we're finished."

"That's a small boat," Scott commented.

"No shit," I said. "We're going out there in that?"

"Well gee, I would've brought you a yacht, but that definitely wouldn't have gone unnoticed," Travis said. "No one will miss this. They weren't even home."

"We don't all fit in that," said Geoff.

"Trey and I will go," Travis replied. "Richard can look after you here."

Geoff was generally congenial, but I was a little surprised when he said okay after witnessing his outburst in Scott's apartment.

Let it go for now, Trey. "There's no motor. Dude, not even oars," I said to Travis. "Why aren't there oars?"

Scott said, "Probably so no one would," fake cough, "steal it. Hey, so how'd you get it here?"

Travis tapped his temple in reply to Scott.

"Huh?" from Scott.

I cut in. "Oh, you know, telekinesis. Simple."

Scott stared at Travis. "Oh."

"I reckon we should get on with this," Travis said. "Ready Trey?"

"Uh…currents out there can be strong, you know. You sure you got this?"

One of his brows arched. "Are you suggesting this river can best my mojo?"

After studying him and deciding he was taking the piss out of me, I grinned. "All right, all right. I trust you."

"Right then. Climb aboard."

I planted a kiss on Geoff's cheek. "Be back soon."

"Okay."

"We'll back off this beach a bit, find something else to do," Richard said. "Draw less attention."

"Good idea," Travis said to that as I wetted my shoes climbing into the boat. Then to me he said, "All right, Trey. Lead on."

"Uhh…that way."

The boat started gliding over the water.

"Thanks," I said. "For helping me. You didn't even give me a third degree."

"You'll be less distracted if we get this sorted," he said, eyes on the water.

"Right. I've got business to finish."

His eyes shifted to me. "Ah, c'mon. You know that's not the only reason I'm doing this."

I gave him a smile.

"Can't have you drowning while going after some dead woman."

If he'd intended that as a joke, his tone taking a dive had ruined it.

"Hey. What's up?"

"Whatever you need to do, do it now, Trey."

Doing my best not to take his dismissal personally, I reached for Myra. "Go...left."

* * * *

Struggling for air.

Choking.

"What's it, mate? Sea sick?"

Tightening around my throat. Hands.

A – a cord. Cord around my throat.

Gurgle.

"Hey hey hey, what's happening, Trey? Talk to me."

Gurgle. Gasp.

The world takes on a grey haze, blackens on its edges, a section of deteriorating film.

"Trey!"

Sting. My face.

Flat brown eyes. No, not so flat. A spark of maniacal fire – but cold all the same. So cold.

I know those eyes.

I know them, and he is going to kill me. Is killing me.

Another sting to my face. Stars in my eyes.

Flash of red and black in my brain.

Shaking.

"Trey, where are you? C'mon, talk to me, talk to me."

Scent. Flooding my consciousness. My nostrils.

"Geoff," I think I gasp.

"What about Geoff? Trey, can you hear me? What about Geoff?"

His smell. Essence.

Warmth.

Wing beats.

The film separates, becomes two films. One I am viewing but no longer the star of. The other, I am, but it's a far more comfortable film.

Different eyes, I see different eyes. Beautiful, inhuman eyes. "Trey, what about Geoff. Is he all right? Are you?"

My voice follows my frantic thought. "Yes. Oh my God, no, no fucking way!"

"Try to take a breath…Good, now take another."

Blinking.

"Jesus, no fucking way!"

"Trey, I need you to level out before you hurt yourself. Come on, you can do it."

I sat up, never knowing I'd gone down to begin with.

"That's it. Nice and even," he said, his eyes seeking mine for answers to yet unasked questions. "You'll be right in no time."

"I was there," I said. "I was in her place. It was worse than at the beach. I saw him this time; Jesus, I saw him! He was strangling me, cold-blooded murder in his eyes. Hitting me, choking me. I was there for all of it."

He waited patiently for me to gather myself a bit more. Waited while I shook off the rest of the nightmare, the vision, the happening. A very real happening that reminded me too much of those girls, that wretched court case.

Too much like a football field.

My body started shaking all over again.

266

"Hey. Stay with me, now. Stay with me, Trey."

"It's...it's..." head shake. "Ah, God." I pressed the heels of my hands to my eyes, trying to push the lingering visuals away.

"It's just you and me, here. I got ya."

"It's not just you and me." It felt like the boat was rocking more than previously. "We're not alone."

"But you're safe. You're safe, Trey."

That's me rocking the boat. Time for a cleansing breath or five.

"That's it, mate."

No, that's not it. The girls went away, but the other part didn't. Finally dropping my hands, I looked at him through the lingering bursts of color I'd rubbed into my eyes.

"Oh my God, he did it."

"Who?"

"He did it, Jesus Christ, he did it."

Travis' eyes continued to ask the question of who.

His name felt like sandpaper across my tongue. "Billy."

The light in Travis' eyes faded.

"That's why." Grabbing his shoulders. "That's why here, why now. William Brantley murdered this woman; she just showed me."

Travis' eyes – they'd gone black. They must've, because there was no color for me to find in the dark, no amber lights, and sure enough when he spoke, I heard the shift in his voice.

"You're positive it was him."

"Yes, I'm positive! I saw that wild look right before he shoved my face in the turf and raped me!"

A purr roiled through him, and seemed to touch me, my nerves, and I felt my body relax.

"He will be judged, Death Dancer."

My eyes closed with the weight of it. "He could've killed me. Jesus Christ, he could've killed me," I whispered hoarsely.

"He cannot hurt you now."

Slow inhale. "No." Eyes opening. "No, he can't. He can't, not now."

"Very good. But now I need your help. I need you to find her and the closure she needs, before I lose all control and go after him to shred him this instant."

His tone commanded me to sit up straighter. "Maybe that's what she wants. Eventually." I looked away and pointed before that went any further. "Okay." Deep inhale. "Okay, that way. I can feel it. Her, I feel her."

The boat started moving, and then Travis, in a tone I was much more accustomed to, said, "What was that about Geoff before? You called out his name."

What was that about? Let me think.

"I – I was struggling with her memories. It was so real, so real. But then I smelled Geoff. Felt him. He…"

My eyes moved to him. Our gazes locked.

"He balances me," I said.

Yes. That was it.

"He keeps one of my feet on this side of the veil, where it belongs," I said.

Exactly it. Everything has its opposite, its balance, just as P.K. said.

But Geoff was even more than that. He was my anchor. He was still standing on the beach where we'd left him, but I'd felt him, scented him, because he was in me and I was in him.

That must've been why he freaked at the idea of me coming here alone. He knew I'd need him, didn't want to be too far away when I needed him.

There was a flash of white, then. It was Travis' smile.

Michel
Madrid

The moment I returned, Gabriel informed me that Kar had heard from allies in Belgium. Miles was disposed of. Lucas had left the country, apparently making for Greece. There was yet no news concerning the other message I had asked Kar to send. Not much time had passed, but returns were sometimes swift, which always pleased me. As my patience continued to thin, I tried to hope for the best – such as a reply before dawn, or for Gabriel to knock me unconscious, as sleep certainly wasn't about to find me, nor I it.

Gabriel settled onto the bed, stretching out his lithe frame. "You had a good walk?"

"Yes. It's a rather nice evening, weather-wise."

"I speak of you and Elise. Your half-hearted bickering earlier reminded me of olden times."

My fingers paused in undoing the buttons of my shirt. "Oh?"

"I must confess that it was pleasant, in its way."

"It appeared to me you grew impatient with it," I said as moved toward the bed to sit upon its edge.

"Somewhat. Yet, it made you happy. This is what I found pleasant."

"Pah." I stood so that I might step out of my trousers. "Useless banter."

He rolled, resting his chin on the backs of his hands, looking up at me. "Banter you always enjoyed with her. All of it affectionate jest at its heart."

"I wasn't precisely pleased with the situation, you realize." I sat once more, at last free of garments.

"Oh please, *mon lion*. You may admit it."

"Pardon?"

"You miss her."

A snort left me.

He slithered across the bed and up behind me, resting his chin upon my shoulder.

"I shall not detest you for it. I do not detest you for it."

I leaned back into him. "Yes, I miss her. Those earlier times." A smile accosted me. "I always fancied having siblings and a father, but I never really did. Half siblings I never knew, a father I saw so few times I can count them on one hand; that's what I had."

"I remember your telling me how you always fancied that you would be a wonderful older brother."

With a slight turn of my head, my peripheral vision took in his face. "Was I, do you think?"

"You were wonderful with her, and firm when necessary. What is said? Two peas in a pod, this is what you truly were."

For the second time in what had morphed into a hellish evening, someone sparked laughter within me. The evening, perhaps, had time yet to continue improving.

"Gabriel, are you honestly all right with all of this? With what I'm thinking to do?"

"I trust you, *mon amour*."

"Even though I'm reckless?"

"Reckless? Yes, you are, yet so often it works out for you in the end." His sudden laugh was softer than a cotton ball. "You lead a charmed life, and I like you just the way you are."

A smile lingered on my face a time before I continued with other thoughts aloud.

"Elise believes I'm going to kill him, Gabriel."

"As she wishes. It makes little difference. However, I am curious as to why you did not divest her of this belief."

I made to shrug. "I don't know. She was worried, and I didn't offer the truth as a bit of comfort."

"Perhaps you wished for her to worry?"

I reached around to find one of his hands. "Perhaps. Perhaps I merely wanted to know that she'd worry at all."

"Perhaps it is that you worry after her, her knowing too much."

"I'm suspicious, you mean?"

"Come now, you know very well what I mean to say."

"People are asking after her. It's better that she return to Belgium. Better that she removes herself from the situation here."

"Where she is less safe, in your eyes." I felt his nimble fingers move through my hair. "You yet have a bond. You cannot be reproached for this."

"Perhaps not," was my whispered response. I rested more of my weight against him. "Enough of that for now, if you please."

"As you like, *mon amour*."

"Moving on, then. We shall have our meeting with him; I'll find out what I need to know, and depending on the answers, we negotiate."

"And when he has served his purpose?"

Fully, I turned, he making room for me as I did so.

My eyes found his directly. "You may at last be able to finish it as you like."

Trey
East River

Travis kicked off his shoes, started peeling off his clothing. Nice view, but "What're you doing?"

"Only one way to find out if there's a body down there," Travis said, **flashing** me a brief smile before standing at the boat's side.

"Hey, w**ait. You** can't see what I'm seeing. Right?"

His head **turned** in my direction. "No. But you said right under the boat, ay?"

"Yeah, but in some spots, it's about a hundred feet down, Travis."

"No worries."

My eyes closed. "Fine – okay, big rock." Probably lots of those. "Wait. Anchor." My eyes opened. "She's showing me a small anchor; it's weighted with an anchor."

271

He nodded and dove before I could say another word, his body silently slicing the water.

I leaned over the edge he'd just vacated, grabbing the side of the boat as it rocked.

So black. Couldn't see a damned thing. Not even a ripple left behind.

"Travis!"

Eyes scanning, scanning. At first, I wasn't certain why I was anxious. Or really, which thing made me more anxious. His actually finding a body? Or his being down in that water with no scuba gear?

Rising to my knees, I said his name again, though I don't know why. Good hearing they might have, but through several feet of water?

Didn't know. And though I *did* know that Gabriel didn't appear to breathe in his sleep that time I came upon him on the floor in his house, I wasn't sure if Travis did. Need to breathe, that is.

Vampires weren't all created equal; the phrase repeated in my mind as my eyes uselessly searched the water. Not so much as a bubble that I could see. Just the normal currents of the river with a slight breeze along the water.

Too many minutes passed. Far too many for the fittest human swimmer. For even a record-holding diver, I thought.

"Shit." I stood, seriously contemplating the idea of diving in after him, to look for him.

"You're a vampire," I said to the dark water. "You'll be fine. Right? You wouldn't go in if you couldn't handle it. Right?"

Nod to self.

But still.

"He is not stupid enough to dive in there if it would drown him, Trey. He can handle the currents, too. Better than you can."

Nod at self. It's not as if the river is freezing, either.

Still.

"Jesus, he's been under forever."

Eyes, scanning, scanning.

Then I realize the boat is drifting. Drifting with no oars. Gifts I might have, but they didn't include moving things with my mind.

"Shit. A really long time..."

He is a thrill seeker. Fuck the boat drifting; Travis is a thrill seeker.

I toed off my shoes and starting skinning out of my shirt.

"Going somewhere, mate?"

Whirling around, I nearly fell on my ass. Or worse, actually.

He was looking at me from the other side of the boat, hands already pulling him up and on the way in.

"Jesus," I said. "You nearly sent me over the side yourself. Fuck. A little warning, dude, a little warning."

He was chuckling as he got his entire 6'2" frame in the dinghy. "Were you going to save me?" he asked. "How sweet."

Waving him off, I sat and proceeded to put my shoes back on my feet.

"I don't need air like you do," Travis confirmed for my spazz of a brain. "For future reference."

"Yeah. Figured that out, thanks. I was being stupid."

"Really. Your concern is touching. But don't go drowning yourself on my account, mate. This river has some gnarly currents."

Nod.

His expression lost its amusement, then. "I found something."

This brought me to my now shoe clad feet. Probably should try sitting still in the small boat, but I was too anxious. Good thing I was used to boats.

"A large bag," he continued. "Maybe like one of those army issue duffels." Beat. "Weighted down with a small anchor."

"Oh God."

273

"There's abso-bloody-lutely a body in it." Beat. "Pieces, packed in what's basically compost."

Hand going through my hair. Myra suddenly back in my head.

"Jesus, Travis. It's her. She's telling me it's her. You *found* her!"

Christ, Billy. You strangled her and *cut* her up in the back of a van. Jesus. As appalling as that was, the thought I was lucky he'd left me alive did even stranger things to my stomach.

I then realized Travis was asking me something.

"Huh?"

"Should we report it?" he asked. "Will this put her to rest?"

"How would we explain it?" I said.

"Anonymous tip?"

"It'd have to be. But then it could take them forever to find her without an exact location."

"Your call, Trey. Do we phone in the precise location?"

"Of a body dumped four years ago?" Head shake. "Suspicious sounding. So many new ways to track calls, now. And at least one person will say they saw us out here. There's always one if you look hard enough. If they look that hard, that is." My brain raced through possible scenarios, while Myra remained eerily silent.

"I reckoned this might be a problem," Travis said. "So I've an idea."

And he silently dove back into the East River.

It wasn't quite forever this time before he reappeared, and as soon as he broke water, he said:

"I freed her from the anchor. It — she can drift. We could likely still phone in a tip later and maybe she'll be easier to find. Or maybe someone else will see her and do it for us. Is this right with her? I'll put her back if not."

As if hearing him, Myra said yes. In my head.

If.

If she could confront Billy, too, she said. That's what she really wanted, she said.

Things she never got to say to him, things she wanted to say to him.

Nod to Travis. "She's fine with it."

I told Myra she'd have to wait. Not just yet, Myra. Not just yet.

Soon, maybe. Soon, I said.

Then she told me about Sandra –

And then I *met* Sandra.

Chapter 20

SEPTEMBER 7

Trey
New York

Geoff was whipping something up on Scott's kitchen. Scott and I, we were sitting on his sofa, where I finished explaining what had still been a bit too much for me to explain last night. How I'd not only fully witnessed Myra's death, but nearly been in her shoes. Hers and Sandra's, because Sandra was desperate to get her story out as well, and while I shuddered with it in that little boat, Travis had held me firm to let me know I was safe. Because of him and Geoff, I wasn't overwhelmed that time, though I wouldn't soon forget the visual, her screams, her struggle.

Billy was quite fond of heavy fishing line, which he kept in the back of the dark blue van he sometimes towed his boat with. Fortunately for me, maybe, he hadn't been much of a fisherman back when he attacked me on that football field.

Or maybe he had just forgotten to bring his fishing tackle with him.

He'd taken Myra out the night of her murder, taken her out in that van, making several side trips between the restaurant and the river, at one point convincing her they should go parking. It'd be just like high school, he'd said. Capture that feeling of sneaking off, breaking curfew, and risking discovery. Oh yeah, the good old days.

Instead of groping and fogging up windows, though, he'd strangled her, beat her, chopped her, stuffed her in a bag of trash and dirt, and taken that bag out in his boat, which, lucky for him, was already at the dock, all gassed up and ready to go.

The van was trashed short days later. A person can get away with a lot when they have money and connections.

Sandra didn't have it much better. Just one year before he met Myra, Billy had strangled Sandra in a cheap motel somewhere off I-87. Face down in pillows, suffocated in all directions, her neck snapped just before she completely blacked out.

Seriously, thank God for Geoff and Travis, because face down – well, I'd started tasting grass, because it was much too similar. He didn't just choke her face down; he choked her face down while taking her from behind.

Much, much too familiar.

He dumped Sandra in a lake. I couldn't quite see which one, yet, but she didn't seem to care too much about that, which was probably why. She wanted what Myra wanted.

To confront Billy.

If I'd been thinking of revenge, the tables had turned. Now I had someone to *avenge*.

Precisely when and where, I had yet to decide. When, where, *how*.

"Jesus, Trey," said Scott. "He's a killer. You're doing business with a killer."

"I'm doing business with Blake."

"And his serial killing, rapist lawyer. They might not even be the only ones, fuck." His hand lifted, coming to the back of my head. "Jesus. To think it could've been your body he dumped."

"But it wasn't," I reminded myself as much as Scott.

His hand dropped, drifted back to his knee. "What're you going to do? How do we get him locked up?"

I leaned back into the sofa cushions. "Don't count on him being locked up. I'm not."

He just gave me a questioning look.

"One vampire already wanted to kill Billy the moment he understood who he was. There'll be two more when they find out, if Billy's still alive when they find out, anyway."

"Travis very angry," Geoff commented through the butler.

"Travis? Is he gonna off him?" Scott asked.

"Yeah, and I can't stop him." My eyes met his. "He's got a real dark side you haven't met. I talked him out of it once, at the first meeting with Blake and Billy. I don't think I'll be so lucky a second time."

"Well." His eyes dropped to his hands. "Will you think less of me if I say who cares? Let him have at it."

"Don't blame you for feeling that way."

His elbows went to his knees. "Eye for an eye. I know it's not right. What's that saying? Eye for an eye, and eventually the entire world will go blind. But…just once in a while, maybe it is right."

"I'm not gonna cry over him, that's for sure. If they kill him, then it's just his time." I stretched my legs out. "I've got to see him first, though. Meeting or no meeting, I've got to see him, for Sandra and Myra."

"So they rest peacefully," Geoff said.

Scott nodded, then said to me, "So, they'll talk through you? Talk to him that way, or something?"

"They can if I let them. They'll see him and hear him, too. They don't have to take me over like Adele, before you ask."

"Okay, okay, I got it. Can't help worrying though, y'know? Anyway, do they just want to have the last word?"

"I don't know. I feel like they want more than that." I stopped studying the wall of photos and looked at him. "One thing I know for sure is I can fuck with him after he's dead."

"You can?"

Nod.

"Put him through hell, make like Satan? In a manner of speaking, 'course."

Another nod.

"You really are a spooky fuck. Remind me not to piss you off in this life."

Smile. "I don't think we have to worry about you making my shit list."

"That's a relief."

My cell vibrated against my thigh. After digging it out of my pocket, I checked the number. "Huh. Don't know who this is. Hang on. Hello?"

"Hello du Bois."

Blood, chilled.

"Brantley."

Scott stiffened.

"Blake wants another meeting," he said in a pissy ass way.

All right. I can do cold-blooded. We're on the phone. Yes, I can do this.

"How much did it hurt to say that just now," you murdering bastard. A glance showed me Geoff's wide-eyed stare from the kitchen.

"You haven't won yet," said Billy.

"What's your stake in this anyway, bub? You're taking this very personally. Another company offering you a closing fee?" you sick fuck.

"I'm concerned that this deal isn't in my client's best interests. Our job is to protect the client's interest, after all, isn't it?"

"Some of us are in it for that. You don't strike me as one of *us*. Either that or you wouldn't know a good deal if it dropped its pants and screamed fuck me, fuck me now."

Geoff's hand went to his mouth.

"What about you, du Bois? You're certainly pushing this deal, hard and fast as you can."

If my sexual reference had triggered anything in his memory, I couldn't hear it in his voice. No, he was merely giving half as good as he got. He gave nothing away, damn it.

"Allow me to elegantly retort: *duh*, Brantley. My clients pay me for that. It's in their best interest."

A few second's silence, which I took advantage of.

"Couldn't find a single flaw in my paperwork, could you?" I taunted. "God, that must've chapped your ass," you pansy-ass waste of skin.

He had no retort. The tension was palpable on the line, however. "We meet at the same location in two hours."

"No. We meet at 8:30 tonight, you – " careful there, Trey. Blood's starting to boil. "You got it?"

"You're not calling the shots here, du Bois. Two hours, or forget it."

"I seriously doubt you're calling the shots either, Billy. I'll phone Blake and set up my own meeting. He doesn't need your help to finish this deal. I'm guessing the board jumped at the offer, no need for him to toss his weight around."

"Someone needs taken down a few notches, and it isn't me."

"Because you've already been knocked down. After all, you're calling me, aren't you? A secretary set things up with Mr. Starke last time. Been demoted, have you?"

"Listen here…"

I listened, but what I heard was someone in the background. Possibly Blake himself.

"I'll speak to you at eight-thirty, du Bois."

My blood had turned to lava. "Yeah, see you at eight-thirty, Brantley." I snapped the phone shut.

Geoff nodded at me and resumed playing chef.

"Well," I looked at Scott, trying not to grit my teeth. "Guess I know the when and where."

He blew out the breath he must've been holding. "Do you need to take him someplace? What about the other guy, the boss?"

"Travis'll help me figure something out. All I know is, it's my last chance this trip."

"Why?"

"Michel wants me back in Paris soon as possible."

"You sure you've told me everything?"

I laid a hand on his arm. "He just wants me home. Really, I think he just wants to see me there when he returns."

"You heard from him since that last call?"

Head shake. "And Travis didn't say if he'd heard from them, either."

"Still worried?"

I let out my own breath. "Yup." I got up, needing to stretch, move, think. "Never a dull moment in Trey-land."

"Apparently not. Well, anyway, I'll keep Geoff company while you're at the meeting."

"Cool, thanks."

"No sweat. I like your man."

"I like you too," Geoff called out.

"Trey, you're making me nervous. Sit still. Or at least stand still."

"Sorry, I can't seem to." My hand went through my hair as I caught his gaze.

"Never seen you pace like that."

281

That slowed me down.

"Sometimes you were twitchy," he continued, "but not spastic like now, not that I remember."

My feet stopped moving. "I just can't help it. Don't know why."

He gazed at me quietly a second then said, "So have you talked to Polly since you've been here?"

"No."

"Don't you think you should? She might be worried."

I pulled my cell out again. "Yeah, well, she hasn't called me."

"Maybe she's been busy."

"Maybe. Or maybe nothing's made her alarm bells go off, which, actually, is comforting."

"There, see, something positive. Maybe talking to her would do you some good, though. She might even be waiting for you to call." He lifted a brow.

I wondered if he knew how on the money his last remark was. She often let me figure things out for myself. Encouraged it. But she still wanted me to ask for help when I needed it. Something I was learning how to do.

Nodding at him, I dialed. "Wait, what time is it – "

"Hello, handsome."

"Hi, beautiful."

"How are things going?"

"Oh, parts are okay. Others are like a bad acid trip."

"Tell me all about it, sugar."

So I did, while Scott and Geoff listened in.

"So yeah," I finished. "The last thing I'd want to face, the bridge *and* Billy in one night."

I'd left out the part about Billy being a rapist. Scott was the only one I'd ever *told*. Geoff had sensed it, and I'd confirmed it, and Michel – Michel probably knew it when he met me. Maybe P.K. had her own ideas, too, but I wasn't getting into it on the phone, so I'd told her that he and I had fights in school, that I hated his guts, and now I'd found out he was a killer.

282

"I honestly hate being right, sometimes," she said after I finished. "But, it sounds like you're handling it. Being right about that makes me a happy girl."

"We like you happy. So what about these women? Any advice on how I go about this?"

"Advice? Not exactly. I think you'll know what to do when the time arrives, and before you ask, you'll know when it's time."

"Well, then. Your vote of confidence is appreciated."

"Sorry I don't have more, handsome."

"No really. Hearing you say that helps. Besides, it's basically what Lucien says, so that's two votes."

The smile was in her tone. "You're welcome."

"Do me another favor?"

"If I can."

"Talk to Scott. I told him," just about, "everything. He may need a vote of confidence, too."

Scott rolled his eyes, then said, "Whatever, but I'll talk to her all the same," while in my ear P.K. said, "Hand me over to him; I'll set him straight. Oh, but first: try not to worry about Michel. I believe he can handle it, too."

I hadn't said I was worried. I hadn't even said much about Spain, since there wasn't much for me to say.

"Thanks, P.K. Here's Scott." After handing him the phone, I made my way to the kitchen to distract myself with Geoff and his food.

Michel
Madrid

We arrived at the private airstrip. Gabriel, choosing to remain in the Jaguar with Kar, left me to escort Elise to her jet, if I so wished. There were yet thoughts unspoken between us, thoughts plaguing me ever more since our previous night's discussion, concerning our business venture.

Or perhaps he left me to it merely because he sensed within me a simple need to spend further moments with Elise. He sensed what I was yet coming to terms with – how much I truly missed her – and that spending time with her had brought sharply to me just how little I could honestly blame her for the past, in the end.

Along we walked, the two of us. Catching her in my peripheral, I could see that so badly did a smile wish to form, her lips twitched.

"It was nice to see the two of you, whatever the circumstance," said she.

"*Oui*, Elise, *oui*."

Her mouth chanced the smile, small as it was, after I spoke. Repeatedly my eyes moved over her face, before at last I offered a few more words.

"I'm glad you came, and not merely because I asked you to."

Her smiled broadened, if briefly. "I doubt Gabriel feels the same way, but that's all right. I understand. I'm sure he's still suspicious of my motives."

"I don't know." I paused. "I think he believes you and is yet coming to terms with it."

Her response to this was a widening of her eyes, swiftly followed by an averted gaze.

"You were attempting to help us with our quest. You really were."

She looked me directly in the eyes as she replied. "Yes. I still regret that I come to you empty handed."

"Not so empty handed," were my soft words.

"What do you mean?"

My lashes lowering, I inhaled slowly, shaking my head. Releasing this breath, my words came on a sigh. "Your heart was in the right place."

Soft was her reply. "Then you believe me as well."

My answer for this was a slight nod, and once again, I found her gaze. "I'll tell you something else. I do miss the way we were. Before. Long before."

One of her hands drifted towards my face, yet stopped just shy of touching it. "So do I," she whispered. "Such good friends, good siblings."

My own hand did not hesitate. Gently, I ran the back of it across her satin cheek as I ceased walking. Closing the distance, she embraced me, and this time her whisper caressed my ear.

"I still love you, Michel. I always will."

"God help me, I believe I might love you as well."

Whisper soft, the caress of her laugh.

Making to step back, I recaptured her gaze in mine. "Elise, I can't say I'll ever forget what you did. I can't say at this moment I forgive everything. Yet, I think I can forgive your reasoning."

She searched and searched my eyes, hoping to see the truth of my statement.

"Yes. I think even in this, your heart was in the right place," I said.

Her lashes made to flutter, and a swift kiss she placed on my lips. After this, she turned and hastened toward the jet. Fleeing, just as I'd fled her home with too much to feel. My eyes tracked her movement up the steps, and when she paused at the top, she turned.

I blew her a kiss and then mouthed the next words, knowing quite well she would easily read them from my lips.

"I love you, my Gemini woman. I forgive where your heart led you."

Within me, a certain tension loosened. Perhaps in taking this step, I'd be better able to forgive myself.

Just before she turned to go inside, I saw the flash of her smile that could not decide where to settle in her emotion, and the one perfect tear, which had escaped to paint her delicate cheek.

See you soon, Prince.

I stood and watched as the jet taxied down the runway, watched as it gathered speed and wheels left pavement. I watched, even, its ascent.

When at last I turned, a sharp pop felt to issue in my chest. Not half a second later, as I whirled back in the direction of the runway, the dark sky blossomed in bright flames after a monstrous explosion of sound that shattered the still night air.

Or – perhaps the events were simultaneous, but I could no longer think clearly as I stood, stunned, of a sudden not trusting my senses, uncertain of what they were telling me. Uncertain and afraid of the great yawning hole that felt to be spreading in my chest, a yawning absence, an absolute silence.

Impossible, my mind railed. Impossible that my eyes were seeing what they were seeing. Impossible that my ears heard what they heard.

Impossible, the utter loss filling me, threatening to consume a deep part of myself.

Gabriel

Sounds assailed my ears, sounds I did not consciously separate as I found myself leaping from the vehicle, Kar soon following. Visions assaulted me, cataloguing themselves, but the only one I found sharp focus on was that of Michel, falling to his knees, his hands clutching at his chest.

Immediately I sprinted in his direction and jumped the fence, the scent of smoke, petrol, hot metal, seeming to fill my nostrils. Briefly I feared that he had been harmed, but swiftly he rose, a piteous wail leaving him, and it was then I accessed all of my speed to catch him up as the firework of sky registered in my brain.

"Michel, no!"

He was making for the runway and he was about to take flight.

"Michel!" I lunged at him just as his feet left pavement, and lifted I was, wind rushing past, for my arms were tightly about his legs. "Michel, there's nothing to be done now!"

Onward he rose, seemingly deaf to my pleas, and the singular thought of stopping him loomed bright, insistent in my mind, in my being. Exerting all of my will, I focused on the ground; I focused on going down, diving down, holding him as firmly as I was able.

Our bodies struck pavement; a struggle ensued; we rolled about on the ground, he in his sudden grief, which washed through me even now, as he desperately, blindly attempted to get away.

I knew that I could not hold him, not for long. I knew that I had been lucky to pluck him from the air, so very lucky.

"Michel, please, *attendre!* It's too late."

"No!" His fractured cry felt nearly to shatter my eardrums, it seemed. "*Non, non non non!*"

Gathering all of my strength, I held him to me. "Michel, please. *Regarde-moi.*" My heart was breaking, breaking for him; I could not bear to see him this way. "She's gone, my sweet. *Je suis désolé,* but she is gone."

His face, awash in the red of his tears, turned at last towards mine. "Oh God, I can feel it; she's gone, you're right." His chest heaved, and one of his hands sought to insinuate itself between us, to grasp the place over his heart. "Oh dear God, she's gone."

Kar's voice reached me through Michel's tortured cries. "My Lords. Forgive me, but we cannot remain."

"Michel," I cooed. "I'm sorry, my love. I'm sorry. Please, come away with me now."

"She's gone," he cried yet again.

"Oh, my sweet. Let me help you, let me take you away from this place of death."

"Pain, the pain," he said, this pain not physical, and he then became akin to a wet rag in my arms, the strength of his emotion overpowering him and alarming me.

"*Mon lion? Mon lion?*"

"Forgive my haste," said Kar. "We must take him away from here; we all must be away before authorities reach us. You and Michel are in no state to deal with them and questions regarding a bomb. I've taken care of the two guards, but more will come. There is movement in the building."

"A bomb?" was my absent reply. I was then vaguely aware of Kar reaching for me. "Away, yes. Away we must."

Rising with Michel in my arms, I followed Kar on instinct only, Michel's anguish flooding me and his red-streaked face flooding my vision; his grief-stricken murmurs babbled like a busy brook in my ears.

"My love," I whispered, tears for him now leaking from my eyes. "Oh, my love, I'm sorry. I'm so sorry *mon ange d'ors.*"

Chapter 21

Trey

Travis, next to me in the cab. Manhattan Bridge this time, on our way to the meeting. The last meeting, I hoped.

"You need to get him alone, then." Beat. "It's good something will be accomplished aside from the deal, what with no computers for me to mess with."

I said, "I'm not sure exactly what to do or what's gonna happen, but I don't know when I'll have another chance. Michel wants us back soon as we're done."

Nod from him. "I know. Likely he'd understand if you needed more time."

"Yeah, but – he sounded tense when I talked to him." More than tense. Upset, tired, anxious, and a bunch of other things.

"Kar said they're returning to Paris tonight."

"Then I really wanna get back there, because I think he needs us. He just didn't sound right, at least not to me."

His eyes stayed forward. "Something else Kar said."

"You're worried too, aren't you?"

"Yes."

"Do you know something I don't about Spain?" I leaned closer. "Something you can tell me?"

Head shake from him. "I don't think that I know much more than you," his gaze flicked to me, "which is a reason I'm worried. Kar was a bit tight lipped last time I spoke to him, said he'd explain when he saw me."

Fantastic. Now I feel just *great* about all that.

"But since I can't do anything about that just now, let's get back to the task at hand." Travis said. "When you've wrapped things in the meeting, give me a call." He tapped his forehead. "I'll get Blake out of your way."

"You're not coming in before then?"

"I don't know if I can control myself," he said low. "I don't know that I can be around Billy for long this time without losing it. I'm already choking on my leash."

Leaning in, speaking just as low. "Do you need one of those purges?"

"It's a cycle just now. It's knowing that he needs to pay. I can't ignore it. My nature can't be denied."

"Aeshma doesn't *like* being denied," I whispered.

Firm head shake from him.

"I risked my ass stopping him – I mean you – before, didn't I?"

"I reckon you did. The urge to fling you across the room hit me once or twice, but I knew you." He patted my shoulder. "It could've been worse."

"Worse. Even though I was the one you were protecting. Sort of. Wanting to avenge, that's the word."

"It's not a mood I can easily switch off. Not until vengeance is mine." He looked me hard in the eye. "It's just biding time inside me until I have it. The longer it takes, the less conscious I am of who's in my way." Beat. "Once on the rampage, I have complete tunnel vision, you might say."

"I'll make note of that. And I vote we change the subject now, okay?" I moved back.

"I've got another one," he said. "When we started out on the river, I was short with you." His gaze swung to me. "I'd like to apologize for that."

"Oh." Light shrug. "No big. You gave me lots of help."

"I know it stung, Trey."

"Yeah, well. You just said you were on a short leash, in a tense mood. I understand."

He shook his head. "That wasn't it, really. After you called, I..." he paused. "It set me to thinking about Keegan. He was still on my mind when I got there."

Keegan. His brother. I debated my next words. Decided to go with them this time. "I had the sense you wanted to ask me something about him before."

He gazed at me a minute then said, "I considered asking if you could contact him."

Just as I'd thought. "I could try."

His head started shaking. "I'm...no. Not just yet."

"Travis?" I shifted sideways in my seat to see him better.

"Hmm?"

"Were you thinking about what happened to him?" I quietly asked.

He looked out the window.

"You don't want to talk about it. That's okay. Pretend I didn't ask."

"We were in Perth," he said after a minute. "Family trip. He wanted to surf. I'd been teaching him."

He spoke so softly; my ears strained for his words.

"The sea kicked up, tossed him and rolled him under. I swam as hard and fast as I could. It felt like forever."

I could barely see his profile for the way he turned his head.

"I finally found him, got him to the beach." He looked down at his hands, which were clenching when I glanced at them. "I couldn't bring him back. It was too late."

291

I wanted to say something, anything to comfort him, but I wasn't confident he could be, or even wanted to be.

"Seven years old." His eyes found my face. "He was seven years old." His gaze returned to his hands. "I was nearly fifteen and an excellent swimmer, but helpless that day. Powerless." I could see the muscle in his jaw tensing, streetlights illuminating him. "After that day I never wanted to feel powerless again."

Epiphany. "That's why you said yes to Clarice. Why you wanted to be a vampire."

His eyes sped to me. "Obvious, ay?" He nodded slightly. "It was high on the list of reasons."

"I'm so sorry, Travis."

Another, smaller nod and a watery look to his eyes. "So am I. I helped raise him, you know. I was supposed to take care of him out there. I always told him I'd never let anything happen to him. Promised Mom I'd – "

"Travis…" Reaching, I touched one of his hands. "You didn't *let* it happen. You did everything you could. I'm sure your parents knew that. I'm sure Keegan knows, too."

He laid his other hand over mine.

We rode the rest of the way in silence.

Gabriel
Madrid

"It's been thoroughly checked, my Lord."

With an inclination of my head to Kar, I led Michel towards our jet. He was calmer in one sense than short hours before, yet this was not saying much, as he oscillated between anger and sorrow, unable to focus on one subject long enough to truly gain a foothold with his thoughts, though at the very least he was speaking. He had not uttered a word for several hours previously, and where he had been limp and listless before, his energy was now kinetic.

"Who," said he. "Who would dare? When I find out, there will be no quarter given."

My arm slipped about his waist as we walked.

"Gabriel, it's so empty." This piteous comment left him as his hand drifted to his chest.

I drew him closer to my side. "I know, my love. I wish that it were not so."

"No, you hated her," he stated, his voice gone quite flat, and he removed himself from my side. "You have pity for her now that she's dead, do you?"

Knowing very well this was no true personal attack, that the harshness now creeping into his tone was everything to do with his being distraught, I remained calm as he stared me down, expecting some manner of reply.

"True, it is your pain that I am the most sorry for. But you must also know that only because I once loved her, could I ever have hated her, Michel."

He merely gazed upon me a moment longer, before his attention shifted to our emissary. "You're investigating, yes Kar?"

"Yes, my Prince. Also, Emanuel is tidying up the situation at the airstrip, sir." This Kar said with a delicacy of tone.

"Good man," my Michel replied quite softly. Then, with more force, "What of Ricco? Has he met his demise, yet?"

"He yet lives, sir."

"Why? Has his luck so improved?"

For this Kar had no reply, and Michel's eyes sped to me.

"I do not know, my love," said I. It seemed best not to mention Lucas Demetrius, unless he did so himself, particularly as there was no new intelligence on the man.

He ascended the steps ahead of me. "If someone doesn't beat me to it, I'll kill him myself at a later date."

"Diego is quite dead, *mon lion*," I offered, thinking that this would please him.

Both of his hands he waved. "*Bien*, yes, fine." He made an abrupt halt. "No. *Merde!*"

"My love?"

"Lucas and Diego were trafficking in weapons, explosives, so Ricco said. *Merde.* I can't question a dead man."

"There is yet Lucas, my love."

Once more, he began to move, waving his hands with his words. "*Oui, oui.* The shadow known as Lucas. I cannot question a shadow, either." His hands then accosted his hair in a way suggesting they might rip it from his scalp. "Damn it, I set her on that jet." His hands dropping, his hair intact, he resumed his ascent.

I followed him up the stairs and ducked into the cabin. "We make for Paris, *oui* Michel? You have not changed your mind, have you?"

Silence greeted me as he took to pacing up and down the very short corridor. Glancing at Kar, I bid him to ready for takeoff, our destination being Paris. After he took his place in the pilot's seat, Michel and I were left to our own devices.

"*Mon lion*, sit with me," I pleaded as I settled into my seat.

His pacing did not cease. "Vicont, I must see Vicont."

"He has yet to reply, my sweet."

"If he had anything to do with her death I'll – I shall – "

So suddenly did he stop, I nearly rose to capture him in my arms.

"She's dead." His eyes, shimmering, found mine. "Dear God, she's actually dead."

In lieu of words, I offered companionable silence.

Yet again, he commenced pacing. "What am I doing, what *was* I doing, and what was I thinking? I can't best him, I never could." His arms wound tightly about his own waist as he continued his circuit. "She was right. She was right."

"She believed in you, Michel."

"This isn't what I mean." He came to a halt, bringing his eyes to my face.

"You may be impetuous, my love, but – "

"*Non.* That I'm giving up. I give up, Gabriel." Of a sudden, he came to his knees in front of me. "I can't take this any longer. I don't know what I'm doing any more." He gestured about his head. "It's a mess in my head, all confused. *Tout.*"

Both of my hands found his face.

"I can't do it, Gabriel."

"Then don't, Michel."

Deeply his eyes searched mine. Several moments passed between us with only the buzz and hum of the jet, its engines, to fill the silence. When he chose at last to add his voice to these other sounds, I was briefly startled; I was startled not for his swift turn of subject, but because of what he said.

"I had to punish myself. That's a reason I did it, Gabriel. A very compelling reason."

I had no need of asking to what he referred.

"I'd been so wrong, caused so much pain," he continued. "And I couldn't even hate her properly, as much as I wished to. I couldn't hate her, because it wasn't truly her fault. No matter what you say, have said, I did it. I made the choice. I didn't deserve your forgiveness, as much as I wanted it, and I knew it. I *knew* it, Gabriel."

My single word reply scarce found volume. "Michel."

He came up and forward, his hands reaching to grasp my shoulders. "Oh yes, there was pain, pain I intended to slice from my person, but it was all of my making and I deserved this as well. I rose to the occasion when an argument reared its head between us, because I wanted you to slap me, cut me, anything." He shook me with his next words. "I needed you to hurt me more than I hurt you."

My hands found the back of his neck and pulled him to me, our brows meeting.

"I know this as much as everything else made it more difficult for you," he whispered. "Caused more time to pass before you forgave me, and I'm sorry for that." Gently, he pushed me back so that he might meet my gaze. "I'm sorry for this, as well, but... I need you to retract a statement. Speak truly to me."

"*Quoi? Je ne te comprends pas.*"

"Say that I betrayed you."

"Michel – "

"I know you said I didn't in my heart, but something of my heart must also have betrayed you – or us, as you like."

Holding his gaze, I was yet uncertain how best to respond. Here, now, I had answers to the questions my mind had not released, but to hear his reasoning made my heart wish to shrink, to shrivel, it wished to rail at my brain for its incessant need for details.

"Surely you've thought it in the time since. Surely you've been far too generous with me," he said then.

"This is highly reminiscent of Trey," were the next words that sprang to my lips. "Why are you so insistent on punishing yourself even now?"

"It isn't about punishment now, Gabriel, I swear. Tell me you haven't thought it. I doubt you can."

"I couldn't live without you, Michel. I – "

"Gabriel, *please*."

The way he spoke these words stayed my own.

"Gabriel. I've realized I can't forgive myself completely if you don't agree that I betrayed you. That's why you left, because of the choice I made."

My gaze fell and my lashes dropped. My reply was slow to come.

"Gabriel?"

Deeply did I inhale. If he were strong enough to hear it, certainly I could find the strength to say it, to answer this need within him, as so often he answered mine. Certainly, I could not continue to belittle the subject, or him, by avoiding the question.

"Yes. I thought it then, as you know, and have thought it since we reconciled." I lifted my eyes, mustering the will to speak as truthfully as he needed me to. "You knew better, should have known, but you betrayed our *love*."

His brows made to crease, though his eyes did not once waver from mine.

"Your heart betrayed mine, it's true," I said. "Yet still, I forgive you. Even you make mistakes."

He near choked on his sharp inhale.

"I know that you'll never again betray me, Michel. It's one of the many reasons I returned to you."

"*Merci*," he said as he drew me into his arms. "*Merci, mon amour. Merci.*"

Trey
New York

Right then, Death Dancer. I have this.

Travis showed up shortly after my 'mental call', just as he'd promised. He'd skipped the entire meeting itself, making the perfectly good excuse of needing to conduct some other fast business. I'd called him almost immediately after sealing the deal, feeling a bit claustrophobic, too much in my head as well as the meeting room.

Blake stepped out of the office with my vampire bodyguard, Travis having lured him with suggestions for proper security and offering a walking tour, which was better for demonstrating his points, as he'd told Blake – but I think the power of vampire *suggestion* had the most influence. In the meantime I gathered up my files, proud of my victories (regardless of everything else) both in the signed contract, and stomaching another meeting with Billy, even keeping relatively cool while two dead women went on in my head, so close to their murderer they could taste it.

But I was definitely disconcerted. Facing Billy, knowing he was even worse than I'd already thought, was one of the hardest things I'd ever done. Doing my best to ignore the person still in the room until I sorted myself, I stuffed my files into my briefcase and snapped it shut. Touched the charm in my pocket for the tenth time or so, thinking *now what*? You're alone with him; he still doesn't know who you are or is pretending not to, so now what? Where do you begin, Trey? Myra and Sandra want their chance with him; you want to find your own peace, so –

Suddenly I felt him. Standing close, right there behind me.

"Not quite as scrawny, but I bet you're still just as queer," he whispered in my ear. "You think you've won, but I still have access to the board members."

I froze. Several desires hit me, but I froze.

Wanted to deck him. Wanted to choke out a cry. Wanted to scream in his face, to kick him in the balls. To faint or throw up or both. To strangle him with fishing line and dump him in a river. But that might have been the girls' influence.

The idea of calling Travis back, letting Aeshma rip him apart right here, right now, was all mine, however.

Billy's low laugh tripped a wire. His words snapped it.

"Still scared of me, aren't you. Which is another reason I'll win in the end, *Trey*."

I slowly turned, but didn't yell. Faced him, but didn't deck him. Didn't even shove him out of the way.

No. I spoke calmly; it was as if some new drug made of cold calculation rushed through my veins. Who injected it, where it came from, I wasn't certain at first, it was so sudden.

"No, I'm not," I said. "I'd bet my life that you still *want* me, however."

A cool smile found me when he didn't respond.

"You want to kiss me, right now. You know you do," I continued, and in fact, reclaimed the space his step back had created between us. "You've wanted me since the first moment I walked back into your life."

He managed a laugh. "You're delusional. That big brain of yours must have snapped that night."

"Hmm. You're right." Nod. "You never *stopped* wanting me." I ran a finger over his lapel. "You probably jack off every time you think of that night in my bedroom." My face, close to his. "Every time you think of me – "

"Fuck you," he whispered.

"Exactly." Sultry smile. "I'm certain the football field is your favorite fantasy. You, in my place, me, the rapist."

He shivered, then shoved me back. "You really have lost your mind."

I laughed. "How many others have there been, Billy boy?" I advanced, which forced him to move back. "How many that you imagined with my face, my body?" He continued to retreat in the face of my advancement. "How many, while you keep desperately pretending you aren't what you are, that you don't get off on it, huh?"

He backed into the long table on the right wall, my unexpected reactions disconcerting him. "I don't know what you're talking about, du Bois."

"Sure you do!" Another laugh. "I've realized why you did it to me, see. I get it, now."

"You don't get anything – "

"Queer boy," I said for him. "If I am, so are you, sweetheart, so are you." I held up a hand. "Let me guess. Fuck you. Right Billy? You always did have *such* a full vocabulary. I bet your father pulled a lot of strings getting you through law school."

I could feel the heat coming off him, but it wasn't merely anger. Some part of him was getting off on this, all right, even as it confused him, what I was doing.

"Go ahead, gloat over your victory, but this won't be the last time we dance, boy," he said.

Which I ignored.

"So let me tell you why you did it, Billy." My hands smoothed the front of his suit jacket. "It wasn't *really* because you thought I'd told your secret. It's because I wasn't *yours*. You. Couldn't. Have. Me. Or *keep* me – this is more precise."

He laughed in my face, but it wasn't very convincing. "All right, go ahead; bore me with more of your pathetic diatribe, if you must. It's providing great comedic potential for later."

That didn't divert me, either.

"Your father would've killed you. The reputation you had would've died. And you were in big time denial." A breath away from his lips. "So you soiled the one thing you couldn't have, tried to own it the only way you could, hoping no one else could touch it then."

"Delusional…" his word came on a breathy exhale.

What's wrong, Billy. The opposite of boring?

"I don't think so," I said. "Of course, you also did it because you're a violent asshole who likes to exert his power, like most rapists. Then there's the fact you were trying to prove to yourself you were still a man, in your own sick way. Well adjusted people don't do such things, Billy."

He grabbed my lapels, yanked me forward, snarled "Get out of my face, fag," and shoved me harder than before, somewhat proving my point.

My feet ate up the distance again, arms flung out from my sides.

"Here I am, Billy, all grown up. You still want me. Go on, admit it. Maybe I've forgiven you." Closer, voice dipping. "Maybe I liked it. Maybe I've wanted you all these years. You never called after you left me there. Why didn't you call me, baby?"

That drug must have been working full tilt, because when it seemed he would kiss me, further backing up my words to him, I didn't revolt.

I didn't even move.

In fact, it pleased me immensely, on a very sinister note. I was *getting* to him. I was in *control*. I had him just where I wanted him.

This. This is what I *needed*. I didn't need him dead, putting him in his place was too satisfying – and now it was time to become the avenging angel, to pacify all interested parties.

"How's Myra, by the way?" my lips asked his.

His head jerked back from my words as if I'd slapped him.

"You dated her about four years ago, right?"

Another slap.

"I'm thinking it didn't end well, Billy."

The mysterious drug in my veins, it connected to the Dead as well as my own dark side, certainly. Their need, their desire. The terrible whisperings and visions of terrible things, from two who wanted their own vengeance, their own last words, their own satisfaction.

This was a win win situation.

Silently, I thanked those on the Other Side, and told them that yes, now. Now we could do it. Right *now*.

"I don't know what you're – "

"Yes, you do," I interjected. "Why, just look at that. You're starting to sweat." I touched a finger to his face. "Getting a little warm for different reasons now, eh?"

His jaw went slack as he gaped at my eyes. I would have bet they were changing.

"Myra, Myra. She wasn't the first – Sandra was – but right now she's first in line," I said. "One of the women you used in your attempts to be something else. But it never worked, did it. Nope, it never worked, so who did you punish? Them, Billy. Them. How did it feel, making the final leap to *murdering* rapist?"

His head shook and shook.

"Oh, you can tell me, baby. No one else is listening. Well. No one you can see, anyway."

Yet.

He tried backing up, but the table prevented it. "You're flipping psycho, Trey. Get away from me or I'll call security."

"What security, sweetheart? It's just you and me here."

"I'll call the police."

"Aww. Are you scared?"

He tried stepping around me.

"Gonna scream for me, Billy?" Grabbing his shoulders. "Come on, *scream*. I'd love to hear you scream, and I'd *love* to hear you explain to your associate *why*."

He finally gave up, gave in to his bafflement. "How do you know their names? How do you know! I haven't seen you since – "

"You raped me." I laid a finger over his lips. "Shhh, shh, shh. I'll tell you, I will. We both will."

He batted my hand away. "What the fuck are you talking about?"

From her ghostly lips to my solid mouth. "I thought you loved me. You were such a good actor."

He stared at me, wide eyed. Even I could hear the change in my voice.

"You told me we'd go away together. To Bali, first. Forget your father, you said. It doesn't matter what he thinks, you said. I love you, Myra, that's what you said, right before you strangled me. *While* you strangled me."

Billy muttered unintelligibly.

"You're trembling, Billy," I said. "Who's scared of whom, now?"

"What the fuck is this?" he stammered. "Where are you getting this bullshit?"

She and I smiled. "From Myra, of course. No one else was there when you killed her; how else would I know?"

"You're insane, do you know that?"

"No. I'm right."

"Insane. Men in white coats insane."

302

"Repeating it won't make it true, Billy. Tell me; do you miss that blue van?"

He did his best not to react to those words. "Cute trick with the voice." He smoothed his hair, trying to resume control of himself, the situation. "Such a shame, though. You clearly have a problem requiring drugs and shock therapy. I'll call the ambulance on my way out."

When he moved this time, I *did* deck him. His return blow came up a bit short, grazing my left eye.

I decided I must not look like myself at all, judging from the expression on his face when I turned my head back in his direction. Myra's perfume drifted to my nostrils, and I wondered if he could smell it, too, judging by the stunned look in his eyes.

"I'd already given up my life for you, William. But it wasn't enough, was it? You literally took it, all of it, in the end. I was never enough. I kept thinking I must have been stupid, not to see it coming." A laugh. Her laugh. "Love is blind, it really is, I guess. But then who would have thought you were a murderer? Why would I have thought you were a rapist? You're really, really good at keeping secrets, aren't you."

Billy scrambled away from me, making a bid for the office door.

He found my body once again in his way. "They're going to find my remains, William. I can't wait to see what your father will think of you. Of course, he'll no doubt do his best publicly to get you out of it, now won't he? His reputation is so damned important. But privately?" Another laugh. "I wish I could be there for that. Maybe I'll hang around a little longer, just for that."

You'll give me that, won't you, Trey? Is this something I can have?

Yes, Myra. That's the closure you really need after all, isn't it? Before you move on.

Yes...yes, it is. Thank you so much.

Meanwhile, outside my private conversation, Billy was reaching for the tough *I'm in charge* Billy.

"You can't touch me. You don't have any idea what you're talking about; you don't know a damned thing. Go ahead, du Bois, keep threatening. It means nothing. Your attempt at revenge means nothing."

"I know where her remains are Billy. I know where you dumped the pieces."

"Bullshit, and if you even think of going to the police or anyone else, I'll sue you blind."

"They're floating along the East River as we speak, you twisted fuck. No more anchor."

His pupils dilated with fear while he continued to pretend he was in control. "Slander, defamation and anything else I can think of, du Bois."

My fingers found purchase on his lapels, yanked him closer, more roughly than he had me moments before. "In case you hadn't noticed, I'm not exactly worried." Smile. "Let me show you why. Let me show you just how much of a predicament you're in. Just how fucked you are, *sweetheart*."

I dropped the proverbial gate and let them all the way through.

Myra's hands, Sandra's hands, they reached for Billy, caressed him. I could see those hands. Whether he could or not didn't matter.

He felt it. He felt it and he started shaking, regardless of his words. "What's this, some new magic trick, you freak?"

"I suppose you could say that. But wait, it gets better. We haven't gotten to the finale, yet. Why, we haven't even started."

He began to move away, but then Myra and Sandra's voices filled the room. He could hear it; I knew he could, because his face drained of blood.

Myra- "Let's go to Bali, baby. We'll go far away; I'll get us a beautiful house on the beach. What do you say?"

Sandra- "Don't be that way, Sandy. I didn't mean it."

Myra- "It doesn't matter what he says. He doesn't run my life."

Sandra- "C'mon, Sandy, you know I love you. I wouldn't hurt you for anything."

Myra- "I'm not lying, Myra. Damn it, I haven't cheated on you, okay?"

Sandra- "Don't be that way, Sandy. It won't hurt, baby. Do it for me."

Myra- "Go ahead, try to scream."

Sandra- "Shut up, bitch!"

"Stop it!" Billy's hands flew to his ears. "Stop it, stop. Shut up!"

"Go ahead, scream, Billy," I said. "Let's see if anyone helps *you*." It didn't matter if Travis and Blake came back in now. Blake would probably just think Billy had lost his mind and Travis certainly wasn't a worry.

"What the fuck is this?" Billy nearly howled. "What the..."

"Consider it the beginnings of your penance, asshole." Wide smile. "Your sins have caught up to you, and it's time to atone."

Myra and Sandra carried on. I could see them entirely. Judging by the terror that struck Billy's eyes, he could now, too.

"What the – the hell! Get away from me!"

I walked away and pulled out a chair, settling in to admire the scene.

Someone did eventually return. Travis, alone. He took one look at Billy and one look at me –

And then his expression arranged itself into something resembling black delight, to go along with his black eyes. Because by this time, Billy's marbles were starting to bounce on the floor as he desperately tried to shut out Myra and Sandra.

"Where's Blake?" I asked, as if making light conversation.

"Two floors down, making some calls. I could distract him for a while longer, Death Dancer."

"Thank you, Aeshma. That would be lovely."

305

* * * *

"Well. I hate to dash off like this, but I've really got to go."

Billy kept on rocking, a ball in the corner on the floor.

"It was great to see you again." Smile. "I had loads of fun, didn't you?"

Whimper from him.

Sigh. "I understand." I grabbed my briefcase. "Guess I'll see you around."

"What-what...how...what are..." his tear streaked face finally lifted from his hands.

Finger pointing at my chest. "What am I? Is that what you're trying to ask?"

Bloodshot, thoroughly haunted eyes tried to focus on my face.

"Let's see, what am I..." I moved closer, squatted. "The tables have turned, Billy. I'm the purveyor of your worst nightmares." I patted his cheek, and he flinched. "And the worst ones yet to come," I said as I rose. "Because I honestly can't say how much longer you have in this world. Not long, I think." Staring down at him. "And then you're *all mine*."

I made my way across the room and out the door, just in time to pass Mr. Blake in the hall.

"Your security man is top notch, Mr. du Bois." He offered a smile. "Quite a few nice perks go with this deal, I must say."

Knowing there may be a mark by my left eye, I stayed to Blake's right, facing the opposite way. "Yes, he's a great perk."

"I assume you and my lawyer hammered out any remaining details."

"We did at that." I moved a bit closer. "Listen, I'm, well I'm not sure how to put this, but I actually think Mr. Brantley might need some assistance. I was about to call for someone."

"Pardon? Has he taken ill?"

I opted to go for the dramatic, since Billy was in a state. Calling it simple anger over me besting him in the deal wouldn't cut it.

306

"Not exactly, not physically. Mmm, has he had a recent shock or something? Some kind of personal issue?" Blake would have an easier time believing me after he saw his attorney, flimsy as my coming story might sound just now.

His brows tightly drew together. "I don't believe so. Please explain your meaning."

"Ah…well, he lost it on me just now. He's quite emotional. I tried to help, but he backed away as if he were scared of me."

His brows amazed me by managing to merge into one. "Excuse me, but he what?"

I carried on with my act. "Frankly, I'm not quite certain myself what just happened, and I'm a bit rattled, I have to say." Taking a breath for effect. "All I can say is that he started acting very strangely. He insisted I leave, and he seemed angry with me." I faced him fully, deciding any mark on my face was to my advantage. "He tripped when he was backing away, and I think his face hit the table. Being concerned, of course, I tried to help him, but he punched me."

Blake didn't have words for this; he just stared at my eye.

"After that, I definitely thought it was better if I left and called for help, maybe."

"He *hit* you?" He searched for some sense. "I know he was displeased with the meeting and my reprimanding him, but I can't believe he'd confront *you*." His hand came to his chin and he spoke more to himself than me. "I suppose he has been somewhat tense with the company's situation lately."

"Stress sometimes makes us do crazy things, Mr. Blake."

He studied me and studied me.

"Yes, it does," he said at last.

Maybe I could lie just well enough when I really needed to, if there was enough truth to go with it. At least to virtual strangers who were human and not psychic.

"But this…this is unconscionable," he carried on. "I can't believe he hit you, Mr. du Bois. I don't know what to say." He glanced toward the meeting room's door. "Perhaps you should come back inside with me — "

"I don't think that's a good idea," I said, adding a shiver for effect. "Besides, it might set him off again."

"You do appear shaken. I'm terribly sorry, Mr. du Bois."

He was, but he was also wondering if I was going to call the police, maybe sue.

"He didn't hit me that hard; I'm fine. We'll just let it go, because honestly," I leaned in, "I'm thinking nervous breakdown."

Blake was quick to recover, I'd give him that. He flowed into professional mode. "Are you certain? I'd be happy to arrange for a doctor to see you."

Shaking my head. "No really, it's fine. I'm more concerned about Mr. Brantley."

"Yes, well." He glanced at the office door again. "It's definitely troublesome. But if he isn't truly ill, I'll reprimand him quite harshly myself."

"Maybe he just needs a vacation," I said, leaning in again. "We all go a little crazy sometimes."

"You're very generous, Mr. du Bois."

Slight shrug. "Occasionally. But also, this deal's important. A little office rage isn't going to deter me or my employer, so don't worry about that, either. After all, it's not your fault." I glanced down the hall as I heard Travis' voice.

"Sorry to interrupt Mr. du Bois, but we do have a plane to catch."

My eyes returned to Blake. "I'm so sorry to dash off in the middle of a crisis, Mr. Blake. If you need to speak to me further about this, just give me a call. I sincerely hope that Mr. Brantley is well, that he merely lost his composure for a moment."

He lightly cleared his throat. "If he does require some assistance, I assure you I'll see that he's taken care of." He was itching to get into that room and find out what was up with Billy, whether he honestly believed my version of the story or not. "Thank you for your understanding and compassion, Mr. du Bois."

"You're welcome. I really must go, now. Good evening, Mr. Blake." I walked away, leaving Blake to witness Billy's condition first hand. It was possible that Blake would have questions for me after seeing him, but I wasn't exactly worried about it.

An insane man's word against mine? A man whose days (maybe hours) were numbered because he was on a vampire demon's shit list?

Not a problem.

Chapter 22

Trey

We ended up on the jet not long after the meeting.

Travis and I had first gone back to Scott's place. I'd been explaining what'd gone down to Geoff and him when Travis got a phone call.

Elise was dead. Blown up. Assassinated, they were certain. That pretty much blew the encounter with Billy out of my mind for the time being.

No love lost between Elise and Travis, but he was upset all the same, on behalf of Michel, because Kar told him Michel wasn't taking it well at all. It definitely seemed even more urgent, getting back to Paris, after hearing that. While Travis stood there making his own calls and arrangements, I spent time assuring Scott I'd be okay, even though it wasn't a

310

certainty, since we had no idea who'd been playing with bombs, or exactly why.

After promising Scott I'd keep him up to date, see him again soon, and reminding him he was welcome in Paris any time, off we'd gone to pack up and head out – Scott saying on our way out that he wished he could come with us, that maybe he could cancel some of his shoots.

But I said no. No, don't do that, Scott, no need for you to get deeper into this than necessary; I don't want you involved, Scott, please.

I was a little nervous getting on our jet.

Because of time differences, Travis could only pilot part of the way going this direction, which meant I met yet another human in his employ – Marco. Marco took over when necessary, and Travis tucked into a special cabin at the tail of the jet, much like Michel and Gabriel's cabin on the other jet, if smaller. Once landing in Paris, he'd said, someone would retrieve him; they'd get him out and safely away in a coffin.

Okay, a crate or something, but coffin sounds classier, as well as normal, in a stereotypical way.

With Marco up front in the copilot seat, Geoff and I had the back to ourselves for a while. We talked more about Billy, Myra and Sandra. About how the women had receded and were content with their confrontation. We even talked about going to Carmona when the dust had settled one day, that maybe I could meet his parents.

And when I told him I'd wanted Michel to call this whole thing off before, he agreed. Naturally, this didn't boost my confidence.

After landing in Paris and having Marco convince me it really was fine to leave Travis in his hands, Geoff and I snagged a taxi. Geoff, being practical, not to mention highly attuned to my mood, decided he'd check in at work after settling his stuff in at his apartment, see about his new schedule – which left me to hot foot it to, you guessed it, their house.

I had to. Had to see about Michel.

The door swung open on its own after my knock and Gabriel was sitting in his chair when I wandered into the front room.

"*Mon* Trey, I am so pleased to see you." He stood and made his way to me, abruptly snagging me for a big hug.

"It's very good to see you, too." I squeezed him back.

He moved slightly away, catching my face between his hands. "I had a feeling that you would come. I was awaiting you."

A small smile formed. Now I knew why he wasn't glued to Michel's side. "After hearing about Elise, I had to. First place I wanted to be. I almost came straight here after landing." I searched his eyes. "How is Michel?"

He lowered his hands. "Back and forth, you might say. Just now he is resting, having succumbed to day sleep earlier."

"He said he doesn't do that often."

"*Non.* I am glad of it, for it will afford him a bit of peace for now."

My eyes dropped and lifted. "I don't know what to say. Obviously he still cared about her."

He gave me a slight nod. "He did. They had begun a true reconciliation before she died."

"Oh," was all I could say.

"Please, have a seat, Trey. Perhaps he will awake soon. If so, it would do him well to see you here."

I made my way to the wingback chair closest to Gabriel – Michel's chair – and sat. Gabriel settled back into his own.

"It must drive him crazy, not knowing who did it," I said. "I'm guessing he's angry and sad at the same time."

"You have learned his personality rather well in a relatively short time." He gave me a melancholy smile to go with those words. "Once he settles somewhat, seeking vengeance will be a priority."

"I figured it would be."

"Kar yet investigates the situation, and now that Travis has returned, no doubt soon Michel will set him also on the trail."

"Not to be insensitive, but – well where does this leave everything else, then?"

He folded his hands in his lap. "This you will have need of asking him."

A nod from me. "I was all for quitting this mission before..." my words trailed off when I realized how what I was going to say might sound.

"Ah, he has already blamed himself, my dearest. He set her on the plane, after all. This is not presently his focus, however, not to worry. The emptiness is yet consuming."

"How long did you guys know her?" I asked, feeling more sadness coming from Gabriel, but it wasn't his own. I knew this sadness was all for Michel, and it wasn't because I'd read it on his face or in his gestures. Briefly, I thought of how I'd freaked when talking to Michel on the phone, before.

Was it the zippy-juice? Were the effects more than physical? Well why not, I thought. They could be, they definitely could be.

"Near three centuries ago it was that he met her," Gabriel answered, dispersing these thoughts. "A few days later, he introduced her to me."

"I didn't know much about her. Just – well, just what happened between the three of you a few years ago."

He said nothing.

Moving on. "Where, how, did he meet her?"

"One of Vicont's many acquaintances had brought her, a human then, for some sport, to make a spectacle of it to entertain the others. It was a *soirée* at one of Vicont's mansions, and Michel was in attendance."

Scowling, that was my response. My opinion of her had been lop-sided. She probably didn't deserve to be that kind of entertainment.

313

"Brothers named Lucas and Declan had abducted her from her own home and tortured her," he continued. "She was but a peasant, then. Michel eventually defied Vicont and intervened. He did not feel the poor young girl deserved such treatment. He felt there was a spark in her worth saving. Vicont merely observed, at first." His eyes nailed mine. "Lucas and Declan had already spilled much of her blood and ravished her body by this time. The only way to save her was to bring her over, which Lucas refused to do. Declan could not be consulted, for he was dead."

From a scowl to a wide-eyed look. "Oh my God. Elise belonged to Michel, didn't she?"

He gave me a slow nod. "Sister, daughter, friend. Sister to me, after a fashion."

"Jesus. I had no idea. He never mentioned it." My eyes lowered. "I remember Travis talking about feeling the absence of Clarice. That it was like a void." My eyes lifted and found his face. "I can't imagine how profoundly Michel must feel her absence." Pause. "Will you tell me more? About her, about back then?"

His face became utterly smooth. "I can tell you that Vicont certainly did not waste much time in taking advantage of her naïveté, though most often she looked to Michel for guidance – even as she hated what she had become, at least for a time. She was not immediately grateful to Michel for her new life and he sometimes felt guilty for saving her, as she truly had not made the choice. Michel had made an emotional, split second decision."

I didn't know how to respond to that. He'd wanted to save her life, a noble thing, but I could understand someone not feeling grateful when they realized they'd become a devil, which is what she must've thought they *all* were back then.

Suddenly Gabriel smiled, if slightly. "But as I said, he had sensed something within her, a place within each of them called to the other. He told her later that if she truly wished it, he would destroy her, though it would pain him to do so."

His smile didn't make sense to me after those words, but again it was like I could sense some subtle emotion, one that matched the smile, so I waited for him to continue, certain his next words would explain it.

"She did not ask it of him, however," he said. "She began to fully comprehend the new freedom that she possessed. No longer a fragile human woman in a world dominated by men, and no longer prisoner to mortal fears, she began to embrace it. She was free to live a life women of the time could but dream of, if they dreamt of such things."

Now the smile made perfect sense. "I get it. True independence."

"Yes, though some yet attempted to keep her in her place," he said, his smile now wry. "Even in this century they did. Some never move on with the times; they never change."

Opting for levity, I said, "Well, *you're* a little dated sometimes, but I like it, because it's mostly the good stuff."

His smile warmed. "The definition of old-fashioned in a dictionary perhaps includes a wood-cut likeness of myself."

Welcome laughter loosened in my chest, more so than it otherwise might've, since I rarely heard him make a joke, and one so modern in its way, to boot.

"I don't know, *grand-père*, sometimes you're very modern. I'm thinking of the way you dress sometimes, specifically."

That beautiful smile of his grew, especially sweet to see considering the situation. "Michel enjoys it, and I must confess that at times there is an appeal in appearing wanton, perhaps shocking to others." One of his brows sharply arched. "I have long been decadent; therefore, I rather suppose that it is no great stretch. The clothing considered shocking has merely changed, not I."

Grin. "I figured that, somehow." The corners of my mouth dropped as my thoughts turned back. "Gabriel, Michel had mentioned a vampire he didn't know. Do you think he was involved in this?"

His face smoothed again. "I don't know. I do, however, now know who he is, as does Michel." His eyes shifted to the side.

Leaning towards him, sensing I might be losing him, I asked, "Gabriel? Who is he?"

"Lucas Demetrius." My head snapped toward the sound of Michel's voice. "Brother of Declan." He made his way into the room, looking for the first time in my eyes, disheveled and less than radiant, wearing a somber, charcoal grey robe.

Before I could even think of responding, he'd crossed to my chair and pulled me up into an embrace. His words were like a sigh.

"Thank goodness you're here. Someone safe and reliable, part of the family."

Hugging him tight in return, I said, "I wouldn't be anyplace else. I'm so sorry, Michel. Gabriel just told me you were her Sire."

He stepped back and gave me a gentle smile.

"Is there anything I can do for you?" I asked.

"I believe you've done enough for me, darling. Quite enough."

"Well. If you change your mind…"

His smile grew, dampened as it was. "Thank you, Trey. For now, just stay a time, if you please."

"I can and will do that." I gestured. "Here, you take your chair. I'll sit on the sofa."

"That won't be necessary." As he said it, Gabriel was already moving to the sofa. Once he was there, Michel settled in, lying back with his head in Gabriel's lap, and Gabriel immediately began stroking Michel's face, his hair.

I sat back in the chair, debating whether to ask anything else about this Lucas or Elise. Not wanting to upset Michel, I kept quiet for once and waited for him to choose a subject.

It turned out to be Elise.

"I remember how afraid she was the night I first laid eyes on her – of course she was; anyone would be," he said. "Yet she fought back, as much as she could." A smile cracked his face. "She even taunted them. How could I resist such a spit fire of a woman?"

I offered a smile in return, but his faded.

"She was barely a woman. Younger than me. There was also a softness to her, then. One she possessed up until the moment she," his voice faltered, hitting me in the heart, "died. One she didn't share with everyone, but I knew it. I knew it well."

I held my silence, letting him go on as he would, feeling this was best, that this was what he needed to do.

His face shadowed. "Lucas tore into her jugular vein. I attacked, but Declan stepped in, betwixt us, and so he died in Lucas' stead. It was too late to heal Elise. There was too much damage, too much blood lost, and so swiftly."

Awful. Horrible.

"Could he have wanted to finish it, all these years later?" Michel said, seemingly more to himself.

Then he settled into his own silence. Gabriel caught my eye and gave me another sad smile. When it seemed neither of them was going to speak up any time soon, I asked a question, delicately as I could, because something didn't add up, didn't make sense.

"Michel? I'm sorry, but I'm confused. On the phone, you said Lucas' name had come up, but you didn't know him. Now you seem to know a lot more about him. What am I missing, here?"

Michel's focus sharply snapped back to me. "Lucas was erased from my memories," he said, the way he spoke raising every hair on my body.

I couldn't speak.

"Vicont," Gabriel said.

Michel picked it up from there. "He violated a sacred trust. Sires and offspring do not tamper with each other's minds. In olden times, covens, clutches, councils, call them what you will, would seek the death of such a violator. The Anima Mundi made the law originally. He told me that. He told me it was one thing vampires across the world could agree upon." He sat up, his hand hitting the sofa to punctuate his statement, startling me. "It's not done!"

A handful of quiet words found me. "Because it's worse than rape."

Both of them just gazed at me.

"It's an utterly personal violation, a complete betrayal, perpetrated by someone who's supposed to love and protect you." I looked into Michel's eyes. "Or at least protect you and respect you."

"Yes, you understand. You understand very well," he whispered, his emotion turning to bitterness, sadness. "The *one* line I thought even he wouldn't cross. I've just discovered he would and *did*, indeed."

Words failed me again. Vicont had done many things to Michel, things I didn't even know about, but this...

This was probably the worst. Wounds heal, bruises fade. Things like this don't. I understood more than I wanted to.

"I still don't have my memories surrounding Lucas, not the true memories," Michel said. "Some were altered, some erased, and we believe he left triggers," he paused. "It's akin to hypnotic suggestion. Lucas' name would be mentioned, yet I'd immediately forget."

I sat back, his words swimming around in my brain. "How did you find out?"

"Elise." A wave of sadness flooded that one word, her name. "She told me."

I just couldn't imagine. It was freaky enough when a vamp tampered with my mind just a little, but what Vicont did to Michel? This was full on fogging. Hell, worse than fogging.

Of all the things swimming in my head, the first thing to break the surface was:

"What are you going to do?"

Michel swiftly rose. "Excuse me," his hand flew to his

forehead, "I can't continue this just now," and he left the room.

My eyes sped to Gabriel. "I'm sorry. I upset him, talking about all this."

"*Non, non.* It's not you, Trey." He left his seat and went after Michel. I was getting out of my own chair when I heard Gabriel in my head.

Please, remain a time. He desires the feeling of you.

The feeling of me. Sitting back once more, I nodded to myself. If knowing I was in his house gave him any comfort, I'd sit for however many hours were needed.

Chapter 23

SEPTEMBER 9

"Gracious, but you got a work out in New York, sugar," P.K. said, refreshing my cup of hibiscus and chamomile tea. "I knew you were holding out on the phone, but that's understandable."

We were in the back room of Poe – my first time seeing it, in fact – where she did readings for people *in the know* and kept personal items, as well as 'special items' she sold, again, to those people *in the know*. She'd closed up shop early and invited me to the room, so I could catch her up on everything I hadn't said on the phone and what I'd found out since returning – and yes, somehow I managed even to tell her what Billy had *actually* done to me.

I felt somewhat at home in her little room; the energy was comfortable. There was an altar covered in pink and blue velvet, white and gold beads, a heart shaped candle, a black candle, a white candle and a crystal bowl filled with water mixed with some rum; she was dedicated to *Erzulie*, the embodiment of femininity and compassion, who was also flirty and fond of high luxury. Did I say flirty? Heck, in Haitian lore, *Erzulie* had three husbands, and they were all big shot *lwas*. In fact, *Ogoun* was one of them.

There was what looked like an alligator skull sitting on a lower, smaller table in one corner, flanked by two jars containing dirt. When I asked her about that, she said it was graveyard dirt. When I said *Gee, why do you need graveyard dirt*, she said, *Oh, for planting anything I'd like to grow.*

I was thinking that meant hoodoo. She still doesn't leave hoodoo instruction manuals lying around, but I felt more confident in my assessment of those jars each second I sat there – and was getting more and more curious about hoodoo, but decided it should probably wait.

"I figured it was better to tell you in person," I said. "And you were right. I managed."

"More than managed, I'd say." She smiled and settled back down on the floor cushion across from me.

After a sip of tea I said, "Guess so. But let's change the subject now, 'kay?"

"Sure. How about this. Scott called me again yesterday."

"Ah. Get another barrage of questions, did you?"

"Mm hmm." She chuckled. "I could barely answer one before he'd toss out five more."

My laugh joined hers. "Somehow, I still think you managed to turn that conversation back on him."

One of her brows lifted.

I set my mug on a tiny table that wasn't sporting chicken bones or chicken feet. "You always avoid saying much about yourself; always shift the subject back to the other person."

She shrugged. "Because it's not about me, Trey."

My turn to lift a brow.

"You met me at a time you needed support and guidance," she said. "The apex of a tumultuous string of circumstances. I'm here for you, or whoever needs me."

I smiled. "Well. Yes, you've been very selfless. But some time's passed now, so what about you?"

"I don't need any help, sugar."

"Hah. That's not what I meant."

"What do you need to know that you don't already?"

I paused, studying her face.

"Actually...nothing that'll change how I feel about you."

She broke into a wide smile. "Good answer."

"But I'm still curious. This woman of mystery thing can't go on forever, you know."

"Why not?"

I started laughing. "Okay, *Michel.* Why not."

"Seriously, you know things about me."

"Tell me a secret. Tell me something you wouldn't tell just anyone."

One of her fingers came to her lip and stayed there a while. Finally, she lowered that hand. "Okay. I'm thirty-four years old."

"Bah." I waved my hands at her. "Fine, never mind."

Her rich laughter filled the small space.

"You don't look it, by the way," I said. "I thought you were in your twenties until Michel said thirties."

"Why thank you, darlin'." Her eyes moved over my face. "Just for that, I'll tell you something else."

"I'm all ears."

"I move around more often than you think."

"Why's that?" I retrieved my mug and sipped my tea.

"I go where I feel called, really. I get a strong urge to be in a specific place, and I follow the urge."

"So three years ago, you had a strong urge to be in Paris."

She nodded.

322

"Have you helped someone in some way each place you've gone?"

Another nod from her. "I try, anyway. But you're by far the most interesting case I've encountered."

"Oh, I feel so special."

Her expression became serious. "You are. I've met people who commune with the Dead in different ways, but I've never met anyone with precisely your gifts. Such *strong* gifts. The conditions of your Mark are very interesting."

I set my mug back down. "You know...Gabriel might have some connection to it. I mean, I don't really know, Michel and I didn't finish our conversation, but Travis said some things..."

"All right, now back up and explain this to me handsome, because now you're the one sounding cryptic. Or just plain confused," she added with a grin.

So I backed up and explained – without mentioning anyone's demon genes and whatnot.

"Interesting," she said when I was finished. "Very interesting. Have you asked your dad about the bargain?"

My head quickly shook.

"You're not ready," she gently stated. "That's okay."

"It doesn't matter, P.K. Whatever he did, it's past, it can't be undone, and it just doesn't matter."

"I think I understand." She reached and touched my hand. "If there was something you really needed to know about it, I'm sure he would have told you by now, anyway."

I'd had thoughts about what kind of bargain he'd made and why. Not liking my thoughts, I'd shoved them aside. There was plenty of other stuff to replace the space in my brain, anyway.

P.K. was just gazing at me.

"It might have been because he didn't think he was good enough for Mom," I whispered. "To keep her, to marry her. But I could be totally wrong, and if I'm not, he was wrong, and – I don't care. Papa would have got me one way or the other anyway, don't you think?"

323

Slight nod from her. "Would you like another change in subject, handsome?"

"Yes, thank you."

"How's Michel?"

"Not good, really. He basically just lost a daughter." My eyes dropped to my mug. "But, you said he'd be okay. On the phone, you said he could handle it." My eyes found hers. "Did you know then? Did you know before it happened?"

"I had a feeling he might lose something, so I read the bones again and it seemed this something might be a person. I didn't want worry you more, and I didn't specifically know who, or when, so I didn't say anything else. And, the path could've changed. Unfortunately, it didn't."

Head shake. "You don't have to explain. I was tense enough, so yeah, good call on your part."

"Maybe I should've warned him." A wisp of air left her, almost a sigh. "Or you could have warned him for me."

"And he still wouldn't have known who to protect, P.K." I slid closer to her, placed my arm across her shoulders. "Remember, you were the first to teach me that if all roads lead to the same place, that's that. They must've all led there, because you couldn't bend the roads any more than I could."

Soft smile from her. "I know. I suppose I was thinking I might have prepared him, softened the blow in some way." She leaned into me. "It's probably better that I said nothing. You're never *really* prepared for things like that." She wrapped an arm around my waist, giving me a half hug. "You're settling into your place well, Trey. Your adjustment to everything is pretty impressive."

"Thanks, Sis."

Her smile reached the depths of her eyes. "Too bad I missed Billy's reckoning. For posterity, all that."

"Uh huh. Posterity, sure." Pause. "I'll write down the details of our next encounter for you."

She leaned back. "You're going back to New York?"

"I won't have to."

Chapter 24

Michel
Algeria

We approached the entrance to the self same fortress that had not so long ago imprisoned Trey. Vicont had insisted upon this place when we spoke on the phone, and his insistence, along with the underlying tension in his voice, more than suggested he was wary and no doubt felt safer in this underground lair. As such, our senses were piqued, as we expected as many, if not more, guards than before. It was therefore not surprising that greeting us, not many steps in, was the appalling sight and rancid stench of two vagrants chained to the tunnel walls on either side. What *was* somewhat surprising was the first guard we encountered, who was standing at the safest possible distance betwixt the two vagrants and holding a rifle – surprising, as he scented as human. Hardly what I would consider threatening.

"Gabriel," I said. "Should I inform him what happened to the last gun-toting man I encountered?"

"You could, yet this would certainly spoil the surprise."

I came to a stop a few paces from the familiar-looking armed guard, ignoring the vagrant's warning growls.

"I suggest you lower your weapon," I said. "I don't know what you think shooting me with that toy will accomplish anyway, other than serve to piss me off."

His mouth offered hints of a smug smile. "I'm sure I could slow you down with a shot to the head. Right through your brain, that would do it."

"That's assuming you could pull the trigger before I rip off your arm and feed it to the beast drooling at your left. He looks terribly hungry; shall we give it a go?"

"Place your bets, gentlemen," said Kar, offering a rare moment of on-the-job jest.

"Better yet," I said to the honey-haired man, "why don't I split your skull like a melon and share your brains with everyone?"

"It has been far too long since I attended dinner theater," my Gabriel remarked.

Vicont's new man rolled his light brown eyes at me. "Enough already. This isn't for you, anyway. You're expected."

"Damned right I am, you little weasel," was my response, along with an accompanying backhand to his cheek. "And don't ever roll your eyes at me again, Tony; I'll pluck them out and play a game of marbles with them, next time."

He recovered his balance just in time to keep the vagrant on his right from sinking his putrid fangs into one of his booted feet, handing me a hot glare all the while.

"Go on," I said. "I *dare* you."

Tony continued to glare.

"Kar? You didn't happen to bring any toothpicks, did you?'

"I'm afraid not, sir. Although I do have a pin in my hair."

Tony's eyes sped to Kar. "What's that you're carrying?"

"It would appear to be a small briefcase of sorts," Kar replied.

"I can see that. Open it up."

"That won't be necessary," I interrupted.

"I'll decide what's necessary," Tony shot back.

I took steps in his direction, until our noses nearly touched. "You are pushing too many buttons, worm. One more and I shall rip out your jugular vein and twine it around your head. Are we now on the same page?"

"This way." He gestured with his rifle, wisely understanding he'd gone far enough and adjusting his attitude immediately.

"I know the way, *rrr*at." Tony, who had years ago worked at the Fall Out, led on, and for all of his bravado, I knew that his mind was offering up a veritable gumbo of scenarios – that is to say, all the ways I might kill him.

"What did he offer you, Tony?" I inquired, not waiting for a reply. "Money, women, status?" I let go with a snort. "You do realize he'll renege on everything."

"Like you didn't," he retorted.

"What didn't I give you that was promised?"

He stopped and glared over his shoulder at me. "Eternity."

"Ah." My lips spread. "You have a poor memory. I never promised you that."

His jaw stiffened and he moved on. "Maybe not, but it's all I wanted, and you knew it."

"Sorry darling, but I didn't think you could handle it. I do possess a scruple or two."

"Certainly Vicont will accommodate him," said Kar, who remembered Tony well, and there was no love lost between them now.

"Yes. Vicont does love making new dolls for himself," I said. "It's not a hobby I share."

Gabriel added, "They have dreadfully short shelf lives, after all."

"Mmm, yes. He dislikes being low stocked."

"If you're trying to scare me off him, get me back over to your side, may as well give it up right now," Tony said.

To which I began to laugh. "Ahah, why on *Earth* would I want you back? Besides, you already know these things. If you think he finds you special, you've certainly lost several brain cells since last I saw you, in which case I *definitely* don't want you back."

He continued in silence. Meanwhile, a different thought struck me.

Kar, remain by the cave entrance, will you? It occurs to me that Vicont may sense too much.

As you wish, my Prince.

Kar turned to head back the way we'd come as Gabriel and I continued forward.

"Hey, where's he going?" Tony barked as he turned and stopped.

"It's none of your concern," I said. "Carry on."

"I don't think so." He took a step in my direction, for which my palm found his chest, knocking him back several feet.

"He prefers open, fresh air," I said, glaring at the mortal. "And I prefer that he watch the entrance. Now carry on; your master is waiting."

Again wiser than I remembered him to be, Tony carried on with escorting us to Vicont's waiting place, which turned out to be the same room in which he'd lost a piece of his heart. This time it was even more impressively lit with various lamps and wall sconces, as if he were attempting to chase away every particle of darkness. I had a better view of his accoutrements, as there were not so many men with him presently – just two to the left and two to the right of his expansive marble top desk, though I sensed many more in locations unseen.

But I cared little for my surroundings.

"Thank you, Tony. Now leave us," said Vicont, rising from his chair behind the desk.

Tony made his exit, whilst Vicont's guards kept their eyes trained on me. As for myself, I was congratulating myself somewhat for not being as disconcerted this time by Vicont's unhealthy state.

"You'll pardon him, I hope," Vicont said, addressing me. "He's yet learning proper etiquette."

"I remember well his personality. My emissary yet stands at the entrance. He too has a good memory."

"He will give Kar no trouble, Michel."

"It hardly matters, for if he does, you'll have another death on your doorstep. A most final death."

"This seems fair enough," came his predictable reply. "My vagrants are always hungry."

"Oh yes, them. Interesting addition to your twisted family." I spared his men a glance. "It would seem your trust in me wanes."

"One is dead already, and blatantly so, Michel."

Gabriel's invisible touch damped slightly the ire that swiftly flared within me. "Do you dare suggest that I killed Elise?"

"I seem to recall your leaving me once before with such intent."

"Yes, face to face, unlike a coward who leaves it to bombs in a poor attempt at keeping his hands clean."

He surprised me by making no reply.

"You must have been so very disappointed," I continued, "when you heard she yet lived after my visit, for you were so intent on manipulating me into killing her."

Weary, the way he lifted his hand. "Your own emotions led you. Still, I didn't expect you'd follow through with it, as after all – your emotions were leading you."

I found myself in need of a moment to unclench my teeth. "So. You did it for me, or had it done, thinking it a favor. No?"

"No, Chrétien. No, I did not. I knew even in your anger that you still cared for her. I realize you believe it doesn't matter to me, who you care for, but she was one of *our* kind."

"Since when did *this* matter to you?"

"She was once family, not a mere soldier or servant, and she was yours. Whether or not you believe I care about even this, it remains that Sires cull offspring; it is not the place of another to decide."

One old law of the Anima he yet adhered to, which also was where his idea of a life for a life came from, was the right of a Sire to cull his own, whether in punishment or mercy. There was only one amendment to this rule. One could be ordered to destroy their child if the child was found guilty of a high crime at a trial. Not so many bothered with trials any longer, as it was a tedious process, and the meaning of high crime was often dependant on the judge. Even so, in past years as Prince, I had adjudicated at a few. These thoughts led me swiftly to the fact that I did have one point to call him on, as I knew the customs quite well.

"You consider yourself royalty as do many others, and royalty are sometimes above this ancient law. Royalty may kill without reproach in special circumstances."

"I did not have her killed, Chrétien, nor did I do it myself."

A moment's pause I needed yet again, as I marveled over the apparent truth of his statement. A pause, as I marveled over the fact it had tasted of truth each time he'd said it.

"*Je m'appelle* Michel," I quietly corrected, relieved in ways I couldn't explain that it didn't seem he had a hand in Elise's death. But now this left Lucas as chief suspect. I could presently think of no other.

"Yes. Yes, very well, Michel. But please, let's not begin this way." He made with a gesture to my right, towards an area where sat three plush sable colored chairs. "We'll sit. We'll speak, just as you wished."

Relieved I may have been, yet there were other matters to discuss, yes. Matters that would not be so simply eased in my mind.

"We need to stop by my place so I can grab the rice." P.K. unlocked the shop door. "Geoff's not the only one who can cook." She opened the door and out we went.

"Sounds cool. I can surprise *him* for once."

She paused in locking back up to look across her shoulder at me.

"What?" I said. "You'll get full credit for the food. At least let me have credit for the idea."

Chuckling, she got the lock in place, then turned to me. "How late did you say he was working?"

"Till about eleven."

"That gives me just over an hour." She moved closer, looking up at me. "We'd better get on the hot foot, handsome."

"Yes ma'am."

We'd barely gone three steps before we spied Travis heading towards us.

"Hey, Trav." I pulled up short when I saw the look on his face.

"Hey," he said. "Hi Polly. You two busy?"

P.K. must've noticed, too, because she immediately said, "Not at all."

"Cool." Nod from him. "Maybe we could hang out?"

"Sure we can," I said. "Now give it up already. What's going on?"

"That obvious, ay?"

P.K. and I nodded in unison.

"Right," he said. "Well then, can we go somewhere first, or something?"

"Do you mind stopping by my place?" P.K. asked. "I just need to grab some rice."

"Oh, you do have plans," he said. "Hey, no worries. Go on about your evening."

"Hang on," I said, before P.K. could reply. "You realize who you're talking to here, right? Like that's gonna work."

"He's right," she said. "Come on, you're invited. I was just going to make dinner. I," she glanced at me, "*we* were going to surprise Geoff later. I was planning to cook at Trey's place."

"Well – " he started.

"We insist," I finished. Dang, was he wired. "We'll keep insisting until you're so irritated you either give in or run away screaming."

He laughed. Not much of a laugh, but he did laugh. "All right. Thanks."

"So tell me, is everyone okay?" I asked. "Did something else go wrong?"

"Everyone's okay." He started walking. "Nothing's wrong, technically. This way, right?"

P.K. and I exchanged puzzled looks as we followed him.

"Travis?" I had to hotfoot it to catch up to him, P.K. bringing up the rear. "What's this *technically* business?"

"Really, everyone's fine, Trey," he said, not breaking stride.

"All right-y then."

He came to an abrupt halt, turned to face us. "It's just that Kar called earlier and they've gone to meet with Vicont."

My jaw slacked.

"Just a meeting," he went on, "but Kar wouldn't tell me what was going on, he always tells me what's going on. I'm supposed to know what's going on. I didn't even know they were planning on talking to Vicont." Beat. "Maybe he didn't know until today, either."

One. Two. Three. Okay, I caught up. "Maybe he doesn't know exactly what's going on." Caught up and now more worried. "Michel and Gabriel went to see Vicont?"

"Yeah. They did." Beat. "Maybe you're right, and Kar doesn't have the details. It's happened before. If he had the details he'd tell me, unless, of course, he was told not to."

"Why would they tell him to keep secrets from you?"

"It's not about keeping secrets." Beat. "Though normally he tells me."

"You're starting to freak me out, dude."

"Sorry, I'm a bit amped."

"A bit? Understatement of the year."

P.K. did a little throat clearing. "Mm hmm. I concur, honey."

He looked back and forth between us, took a deep breath and let it out.

"Kar said it was no big thing," he said and pivoted, walking again. "I just wish I were there, that's all. I don't like not being there."

P.K. and I exchanged another look and set about catching up to him again.

"Kar can handle things, don't get me wrong," Travis said. "Nothing to do with that."

"Of course he can," I agreed.

"I just don't understand what's going on." He stopped again, turned. "Or why they…"

"They what?" P.K. and I both asked.

"Not important." And off he went again, us humans getting a good workout before dinner.

"Hey, slow down, explain." I made it to his side. "Please."

"We'll talk at Polly's. Or wherever."

He was so amped that my hairs felt like they were standing on end. When I looked at P.K., she was lightly rubbing her arm.

"Okay," I said to Travis. "We can do that, yeah." Yes, we'll just go right along and figure out how to calm you down eventually. Maybe.

But probably not.

333

Chapter 25

Michel

Gabriel was directly to my left, Vicont across from me, and suddenly I found myself lacking a starting point – perhaps as there were so many ways *to* begin. Vicont, for his part, merely gazed patiently at me, which in its own way was maddening, disconcerting. For a moment, I held that cataract gaze; for a moment, the lines about his eyes were too evident, and for a moment, I lost myself in a vision of starlit eyes, the grey crisp, magnetic and lively, dancing with...

This vision, it was from a time when I trusted him, trusted him not to violate me, even though those eyes danced with devilry as well. Violated me, he had, and yet I wasn't currently seething with anger, but rather, a nearly profound sense of sadness and loss, a different sort of loss than what I felt over Elise. It was akin to when as a child, or perhaps adolescent, one loses their last shred of innocence, their image of a safe little bubble insulating them from the world, popped.

The moment one realizes one's parents are just as human as themselves.

I broke our mutual stare and my eyes found Gabriel's hands, which were folded neatly and resting on his left knee, his legs crossed just so. I studied the jewel that adorned his right ring finger, a match for mine, save for the color of the stone – rings exchanged on a distant Valentine's Day.

It was also on Saint Valentine's that Elise had died and been reborn. With this memory, my eyes rediscovered Vicont's. Impulsive, yes. Yes, I was, and here I was without a true idea of what I thought to walk away with, but here too was my Gabriel, with me every step of the way.

"Michel?" His brows made to lift.

I chose my starting point, wondering even as I said it if it would be shocking to anyone present, anyone at all.

"I've been seeking to destroy you."

"Pardon?" His forward lean was slight, but unmistakable. Gabriel, however, was a statue. "Destroy me?"

"I've already acquired six of your companies."

Vicont's brows managed to find a higher resting place on his forehead. But then, in a moment most surprising to me, he began to laugh – though even his laughter was less marvelous than I remembered, given his state.

"Do you not believe me?" I inquired, uncertain as to whether he was laughing at me, yet quite certain I'd be irritated if so.

His laughter trailed off, like slender curling wisps of cigarette smoke. "I believe you. I not only believe you, I already knew. I'm amused, delighted, and bit surprised that you chose to tell me yourself."

Feeling disappointed that his spies would of course always best mine, disappointed with his reaction, which was opposite to what I'd hoped, and feeling somewhat defeated yet again, I reached for some of Gabriel's steely reserve.

"So then, Lucas is working for you?"

Any trace of humor within him swiftly dissipated. "Who?"

"I'll say it very slowly, so there's no mistaking the name."
I made a forward lean, a touch of anger now flirting with my
person. "Lucas. Demetrius."

His nostrils flared somewhat, his inhale slow, measured.

"Ah, now that's a reaction I expected."

"Lucas is not working for me," Vicont said, appeasing me
somewhat by not feigning ignorance of the man. "Lucas and I
have not been colleagues for some time."

My brow arched with my reply. "Why don't I believe you,
hmm?"

"You believe little to nothing of what I say, Michel."

"True enough." I leaned back. "But you see, I know."

"I'm at a loss as to your meaning."

A bit of anger overtook me, and my hand slapped at the
chair's arm with my churlishly flung statement. "You went to
great lengths to expunge him from my memory, *Father*."

Yet again, his nostrils flared. "Forgive me, but I deemed it
necessary at the time."

"Thank you ever so much for not making a mockery of it
by denying it. As to forgiveness, you'll pardon me if I say *go to
hell*."

"Necessary, you say," Gabriel interrupted, Vicont's
admission causing him at last to twitch. "You deemed it
necessary to risk injuring his mind beyond repair?"

With those words, my eyelids dropped. I heard Vicont reply.
"It was never beyond repair, Gabriel. I'd not do such a thing
to – "

"Not do such a thing, oh, how *sweet*!" My eyes found his.
"You'd not damage me beyond repair, so I shouldn't let a little
thing like you *erasing my memory and placing triggers* bother
me. This would be your logic, yes?"

"Michel, please – "

"Please what? Please see that I had no choice, Michel?
Please see that I'm your Sire and I deemed it my right, damn

336

the sacred rule, Michel?" My hands were gripping the chair by this time. "Please see that Lucas was so important, I'd violate even my son's mind?"

One of my hands flew to my face; it found my eyes and covered them, for I was very near tears.

"I'm...sorry," he whispered.

"Why was he more important than me?" I dropped my hand, no longer caring if he saw the tears he could surely sense. "What was so special about him that you'd violate me this way? Me, your supposedly most precious, priceless child."

Gabriel's hand bridged the short distance between us, finding mine to give it a squeeze, and then a lingering touch.

"I simply couldn't have you killing him," Vicont said, his eyes lowering. "I knew very well there would be no way to talk you out of it."

"Business, wasn't it," I said. "Business and what he could do for you, always your number one priority. Who can best help me take over the world, your constant query, your constant search."

His eyes rose to meet mine and for a moment, I thought I did see true sorrow in the depths of his gaze.

But it was too late for that. "This is why it went so wrong between us, Vicont. I didn't want what you wanted, I wouldn't be the General you hoped for, and so you forsook even me. Already, I hated you for this; already, I despised how envious I was when I was yet so young, of all the attention you gave to other matters after telling me how damned special I was. Now I discover you went so far as to *defile* my mind, damn you."

"I did," was his simple reply to my emotional outburst. "Yes, it was my fault."

I found myself at a loss for words, where before there had been too many.

"You've remembered everything, have you?" he asked me then.

"Hoping I haven't, are you?" I retorted.

He merely offered a shake of his head.

Gabriel's hand sought to squeeze mine once again, and I drew in a deep breath.

"Elise told me what she knew, but how can I trust this is all there is?" I said. "What else have you taken from me? What else?"

Again, his words were soft. "I'll trip the switch, Michel. I'll give you the trigger that returns your memories in full."

How I longed for it. "Why didn't you do this for me before? Especially if Lucas has no place in your world, hasn't had a place in your world as you said, for some time."

"After all this time, I thought I'd spare you the memory of what was, for you, a terrible night."

This sounded too much like Elise's explanation, an explanation I had an easier time believing, and a laugh left me of its own accord, a rather strange sounding laugh even to my ears.

"We've been quite occupied with fighting as well, Michel. I wasn't inclined to sympathetic gestures."

"Now that, I believe."

"I'll return what you've lost this very night."

"If?"

His brows made to knit.

"I'm waiting for you to say what you want in exchange, Vicont."

His head shook. "Nothing, Michel. Nothing at all."

Words again abandoned me, though a thought raced through my head, which Gabriel spoke to before it could find its path to my lips.

"How can he trust that you won't, instead, erase more? We have no idea what other traces of you linger in his mind."

A very good question indeed. Though it was a question whose possible answer frightened me.

I could hear P.K. rummaging in her kitchen, and I could see Travis pacing a tight pattern back and forth in the hall, if you could even call it a hall. He was pacing like a caged lion.

Make that cheetah.

"It'll just be a minute," I said. "Then we can walk some more, okay? 'Cause obviously you need to walk."

"I shouldn't be here." Back and forth he went.

"I know you want to be with them. Believe me, I can feel how much you want to be with them, but hey. I'm sure they'll be back soon."

Back and forth. "No, I mean I shouldn't be here, in this apartment. It was a mistake."

"It'll just be another second."

Back. "I shouldn't be around the two of you." Forth. Then he made a beeline toward the door.

"Hey, hang on a sec." I strode in his direction, intent on soothing him if I could. Didn't take long to reach him. "You needed the company. It's cool, that's totally fine. We're here for you."

Too late, I realized the air had thickened, weighed much too much. Noticed a bit too late, in my concern for him, that every hair on my body was not only standing, they were practically tingling.

Too late, because he'd already whirled and grabbed me, pinning me against him just as I registered the wild energy filling the room.

"You're afraid." He sniffed. "I smell it."

His pupils were oblong slits. His irises were shattered amber, shattered pale, palest wheat. His fingers gripped the back of my neck and his other hand gripped my arm.

Then there were the four fangs baring themselves in my face and his statement before had come out a growl.

"Um. Yup, yes, okay, you've startled me, Travis. Maybe you should go now, yeah. No problem, we'll be fine."

"I've got the rice." P.K.'s voice came from what I hoped was still a safe distance, if such a thing existed around vamps. "See? We can all go now."

Nice attempt on her part, but his wild eyes didn't leave me. "It smells good."

Swallow. Don't think he means the rice. *Fear* smelled good to him. Now to figure out how to stop being afraid and get rid of the scent.

"Travis. You're still aware who I am." There. Don't be afraid, Trey. He knows who you are. "You *know* who I am, so you're not going to eat me, no matter how good I smell." Right. Abso-bloody-lutely not. I hope.

My spine straightened a little. Yeah, be the alpha, Trey. My spine straightened some more.

Until I felt what I guessed was a claw pressing into the flesh of my right arm.

"Travis," P.K. said. "My cooking smells even better. Let's go make a late dinner for Precious; he'll be home soon."

Bless her. We'd found a situation where she wasn't calm and collected, the only way to explain how she'd forgotten some vampires freaking hate the smell of human food. But I appreciated her intent all the same, gave her points for trying.

Even if her voice had wavered.

The wild cat with sharp claws stared at me, and I thought, *oh shit.* I'm not sure he knows who I am anymore. Then my skin parted for at least one of those claws, but I didn't dare say ouch, just mentally tracked the warm trickle as it made its way to my wrist.

He inhaled. Deeply.

P.K. might've been holding her breath, since she didn't say a word.

"Travis," I said as firmly as I could, mustering my courage. "Back off. You're hurting me."

His head tilted, and his eyes were what I could only call feral.

"I said back off; you are *hurting* me."

His head tilted the other way.

"God damn it, if you want to taste me sometime, I'm all for it, but you're sure as hell not doing it right now, not while you're Beasting out on me, *mate*." Quick prayer to Papa, Lucien, and anyone else listening, that my next move wasn't going to be a mistake. That it wouldn't just egg him on. "I am your *friend* and you are my *guardian*." My arms jerked up, my hands found his chest and I shoved him as hard as I could. "So yous best back off nah, ole man."

One. Two. Three.

Okay, no mauling commenced. And there's space between him and me. But he's looking at me like he doesn't recognize me.

Travis moved farther back, farther away, just as it hit me that Papa had not only heard my little prayer, he'd told Travis to back off himself.

A visible shudder ran through his muscles, as if he were straining, and he suddenly looked at his hands, which were still sprouting Beast claws, then glanced at P.K. and high-tailed it out the door.

"Well," P.K. said. "That was...interesting." Then she was by my side. "You all right, handsome?"

"Er, yeah." Nodding. "Yeah, I think I'm pretty good, considering."

"Let me get something to clean that up, hang on." She trotted toward her bathroom while I got a look at my arm.

Not too bad. Small puncture. Could've been worse, much worse. Heck, I'd cut myself a lot worse than this. It was just a scratch, sure.

I sank to the floor, adrenaline leaving me. "Jesus H. Christ on a rubber crutch."

P.K. came back, hurrying to my side, sitting on the floor with me. "I don't suppose we should go after him."

"I'm thinking no. We absolutely shouldn't."

"You were very brave." The scent, then the sting of alcohol hit me.

"Didn't have much choice. Besides, I dealt with," careful, Trey, Aeshma's a secret yet unexplained to her, "an intense mood shift in him once already, back in New York."

"'Scuse me, you what?"

"He really, really wanted to kill Billy. I had to stop him so I could get back to the meeting."

"Oh. Right. You said before that Billy would likely end up dead. You didn't give me every detail, obviously."

"Later."

"Fine, fine. It was great when Papa showed up a minute ago."

Nod nod.

"I'm really glad he helped you."

Nod nod.

"Because let me tell you, I was trippin'."

"You did an admirable job of hiding it. Except for when you told him your cooking smells better."

She slapped a band-aid on my arm. "It *does* smell good."

"Not so much to someone on a blood diet, chile."

"Oh. Well. You might have a point, sugar." She finished with my arm and looked into my eyes. "Off to your place, now?"

"Why the hell not. Things can't get any weirder between here and there, right?"

We just looked at each other a second, then said:

"Yes, they can."

She said, "Do you really think he'll be all right?"

Wow. She was definitely still at a loss, even if I didn't suppose she could sense every damned thing.

"Admittedly," she went on, "I'd rather not go after him, but I'd like to think he's okay."

"I'm sure he'll be okay. I think he ran out to protect us from himself. He was saying just before that he shouldn't be here." No, it wasn't so much Travis I was worried about.

It's what's making him so antsy that concerns me.

Chapter 26

Michel

"I took nothing but the memory of Lucas," Vicont replied. "I did nothing but assure that Michel would not remember him under ordinary circumstance."

I repeated the question. "Why should we believe you?"

"You have, of course, only my word," he said, spreading his hands.

"Which is worth so little," I spat.

Silence, this I received in return.

"You truly know nothing of Lucas' activities as of late?" I asked then, hoping yet to attain some bit of useful information, and in need of dropping the subject of my memory, for now.

"I swear that I do not. I would in fact be quite interested to know what it is he's done to earn your notice."

I contemplated him, studied his face, his expression.

"He was spying on Elise. Spying on me, I believe, and collaborating with a traitor."

He contemplated me in return. "If you like, I'll have the matter looked into."

Certainly, my brows lifted. "You're full of offers this evening, aren't you? Still hoping to gain my forgiveness, and rather desperately, it seems."

"Is this not what you came for, the wealth of my resources?"

Laughter let loose in me once again, this time near uncontrollable. "After all I've said thus far, this is what you believe?" I made with a shake of my head. "You are not so dense, nor naïve." More queer-sounding laughter accosted me, and though I could feel Gabriel looking at me, no doubt troubled by my demeanor, I couldn't stop myself. "And I can assuredly handle my own affairs, all the same."

"But you *are* after my resources, Michel. Other resources."

As abruptly as it had begun, my laughter died.

"I was. I no longer care, and so I told you. I'm not surprised you already knew."

"Ah, I see, this is why you told me, mmm." He curled a finger beneath his chin. "And not because you were already caught, yes, I see."

A nerve in my jaw twitched.

"Honestly, Michel," he continued. "I'm unsure what you and Elise thought to accomplish. However, I am prepared to forgive you."

"How magnanimous of you," was my dry reply.

"I'll pardon it, though I really should punish you in some way. After all, I can't have everyone believing I've gone soft, as they say. Or that I grant you special favor."

"So now we come to it." My eyes narrowed themselves, and Gabriel tensed. "Firstly, I can't even recall the last time you granted me special favor, as you put it. Secondly, I'm not yours, save on technicality. I haven't been for a long time, and everyone knows it, so you may as well get on with it and punish me as you would any other, yes." Dramatic was my pause. "Speaking of punishment, I wonder what the Anima would think of what you did to me."

Briefly, so briefly, his eyes sparked. He then smiled, and were I not so disillusioned with him, I might have found it attractive. Thank the gods I *was* disillusioned, as I couldn't stomach finding anything about him attractive at this time.

"Ah, Michel. We both know they'll never find out. Also, I haven't forgotten," his palm came to his chest, "what of mine you yet possess. Furthermore, you did inform me directly of your activities – and six companies? A paltry sum. I'm not about fighting you."

I arched a brow at him.

"Tell me, Michel. Enough of this prattle, this pretense of conversation we're having. Why *did* you come, and why is it really that you told me of your attempts to," he made with a dramatically languid forward lean, "take over everything."

Trey

"Geoff'll probably be here in about twenty minutes," I said, sinking into the sofa.

"I'll get the food started. It'll just be even later than we first expected, that's all." She made her way to my kitchen.

I kicked my feet up on the coffee table, ran a hand over my face. We'd made it to my apartment without incident and hadn't seen a trace of Travis. Picking at the band-aid on my arm, my thoughts returned to Michel and Gabriel, what could possibly be going on between them and Vicont. Where were they, why were they talking to him, and what was the rest of the sentence Travis had started.

Why did they...

Why did they what?

"Don't you have a sauce pan, handsome?" P.K. called from the kitchen.

"I'm not much of a cook, beautiful."

"Everyone has a sauce pan, Trey."

"I'm not everyone." Pause. "Sure you can't find one? Geoff's brought stuff here."

I heard clattering and clanging.

"There's an omelet pan."

"Well there you go."

"It's not the same thing."

"See? I know nothing, nothing at all." Pause. "But hell, isn't that close enough?"

"I'll make do."

"Geoff can cook with anything, you know."

"That he's well versed in the cooking arts tells me he'd want the right pans, too."

"Sure, but he could do without. That's the sign of a true cook, yeah?"

"You can just hush up, now." Clatter, clang.

"I bet the only thing you know how to cook are voodoo spells."

"Don't make me come out there and hex you, chile."

"Whatchoogonna do, make me sneeze every time I try to insult you?"

"You're rolling your eyes, aren't you? I bet you are. I'll knock those eyes out'chore head, watch 'em roll across the floor, little boy. Just keep up, nah."

Much needed chuckle from me. Shame that didn't last long, since my brain was intent on other things, but then whose wouldn't be?

"Fuck." I sank further into the sofa, running a hand through my hair. "I wish I knew what was going on."

"Calling them seems out of the question." Her voice was closer. I shifted, turning my head to look at her.

"Doubt anyone would answer," I said.

347

She folded her arms across her chest. "Well. I'm sure we'll know when we're meant to know."

Dramatic eye roll from me.

"Remember what I said I'd do with your eyes?"

"I'm sure some people fall for that, but I'm not one of those people. I've just been humoring you all this time."

"What? You lost me."

"What you said about knowing. Say it with just the right expression, an authoritative manner, and real fast? It probably sounds all wise and shit to some people, instead of what it really is – nothing."

She gave me the hairy eyeball.

I winked.

"Maybe I'll just get back to cooking." She spun and headed back to the kitchen.

"C'mon, it was funny." Short pause. "And true. Totally true."

Bzzzt.

"Saved by the buzzer," she called out, not managing to keep the humor from creeping into her voice.

Chuckling, I got up and headed for the intercom, pressed the talk button.

"Yes? Who's there?"

"It's Travis."

"…oh."

"Mind if I come up?"

Hmm. Let's think about this, weigh the pros and cons. Pro: I want to know what's going on, and he might be able to tell me something. Con: He clawed my arm and nearly made me piss my pants. Pro: He's back, so maybe he's okay. It'd be good to find out for sure. Con: He nearly made me piss myself.

"I'm better now," he said. "I wouldn't come back if I weren't."

Pro: He used the intercom instead of showing up at my door. That has to count for something. Though it could also be a con.

"I'm really sorry about before, and I won't blame you if you say no, Trey."

Ah hell. I can't say no to that. Besides, he's my friend. As if I was going to say no, anyway.

"Okay, I'm buzzing you in."

Short minutes later he was outside my door, which I opened a crack.

"Let me see your eyes, dude."

He peeked back at me with normal looking eyes.

"Okay." I swung the door open and let him in. "Sorry," I said as I closed it behind us, "but I just had to check."

"No worries." He turned, took one look at my arm, and his expression fell. "I'm so damned sorry."

"It's no big. Really. Just a scratch."

"I shouldn't have gone with the two of you in the first place."

"Well, you did, and it's over, so sit down and stop wallowing in it, because it's freaking me out, since it's so unlike you."

He cracked a smile and sat down in the spot I'd previously vacated. "You're a darl'."

"Yeah yeah, I know." I sat on the other sofa, facing him. "I'll even give you a minute before I start on the third degree."

He relaxed a bit more. "Thanks."

"Welcome back, Travis," P.K. called out.

"Hey, darl'," he called back.

"That sounds much better than before. I might even come out of this room for a minute."

"I'm very sorry that I scared you, Polly."

She made an appearance. "We're all in one piece, and you're so damned handsome; I guess I'll have to forgive you this time."

He returned her smile, then refocused on me after she left the living room. "See, much calmer now, Trey."

"Should I ask why, or rather, how?"

"Probably not."

"Fair enough."

After staring at him a minute, I said, "Okay. Let's start at the end and work our way to the beginning."

He just looked at me.

"I'm gonna ask what you did after you left P.K.'s, regardless of what you just said. So. What did you do?"

"I hunted," he immediately said, nice and direct.

"And killed?"

"Bingo."

"Well then." Nod. "Kinda figured. Was, or is, it enough?"

"For now."

"Right." Another nod. "Duly noted. When I asked you in New York if you..." I paused, remembering who was in the kitchen.

"Needed to blow off some steam?" Travis prompted.

"Yeah." Lowering my voice. "Seemed like you were saying no. Just a cycle, you said. Not to be insulting, but you sure about that?"

His expression was contrite. "It pounced on me unexpectedly back there."

Brow arch.

"I knew that I needed to leave, that I was getting much too tense, but I still wasn't expecting to suddenly snap like that."

"I probably shouldn't have chased you."

"You didn't know what would happen."

"True. I wasn't expecting you to snap, either. I'm sure it could've been way worse, huh?" Another brow arch.

"Yes. Which means I should probably blow off some steam in a big way sometime soon, yes."

I slid forward in my seat. "Mm hmm. All right. Now, can you explain more about Michel and Gabriel, all that? What *really* has you so upset?"

"Didn't I already say?" His brows tangled.

"You were like, hyper-Travis. Dude, I can keep up with Geoff better than I could you, earlier. I've never seen you that way."

He took a breath.

"Hang on," I said. "If telling me is gonna make you freak out again, I'll just have to deal with not knowing."

Slight shake of his head. "I'm honestly okay for now."

Brow arch.

"You have my word."

"Okay."

"Here's what I know," he said. "Not long after sunset Kar, Michel and Gabriel left for Algeria."

My brows shot up.

"Yes, they went to the same place Vicont held you prisoner."

P.K. reappeared, stood quietly with her eyes trained on the back of Travis' head.

"Kar said that Michel needed to talk to Vicont about something," he said. "That he'd sent a message to him when they were still in Spain."

P.K. and I exchanged a look.

"It was before Elise died," Travis said.

So much for my next question. It wasn't about Elise, apparently.

"So here's what bothers me, Trey," he continued. "From Kar I know that Michel was already upset, acting strange, before all this with Elise. You have some idea; you said he was tense on the phone."

"Yes."

"Kar said that Michel had learned something that completely unnerved him, but he wouldn't tell me what it was."

Not good.

"And, before they left, Gabriel snuck into the crypt under Notre Dame's square."

Brows up again. "Huh? Why would he do that?"

"Kar said Gabriel was retrieving something."

Frown. "What would he need from there, limestone? I mean, it's an archeological...Oh man. Wait. Do you think he – "

"I reckon so."

"Why wouldn't Kar just say so?"

"He didn't want to say much on the phone, and Michel was in a hurry. But I can't think what else it would be." He lifted and dropped a shoulder. "For all I know, Gabriel's hidden other things there, but the fact they went straight to Algeria – "

"Holy shit."

"Right. And the big question is: what's he going to do with it?"

"I give up!" P.K. flung her hands out. "What on *earth* are you talking about?"

Chapter 27

Michel

After a glance to my husband, I returned Vicont's steady gaze and drew breath.

"I told you to see if you already knew. I told you, hoping to shock you, to disconcert you. Obviously I lost that round."

One of his brows made to lift. "And why are you here, Michel?"

"Besides my lost memories and Elise, you mean?"

He handed me a strangely patient look.

"To negotiate, Vicont, which is another reason I confessed – so you'll know I've decided to go about this legitimately."

His other brow joined its twin.

"Ah. Not the same shock I'd hoped for," I said, "but it's better than nothing."

"What precisely are we negotiating?"

"You leaving me and mine alone. Forever."

He handed me a wry look. "Why would you now take my word on anything, if I did promise such?"

"Likely, I shouldn't. However, I have something I know you want."

He made a thorough study of my face. "What are your terms?"

"You'll make no bid for Belgium and let go of your designs on any part of France. Both countries are to be mine. You and your people, then, will observe proper custom when dealing with these countries."

"France is not all together disagreeable, but Belgium was never yours; it never much interested you, Michel."

"It's half French."

He let go with light laughter. "Truly, why Belgium?"

"Elise wished it."

"This is news to me."

His admission pleased me. "She first informed me years ago and then again before…" but here my newfound confidence wavered as wounds, once again fresh, bled. Only now, it wasn't Elise who made them bleed. "She always wanted me step into her place should anything happen to her."

"Others in the country may disagree, Michel."

"I am yet in possession of her will. I'm prepared to assert my claim. Besides, they know you've had your eye on it, and most find me preferable."

Once again his finger curled under his chin as he contemplated me, contemplated my words.

"You don't care about Belgium, Vicont."

"Its location is rather advantageous, you must agree," he countered.

"I will not have you in charge of a country so *close* to me and mine." Nor one that was once ruled by a woman who wished you dead, Vicont.

"Will you rule it yourself?" he asked.

Not for Eternity, I thought, yet did not say, as this was none of his concern.

His chin made to lift. "France was always to be yours, you realize."

"We agree, then?"

"On France, perhaps."

Gabriel said, "What we offer is worth the price of both countries."

Vicont's water-grey eyes briefly glinted with something of their old character as they shifted to my dark angel.

"Pardon me," he began, his tone carrying a measure of sarcasm, "for speaking ill of the dead, but even you know that she had no business skill. Her assets were not truly hers alone."

"I am quite aware of this, yes," Gabriel replied.

"You are not merely asking for symbolic rule. You're asking for control of my interests, as I know Michel won't suffer me doing business in his territory."

"Yet another thing I am quite aware of," came Gabriel's dusty reply.

"You think what you offer is worth this?" Vicont inquired, directing his gaze to me.

"Oh, I think so," I said. "Very much so. But I'll sweeten the deal and offer fair price for your companies."

"Really now." His fingers came together, creating a steeple beneath his chin.

"You're aware that I'm no pauper."

"Of course you're not."

"It will, however, be fair market value, as I said."

"Mmm."

We three then sat in thick silence for a few moments, and my thoughts wandered to words spoken betwixt Elise and myself, words of how negotiating with Vicont was futile, how not even possessing a sliver of his heart would help her win.

I hadn't said this merely to discourage her at the time, nor because I was irritated. I had meant those words. I wasn't fully confident now, would not be even with witnesses or other leaders present to sign papers and seal it in blood. But this was all I had left in me; I was so weary of the fight.

Though if Vicont made and then reneged on this particular deal, I'd be within my rights to kill him. Many *might* honor this code. This didn't ensure absolute safety for my family, there would always be rogues, but...

The *Ancients*. If they were aware of this bargain, it might help me later on. No one could legitimately come after me then, not *legitimately*, and so many feared them. The Anima Mundi were the vampire equivalent of Satan, the Anti-Christ, to hear some speak of them.

I'd never had this advantage before, never before possessed a proper bargaining chip. No mention need be made of our past grievances; a record and witnessing, this would do, it was better than nothing at all.

"Where is it?" he said at last, breaking my near reverie. "I agree to nothing without seeing it first."

What he asked for was with Kar. I had wanted this done, over with, as quickly as possible, and I knew Vicont would make this demand, so Gabriel agreed we'd bring it with us. I'd also harbored thoughts of taunting my Sire. To have it close, but so out of reach.

Sparing Gabriel a glance, I made the mental call to Kar. A moment later, he arrived, briefcase in one hand, his other brushing at the silk of his maroon suit jacket.

He inclined his head in Vicont's direction. "I fear your human found himself on the dinner menu."

The back of my hand came to my face to conceal my sudden involuntary smirk. I wanted to thank Kar, to kiss him for the moment of humor, but held my place.

"He attempted to divest me of the case," Kar explained, certainly sounding less than contrite. "He tripped and found himself in a vagrant's mouth."

Much of Vicont's focus, however, rested on said case. "No matter." He made with a wave of his hand and his pupils dilated, his senses piqued. "It's in there?" he asked in a whisper.

I rose and made my way to Kar. Once there, I took the case from him. I turned to face Vicont once more.

"Yes," I said. "You know it is."

"Show me." His body half lifted from the chair.

"Agree to the terms. We shall list them out on paper."

"You must first show me."

A sliver of pity stabbed at me, which I quickly shoved aside. "You know that it's in here. Now make the deal. Agree to the terms." My eyes swept the room. "And if any of your men make a bid for this, I'll destroy it on the spot."

His next breath was a rasp of sound. "Belgium is yours." He had come to be fully standing, and now took a step in my direction. "France is yours. I will observe the customs."

"Ah, ah." I gestured toward his desk. "Now you make a call."

He had taken another step, but my words caused him to halt. "A call?"

"To the Ancients. Inform them of my new position and relay the details of our arrangement. Inform them a Pact is being made."

His expression reflected his disbelief. His guards could not contain their discomfort. It was as if I'd uttered a curse, and four incredibly superstitious men were quivering with the desire to cross themselves, say a prayer, and throw salt over their shoulders, and all this just for a start.

"Ah, now there's a nice bit of shock," I said. "I can see this is the last thing on earth you expected to hear me say." His reaction was a pleasant surprise. I'd wondered that he wouldn't merely laugh at me as he had earlier.

He yet gazed at me in silence.

"The Anima Mundi are the only ones whom you will acknowledge as an authority above you, and you are one of few existing who has met with them," I said.

His reaction had bolstered my confidence. He was afraid; I could taste it.

"The very idea of them always frightened you," he said. "And irritated you. You refused to bend your knee to the Ancients. Never would you ready yourself to make the pilgrimage with me."

"I tired of your attempts to turn me into the Vampire God you longed for, the God you wished to present to them. Tired of your attempts to please some faceless Order through me. But I have rethought my position and I'm a big boy, now. They're not boogie men from some children's fairy tale." I paused. "Or are they?"

"You know what they are, Michel."

"Yes, I know damned well what you told me, and I know the rumors." A step closer to him did I take. "You still wish for special favor in their eyes?" I gestured to myself. "Well here I am. Give them a call, and I'll speak to them. I'll even put in a good word for you."

His eyes turned to Gabriel.

"I assure you that it was his idea," my lover stated quite proudly.

Gabriel hadn't known. *I* hadn't known I would make this move before arriving. It was true that I'd spent much of my *own* life either fearing the Anima Mundi or doubting their existence. I'd also never known how to contact them, how to gain an audience with them. Vicont had never offered information regarding this. Once it was clear I'd never be what he wished, he stopped speaking of them altogether.

Lightly, I shook the case. "If you want it, make the *fucking* call, Petrov. I have two witnesses. You have four. Make it a conference call, if you please. It will go so much more quickly that way."

"One does not simply *call* the Anima Mundi," he said, his eyes shifting back to me.

"You'd best find a way to summon them, if you ever wish for me to open this case."

"Be reasonable, Michel. They do not trouble themselves in the petty affairs of those lesser than themselves. They have long left such affairs to we common people."

"So you have always said. I'm not asking them to appear; I'm not asking them to fight my battles and they need not know about our past. I am asking only that you have them record this Pact. A simple enough thing, isn't it? Will it take too much of their precious time, do you think?" I looked hard into his eyes. "Or is now when you tell me they no longer exist?"

And that I have no upper hand to speak of?

"Or is it that you've never met them yourself, and you lied to me, as his your habit," I added, stiffening my spine. "Do you not know how to contact them, Vicont?"

Very slowly did he pivot, and very slowly did he make his way to his desk. In the meantime, I suffered through the pregnant pause.

Trey

P.K. sat on the edge of a chair, just staring at Travis and me.

"You wanted to know," I said to her.

"What happens if he destroys it?" she asked Travis.

"He'll never recover. He might even degenerate a little more."

Her hands fanned the air. "What are the political ramifications when it comes to vampires and people they hang out with?"

"Oh," he said. "Possibly some big skirmishes."

"War. He means war."

"Not as much of a war as if he killed him," Travis offered.

One of her palms came to her cheek. Nearly slapped it, actually. "Big time, Trey. Too big in scope."

"I know, I know. But it's not like any of us can stop him if that's what he wants to do. Oh, damn." Possible epiphany. "I know what tripped Michel out. I know why he might be there."

"What do you mean?" Travis asked.

"What Kar didn't want to say on the phone. Michel found out that Vicont erased some of his memories."

I was sorry I'd said it when I saw his eyes flash black.

"He what?"

"Uh…" well, too late now. "Vicont fogged Michel's mind. Something to do with a vampire named Lucas Demetrius."

Black flashed again, stayed a little longer.

P.K. got up, hurried over, and sat close to me.

Travis' nostrils spread with a sharp inhale, then a slow exhale.

"Your food is burning," he said.

Blink. From P.K. too, I'm sure.

"I didn't smell – vampire, right. Damn it." She flew off the sofa and fled to the kitchen. "Damn, damn and fiddle-sticks," we heard then.

I was keeping a close eye on Travis, though.

He lifted a hand. "No worries. But you might want to change the subject, now."

"Yeah, that seems prudent." Think think. What the hell can we talk about? "So how about that Anima Mundi, eh?"

"Where did you hear that?" he demanded.

Oops. Bad move? "Michel mentioned it."

"He did?"

He looked *real* surprised. "We were talking about Vicont and all that *special* stuff." Half second's pause. "I take it you've heard of them."

"Everyone's heard of them; they just don't talk about them."

"Well, not to be a smartass, but obviously someone's doing some talking, otherwise everyone wouldn't have heard of them."

I got a level stare for that. Guess kid gloves are still required.

"Right," I said. "I knew what you meant. And I guess we'll change the subject again, since no one talks about them."

Stare.

Yeah, shut it, Trey.

"Did he tell you…" he started – and didn't finish.

"Tell me what?"

"Nothing."

"Geez, are they really that scary?"

"Why do you ask that?"

"Michel acted like talking about them would literally summon them, and he didn't like the idea one bit."

"They're vampire boogie men, mate. People think they're all-seeing, all-knowing." He cracked a small smile. "Which is one reason for their name. Do you know the words?"

"Yeah, I understand the Latin: *World Soul*. So are you afraid of them too?"

He shrugged. "I haven't heard enough stories to fear them. But I have to take it seriously, because most everyone else does."

"So c'mon, then. Did he tell me what? The suspense is killing me."

"I don't know if it's for me to say." He spread his hands. "Sorry."

"Damn it." I sat back. "Never mind me; I'm just frustrated about being in the dark."

"Lawd, this is a mess," we heard from the kitchen.

"Good thing you don't have a nature like mine." He smiled a bit more.

"I dunno. I might go all voodoo freaky on you."

"That could prove interesting."

"Pff."

He looked at me a minute, got up and made his way around the coffee table, and then sat next to me.

"All right. Did he tell you he once thought Vicont was one of the Anima Mundi, but that he got kicked out of the Order?"

Jaw. Hanging open.

"I'll take that as a no."

"*Was* he?"

He shook his head. "Michel only thought that when he was really young, and Vicont probably did nothing to discourage it. Vicont just *wishes* he were part of the group."

Sitting up. "But if other vampires think he might be…Shit, that could explain why some of them do whatever he says."

"Maybe."

"Why some are afraid to go against him."

"Logical."

"Michel probably seems like a, a – blasphemer, or something, to them."

"Yes, they're like gods to some, and I reckon he might. On the other side, to some he appears even braver, like a trailblazer. *Vive la révolution*, ay?" Beat. "Likely he seems a little crazy to some vamps, though."

"Suicidal, yeah."

He patted my back. "Ah, Trey. I think it's mostly fairy tales. It might be true they're the ancestors of us all, but some of the other shit is probably just – shit."

Blink. "They're the origin of the vampire species?"

"Maybe. Personally I don't dwell on that sort of thing."

Hand up. "That's fine. Okay, hypothetically speaking then, just how freaking old are they supposed to be?"

He studied my face. "You don't want to know. That even scares plenty of vampires."

A crash issued from the kitchen. The kind that signals broken glass.

"I wonder if the waters just got too deep," I muttered.

"Eh?" He glanced in that direction, then back to me. "Oh. Maybe you should see if she's okay."

"I got it!" she called out. "Really, I've got it. I just hope this glass wasn't an heirloom. Didn't look like an heirloom, but it could've been."

"Nah. Just don't cut yourself." Then to Travis. "For real now. How old."

"I've heard thousands."

Crash.

"Jesus," I called out. "Could you please not freak on me now? Travis already took care of freaky for the night. Seriously,

I'm the only one not freaking out, and that's just weird."

Right then my door opened, and Geoff walked in. "Hi!" Then he pulled up short. "Why you both look at me funny? Something is on my face?"

Then we heard P.K. say, "My grandma is going off something fierce in my head, Trey. I can't be cool all the damned time. But I'm still sorry about your glasses."

Geoff looked in the direction of the kitchen, looked back at Travis and me, and said, "What wrong with her?" His nose wrinkled. "Ew, did you try and cook?"

Chapter 28

Michel

Vicont's guards tried their best not to stare in disbelief, at which they failed. From beside his desk he looked to me, an appeal in his eyes.

"I can't contact them directly," he said. "I can have a message sent, requesting an audience."

"It was all a fable," I replied, and his men exchanged furtive glances.

"Michel…"

"Kar, would you be so kind as to lend me your hands?"

Kar turned to me and lifted those hands, his arms creating a cradle of sorts.

"*Merci*." I placed the case on his arms and opened it. The room itself then seemed to tremble, to strain, with its own held breath, its desire to express a reaction.

From the cushioning of the case to the smoothness of my palm it went: a pound of flesh.

"Contact them, or this is the last time you ever see it, Vicont."

His eyes were riveted to the section of his heart I held, his reflexive breaths thrumming in time with the slow shadow of a pulse I could feel throbbing in my open hand. What yet remained in his chest begged to meet with its missing part; it was as if the two pieces reached unseen for each other along mystical bonds.

"Michel." He so desperately wished to move, to close the distance between us, yet dared not. "Think on this. I can only relay a message. Do you truly think there's an easier way?"

Now I was certain. He wasn't lying to me. Had I thought contacting the Ancients would be so simple? Not truly, but it was worth it, pressing him into this corner, and gods help me, I'd harbored the wish that it could be so simple.

"Very well," I said. "Send your message. Only after we meet with them may you see this returned to your person, not one moment sooner."

His hand, as if pulled by a string, lifted, his fingers seeking to touch the dense flesh sitting on my palm.

"You're better suited for ruling. Perhaps I should thank Elise's killer," he whispered.

My blood chilled twice over. "What?"

Certainly, he misspoke; certainly, he was so entranced, so romanced by the closeness of his pound of flesh, he misspoke.

"And now we come to this," he continued, oblivious to me, it seemed. "Yes, I should thank Lucas."

My blood simmered; it threatened to boil. "You son of a whore."

His focus swiftly snapped back to me. "No, you misunderstand."

"You filthy, lying, son of a fucking whore." My fingertips began to tingle; my very flesh began to tingle.

"Michel, I didn't – "

He cried out as my fingers convulsed, curled and squeezed, clamping down mercilessly.

"No!"

Before he could reach me, it burst into flame, a flaming ball I launched across the room.

"Damn you!" He cried, scrambling in the same direction, pawing frantically at the air, at what were already ashes.

Hell itself sought to break loose both inside me and around me, all as if in a blink, and I could scarce form thoughts any longer. From a growing distance I could hear Vicont. It felt as if the devil himself was trying to consume me.

"Damn your eyes! I didn't do it! Lucas is attempting to destroy us both!" Anger flared brightly in eyes that now loomed close, his weakness no match for the emotion. "But by the Ancients I smiled when I heard she was dead. Oh yes, Michel, I was immensely pleased. I shouldn't have let you save the bitch!"

Everything in my vision blurred; it blurred then flashed so brightly it was like staring into the sun.

Gabriel

Of a sudden, the air felt to crackle; I could feel Michel also along our bond, his swift red rage coloring his words.

"You son of a whore."

Already I had vacated my seat and already one of the guards had taken a step.

"No, you misunderstand," Vicont hastily replied, realizing his mistake.

"You filthy, lying, son of a fucking whore." These words left bright red electric trails.

I moved closer.

"Michel, I didn't – "

366

Vicont's words soon became a cry and I was aware of the dimming light, ever dimming, and movement I felt in Kar, the briefcase falling to the floor. Vicont's anguish soon mixed with anger, as on he ranted.

"No!" he screamed, rushing across the room. "Damn you!" Rushing, hands seeking, and soon all was movement, commotion, all sprang to life, as the guards left their posts, intent on battle. I myself was in motion, found myself soon locked into a fight, all the while keenly aware of Michel's expanding aura, feeding on the electrical currents as it was, his power gathering in strength.

Above all this, above what threatened to overload my senses between traded blows with faceless men, could I hear Vicont.

"Damn your eyes! I didn't do it! Lucas is attempting to destroy us both! But by the Ancients I smiled when I heard she was dead. Oh yes, Michel, I was immensely pleased. I shouldn't have let you save the bitch!"

An object bearing the shape of a head flew past, from the direction I felt Kar to be fighting, but I was then blinded for a moment by a flash; the flash of a thousand or more bulbs.

My Michel had lost his final sliver of restraint.

Instinct guided me as more bodies crossed my path, bodies I could not yet see for the tracers the shock of light had left in my vision.

There was then a thunderous roar, a growl, which vibrated me flesh to bone, this sound issuing from *mon lion*.

"You I could forgive, but not her, Michel!" was the following shriek. "She deserved to die!"

It was all such a blur in time; indeed time no longer existed. My hand would connect with bone, my foot with stone; I found myself on the floor and yet felt myself moving through the air.

And the sounds, there were too many sounds. Curses, growls, snarls, shrieks, and above all, the inhuman pitch coming from Michel.

"My Lord!"

Was it that someone was calling to me?

"My Lord, come with me!" These words carried more volume; they were closer still. Hands I felt on my body, hands I nearly crushed before understanding that they belonged to Kar. "Please, come with me now."

My eyes cleared. What they saw were severed limbs, great splashes of blood, quivering flesh; they saw a man enveloped in a film of living gold, blue flame dancing through it, in whose grip was another man.

"My Lord, we must flee!"

My senses separated the chaos, thousands of neurons communicated. "No. More come, I feel it, like cockroaches emerging from dark places in droves."

Arms wound tightly about my waist, arms that dragged me backwards.

"No! I will not abandon Michel!"

"We are not abandoning him!" Suddenly, Kar let me free. I whirled in time to see him spin and kick, decapitating yet another foe. As I took this opportunity to move toward Michel, Kar accosted me once again.

"We're not abandoning him, Gabriel! I'm trying to save you *from* him." With uncommon strength, he forced me back, even as I thought to struggle. "I can't let you stay here!"

All other thought was lost to me, save one, then. Michel would be devastated. Never would he forgive himself.

No longer did I struggle. With Kar, I fled. We fled a room that had become a giant Tesla coil and ran down the tunnel, voices from behind us signaling more, still more of Vicont's men, had leapt into action, and all seemed intent on that room; none appeared to notice us.

I thought to turn back. "Michel..."

"Don't stop now, Gabriel, I beg you." Kar took hold of my arm; he steered me forward easily, as I forced myself not to resist.

On we ran, and all the while it felt as if an electrical storm nipped at my heels, that should I hesitate for one second it would engulf me, vaporize me.

Soon we encountered the two vagrants, who whined and snarled, straining to be free of their chains, hysterical in their movements, but these we ignored, running on still, running until we spilled from the mouth of the tunnel into the night, not stopping until we were several meters away.

The wind was voiceless. My gaze lifted. The sky was moonless. Clouds collected above the mountain's peak. My gaze fell once more to the lair's entrance. Not a living thing passed through.

We waited.

Chapter 29

Gabriel

We waited. The silence of the desert disconcerted me terribly in comparison to the turmoil within the mountain. In comparison to the rage unleashed therein, which raced to reach me, the feeling of it, along invisible tethers, electrifying my nerves.

I could feel the rumblings within the mountain. I could taste the fulminating energy.

"Gabriel."

My gaze refused to leave the dark entrance. My attention refused to divide.

"Gabriel..."

A touch there was to my shoulder, and then once more, another touch.

"Yes."

"Did you hear Vicont's comment?"

"Are you attempting to distract me?"

"Yes."

I could hear distant screams.

"Try harder, Kar."

"He all but named Lucas as her killer."

"Yes."

"If Lucas wasn't working for him, if he wasn't lying about that, then he possibly had information."

"You state the obvious."

"I'm aware. Shall I try harder?"

"As you like." It seemed I vibrated, yes; this was the feeling, or one of many.

"Doubtful that any will leave that mountain alive."

At length I looked to him.

"Whatever information he had is certainly lost, Gabriel."

"There's nothing for it. There was no stopping him, Kar."

"Did you want to stop him?"

My gaze returned to the mound of earth that I wondered might give a shock if touched.

"No," I said.

"Neither would I. But it doesn't matter, likely. Vicont was clearly withholding the information."

"And would have continued to do so."

"Lucas will be dealt with. There will be no stopping Michel on that score, either. No stopping any of us, I promise you."

Lightning split the sky. My vision dimmed; I gasped. I lost sense of my body.

"Gabriel!"

It was so dark, a darkness all-consuming.

"Gabriel, speak to me."

It came to me that his hands were at my face. As swiftly as I'd lost sense of everything, everything returned, and I found his gaze boring into my eyes.

"Gabriel?"

The silence, it was deafening.

"I think it's over, Kar."

I began to rise, coming off my knees, Kar aiding me, and once standing, our attention moved back to the great rock, the mountain. The mountain that to my eyes faintly glowed. My stare was then rewarded by a lone figure emerging, staggering a few steps, a few steps more. By his next step, I was at his side, capturing him in my arms.

"*Mon ange.*" I stroked his face and smoothed the now wild mane of hair away from his eyes. "*Mon ange.*"

All of his weight shifted to me; he collapsed in my arms.

"I'm …free," he said, his feebly spoken words reflecting how drained he was. "We're free. I'm free, Gabriel, I'm free."

Trey

"Let me help you clean up, Precious."

"You don't have to," Geoff replied to P.K.

"Don't let her touch anything, baby. She already broke two glasses."

"Hush up, you. I said I was sorry."

"Come come, we do dishes." Geoff looked at me. "Don't worry, I keep two eyes on her."

"Good idea."

He and P.K. gathered up the dishes and headed for the kitchen, leaving Travis and me to sit and keep waiting for whatever it was we were waiting for.

We'd filled Geoff in on the latest, adding another confused person to the list, and he'd taken over the cooking duties after first scolding, then teasing P.K. to death about her failed attempt. Then we'd sat around trying not to talk about Algeria, since it would've been useless as hell.

"It's getting very late," Travis said. "Or early, however you want to look at it."

"Dawn's still a ways off. You thinking of leaving?" Narrowing my eyes. "Need to hunt again?"

"I might, if this keeps up." He stood.

"You put up with an assault to your nose, too. If you need fresh air, I understand."

"I reckon I do." He headed for the door. "As soon as I hear anything, I'll let you know."

"Okay."

He stopped at the door and looked back at me. "You should try to get some sleep."

"Don't think that's happening for a while, yet."

"I hear you. Well, see you. And thank you for being so cool about everything."

Shrug. "I'm alive; it's all good."

He smiled, opened the door, and started out. Then stopped.

"What's up?" I said.

He didn't answer. I saw him reaching into his suit pocket, and out came his phone, which went straight to his ear.

"Kar. What's going on?"

Kar? Damned right I immediately started eavesdropping. Even got up from the sofa to get closer.

"He what?" Pause. "They what?" Longer pause. "And then?" Really long pause. "You're serious." Pause. "Where are you now?" Pause. "I will." Short pause. "You too."

His phone went back into his pocket and he came back through the doorway, an incredulous expression forming on his face.

"Well, don't just stand there," I said. "Tell me before I bust."

"They're on their way home."

"Yeah, yeah, and…?"

"Vicont is dead."

"Oh…Wow."

"Michel killed him, killed them all." He began to smile.

Crash.

We both turned our heads. P.K. was standing not far from a sofa.

"Dang it," I said. "I thought you were keeping both eyes on her, Geoff!"

Chapter 30

SEPTEMBER 13

Trey

"His memories are coming back," I said after the waiter dropped off our coffees. "It's like breaking a spell, maybe, you know? Vicont's dead, so his influence is gone."

Michel had finally felt like talking a few days ago, so I'd finally gotten the story. The whole story, because Gabriel filled in the parts Michel was sketchy on. Then it was up to me to bring the important humans in my life up to speed.

This marked the third time I'd had the conversation, Geoff being first, Scott second, because he'd called just before P.K. and I got together for lunch. Talk about redundant. Should've gathered them up and gotten it done in one shot. I was getting good, though. I was at the end, and it'd taken me half as long as when I told Geoff.

"That makes sense." She sipped at her coffee. "Is Michel handling them okay?"

"I don't think he likes reliving that night. But it's starting to look like that's all he lost, so he's happy about that."

She nodded. "That's good." She set her mug down. "So. About this Lucas."

"Travis is hunting him already. Actually, they're all going somewhere tonight."

"Are they worried about war?"

She looked concerned.

I sipped my coffee. "I wish I had an answer, P.K. They all do. But so far things seem quiet, and everyone who matters probably knows Vicont's dead."

"What about those Ancients? I'm worried about Michel."

Mug, down. "Yeah. So was I. No one called, though. No message was sent."

"But if Vicont actually knew them…"

Head shake. "I dunno. Michel doesn't think it matters anyway. He's not convinced they gave a damn about Vicont. Hell, he's still not so convinced they exist."

Her brow arched. "Okay. Now what do you think?"

"I think he's still weirded out by the idea of them." I lifted my mug. "And I think it might be okay as long as someone doesn't start a damn war over this. I also think it's probably all worth it, because Michel's happy to be free of Vicont. Shit, they're all happy about that part of it."

"You said they all hated him. I don't begrudge them their moment of happiness." She drank more of her coffee. "Besides. Nothing we can do about it. It'll be whatever it'll be."

"Yup. But hey, Michel's a King now, two countries. That's gotta count for something."

"True dat. So he's got more allies, more power. Must count for something, sure."

"Sure."

Moment of silence. We had no idea right now how much power Lucas had. But it looked like neither of us wanted to talk about that.

She steered us away from the war talk. "You said they're *all* going somewhere tonight. Really? All of them?"

"Well, not *everyone*. Michel, Gabriel and Travis." Grin. "We get to try and keep up with Shane and Dane for a night."

"Lawd, those boys plum wore me out."

Southern was kicking in again big time, and I liked it.

"Oh. Did they now?"

"Not like that, honey. They're children!"

"I think they're of age." Wink. "In some countries."

She shook her head at me. "They are seven*teen*."

"Like I said."

"A bit girly."

"Yeah. They're pretty."

"Oh, they are, yes they are. But not really my type, never mind the age."

Swig of coffee. "Technically, they're a lot older than you. So I heard, anyway."

"Give it up, sugar."

We both chuckled.

"Isn't this nice, not freaking out?" I said.

"Mm hmm. We'll see how long it lasts."

"I hope a long time. Seeing you freak out is too weird for me. Besides, I'll run out of glasses."

Her smile grew, warm, loving, and she lifted her mug. "Here's to hopefully not having a reason to break any more of your glasses."

"I'll drink to that." I'm not confident of it, but I'll drink to it.

Clink.

"Where are those three going, anyway?" P.K. asked me then.

Head shake. "Dunno. Said they'd fill me in when they got back." Contemplating. "Crazy how Michel can be two things at the same time."

"Meaning?"

"He seemed displeased about this trip, but at the same time, happy to be going, excited in some way."

"You're right. That's a bit crazy. Of course, not being human, I'll accept it as normal for him."

I felt a smile grow. "You're wrong. It has *everything* to do with him still being human. Anyway, it'll be a good distraction for him."

"He's still grieving, isn't he?"

"Yes. But he's a lot better."

She smiled a little. "I'm glad. Oh hey, so did you get any more of Michel's theory about Gabriel when you talked to them?"

Oh yeah. That. Heard about that after being told about Michel cutting loose with an electrical storm in the mountain – the part I left out when retelling the story two of the three times.

"The theory," I said, "is that Gabriel's father was being ridden by a *lwa* when Gabriel was conceived. Michel's really taken with the idea that Gabriel carries the essence of this *lwa*."

"My, my my. Was it Ti-Jean-Petro?"

"Mm hmm."

"Where did Michel come up with this theory?"

I drained my cup before answering. "From bits of Gabriel's memories, things he's said and done over time." A smile broke free. "But I'd say we can't call it a theory anymore."

She finished her coffee, too. "Why?"

"When Michel was talking about it," I smiled, thinking of how Gabriel smiled at the time, "Gabriel remembered his father telling him something like that before he died."

A smile slowly crossed her face. "Lawd, your family line grows more interesting by the day, darlin'."

Leaning on my hand. "True dat. Wanna know something even more interesting?"

"I surely do."

"Supposedly Erzulie was riding his mother at the time."
"She do get around, chile. She do get around."

Epilogue

Michel

I landed on the window ledge and peered through the glass. The human I sought was rummaging through a medicine cabinet, a glass of water, or possibly vodka, sitting on the sink. I couldn't be certain, as scenting through the double paned glass was difficult, even for me.

He found what he was seeking; a small, white plastic bottle with a white cap, which he removed, and he shook two little blue tablets out into his hand.

"Valium, hmm?"

I watched as he swallowed these down with a healthy swig of liquid and then made his way out of the bathroom.

With a second's concentration, the window lock gave way for me. I slid the window open and crawled through, stopping, once inside, to glance at the bottle.

"Valium and," I inhaled, "yes, Vodka. Oh. You poor little man."

I was smiling as I wound my predatory way to his living room, the space ample. I surmised he was well paid or well kept, as apartments in New York with so much floor space did not come cheaply.

He halted mid-stride, not far from a large leather couch, pausing as if listening. This wasn't surprising. I wasn't attempting to conceal myself, not truly. I *wanted* to frighten him, after all.

So it was that when he turned, I came forward, and to his eyes, it must have seemed a magic trick. A specter suddenly appearing.

He flinched, he moved back. "What the – who are you, what are you doing in my house?"

"Why do people always say that, even when they clearly don't live in a *house*?"

He remained frozen, his flight reflex not yet moving his seized muscles.

"No answer?"

My, his baser instincts were sluggish.

"Boo!"

That did it. I wasn't precisely attempting to hide my nature, after all. Off he went in the direction of what I surmised might be a bedroom. His sudden yelp of surprise was immensely amusing.

"Excuse you," I heard from my darling Gabriel, who no doubt caused the yelp.

"Who, what…I've got a gun, I'm warning you."

"Not on you," I said, moving up behind him. "And really, does *everyone* have a gun these days? What is it with all the guns?"

It seemed certain he would faint after I smiled. Ah, yes, my fangs were highly visible, all eight of them. This was no doubt why.

He made a bid for the living room, which I allowed, though Gabriel and I followed.

"Going somewhere?" I said.

"We have only just arrived," Gabriel said.

"I'm-I'm calling the cops. You – you'd better get out." Indeed, there was a phone in his hand, his shaking hand.

"They'll be much too late," I said. "I'm not about to give up this chance at, what is it you say? Blowing off steam." I offered a wider smile.

The phone fell to the floor.

"Tsk. You've been a *naughty* boy, William."

"Who-who are you?" He moved back a step, another step still.

"Friends of a friend."

"You have met my Trey, no?" Gabriel said.

The human turned and lunged for the front door. He threw it open. He found himself face to face with Aeshma.

"Good evening, William Brantley. Remember me?"

Acknowledgements

'Alawston'. Melissa – your constant support and feedback are priceless to me. Thank you for always being there. Kyle Cassidy – I forgot you last time! Mom and Dad. Jody Glendinning – cyber-stalker extraordinaire. Hee hee.